is the fourth lively adventure in
Esther M. Friesner's
CHRONICLES OF THE
TWELVE KINGDOMS

MUSTAPHA AND HIS WISE DOG
SPELLS OF MORTAL WEAVING
THE WITCHWOOD CRADLE
THE WATER KING'S LAUGHTER

"Full of magic, intrigue, and romance . . . An
example of an exceptionally well-created world. The
characters are lifelike and engaging . . ."
Dragon

"Refreshingly well-told fantasy . . . filled with
delightful humor . . . she will almost certainly be one
of the more popular fantasy writers in the next few
years."
SF Chronicle

"Engaging characters and an intriguing plot"
Library Journal

"Whimsical, inventive, great fun to read"
Peter J. Heck, *Newsday*

Avon Books by
Esther M. Friesner

THE CHRONICLES OF THE TWELVE KINGDOMS
MUSTAPHA AND HIS WISE DOG
SPELLS OF MORTAL WEAVING
THE WITCHWOOD CRADLE
THE WATER KING'S LAUGHTER

The Water King's Laughter

ESTHER M. FRIESNER

AVON BOOKS ◆ NEW YORK

For Susan Shwartz and Judith Tarr,
Good Friends and Terribly Nice People

AVON BOOKS
A division of
The Hearst Corporation
105 Madison Avenue
New York, New York 10016

Copyright © 1989 by Esther M. Friesner
Front cover illustration by Keith Parkinson
Published by arrangement with the author
Library of Congress Catalog Card Number: 89-91201
ISBN: 0-380-75410-X

First Avon Books Printing: October 1989

AVON TRADEMARK REG. U.S. PAT. OFF. AND IN OTHER COUNTRIES, MARCA REGISTRADA, HECHO EN U.S.A.

Printed in the U.S.A.

K-R 10 9 8 7 6 5 4 3 2 1

Prologue

WET BEHIND THE EARS

"Mother! Father! Help! Save me!"

A gust of dragon's fire curled past Timeo's left ear, making the boy run faster than he'd dreamed possible. His sides ached, his long, coltish legs felt ready to drop off, his eyes were blurring with sweat streaming from his brow, and yet he still summoned up the wind to howl for help again.

"Father! Mother! *The dragon's after me!*"

The boy's cry caught an east bound breeze and wafted over the towers of Dureforte Keep, dropping into the Lady Mizriel's special garden. Mizriel of the White Hair looked up from where she knelt, tending a patch of hope-lies-longing. Her small hands were filled with the tongue-shaped scarlet leaves, and the sap of snapped stems had dyed the ends of her silvery hair pale green. She heard the terrified voice of her only child, and her reaction was immediate.

"Oh, for—! There he goes again. And at the most inconvenient time, as usual. I swear, the boy plans it this way." She dropped her gleanings into the round, shallow basket at her side. "Lymri, are you deaf? Your son is in trouble."

From his place beneath an arbor of trailing wantever vines, Lymri Riverborn spared his lady wife a fond glance of gentle reproof. "He's your son too, my love. And you do have the greater powers for getting him out of a situation like this. I am but a minstrel—" He passed his fingers over the strings of the lute upon his updrawn knees. "What our boy needs at this moment is the aid of a sorceress."

1

"Just like every man alive: excuses, excuses, excuses. No consideration whatsoever." Mizriel pushed herself up from the flower bed and snapped out a spell of transportation. She vanished at once. The empty air seemed to crackle with vexation when she was gone.

"I'll be along right away, darling," Lymri murmured to the empty air, and went on seeking a rhyme for "bountiful."

Timeo had no breath left for shouting, nor any for running. He had made a circuit of the western lawn in headless-chicken style, circling and weaving and zigzagging over the turf when such maneuvers made no difference at all. There was nothing for him to hide behind on the smooth and featureless sward, no way to throw his pursuer off the track. Any advantage of distance he'd had when this undesired race began had been devoured by the nearly flat terrain. The dragon might have found it harder going over steep or rough ground—a wingless, spoiled, and fat young worm he was— but on the straightaway he quickly closed the gap between himself and his prey.

Timeo wasted a backward glance. No miracle of vanishment had occurred—the small mountain of multicolored scales was still after him, jaws gaping to a roar. A lick of flame spattered the air between himself and the beast. The boy sobbed, feeling as though his lungs would crack, and managed to catch his foot on the one rock left marring the lawns of his parents' castle. He squawked, flapped his arms out to grasp nothing, and fell on his face atop a shattered mandolin. He had come full circle, back to where the unfortunate chase had begun. It looked likely to end here too, a thoroughly unpleasant termination to nine years of mortal life. Behind him, Timeo heard the dragon utter the reptilian equivalent of a chuckle.

It was foolish, useless, but Timeo closed his eyes and threw his arms over his head. They would be barbecued all of a piece with the rest of him, but he was a child with the childish instinct to hide, even when hiding was worthless. He felt the earth shake rhythmically beneath his belly. The dragon was coming closer, slowing his pace. Why run when there was no need? His meal wasn't going anywhere.

Timeo's feet began to sweat as the first heralding touches of fire lightly broiled the soles of his shoes. The stench of roasting leather was nauseating, and the thought of how he would soon be likewise done to a turn made the boy cry.

"You're a nasty, mean, vicious, ungrateful animal!" Timeo pounded his fists on the grass. He always got angry whenever he cried. Tears made him feel so stupid. "I should have left you to rot of boredom! You don't deserve to be cheered up at all! I'll—I'll put a minstrel's curse on you, you beast! I hope your ears fall off!"

"Dragons don't have external ears," Mizriel said, stepping out of the cool cloud-cast shadow that fell over the boy suddenly. The white-haired sorceress looked up past her son's lean body to confront the great worm. "At least this breed does not." She clapped her hands sharply. "Go home! Go back into the forest! Off with you; off, I say."

The dragon paused in place. He was of the four-footed kind, with a chest like the prow of a ship, short legs ending in feline clawed paws rather than hawkish taloned feet, and a serpentine neck and head surmounted by a waving fan-coral crest. His jaws were sufficiently long and capacious to snap up the sorceress in two bites, her son in one.

But he was not stupid. He knew Mizriel of the White Hair for what she was, and all dragons had a healthy respect for magicians. He had seen her power in action enough times to appreciate its strength, and had observed further that she never used it to oppress or coerce other beings. For this, he had come to love her. He lowered his head submissively to the grass, rolling the star-pupiled green eye that was his best feature (he had only the one). Soft little imploring sounds welled up in his long throat.

Mizriel of the White Hair stepped onto the beaky promontory of the dragon's snout and crouched down to caress the horny yellow outcroppings surrounding his nostrils. The softer tissues within flared orange with pleasure.

"There, there," she said softly. "I don't really want you to go. But what can I do! This is the third time in as many months that you've almost eaten my son, Timeo. It's simply not acceptable behavior. We can't have you staying on with civilized folk if you're not reliable in social situations."

The dragon snorted and curled his tail high in the air. It was a most flexible extremity, delicate and finely articulated, capable of the most incredible gyrations. By long and patient effort Mizriel had worked out a private language of tail-signs with the dragon. He could understand human speech but lacked the physical means to reply in kind. Sometimes Mizriel would conjure an illusory tail of her own to keep the conversation on an equal footing.

Now, seeing the dragon sign his desire to communicate, Mizriel said, "Yes, Shkaah? You have a reason?"

Timeo sat up slowly, brushing bits of wood and curls of mandolin string from the front of his tunic. He had a disquieting chill in the pit of his stomach as he watched his mother summon her own tail—sky blue and rose to match her gown—and confer silently with the dragon.

After a time the sorceress made her false tail vanish. "I see," she said. She did not look pleased. "Timeo . . ." From the sound of her voice, she had forgotten how close her only child had just come to being crisped and crunched.

"I was only trying to make him happy!" Timeo waved the biggest splinter of ruined mandolin he could find. "Look what he did to my instrument. I bought it with my own money, too!"

"And if I ever catch the peddler who sold it to you, I may feed him to Shkaah."

The dragon wig-wagged his unwillingness to eat peddlers. He still had some difficulty evaluating the more dramatic forms of exaggeration in human speech. As Mizriel was explaining that she really didn't mean it, Lymri came sauntering over the green to complete the family circle.

"Got here in time, I see."

"Wipe that silly grin off your face, Lymri!" Mizriel's hair was charged with the power of a storm cloud: It rose up from her back and spread itself into snowy wings that made her angry face all the more impressive. "You're not going to put it off with a song or a jest any longer. The time has come." She pointed stiffly at Timeo. "*Tell* him!"

The little minstrel looked from his wife to his son to Shkaah and saw that he had no choice. "Come with me, Timeo." He pulled the boy to his feet and rested his arm on the thin shoulders. "We have to have a little talk."

Timeo went gladly with his adored father. It was a relief to get away from Mizriel. He loved his mother too, but love and understanding were two separate things. She might love him as much as he loved her, yet she seemed to understand Shkaah's tail-speak better than his own simple explanations.

Lymri walked his son back into the great castle of Dureforte Keep. In the cool shadows of the hall, under the watchful eye of old Lord Blas' portrait, Lymri had the boy sit down on one of the long oak benches.

"Son," he said, "you've got to stop teasing the dragon."

"I wasn't! I was singing to it. I thought it looked bored. I sang it the 'Ballad of Rundel's Lady and the Worm of Greyfall.'"

Lymri sighed. He had heard his boy's singing voice more than most. Fatherhood entailed certain sacrifices. The dragon, however, was none of Timeo's kin. "Abridged version?" he asked with dubious hope.

"Oh, no, I'd never do that." Timeo shook his blond head emphatically. In the semidark it had a little of the luminous quality of his mother's platinum hair. "Every verse and all the choruses. I was up to the fifty-sixth when the beast smashed my mandolin."

Folding his hands behind his back, Lymri began to pace slowly before his son. Timeo swung his legs on the bench and waited. When the silence grew too long for his liking, he asked, "Didn't you always tell me that a good minstrel has to have a good memory? That's why I always do the full versions of every song I sing."

What you do to a song, my son, would only be called singing by one who loves you dearly, makes allowances, and is provided with sufficient rag stops for the ears, Lymri thought. *Alas, the wise are right when they do say that sons favor their mothers. Mizriel couldn't carry a tune in a dray cart the size of Dureforte.*

He said, "You'd do better to look to your lessons, Timeo. Sums will serve you better than songs. The future lord of Dureforte Keep will be able to hire as many minstrels as he likes, but no one should tend the estate accounts for him."

The boy's lower lip went out. He stared at the floor. "I don't want to be the lord of Dureforte Keep, Father. I want to be a minstrel, like you."

Lymri sat beside his son. "I fear you have little choice there." He hugged the lad. *My poor Timeo,* the singer thought. *Your mother's heritage is a heavy burden for you—a trust her family's held from the kings of Norm for years untold. Only Lord Thaumas' domain in Lyf can rival this one for size. Aye, rival's the word. There will always be danger from the north.* Aloud he said, "The lords of Dureforte Keep are kings in all but name. It's finer to be a king than a minstrel."

Timeo shook his head stubbornly. "It's finest to be both. *You* are. You're Dureforte's lord now."

"I leave the keep's rule to your mother. I help her where I can, when asked." Lymri stroked his small, thick moustache thoughtfully. "That's as it should be. I'd make an indifferent king. My spirit is called elsewhere."

Timeo knew what his father meant. He saw the small man's hands wander to lift his lute strap over his head and lay the instrument in his lap. The boy wondered whether he and his mother together had spent as many hours on his father's knees as that big-bellied lute.

"Well, so is mine!" Timeo protested. "I don't want to lord it here any more than you do, Father. I'm a minstrel, and I know I have a minstrel's heart. It's just like you sing about Tyveen of Sigraton. He knew what he was!"

Without hesitation or permission, Timeo snatched the lute from his father's hands and set it on his own lap. He twisted the pegs very grandly, for show, then burst into song:

"The best of music's daughters,
The best of music's sons,
Are not so very best as he,
Tyveen of Sigraton.
His songs can charm the waters,
His ballads bind the birds,
Because he makes fair music,
And also uses words.
He plays upon the cittern,
And also on the lute.
There is no task a fighter has
But Tyveen too can doot."

The moment Timeo paused for a breath between verses,

Lymri made his move quickly. The lute was out of the boy's grasp before another line could hit the innocent air.

"'Doot'?" asked Lymri as he inspected his beloved instrument for harm.

"It's really '*do it*,' Father, but it doesn't rhyme if you pronounce it that way." Timeo looked proud. "I made that song up myself."

"Aha. What a . . . surprise." Lymri put his lute out of harm's way. "You know, Timeo, there's no law says a lord may not continue to compose music. As a pastime, not a career. You have an obligation to your family. You really must keep your eyes fixed on a future with you as Dureforte's lord; for the family's sake."

Timeo looked ready to weep. "A pastime?" He sounded piteous. "That's something grown-ups do that they don't have to, because they're not very good at doing it in the first place. Like Mother's cooking. *You* don't practice minstrelsy as a pastime, Father. You're good at it. You're good enough to earn your bread that way. Everyone *looks* at you when you sing in hall. They don't just do it to be polite. I've watched them. When you sing 'The Triumph of Elaar' it's as if you've carried us all away beneath the waves, and we're all holding onto the song like a rope of gold. They *applaud* you, Father. That's what I want. I want them to look at *me*, to applaud *me*." His head drooped. "Silly. I'll never be good enough for that, will I? I'll be lord of Dureforte Keep, and I'll get fat, and sometimes I'll play one of my songs and the servants will say it's good because they'll be afraid not to, and when I die, no one will remember my name or know I ever made a song."

He sobbed, and hated himself for it.

"Now, Timeo . . ." Lymri began.

"Well? Did you tell him?" Mizriel demanded as Lymri came back from the castle.

"Where's Shkaah?" Lymri asked, doing his best to fudge over the question.

"He decided it would be better to return to the eastern woodlands now after all. It will only grow more difficult for him to go back and survive there the longer he lingers hand-fed here. It's a shame—there are no dragons native to the

Twleve Kingdoms these days that I know of, though there are tales concerning the Naîmlo Wood . . . I had hoped to learn more about the creatures from Shkaah. Oh well, I want what's best for him.''

"Then Timeo managed to do some good after all, forcing Shkaah to a decision.'' Lymri immediately was sorry he spoke.

His sorceress-wife pounced. "You *did* tell him?''

Lymri looked helpless. "My dear, I hadn't the heart. I told him he had . . . promise.''

"You what?''

"And I suggested he keep his gifts under wraps until he had practiced quite a deal more and found the proper audience to appreciate him. Mizriel, what's the harm in the boy nourishing a dream of minstrelry? He does play stringed instruments passably well.''

"Fine. An artistic accompaniment to a cat's wedding. The boy sings as if he has a grudge against all sense and sweetness in songs. Lymri, sometimes I think you need lessons on what it means to be a human being. You have enough good intentions in you to supply an army of village idiots. There is nothing worse than someone who *thinks* he can sing, unless it's someone who *thinks* he can act.''

"Now really, love, with the dragon gone, he can't get into any more perils *thinking* he can sing.''

"Mother! Father! *Help!*''

Timeo's parents turned to see their pride come running towards them over the lawn, a cittern strapped to his back. It gave him a double wallop for every step he took, but he did not waste a moment to slow down and readjust its position. He hadn't the time to spare.

Baying for his death, the pack of sort-breed castle dogs came snapping at Timeo's heels. They were led by an enraged buck rabbit and followed by the head cook of Dureforte Keep. The rabbit managed to leap ahead and gash Timeo's ankles every once in a while with cunningly sharp teeth.

The spectacle of her boy pursued and harried by what should have been that night's supper was too much for Mizriel. She stood as one lightning struck and let the whole rout rush past her without doing a thing until Lymri nudged her. In a dazed afterthought, she raised her arm to cast a holding spell over dogs, cook, and bunny. Timeo kept running. Watching him go, Mizriel recovered herself.

"No more perils, did you say?" She pursed her lips at her husband.

Lymri shrugged. "I am a minstrel, not a prophet. And as I'm a father too, I'd better go catch our son before he runs all the way to Heydista." The little man took to his heels before his wife could say anything else.

"You *tell* him he can't sing!" Mizriel shouted after him. "This time you *tell* him or I will!"

But the wind took her voice and carried it far away.

Chapter I

SOAK HIM FOR PLENTY

Timeo ducked a flying rock and answered with a heavier one. "Clear off there, you misbegotten trash! Show me the color of your heels!" He stooped to pick a hoof-split piece of cobble from the street and struck a threatening pose. "Or would you rather I showed you the color of your brains?"

The pack of four urchins paused, their hands scrabbling in the road for missiles of their own, and took the measure of their foe. The odds had shifted. He was a youth full grown, and fortune had placed a formidable chunk of stone in his hands. With a silent communion of glances, they agreed to run.

"Gutter scum! Slut ware! Cowards!" Timeo flung insults after them instead of rocks, though he would have loved to pursue them with heftier arguments. However, as a student of the Course General, he had the honor of the university to consider. This code of proper comportment would be ill-served by chucking cobbles at street brats, unless in self-defense. The tenuous balance of amity to be maintained between the students of the university city and the nonacademic inhabitants of Panomo-Midmists was to blame.

Lixan Promezas, Timeo's professor of the Introductory Philosophy of Survival, had phrased it best when he told a packed lecture hall: "Gentlemen, for some townsfolk, the academic gown commands respect; for some it is a galling reminder of all they do not know and will never learn; and for some juvenile members of the community—whatever their age—it is a silken invitation to horsepat hurling contests. No one will blame you if you strike back, *within reason and with sufficient justification.* But before you decide to crack a few small skulls, you would do well to recall that the snot-nosed brat you toss in the River Salmlis today may be the son of the tailor who demands your confinement in debtors' prison for an outstanding bill tomorrow. And a few of your classmates and—ahem—faculty members too, if he is an overly fond parent. There is more than one way,'' he concluded, ''to be a credit to this university.''

It was hard advice to follow, but pragmatic. Not every student was as well provided for as Timeo. Most lived hand-to-mouth between scholarship payments, academic prize awards, and infrequent arrivals of aid from home. The prestige of Panomo-Midmists rested on her students, but the survival of those students rested on the goodwill of her shopkeepers.

Timeo caught several of the merchants of Eluman Alley eyeing him closely. For all he knew, one or more of them might be blood kin to the brat pack he'd chased away. He gave them all a sickly smile and dropped his rock. Most of them shrugged and returned to their daily routines, but Mistress Bruling of The Prudent Surfeit bakeshop motioned for him to approach.

''Here.'' She thrust a large, paper-wrapped parcel into his hands. A savory smell rose from it to tantalize his nostrils and make his mouth water.

''Lamprey?'' he asked, hardly daring to hope.

''Wi' herbs and bacon. Fresh f'um t'oven.'' Mistress Bruling wiped her floury hands on her apron before brushing a few test crumbs from her bristly brown moustache. She always made it a point to sample her own wares. It was hard to say whether she was farther famed for that lush growth of lip fur or for her lamprey pasties. Many a starving student of the Course Artistic had staved off final perishment by presenting the good bake wife with a sonnet extolling her subnasal ornament as a mark of rare beauty not found in every woman.

Timeo tried to balance the package on one arm while fumbling for his belt pouch. ''I think I've enough to pay for them, Mistress Bruling, but if I haven't the coin on me now, I can just run over to my dormitory—''

"Get off that!" Mistress Bruling planted hands on hips, eyes blazing like two rum-soaked juniper berries afire. "Don't they teach you study-sprats nowt about t' gracious way t'accept a gift when it's give you? Call it payment for running off that naggle o' ruffians. A gift for t' both o' you, mind! See as the boy gets his share or—" She made the motions usually reserved for mincing the larger cuts of beef into pasty filling.

"Oh, Mistress Bruling, you know I'll make sure Keri gets—" Timeo paused and glanced up and down Eluman Alley. "Say, where is he?"

"That's t'other reason for t' gift, young sir." Mistress Bruling jabbed a thumb back into the fragrant shadows of her shop. "Payment 'tis t' get him out f'um underways o' my work. It's under t' counter you'll find him, and obliged I'd be was you t' remove him frowt."

The Prudent Surfeit was a half shop, as such were called, with more than two-thirds of the cramped interior reserved for the proprietress' workplace. There was hardly room for the customers to come inside, and it was only the reputation of Mistress Bruling's wares that kept clients waiting outdoors for service in all weathers. Though Timeo had grown into a surprisingly tall young man, he was skinny. Still, even he found it hard going to fit himself inside the bakeshop when Mistress Bruling was in residence too. He edged along the narrow strip of flooring, his back sawed by the edge of the counter that ran lengthwise through the shop, until his plump guide had to open the gate that would let them pass through to the cooking area. It only swung outwards, which meant Mistress Bruling had to back up, which in turn squdged her ample hips into Timeo's belly.

"None o' that!" she growled.

"It never so much as crossed my mind," the young man squeaked, bearing the package of lamprey pasties high and trying to wriggle away.

"S'prise me did anything ever cross it," the fair Bruling grumbled. "Desert o' Thulain sees more traffic, I'll be bound." She got the gate open and pointed dramatically to the other side, where a bake oven and a flour-dusted table took up most of the room. "Get 'im out!"

There was much Timeo would do for lamprey pasties, but there were limits. The university's Course General treated with Philosophy, Lower Mathematics, History, Theology, Self-Defense, and one elective subject. At this moment, Timeo wished that instead of Music he had chosen Irrational Physics (a segment of the Course Sorcerous). There was no logical way on earth—or at least in this narrow shop—that he would be able to get past Mistress Bruling and through the gate in the counter.

Then he heard Keristor crying.

"Hold these!" He shoved the packaged pasties back at their donor, missing her hands but balancing them tidily atop her bosom. Gathering his long legs under him like a grasshopper, he vaulted the counter and came down on the other side. His good intentions outweighed his grace. He landed with one foot on the floor, the other doubled up on the edge of the worktable. The table was heavy wood and would not tilt, but the flour strewing its top was less stable. Timeo's foot shot straight out, launching Mistress Bruling's rolling pins and pastry cutters across the room. He banged the back of his thigh on the table top, and clunked his head soundly when both of his legs decided they would rather be together again. A cloud of flour rose up to cover the disaster.

"You all right?" Mistress Bruling inquired of Timeo's white-powdered shoe soles.

Timeo lay admiring the workmanship on the underside of Mistress Bruling's counter. His ankles rested comfortably against the edge of the worktable, and his whole body was folded into a tipsy V, but he felt strangely averse to moving just then.

"Sweet Sarai, he's been and killed himself!"

He heard Mistress Bruling's horrified exclamation with equal indifference. For the first time in his life, Professor Promezas' lectures of Philosophy were beginning to make sense. The professor himself had kindly agreed to appear floating in midair under the bakeshop counter, in multiple aspects, and Timeo didn't want to miss a word he/they said. Only when the venerable teacher stroked Timeo's cheek and let his many faces melt into that of a dark-eyed little boy did it seem like a good idea to sit up.

"Timeo?" The boy's heavy eyelids made him look even more worried than he must have been. His ginger-brown hair was thick with dirt and a more recent dusting of flour.

"I'm all right, Keri. Really, I'm fine." He clasped the boy's aimlessly wandering hands between his own. "What about you?"

It was a foolish question. The bruises on the boy's flat face were plain to see, as was the trickle of dried blood from his nose. When Timeo pushed the lad's hair out of his eyes, he saw a gash that must have been left by a thrown stone. "Bastards . . ." he breathed.

"Worse'n that, damn them purple!" Mistress Bruling leaned over the counter, entering the conversation upside down. "Born sideways on t'blanket meself, I was, and not a pinch on them lot, so don't go lumping 'em with honest by-blows! If I hadn't been up t' my elbows in forcemeat, I'd've give 'em all a lesson with my paddle, didn't you happen along." She snorted. "The idea, picking on a poor lackwit like that. They should be ashamed o'—"

"*Lackwit?*"

Timeo never did know how he got onto his feet so fast. He had no memory of worming past Mistress Bruling a second time, yet when the red haze cleared from his eyes, there he was, standing in the street with Keristor, giving Mistress Bruling some unorthodox suggestions for the storage of lamprey pasties.

"Fine thanks!" the proprietess of The Prudent Surfeit cried. "This is what comes o' being human to a gown-get!" Her fellow merchants came to their doors to support her as she railed against Timeo.

"Human! Who set you up as a judge of humanity?" Timeo shot back. He put one arm around Keristor's shoulders. The boy was almost as tall as his protector, but he cowered like a child. "Calling him a lackwit to his face, is that human?"

Mistress Bruling guffawed. "What's he know of it? Doesn't mean any more t' him than good day to a dog. Not as I'd stand still to see those street brats throw rocks at a helpless animal either. I *care* about the poor dumb beasts," she informed her avid audience.

"Family feeling, no doubt," a chill, clear voice spoke from above. The spotty sunlight in Eluman Alley was blotted out for a heart-stopping moment as vast wings overspread the tilty buildings. Mistress Bruling and her fellow merchants gazed up open-mouthed at the clashing metallic wings and cruelly curved talons of the lion-bodied monster now descending into their midst. Lesser souls shrieked and fled. More seasoned residents—especially those used to collecting past-due bills from professors of the Course Sorcerous— merely retired to the shelter of their shopfronts and prepared to fight, run, hide the receipts, or serve the new-come customer, as occasion dictated.

The beast folded its wings as it came to rest on the cobbles. Those merchants who had lingered to watch now saw that it was an even odder compendium of creatures than distance suggested. Besides the body of a lion and the wings of a great bird it had a horse's tail and mane. Unfortunately for a fully terrifying effect, this last grew out of the head of a gigantic gopher. Somebody chortled and the beast gave him a hurt look.

Its white-haired rider slipped daintily from her silver saddle, shaking beads of melting frost from her midnight-blue traveling cape. "Really, Timeo, brawling with hucksters in the street—! Is this what I'm paying for you to learn?"

"Mother . . ." Timeo's voice sounded as watery as his knees felt. His mother's accusing stares always did that to him. Since he'd gotten his full growth, he was a head taller than she, but he never looked on that pinched, pale face without feeling five years old again and caught committing some unnamed crime.

"Well? No explanation?" Mizriel rested one hand on the saddlebow, and her conglomerate mount whistled and clashed its teeth nastily. She looked from her son to Mistress Bruling, who had remained petrified on the spot ever since the little sorceress' unscheduled landing. "And you?"

Mistress Bruling babbled out a slanted version of what had transpired in Eluman Alley. She was capable of spicing her tale with as much imagination as her lamprey pasties, so that by recitation's end, she had the sympathy of all her hearers.

"I see," Mizriel said. She returned her eyes to a quaking Timeo. "For a single word ill-chosen, you harangue this honest woman in public. As if you never erred by one word yourself, naturally." To the slowly gathering crowd she added, "I have been known to mistake a word here and there myself, in the course of practicing my art." She smoothed a tangle from her steed's mane.

"She called Keristor a lackwit, Mother!" Timeo's protest might as well have been addressed to a cobble.

"I am not deaf, Timeo. I heard what she called him. Also what you called her. Haven't I taught you that it is a sign of little mental invention to use insults that depend entirely on your opponent's physical flaws?"

"Called me fuzz-lip, he did," Mistress Bruling mumbled through fingers concealing the lip in question.

Mizriel of the White Hair gently removed the bake wife's hand and touched the moustache with the tip of her little finger. It vanished traceless. A gasp went up from many throats, and curses from those students in the throng who had been laboring over rondelays to the departed whiskers.

"Now, Timeo, let us go back to your dormitory. I want a word with you. In private."

Fell of Glytch lounged among the plump pillows of the curtained bed and inquired, "Any sign of him yet, Ovrin?"

The young man leaning out the open window had to twist his torso slightly to pass his massive shoulders back into the room. "None." He ran a nervous hand through his red hair and helped himself to a beefruit gourd from the packed basket on the nightstand. "Nor of Keristor either."

Fell yawned and scratched himself through his brown fustian tunic. "Quit your worries."

"You can say that when you know Keri's not—"

"Your little brother can take care of himself. It's our chum Timeo needs the keeper." He chuckled and winked. "Good thing he's got us to look after him, hey?"

Ovrin looked sorrowful as he munched the beefruit. "Wish it didn't have to be this way."

"*That* again?" The gourd was slapped from his lips. Fell

was out of the bed with a tumbler's swiftness, black hair and eyes wild. "And what other way'd you have it? Picking crumbs from between the pages of your books with a wet finger? Playing lick-tail games around some of our great and grand professors' courts of scholars? Selling yourself as experimental subjects for every jackstraw puppy mage in the Course Sorcerous? You *and* your brother!"

Fell was wiry, all city-bred sinew where Ovrin had a plowboy's muscular physique. The redhead didn't need to listen to such abuse—he could have crushed both Fell's hands in one of his own—but instead he just shook his head. "I couldn't go back to that. For Keri's sake."

"Then what's gnawing at your bones?" Fell relaxed, his smile lazy. "It's not like we're stealing old Timeo's coin. We never take but what he offers, and if a man can't spread his better fortune among his friends, what's life worth?" *A fortune he did nothing to earn*, Fell reflected bitterly. Behind his lazy smile were knife-edged thoughts, long honed on envy's whetstone.

"But we're *lying* to him, Fell! We're always and ever telling him lies!"

"Huh! No more than he wants to hear." Fell cast a sideways glance at the lute in the corner. "No more than all his teachers do when they give him passing marks. A year more tuition to come into their hands for *that* lie. What we take's a piddle by comparison." Fell's sooty brows drew together. "A piddle, and I'm tired of living on that, I'll tell you. There must be a way to draw more off him. There must . . ."

A fiery white star burst into the center of the room and three people were suddenly there. Keristor broke from Timeo's encircling arm and ran to his brother's bear hug.

"Out," Mizriel said.

"Ma—ma'am?" Fell was seldom at a loss for words, but this was the first time he had met Timeo's mother.

"Now." She turned her hands palm up, and two small animals that looked like quill-bearing turtles perched on them. They snapped their beaky jaws at the interlopers.

"Timeo, we were just waiting to talk to—"

Mizriel set her pets down on the floor. They went straight for Ovrin and Fell, quills bristling, claws digging up showers of splinters from the floorboards. Timeo's fellow students ran from the room, yanking Keristor with them, and slammed the door.

Mizriel made a sour face as she toed the half-eaten beefruit gourd. "I can't say as I care for your friends, dear," she said. "When your mother comes all this way for a visit, the least they might have done was introduce themselves. Oh, well." She spread her black skirts over the arms of a chair and sat down.

"Let's talk."

Chapter II

NOR ANY DROP TO DRINK

"Think she's gone yet?" Ovrin asked Fell as the two of them lounged among the ivy plants beneath Timeo's window.

Fell hauled himself to his feet and chinned himself up on the windowsill for a look inside. A purple fireball zoomed past his head. Automatically he ducked it, only to be hit full in the mouth by a puddinglike creature with a perch's face. It globbered mournfully as it flew away. It was followed in flight by a swarm of outsize winged spiders that tickled their way over Fell's neck as they passed, making him lose his grip and tumble screaming into the dirt. He brushed himself off.

"No," he replied with great dignity.

Ovrin sighed. "I wish she'd go." He glanced across the courtyard to where his little brother was observing the comings and goings of an ant colony. Mizriel's gopher-headed steed was in turn observing Keristor as if he were a meaty carrot. This did not appear to bother the boy at all.

"At least the horror's safely tethered," Ovrin said to himself. "As if that'd make a difference to Keri."

Keristor was capable of long, uninterrupted periods of concentration, but when his elder brother asked him what he found so fascinating, he just smiled. There was an age difference of only three years between the brothers, and a gap wider than the cold spaces between the stars. Ovrin found it a little frightening, not knowing what was going on behind that placid face, those eternally dreaming eyes. It was as if his little brother viewed the world as a noisy, unnecessary interruption to whatever was the true reality.

Maybe he saw the gods. *God-touched* was the kindest name applied to children like Keristor, and village superstition claimed that since the gods had departed the Twelve Kingdoms, only certain individuals had the sight to follow them wherever they now roved. How else to account for Keristor's unstintingly mild disposition, his wandering gaze, his total uninterest in nearly everything but his own private passions? God-touched.

Lackwit. They had called him that too, and worse, when the brothers lived in Lascoe village. Old women at the milk stool made finger signs at his back to keep the evil eye off their cows. Pregnant and nursing mothers hustled themselves and their babies out of sight whenever they knew Keristor was coming, as if the boy carried blight, and spat in his shadow when they weren't quick enough to evade him. Children too old to be tainted would taunt him, thinking he couldn't tell kind words from cruel.

They were wrong.

A loud crash and a series of piteous squeals from the open window distracted Ovrin from his thoughts. "And I thought my old mother was a terror," he said. "Sarai All-Mother keep her soul."

Fell chewed a hangnail. "Gods alone know what any man's mother'd put him through if she were a sorceress like the Lady Mizriel. Poor old Timeo. As I heard it, his da was all right—a minstrel sweet-voiced enough to lure birds to the hand and ships to the rocks—but he died not a half year past. He was all that could keep our friend's lady mother partway human in her temper. Oh, but she loved him true!" He cast an arm over his brow and struck a swooning pose popular with romantic heroines from the illustrated broadsheet street ballads. "You remember how Timeo looked when he came back to school after his father's funeral?"

Ovrin shuddered. "Did you see her eyes? Colder than anything, not a drop of feeling that I could see. Hard to picture that fish loving anyone."

"She loved her husband, right enough." Fell gave a mocking chuckle. "And her art, maybe; and that's all, if we can believe what Timeo tells. But who cares whether she's summer sun or winter ice so long as she doesn't freeze up her purse strings towards our good friend, hey?"

"I guess." Ovrin still looked sorrowful. His own mother's face swam out of memory, so worn and marked by the care of two growing sons—one god-touched, one always hungering after bookish things—and no man about the house to ease the burden. Her tongue was often sharp, but she never tried to beat sense into Keristor nor practicality into Ovrin. She worked hard, silently, so that her eldest might have the lessons his soul craved and her youngest might learn—slowly, so slowly!—to do for himself. It was work she died of.

"Here!" Fell punched Ovrin's shoulder. "Wake up! It's bad enough one of you's always in the clouds. At least Keri's got an excuse. The witch can't stay in there forever, and when she leaves, we'd best be ready."

"Ready for what?"

"Why, to pick up the pieces, of course!" Fell made an expansive scooping motion with both hands, but only he knew whether he was gathering up the shattered fragments of Timeo's self-esteem or the scattered coins of Timeo's allowance.

"Mother, I—"

A white flare exploded inches from Timeo's nose, dazzling his sight to dancing black dots. He rubbed his eyes.

"You'll get your turn to explain yourself soon enough, young man," Mizriel said, her mouth a small, severe line. "The least you could do is stop interrupting your mother. The gods know, you made enough noise when you were an infant. You'd think you'd quiet down somewhat by this time. Noise and mess." She cast a distasteful eye about the cluttered dormitory room. "If the university gave awards for those two *virtues*, I'd finally know some pride in my son. Pride!" She laughed bitterly. "Something I've known precious seldom from the day you were born."

"I didn't ask to be born," Timeo muttered.

"No one asks for sorrow," the sorceress retorted. "They

get it all the same. It's the mark of man to make something better out of it. Puppies whine." She settled herself more comfortably in the big armchair. "Now, where was I? Ah, yes. This." She plucked a parchment from inside her wide black belt and smoothed the folds. "It would seem I have something to be proud of after all. Your professor of Minstrelry, Applied and Theoretic, informs me that your original composition, 'The Fatal Bearpaw,' has won the departmental prize for Most Humorous Tirralay."

"What?" Timeo snatched the notice from his mother's lap. His eyes widened as he scanned the lines. *"Most humorous?* Great Insar, are all the old men mad who teach here? That song was about how my Aunt Ursula slew Morgeld's evil servant, Captain Tor! Call that *humorous?"*

"And a tirralay, too. You may imagine my feelings." Mizriel's voice was dry. "You know that I was there when it happened. That same Tor was about to kill me, and very nearly did, until my sister stepped in." The air about Mizriel's armchair acquired a reddish tinge. "It's not so much the embarrassment of hearing one's near-death turned into a tirralay." The rosy aura deepened in hue. "It's not the anticipation of hearing your aunt's reaction to this 'honor' of yours." The red light began to pulse in waves like heat-heavy desert air. "It's not even the fact that your late father's ballad on this very theme is made ridiculous by its inevitable association with your own *creation."* A crackling emanated from the white-haired sorceress.

"But who in Mhispan's name gave you permission to study minstrelry?" Mizriel shot to her feet just as a bolt of flame lanced across the room and smashed Timeo's lute to burning splinters.

"Here," said Fell, passing Timeo a tankard. "Drink this."

Timeo sat at the rickety corner table, head in hand, and downed the offering without bothering to ascertain what it was. It seared his throat and reduced him to choking, spluttering tears. Ovrin pounded him on the back until he recovered.

"Gods, what *was* that?" he demanded when he could speak. "Not this tavern's ale!"

"Of course not." Fell pursed his lips. "My cousin Sterion does all the brewing for the Chuckling Bear himself, and there's not a tavern in all Panomo-Midmists can touch his brown and bitter. You've been drinking it these past seven rounds and no ill effects, but you look like you could use stronger waters, so I had Steri pour you out a measure of Sumnerol *jurav*."

"Isn't that the stuff those fisherfolk distill from blubber? And use to cleanse wounds?"

Fell shrugged. "Steri just imports it; he doesn't ask its pedigree. It's good for what ails you."

Timeo's head sank back into his hand. "Will it make my mother understand me? Or send her back to Dureforte Keep?"

Ovrin put his arm around Timeo's sagging shoulders. "You can always change your courses back to the way they were once she's gone. Let her think you've dropped Minstrelry, then take it up again."

"No good." Timeo's sigh would have broken a banker's heart. "I know her. Soon as I agree to drop Minstrelry, she'd be off to the university governors and lay a curse on them all that'd take hold the minute they switched my courses back the way I want them."

Ovrin scratched his head. "What's to stop her from threatening to curse them now, unless they take you out of Minstrelry and keep you out?"

"Nothing on her part, I'll say. It's only what'd happen to her if she tried it." He jerked his thumb at the portrait hanging above the tavern's common room fireplace. A fair young woman with long, straight, sunny hair stood holding a lance from which a cloth of silver banner flew, its embroidered golden harp plain to see. Her other hand propped up an azure shield on which was an open book, argent, with the motto "Here Truth Shines Brightest."

"The gods be thanked for our wardlady, Fortunata," Timeo said. All the students at the surrounding tables heard him and raised their glasses in her name. Even the barmaid of the Chuckling Bear paused in her rounds to murmur praise for the witchborn lady whose special care was the kingdom of Clarem where Panomo-Midmists lay. "If anyone dares try to coerce the university students or faculty, she'll take them in hand. My mother's a sorceress—a mage by study and aptitude—but the Lady Fortunata is sister to Ayree, Prince of Warlocks, and has greater powers by birth than Mother can ever hope to learn.''

''I don't understand.'' Big Ovrin looked genuinely bewildered. ''If your mother can't coerce them into changing your courses for you, how can she force them to keep you from changing them back?''

''The year's almost sped.'' Timeo gazed dully into the bottom of his empty tankard. ''The Havror Fenn's on us in less than two weeks' time. No course can be changed during or after that festival, and university rules forbid swapping courses back and forth without a two-week interval between.''

''University regulations can be more effective than any witch's curse,'' Fell agreed. ''Another round?''

Another round was brought, though the barmaid proved recalcitrant at first. ''Your friend's had plenty,'' she said, pointing at Timeo. His head had slid out of his supporting palm and now rested with his sharply pointed chin wedged into the empty tankard.

''Nonsense. He can hold his ale.'' Fell was staunch in Timeo's defense.

''Pay for it, too,'' Timeo put in, though the words came a little hampered by the tankard's hold on his lower jaw.

''I shouldn't wonder. The night's order from this whole table's been going on your slate, steady.'' She balanced her serving tray on her head while she readjusted the set of one of the water lilies adorning her long, black braid. The plait fell well below her slender hips, a chain of flowers that nearly dragged the floor.

''What's that to you?'' Timeo grunted.

''Nothing. Ale's as good a grave as water.'' She grabbed the tankard from beneath Timeo's chin and yanked. It came off with a moist *pop*. She tossed it over her shoulder without looking. The students watched in delicious tension as the heavy wooden drinking vessel sailed through the air end over end, only to plop unerringly into the tub of soapy water behind the bar.

''Huzzah, Cattail! Your aim's as keen as ever!''

''Cattail?'' Timeo muttered. He gazed up at the buxom

young woman through a groggy haze. She seemed to undulate as she passed from table to bar and back to the table with their drinks. "Fine name f'you too, with that black swisher trailing down your backside." Here he burst into noisy giggles. Ovrin and Fell joined in dutifully.

"Huh! Another student wit. That makes sixty-five this week alone." The tray was back atop the barmaid's head, laden with the orders of several other tables. It rested there unmoving, though she tossed her head indignantly and made sweeping gestures to underscore her every word. "Only the last sixty-four had the balls to call it my *ass*, not my *backside*, little boy."

"See here—!" Fell began. He rose from his place to put on a great show of defending his friend's honor.

Cattail planted one finger on his breastbone and shoved him back into the chair without even shaking her tray.

"You—you— I'll have Steri fire you, bitch!" Fell spluttered.

"Oh, will you?" Cattail's thick black brows rose in unvoiced laughter. She called the tavern keeper from his place behind the bar. "This sprat says you're to fire me."

Anyone seeing Fell and Sterion side by side would marvel to hear that these two men shared common blood. Sterion was taller, brawnier, and fuzzier than his cousin, with a single sooty eyebrow that grew enthusiastically in tufts and featherings above his small red eyes. He was also more straightforward in his speech than the student.

"Mind yer own business or I'll crack yer skull, Fell." Having uttered this simple admonition, he returned to his taps and bottles. Cattail wore a cream-glutted smile.

It was an irritating smile for sober men to see, but for a man deep sunk in the potent mixture of Sumnerol *jurav* and home-brewed brown ale, it was provoking in the extreme. Timeo stood up and roared.

"What did you say, little boy?" the barmaid inquired lightly.

"I said that you may trust your bullying bedmate to protect your employment for you from now until the gods return, but within the week you'll wish with all your heart that you were as far from Panomo-Midmists as possible!"

"A threat?" Cattail's brows took wing. A charming

dimple showed beside her thin mouth. "Will you be brave
enough to take on Master Sterion in battle?" She considered
Timeo well as he swayed there, his hands holding on to the
table's edge because it *would* pitch and yaw so violently.

"The only battle that truly counts, wench! A battle of
wits! And my quarrel's with you, not him. You are doomed,
poor slut. I shall destroy you utterly in song!"

Not everyone in the Chuckling Bear knew Timeo. For that
reason, the laughter was not general.

Timeo took the small swells of mirth for encouragement.
"Before tomorrow's sun sets, your name, appearance, and
personal shortcomings shall be known to every student in the
university, to every hoary-headed professor, to every unaca-
demic wretch who serves us in tavern or marketplace! Your
face shall be on every tongue! I vow this in the name of me,
myself, Timeo Landbegot, and all my lineage!" He thrust a
clenched fist at the roof and fell over backwards into Ovrin's
lap.

"Bring me a lute," he mumbled. "Give her a taste of
what she's in for."

Fell gave Ovrin a short, sharp nod. Between the two of
them, they propped Timeo up in his own chair and passed
from table to table, seeking the loan of a stringed instrument. It should not have been a hard item to find. The
Chuckling Bear was a favored tavern among students of
Minstrelry and Jest, though it did not have the same status
as the Singing Bird, popular with more serious musicians.
Lutes, citterns, lap harps and zithers abounded, but none
were offered to Ovrin and Fell. Those who didn't know
Timeo, refused to lend something so expensive to a drunk.
Those who did, refused on the grounds of self-preservation.

"I want to have my drink in peace," one youth grumped,
plunging his needly nose deeper into his cup. "Got a 'xam
t'morry, no chance but be ploughed, and I don' wanna think
'bout it. One skree outa that'un's throat'd be 'nough t'
frighten off th'effects of all I've drunk t'night an' every drink
I downed th' past six month besides."

"It's only for a moment," Ovrin begged. "He's too drunk
himself to sing long. We'll give it right back to you!"

"Har! That you will, sure . . . 'less some dainty soul sees
fit t' smash it flindery once that'un starts his song. 'S been

known t' happen. Done it myself a time or two." He drew himself up proudly. "Name o' sweet music, I did it! Now squak off, the pair o' you."

Ovrin was persistent. "If someone does happen to break your lute, Timeo will buy you a new one—the finest! He can afford it."

The beery student pulled down the skin beneath one eye and twisted his mouth. "Think I don't know that, too? Whole damn 'versity knows it. Knows that's why you two hang 'round 'im like flies 'round fresh shit."

"Why, you—" Fell's fists clenched in anger, then unclenched in short order when he evaluated the size and number of the student's table mates. He tasted acid in his mouth, the sour shame of hearing the truth about himself. What stung worse was knowing Ovrin only leeched on Timeo for Keri's sake. Fell played the toady because it seemed the softest road. When he stumbled over the inevitable sharp stone, he wasn't the sort to try a different path. With a glib mind's special sorcery, he turned self-loathing into hatred. *What I am is Timeo's fault,* he thought. *These affronts I must suffer, I bear on his account, curse him. But someday* . . . He swallowed bile and put on a conciliatory face for the man who had insulted him.

"You've got no right to say such things. We're as poor as you," Fell said lamely.

"That's your own fault," remarked one of the needle-nosed student's companions. "When a man's got a fat pigeon in his lap and doesn't know the proper way to pluck it, who's to blame if he starves? You wouldn't be crying poverty if you had greater influence over such a rich tidbit as old Timeo."

"Influence?" Fell and Ovrin repeated together, although with different intonation.

"Rich?" Cattail asked, having drifted over to eavesdrop.

"Only son o' Mizriel o' th' White Hair an' Lymri Riverborn," the needle-nosed student told his beer. "Sole heir to one o' th' biggest damn domains . . . near a kingdom!"

"Landbegot and Riverborn," Cattail mused, setting her tray down. "Odd names."

"Likely 'twas his father give him his name, t' c'fuse th' shame o' his own finding. Make 'em sim'lar, so folk'll think 'sa fam'ly tradition, 'stead of a bastard's catch name. A foundling, that's what Lymri Riverborn was. Ever'body knows it. Found right here, th' bank o' th' Salmlis, near on forty years past.''

Cattail stiffened where she stood. The student didn't notice.

''Sweet-voiced? Hoo! Lymri Riverborn's still a legend for his songs. Now he's dead, shouldn't be s'prized did you hear 'em calling him a demigod 'thin ten year. But his son?'' The student made a rude noise with his tongue and splattered beer all over the table.

''Hey, Pesken, have a care!'' The student who had spoken of influence blotted droplets from his sleeve, then returned his attention to Ovrin and Fell. ''Yes, you heard me right,'' he said. ''I'll be willing to put coin on whether or not you've influence enough on Timeo to gull him good and proper.''

''We don't really gull—'' Ovrin began.

Fell cut him off. ''Name your wager.''

''Ten that you can't convince the poor booby to enter the Havror Fenn.'' The young man smiled. ''I'm willing to wager that even Timeo has more sense than to lay himself open for public humiliation on such a grand scale.''

Timeo lurched to his feet. He had heard nothing of the tavern conversations, but the ale and the *jurav* had obviously been carrying on a lively dialogue inside his skull all this time. ''Since you insist, my friends, I shall sing unaccompanied!'' he declaimed. He bleated through four lines of a tuneless song in which he compared Cattail's raven hair to a pregnant weasel before throwing up.

''And he has to be sober!'' the setter of the wager added hastily. ''Stone sober when he performs in the festival, or the bet's off. It's your influence, not the liquor's, that we're to measure.''

Fell winked at Ovrin, who just looked miserable. ''Done and done.'' He sealed the bet with a handshake.

Timeo's eyes watered terribly as he fought to regain mastery of his treacherous innards. Doubled over in his chair, he blinked at the tears. As his vision cleared, he was astonished to find the barmaid Cattail kneeling at his feet. His stomach lurched in fear that she might treat him after the manner of an empty tankard. He was in no condition to defend himself.

"I—uh—hope you didn't take that pregnant weasel remark seriously," he stammered.

"I shall treasure it always," the barmaid cooed. Her luminous black eyes swam with adoration. "To think that I, a humble barmaid, should be worthy of your exquisite voice!"

Timeo blinked some more, though his eyes had stopped watering. "Exquisite voice?"

She clasped her hands about his knees and murmured, "I don't suppose you'd be kind enough to favor me with another song? Outside." Her fingertips casually tickled the insides of his thighs. "Where it's cooler."

Timeo's disbelieving consent was rather lost as he was sick a second time. Cattail hustled him out of the Chuckling Bear while Fell was still nailing down details for the great wager.

Chapter III

REED MY LIPS

Although a light rain was falling and clouds covered the sky, Timeo saw nothing absurd about Cattail's insistence that they go down to the riverbank to view the moon. He was too bemused by the lovely barmaid's sudden appreciation of his musical gifts, to say nothing of the lingering *jurav* fumes whispering wild tales through his brain. Everything made perfect sense if you didn't stop to think about it.

"—And so it was my father gave me my first lesson," he said, leaning heavily on Cattail's shoulder as they approached the riverside promenade. Willows overhung the gray brick walk, sending rivulets of rainwater trickling down over any strollers who passed beneath their frondy branches. Timeo's hair was half soaked already.

"I think it was nasty of those folk in the Bear to call your father a bastard," Cattail said, contriving to snuggle herself even deeper into Timeo's embrace.

"Oh, but he was!" Timeo shoved a dripping lock of hair out of his eyes. "He often told me about how he was found in the reeds hereabouts. It's as good a place as any for a husbandless woman to bear her baby, though not always a safe one. That's what his foster mother always said."

"His foster mother? Then his true one gave him up?"

Timeo looked solemn. "Not willingly. He was wrapped warmly and dressed prettily when he was found. Show me the mother lavishes such care on her babe if she means to abandon him! No, I still remember my grandam telling the

30

tale after she came to live with us at Dureforte. I was four
the year she died, but I can remember. She said that no
woman dresses a child—even a bastard—in such finery unless
she's keeping him. But that unlucky soul birthed my father
within sight of the Lands Unknown, and the evil spirits that
dwell over the water have been known to carry off mortal
women. Weakened after a birth, how could she have fought
them off? Poor thing, she was probably scared half to death
besides. They're all monsters and horrors, drinkers of blood
and eaters of human flesh in the Lands Unknown.''

He gestured dramatically out over the river. Cattail looked
to where he pointed. The River Salmlis was dotted with the
falling rain, but the air was clearing. It was hardly more than
a gentle mist coming from the clouds, and you could see for
leagues up and down the riverbank.

But across the waters there lay a thick fog, and the falling
rain could do nothing to dispell it. It was a chill bank of
earthbound cloud, its blue-gray roils forbidding.

''There are legends of the Lands Unknown,'' Timeo said.
''Legends that say it was once a pleasant land, as open to
trade and travel as any of the Twelve Kingdoms. But evil
came over it, and no one who sails across the Salmlis to that
hidden shore is ever heard from again. The mists and fogs
straight from the night-spirits' realm covered the land, and
honest folk were driven out.''

''Who drove them?'' Cattail asked.

''Why, the Waterfolk, of course. They're not like Elaar's
people, who dwell beneath the salty waves. Capricious,
wicked, entirely unreliable, the Waterfolk are. It's said that
the reason for the evil was that they pacted with the night
spirits, even mated with them! They haven't any more
restraint than fish when it comes to breeding and about as
much sense of who their fathers are.''

''My. How do you come to learn so much about a land
and people no one ever visits?'' Cattail's voice was oddly
flat.

''There are old men and women in every corner of
Panomo-Midmists who'll claim they hail from Salmlis'
western bank, and speak freely of all cruelties the Waterfolk
visited upon them, until they had to flee or die. I'm surprised
you don't know.''

"That's what I get for staying out of corners." Cattail shrugged, causing Timeo to take a misstep and twist his ankle. "Tell me more about your father."

"What?" Timeo balanced unsteadily on one foot while he rubbed the injured one. He was not fit for such exertions, and tumbled into a puddle under the willows.

Cattail was kneeling beside him again, her pale skin almost glowing in the dim light. His hands reached up to stroke her shining hair, and she did not prevent him. Her cheek was very dry and soft, her hair dry and silky. Only her clothes were as sodden with rain as his own.

"How do you do that?" Timeo wondered.

"Do what?" Cattail asked, making her eyes wide.

"Your skin—your hair—your—"

"I thought you were going to sing for me," the barmaid said, pouting. "But you're like all the men. Think you can just rain compliments on a girl and she'll melt. I've heard enough pretties about my hair and my skin and my what-have-you. What I'd *like* is a song."

This was a greater wonder to Timeo than all the anomalies of nature combined. He sat up straighter in the puddle. "I—I don't have an instrument, but—" He cleared his throat and sang:

" 'Who art thou, sweet maid of twenty,
Underneath the willow tree?
If I give you gold aplenty,
Wilt thou come away with me?'
'Oh no, sir, you rank me cheaply.
Gold shall never buy my love,
As if I were a mere sheeply,
Or a cage-pent turtledove.
If my love you would inspire,
Here is one thing you must do:
Fame in battle first acquire—
Nobly die, then I'll love you.' "

The rain stopped abruptly. Timeo studied Cattail's frozen smile cautiously. "That was an impromptu. Did you . . . like it?"

"Sheeply . . . is the diminutive?" Cattail replied between clenched teeth.

"You *knew!*" Timeo was breathless with delight. "You're the first—I mean, my father always did encourage me, and Ovrin and Fell never fail to say kind things about my songs, but the only ones who've really seemed to understand them straight off, without a lot of tedious explanation—and you shouldn't have to explain *real* poetry, should you?—the only ones who understand are you and—"

The drooping willow branches shook, though there was no wind. Cattail's head jerked, and for an instant Timeo imagined that her pitchy eyes glowed green. He dismissed it as a trick born of moonlight and *jurav*.

"Who's there?" she barked. A blade was in her hand, a knife made of sharpened bone with a water lily carved on the pommel. "Come out!"

The willows stirred again, and a tall, lean-shanked boy of around fourteen shuffled through the leafy curtain. He stared slack-mouthed at Cattail with solemn, hungering eyes, as if he meant to drink down her image with the rain and leave her no skin to hide her spirit in.

"Keristor! What are you doing here?" Timeo scrambled out of the puddle and forced the boy to turn around and look at him instead of Cattail. The barmaid sheathed her knife.

"I followed you," Keristor said, volunteering nothing more.

"Your brother—didn't he tell you to wait on the bench outside the Chuckling Bear? Look at you! You're soaked right through. If you'd have stayed where you were put, you'd be dry now. There's a good overhang from the second—"

Timeo stopped. There was no way to tell whether any of what he said was making an impression on the boy. He sighed and patted Keristor on the back. "Ovrin will be worried. We'd better take you back to the tavern."

He started away from the river, guiding the boy towards the lantern-lit maze of streets. He only paused when he realized that Cattail had stayed on the bank.

"You go on," she called cheerily, holding her skirts high to wring water from the hem. "I've an errand."

"Will I see you again?" Timeo's plaintive question

trembled among the willow leaves. His eyes rested on her naked feet, toes longer and finer than many a highborn lady's fingers.

"The tavern's where I'll always be, and well you know it." Strong, slim legs gleamed bare as she winked at him. "Fancy-free students—well, they go where they like."

"I'll be back!" Timeo cried, leading Keristor away. "Tomorrow night, I swear it! And I'll have a new lute, and a new song, just for you, my lady!" The streets swallowed the two young men.

"Mother of Waters, give me the strength to hear it without screaming," Cattail muttered. She waited until she was sure that Timeo and Keristor were far from the bank, then girted her skirts up between her legs and leaped out into the river.

She landed flat-footed on the water's surface and glided forward over the rippling current as though winter ice held the Salmlis frozen. Taking care that each step should be heel first, she raced upstream, never raising so much as a splash. She did not stop until she was past the fashionable promenade and alongside that section of riverfront properties popular with the more disreputable and unfashionable elements of the university city.

There were no lovingly tended groves of willow here, no brick paths, no hands to uproot the thick clumps of reed that obscured a free view of the Salmlis. When she came to an especially dense growth of these plants, Cattail at last returned to the shore.

She knelt among the green stalks and placed her lips close to the river mud. *"Zibethica! Zibethica!"*

The reeds stirred under her breath, then shook faster and faster, until a tussock of them was rattling in a gale of its own imagining. The stems blurred together as they shook, and a golden skinned woman wrapped in the mantle of her own ghostly yellow hair materialized in their midst.

"This had better be important, rousting me on my night off, young lady!" she snapped at the barmaid. "I've pulled over to the Philosopher's Mistress, and if I never meet another wizard who asks me do I want to see his magic wand, snicker-snicker, I'll die happy."

"You judge, Zibethica," Cattail replied, and told her of the night's happenings.

The lady among the reeds went from indignation to puzzlement to passionate interest. "Are you certain? Can he possibly be—?"

"If only his voice were not so . . . unique, I would wager my life on it."

"He is his father's son, in spite of that." Zibethica turned smug. "He's not full-blooded, after all, and his mother sings like a turnip."

"How could you know?"

"Unless there are two sorceresses named Mizriel of the White Hair, I do. She ordered a hot bath when she arrived at the Philosopher's Mistress, and I brought up the pails and soap. No magic allowed abovestairs, you know, or the whole inn would be a spiderweb of tangled spells. Too bad, or those mages could magic up their own baths, soap and all. She sang in the tub while I poured the water." The reed-spirit made a face, remembering. "Yes, if he is Lymri Riverborn's son, he is the one."

A suspicion crossed Cattail's mind. "Why do you sound so *very* sure of this one's father having been the babe? More than one bastard was found along this river in that year, or I don't know human nature."

"Really, Cattail, you are so frightfully *young*, sometimes. So foolishly enthusiastic. The moment I heard you'd joined us, I thought, 'Oh dear, now she'll expect to right things within a fortnight.' Years have passed, dear child. We haven't just been sitting about, waiting for you to tell us of a nice young man with a father surnamed Riverborn. We've kept what watch we could over Lymri, waiting for the proper time. The pity of it is he died before that time might come." A tear ran amber down her cheek. "He was the dearest babe."

"At least he left a son." Cattail was grim. "And the time grows more favorable every day. We might even enlist the sorceress' help. Magic on our side . . ."

"Ask her for it, then, if you wish." Zibethica sighed. "She won't be the first mage we've sounded. The spell of disbelief is still as strong as ever, and Elaar's Daughter weaves the net fine and tight."

"Still, I will try." Cattail sounded determined.

"What harm is there in trying?" Zibethica yawned, and sank back into her reedy bed.

"What harm is there in trying?" Fell purred, pushing a mug of freshly drawn ale into Timeo's hand.

Timeo pushed it right back. His mouth felt full of caterpillars, and he didn't like the way the group of students at the next table were staring at him. If they were hoping to see him throw up again, he was going to disappoint them.

"This is the Havror Fenn you're talking of, Fell," he said. "The highest festival of minstrelry and jest in the whole calendar. It's not just university students who enter the competition. Singers and players from all over come to try for the crowns."

"And you're here already, so you won't be exhausted after a long trip," Fell pointed out.

"What harm could it do, just trying?" Ovrin added.

"No harm, I guess . . ." Timeo stroked his beardless chin. His two companions glanced at the table full of witnesses, their faces growing longer by the minute. "No harm really . . ." Ovrin and Fell grinned.

"I'll tell you what: I need a new lute anyway, and I've run through my allowance for this quarter. I'll ask my mother what she thinks of this," Timeo said.

Grins and glumness changed sides in the blink of an eye.

Chapter IV

WATER OFF A DUCK'S BACK

"Good evening, sir." Cattail dropped a shallow curtsy to the proprietor of the Philosopher's Mistress. He was a man of general good humor, and a joyfully waddling testimonial to the excellence of his tavern's kitchen. "I should like to see the Lady Mizriel of the White Hair, if you please."

"It may please me, but I doubt it would please her much, my lass." The gentleman smiled broadly, and the lines of merriment creased themselves all the way from his full, red lips to the back of his hairless head. "You never can tell what will please the clientele who prefer my humble inn." He tapped his chin with the mouthpiece of his long-stemmed clay pipe and shifted a step to the right, discreetly yet effectively blocking Cattail from the staircase. "Take it you know whereof I speak?"

"I am not afraid of mages, sir."

" 'Deed?" The host's nut brown eyebrows were the only claim to hair his head could boast, and now they soared. "Met many of them over breakfast, have you? Or *before* they've had their breakfasts of a morning? That's when they're fiercest. Oh, they're pleasant enough to bid you good day in the street, but by and large I wouldn't step on anyone's shadow in this house."

"Still, it is well past the hour of breakfast now, and I would like to see the Lady Mizriel." Cattail remained firm.

She had put on her best skirt, her most finely embroidered blouse, her crispest petticoats, and had bullied Sterion into giving her the whole day off. She would be switched if she'd waste all that effort and have to endure Zibethica's twisty I-told-you-so smile besides. She heard whistling from the tavern's common room, and glimpsed the reed-spirit through the open doorway off the front stairs hall. Zibethica was hard at work, scrubbing down tables. She caught sight of Cattail and winked.

The host of the Philosopher's Mistress sucked on his empty pipe. "You have spirit, my lass. I shall do what I may to put you in the lady sorceress' way." He drifted towards the common room. "Room three."

Cattail dropped him a deeper curtsy and hurried past him towards the stairway. He shot out a plump, ruddy hand and seized her by the elbow.

"Your pardon," he said to her indignant look. "I nigh forgot: You must wait. There's someone else with the lady presently. Even so brash and fine a lass as you wouldn't be reckless enough to interrupt a private chat."

"Who's with her? Another wizard?"

The proprietor chuckled. "Bless you, this isn't the Merrie Manticore of Cymweh port, where the wizards and warlocks cluster so thick in the common room that they shoo 'em out like flies! Here, step up to the bar and sample a draft of my autumn ale while you wait, compliments of the house." Gallantly he steered her into the common room. "It's only her son she's seeing. Family reunions never last long"—he laid a finger beside his bulbous nose—"though they often seem eternal to those caught up in 'em."

Timeo paced the length of his mother's sumptuous room for the eleventh time. "All I asked was why *can't* I have the coin?"

From her place on the window seat, Mizriel replied, "And all I asked was why you need it?"

"Expenses."

"Debts?"

"No!" He was stung. "You know I promised Father I'd never be like the Wastrel Scholar."

"Your father . . ." Mention of Lymri worked strange,

swiftly shifting changes across the sorceress' face. Her lips trembled from the brink of tears to the edge of ancient laughter and over into complete exasperation. ''It was trial enough when your father wrote soppy, moralistic sludge like 'The Wastrel Scholar' and 'The Gamester's Virtuous Daughter,' just to torment me, but he ended up believing them too!'' The anger receded as the tears returned, this time to overflow her eyes. ''My poor love . . . and now where shall I hear the songs that will let me believe?''

''Oh, Mother!'' Timeo sat beside Mizriel and clasped her hands. She leaned against him and wept on his shoulder.

''Why did he die? Why?'' Her fingers dug into Timeo's arms. ''There was no sickness I could see. He grew sad, that was all. He wandered from the castle more and more often with every passing day, his eyes forever looking to the west. That, or else he'd linger beside the River Carras and stare downstream from dawn to dusk. What did he hear? What did he seek? What did he wish to follow?''

''Did he never say what was troubling him, Mother?''

The sorceress' white hair was unbound, the wavy cloud falling over her face. ''Never so that I could understand.'' Her words came muffled.

''How long—how long did this go on? I remember finding him well when I returned home for last harvest.'' Timeo again saw his father perched high on the hayrick, his lute laid aside in favor of the shrill box fiddle that plucked bright notes of a peasant dance from the air. The harvest queen shinnied up the briar pole to kiss her king, and more than one of the blithe and buxom country women of Blas' domain clambered up the hayrick to steal their own kisses from the elfin fiddler.

''Even then.'' Mizriel lifted her head and gave her son a hard look. ''When you came home, it was as if he took new life. The melancholy left him—for good, I prayed. But the moment you went back to this accursed town, he fell into gloom once more. He even stopped going down to the riverside to bathe. His sorrow deepened, and drowned him. He could not stir from his bed one morning. His whole body burned with a fever that none of my herbs could touch. I never felt skin so dry! It almost crackled under my fingers, yet when I came to lay damp cloths on his forehead he motioned me away. He said"—a harsh catch seized her voice—"he said that it was cruel to keep him. Then he asked for you, and died."

Timeo was unable to speak. He scarcely felt his mother's slight body pull roughly from his arms. His father's merry face filled his sight, and the sweetest voice in all the world seemed to sing all at once the old songs of joy and sorrow, love and longing, brief lights struck against the darkness, and long farewells that still kindled hope from the spark of promised return. "I never knew he asked for me," he said half aloud.

"You were his life!" It came as an accusation. "You were all he cared for, from the day you were born. You never knew . . ." Mizriel gave the words a bitter twist. "If you had known, that wouldn't have stopped you. You'd still have filled your empty head with wild ideas of being a singer, wandering the roads in all weathers, trying to make the crowds at village fairs still their chatter long enough to hear some half-cooked songlet of your making. Dead heroes and departed gods! Ladies so fair that they never needed a brain in their heads! Not a mention of backache at planting time or taxes to be paid or babies dying in the cradle, no! And for *that* you would have left the land that is your charge, by bloodright! For that you left the father who loved you!"

"My father understood—"

"And that is what made him a poet! What have you ever understood, Timeo? Responsibility? Duty?"

Timeo's face flushed uncomfortably. He had come hoping to get a few coins from his mother and a bit of counsel concerning whether he should enter the coming competition. Instead he had gotten a hideful. For all that, if he were to take part in the Havror Fenn, it must not be with a borrowed instrument. Ovrin and Fell both insisted he was good enough, and he liked to think that he might be. They were counting on him. He needed the money.

"I'll take over my duties in the domain as soon as I finish my studies, Mother. You know that." He hoped to placate her.

"And what good will you do the land with tirralays?"

He shuddered. Mizriel of the White Hair never forgot and

never let go of his past failings. He wondered whether all mothers were like that.

"A good lord should have some culture," he said weakly.

"Ambra shield him, this is your poor father's fault. You were pig-blind set on music, and he never did you the kindness of speaking the truth of things before he died. That was the softest excuse he could give you, I suppose, that folderol about lords needing culture. Set a lord with culture against the man strong with a blade and they'll be burying the lord and his *culture* in little sticky bits all over the landscape! And the man who knows how to make figures dance to his tune will bury lord and bladesman alike, and build a new law court over their tombs."

Timeo's head sank lower and lower under his mother's sharp speech. "I'm sorry," he managed to say, and slowly rose to take his leave.

"Just a minute! Where do you think you're going?"

"Back to my rooms."

"Without what you came for? Did your expenses vanish?"

"I don't want to trouble you."

"I'm your mother. I'm old friends with trouble." The little sorceress strode across the room to a chest of drawers and rummaged through the top one until she had a chamois pouch in her hand. "I'll not have it said that I stinted you in any way. That would reflect poorly on our domain, and wouldn't Lord Thaumas' bitch daughters make a deal of that! Here." It jingled as it fell at Timeo's feet. "That should keep you until next month, I trust."

Timeo stood staring gratefully at the windfall. "Oh, thank you, thank you, Mother! I shall dedicate my very first song at the competition to you!" He stooped to pick up the purse.

A dainty foot slammed down on top of it, narrowly missing his fingers. "What competition?"

"The Havror Fenn. The festival of high minstrelry and jest supreme."

"Tell me that what you just said is a jest. Please."

"Well, to be frank I haven't decided yet whether I'll enter the competition or not," Timeo admitted, straightening. "I was thinking about it, and I figured that I'd best be safe and get a new lute just in case I do—"

"*Helagarde's halls!*" Only the no magic abovestairs rule

kept Mizriel from loosing the more concrete manifestations of her temper. "Have you the desire to play the complete fool before so many witnesses? To skreek and yowl those idiot verses of yours out in *public?* Well, I see I still have all the sense in the family, and I won't allow it! Timeo, I forbid you to enter the Havror Fenn."

There was something about the word *forbid* that wrought its own magic. Timeo's eyes and mouth narrowed. "The Havror Fenn is open to all comers."

"Most of whom have the brains to know that they sound like a cat caught in a churn and don't need an audience's laughter to prove it."

"Is that what you think I sound like?"

"I'm only speaking for your own good."

"For my own good or not, you can't forbid me to enter."

"I can hold back the price of a lute." Mizriel's small, sharp chin came up. She had fighting blood in her veins.

So did he. "Hold it back, then! And hold my inheritance with it! I'm entering the Havror Fenn!"

He clomped out of the room, with Mizriel whipping after him. As he lolloped down the stairs, she leaned over the upper storey railing and yelled, "The day you find one creature in this world who *honestly* craves your songs, then I'll call you minstrel! And you know where I am when you want to apologize!"

"He might not." Cattail glided out of the unoccupied room at the head of the stairs.

Mizriel's hair was falling in damp wisps over her forehead. "How does your master reward eavesdropping wenches?" she snapped.

"I wouldn't know. This isn't my master's tavern. My lady, I am a friend of your son's, and—"

"Your friendship's due for an unexpected death. Timeo forswore his inheritance. He hasn't a copper to curse."

Cattail frowned. "What's that to me? I don't care about his money."

Mizriel laughed harshly in her face. "Don't tell me you love him for his songs alone!"

The barmaid of the Chuckling Bear seemed to grow more and more perplexed by the turns this conversation was taking. "My lady, my honor will not let me lie to you,

especially about your son's . . . singing. If you will hear
me out—''

Mizriel pulled her hair back with both hands. She felt
foully hot and wanted nothing more than a cool bath just
then. She had no time to spar with this slut—the gods knew
where Timeo had picked her up! The girl had obviously
come seeking to cadge money with some tale of a broken
heart or worse. Mizriel was in no humor for tales, and
proceeded to give Cattail a curt, vibrant character analysis
for the whole tavern to hear. Then she flounced back to her
room, leaving the barmaid steaming silently in her wake.

Below, among the spectators, Zibethica was wearing that
twisty smile.

"Innkeeper!"

Swathed in dripping hair, a soft blanket, and nothing else,
the lady Mizriel bellowed down the stairwell. The proprietor
of the Philosopher's Mistress puffed up the steps and asked,
between gasps, how might he serve?

"How much must I pay you to have the no magic abovestairs rule lifted for me, pray?'' The little sorceress' voice
was on a dangerously tight rein.

"My lady, the rule holds for all, witchborn and wizardly
alike. Even the lady Fortunata honors it when she graces
these premises. Even her honored brother, the most noble
Ayree, Prince of—''

"Then *what* is *this?*'' The Lady Mizriel thrust a wriggling
fish into the tavernkeeper's startled face.

"It is—a pickerel, I believe. Possibly a small muskel-
lunge.''

"It can be a Kestrel salmon, for all of me. The salient
fact is that it is a *fish* and that I found it in my smallclothes
drawer after my bath!''

The host furrowed his brow. "Alive?''

"It's living now, isn't it? And it wasn't lonely while it
waited for me to find it. Every one of my—my most intimate
garments is presently inhabited by a living, flapping fish! If
witchery didn't put them there and keep them breathing all
this time out of water, what did?''

"That I can't fathom.'' The innkeeper scratched his bald
pate. "Our policy bans wizardry and witchborn sorcery, yet

there might still be . . . My old mother would tell me stories of beings and things . . . things that *are* magic 'thout *using* magic.''

"Riddles." Mizriel curled her lip.

"Just as you say, my lady. I'll clear out your drawers. Zibethica! Fetch a withy basket up to number three! A big one!" A happy thought made him pause and shout: "And change the dinner slate, Zib, my girl! It's fresh-grilled fish tonight!"

Chapter V

DON'T GO NEAR THE WATER

"Maybe we can turn this to our advantage," Ovrin repeated. He and Keristor watched Fell count out the last of their coppers into the vintner's palm, under the sharp eyes of that worthy man's wife.

"Short one," she said briskly.

The vintner attempted to placate his mate. "Now, wife, we've dealt with these young men before this, and they've always been good for—"

"They've always paid cash! How'd you know to trust their credit?" she shot back. "Something's gone wrong for them, and I won't have you bear their troubles with your own." She turned to the students. "It's pay in full as before or go elsewhere!"

The vintner returned the coins one by one, looking most apologetic. "You do understand, lads?"

"I understand that more than grapes are squashed in your house," Fell replied gracelessly, and stalked up the street with Ovrin hurrying after, dragging Keristor with him. "There's the advantage!" the dark-haired student growled as his legs devoured the distance between the wine shop and home. "There's what we glean from Timeo's crack-headed pride! No wine tonight, nor from now on, until he goes cap in hand to his mother. Well, I'm going to see that he does, you mark me!"

"But Fell—" Ovrin was panting. Though he was more muscular than his companion, the sedentary student's life had sapped a lot of his rough peasant energy. "Fell, if he makes it up with his mother, she'll insist that he renounce the Havror Fenn and then where will our bets be? Since word spread, we can't go into a tavern without half a dozen folk wanting to get a piece of the wager."

Fell did not slacken his stride. "Everyone knows how high Timeo's used to living. They're betting that he'll sicken of the real student's life and do whatever his mother bids him, just to get back into silks and gravy. And I'm not sure but they're right."

"He seems to be bearing up all right so far."

"Because he's living on *us!*" Fell stopped short and shouted his anger. "Because he's holed up in *our* lousy room, gobbling down whatever food *we* can purchase, and stealing *our* sleep with his twanglings!"

"It's no more than we used to do to him." Fell's venomous glare forced Ovrin to add: "Isn't it?"

"With the difference that *he* could afford to share what he had! Gods, I could strangle him gladly. The fool overstepped it when he withdrew from the university. At least his rooms were paid up until the end of term, and we might've pawned the fittings, but no! He must make the grand gesture! He must depart his mother's rule with only the clothes on his back!"

It was nearing noon, and the street where Fell loosed his feelings was deep in the merchants' district of Panomo-Midmists. There were many passersby ready and willing to pause and be entertained by his rantings. The lanky student suddenly became aware of the spectacle he was making of himself. He shut his mouth with a near-audible snap, lowered his head, and plowed on up the street. Ovrin and Keristor were only able to catch up with him on the threshold of their lodgings. Even then Ovrin had to use both hands to hold Fell back on the doorstep.

"If you persuade him to apologize to his mother, how will we pay off the wagers we've already made?" he asked, eyes frantic.

"Calm down, calm down. Think I haven't thought of that, you great ox? When Timeo's back in his dam's good graces, he'll have coin enough for all that and more. We'll make up some story about needing the money for Keri, there. Old Timeo's soft as butter when it comes to your little brother. The gods be thanked for touching him, I say! We'd never have as sweet a string to harp on if he had his full wits about him.''

Fell smiled blandly at the boy and patted him on the head with all the love a man might lavish on a hound he means to sell. Keristor returned the smile wholeheartedly. ''We're going to eat now?'' he asked.

''Soon, Keri, soon. Yum, yum.'' Fell made broad gestures of spooning up and chewing food out of an invisible bowl, then rubbed his flat stomach and licked his lips.

''You don't need to do that when you talk to him.'' Ovrin gave his companion a warning look.

''Why not? He'll grasp what I mean better this way. Won't you, Keri?'' Fell tapped his temple. ''You understand?''

Keristor looked confused. His smile vanished and he turned to his big brother for help. Fell laughed.

''Never mind. The lean week's done. Follow my lead and we'll be fine.'' He opened the door to their lodgings.

Scholarship students did not live in the vine-covered quadrangles reserved for more affluent scholars and faculty. The university preached equality of minds, but equality stopped outside the classroom door. The first lesson many a youth learned was that the purse was the mightiest preacher of all. Those whose awards covered tuition only, or just partial room and board, soon scrounged up lodgings with willing townsfolk.

To take in students, with their attendant reputation, a landlord or lady had to be very poor to be even slightly willing. Ovrin and Fell's landlord was *very* willing. They found Timeo on hands and knees on the straw pallet he shared with Keristor. He had an old shoe in his hand and was whapping the coarse mattress ticking with savage abandon.

''Working on a new song?'' Fell inquired.

Timeo looked up sharply. ''Do you know there are *bugs* in here?''

''Only discovering that now?'' Fell longed to strike that

incredulous look from Timeo's face with the back of his hand. *Swaddled in gold. I could lend him a scant week off my own childhood that'd teach him brotherhood with bedbugs and fleas.* And *the plaguey rats that carry them. Gods, what justice—?*

"I thought it was the dust making me itch so," Timeo said, scratching at the welter of bites on his chest and arms. He sat cross-legged on the pallet. "We must complain to your landlord."

Fell roared. "And then where shall we sleep tonight? Gubbo the Sot, they call our noble host, but even a sot knows it's easier and cheaper to change lodgers than change flea-ridden bedding. Wake up, Timeo! See where you are!"

Timeo was crestfallen. "I never knew you lived like this. I wish I'd done more for you when I still—"

"But you can do more, Timeo!" Fell was instantly on bended knee beside him, insinuating soft words in his ear. "We didn't want you to learn we lived like this. You know that we'd rather die than impose our misery upon you—you may imagine how poor little Keri suffers, and him without the sense to turn his discomfort to words!—but now you've seen for yourself. Horrid, isn't it?"

Timeo gave no argument there. "What can I do?"

"There will be other years," Fell purred. "Other festivals. How would you manage to enter this Havror Fenn anyway? You haven't the price of a decent instrument, and that old harp you picked up will fall to pieces on the third chord." He pointed to the battered handharp that Ovrin had managed to provide when Timeo first moved in with them.

Timeo sighed and scratched. "You may be right." He looked up, face the mirror of misery. "She'll never let me forget this, you know."

"Never is such a long time . . ." Fell wheedled.

"Where have you been?" Cattail demanded. She tried to contain her excitement at seeing Timeo again, but she had lived in a state of near panic for too long since the day he dropped from sight. She had used every spare moment she had to hunt him in his rooms, in the usual student haunts, even daring the echoing stone halls of the classroom buildings. It was as if a whirlpool had sucked him down.

"Jurav." Timeo's eyes were flat. He slapped a coin on the table.

Cattail ignored it. She set her tray aside and pulled up the chair opposite him. "You look fresh from a funeral. Someone die in your family?"

"Me," he replied. *"Jurav.* A double."

"Tell me what—"

Timeo scraped his chair away from the table and stood up. "Serve me or I'll go where they do."

Cattail's pretty face screwed itself into a pugnacious knot. She picked up her tray and slammed it on top of Timeo's coin as she leaped to her feet. *"Sit!"* She picked up the tray and held it at the proper angle for bashing his head on the next downswing.

Timeo was so flabbergasted that he obeyed. Drinkers at nearby tables prudently looked the other way. The barmaid's temper was clearly well-known.

"Better. Now stay there and I'll bring you a drink. Then you'll talk." She whisked herself to the bar and returned with a flagon of ale. *"Jurav* can't share space with a belly full of self-pity, but one measure of ale cheers a man. One, mind! Drink it off and tell me what's wrong."

She heard him out in silence while other customers called in vain for her attention. Sterion tried to prod her into service but the gimlet eye she gave him sent him scampering to wait her tables himself. Timeo observed this with proper awe.

"How do you manage that?" he asked.

"What, Sterion? He's nothing. Go on with what you were saying, Timeo. You apologized to your mother and—?"

"But he's so *big!*" Timeo insisted. "And you're such a little woman, yet he seems afraid of you."

"You're not afraid of me, are you?" It was a dare.

"N-no. A little—a little surprised by you, sometimes."

"Good. I wouldn't have you be a coward. This world's split between fearers and fighters. When you're afraid of something or someone, it's like surrendering a piece of yourself that you can never get back again. You're worse than a captive, then, you're a slave."

Timeo was ashamed before the barmaid's passionate words. "I think . . . I'm afraid of my mother. A little. I should never have given in to her. A true artist is supposed to undergo hardships gladly, if something beautiful comes of it. I couldn't. I took back my inheritance as pay for quitting the Havror Fenn. I sold my songs for a clean room and a full stomach. I hold the most costly hand harp in all this city, yet I'm not worthy of it. I'm afraid of my mother, and of poverty too. I'm twice a slave."

"Horse dung," Cattail said. She sidled her chair nearer his. "All singers must be petty mages, masters of illusion. If a starving poet sings of suffering, where's the art in that? But when a wealthy man strikes the strings and makes you believe he's suffered—ah! There's magic for you!"

Timeo shook his head. "There is no magic in me." He felt around beneath the table and pulled up an exquisitely made hand harp, the sort meant to be balanced comfortably on one knee. Its golden wood and silvery strings shone with their own special light, and the air around it trembled with eagerness to embrace its music.

"The favored instrument of the ancient epic bards," Timeo said sadly. "They say that when Insar walked the Twelve Kingdoms, this was his favorite. It's meant for a man like my father—someone who can draw tears from the heart and breath from the soul."

"Why did you buy it, if it brings you no joy?"

"I didn't. It was a gift from my mother." Timeo's lips curved into a lifeless smile. "A token to seal the new understanding between us. She tells me what to do, I do it, and I get presents like this." He held up the harp and stared at it, self-loathing in his face. "What am I doing with such a toy?"

He would have cast it far across the room, no doubt to break against a roughcast wall, but Cattail seized his wrist and forestalled him. "You will sing with it," she said in a way that allowed no argument. "You will sing for me."

"I will not sing any—"

She raised the tray a handspan from the table and stared at him so that he could not mistake her intentions. "I said, you will sing for me," she repeated sweetly. "Let me hear your latest song, minstrel."

Timeo was at once thrilled to hear himself called by that honorable title and confused by Cattail's request. "I haven't—that is, I was working on one, but—I was writing an epic about a legendary prince whose death destroys an empire, but it's not finished quite the way—"

"We don't need dead princes," Cattail said sarcastically. "Have you nothing more hopeful to offer me?"

"I've not exactly been living with hope in my belt pouch these past several days."

"What you need is inspiration." She took his hand and stood up. "Let's go for a walk."

Timeo's own desires were never questioned. His will was too freshly crushed for him to offer Cattail the slightest argument. He even waited docilely by the tavern's front door while she did something very peculiar: She raised a dipper of water from the traditional wayfarers' bucket to her lips, whispered something into the liquid, and tossed the whole dipperful out onto the cobbles.

"Shall we?" Her smile belied anything unusual in what she had just done, and Timeo wasn't sure he wanted to know.

This time, it was not raining, though one of the heavy river mists that gave the city its name had drifted up from the Salmlis. Lanterns were fuzzy balls of light in the darkness, and a dank smell weighed down the airier scents of newly cut grass and blooming lilacs.

Timeo hugged his harp close against his body, his cloak covering it. "All this damp isn't good for the instrument," he said. "Couldn't we go back to the tavern?"

"No." Cattail's hand shot through the crook of Timeo's arm and tightened him to her side. Although they walked so closely together, Timeo wondered at the way her face appeared to soften and blur in the mist. Her features grew sharper, and the line of her jaw frilled slightly, as though she wore an exotically fluted collar. Then he blinked, and the illusion vanished. The barmaid smiled at him.

"We shall go back after you've sung; not before."

"Well, if that's all . . ." Timeo stopped in his tracks. He was aware of the soft lapping sound of the river, though their promenade had taken them downstream of the town's formal riverwalk. He was unfamiliar with this part of the city, and the reek of dead fish was very thick in his nostrils. The sooner he sang, the sooner he might escape from this strong-willed wench. He twiddled his harp into tune and struck a flimsy chord.

"She was so sweet and fair to see
That all men knew her fame.
A precious gem of modesty
And Gripsa was her name.
She always was a likely girl,
She always would agree,
With every knight or page or churl
From any family.
For she ranked men as good and great
And wiser far than she,
Wherefore she'd never remonstrate,
But say, 'Yes, dear, I see.'
She never said an angry word,
She never man did chide,
Wherefore it was not too absurd
That she was soon a bride.
But woe, alack, that wedding day!
Alas, sweet Gripsa's doom!
For this dear maid, so people say,
Did die and sleep entombed.
Oh, why did Gripsa have to die?
It happened long ago,
And was because—well may we sigh!—
To Death she'd not say no."

Timeo had begun the song reluctantly, but as the words and music flowed, the old exultation filled him until by the song's end, he was belting out each verse with vigor. The hand harp creaked at the joints under the assault of his fingers, but he forced it into submission with professional mid-song tunings. When the battle to the death between Timeo and music was over, Timeo was clear victor. Music never had a chance.

"You know, I feel much better for that," Timeo remarked, the sparkle back in his eyes. "How did you like—?"

Cattail's opinion of "Gripsa's Lay" was never voiced. A

scream rent the night. The barmaid's nails drove into Timeo's arm. "The river!" she cried. "Hurry!"

Her urgency overwhelmed him. All sounds seemed to come from far off in the mist, yet Cattail knew at once from where the scream had come. If he doubted, there were soon additional shrieks, wailings, and cries for help coming up the bank. Clutching his harp, Timeo ran.

By miraculous chance, the cries came from the one patch of riverbank the mists did not obscure. Four men armed with dragnets and gaffs stood leering down at their victim, a marvelously beautiful woman with a fish's red-gold tail. One net was already over her, though its mesh was insufficient to conceal her glorious, golden hair or the blushing ivory of her breasts.

"Pull off that net, Bukor, and let me have a go," the beefiest fisherman commanded. "I 'uz the one as caught her."

"Gonna breed y'seff to a fishie, Temble? Have lots o' spratlings f' babies?" Bukor was a weasel in a fisherman's smock; his mindless tittering grated Timeo's nerves.

"We'll all have a go!" the third man shouted. He wore a scale-stained leather apron over his bare chest. "Allus did wonder how the fish folk managed. Scientific, I am."

"Randy bastard, you are," said the fourth. "No matter. It's not as we 'uz tuppin' a real lass 'thout by-yer-leave." He chucked the captured water-sprite under the chin. She cowered and moaned.

This was too much. Timeo leaped out of the mist into the clearing. "Let her go!"

The fourth fisherman calmly beaned him with a gaff and tossed him back into the fog. "No keeper," he said with a shrug. The others guffawed.

Timeo's head cleared remarkably fast. Cattail's cool hand was on his brow, but he cast it off angrily. "I'll kill those—"

"They'll kill you, if you go it alone." The barmaid was only stating facts. "And that poor ondine as well."

"Ond—?"

"Not that she won't die anyhow, from what they're planning. But if you attack without thinking, they may cut their losses and her throat at the same time."

"I can't just let them have their way with her! She'll die, you say! I'll get help." He scrambled into a runner's crouch, but again Cattail restrained him.

"By the time you find the night watch or an open door at this hour, they'll be done and she'll be floating down to the Opalza Sea. I'll fetch help. You stop them."

Timeo examined the barmaid's dark eyes for some telltale sign of insanity. "Me, stop them? But you just said—"

"Fight them alone and you die. But I did not mean for you to fight them alone." She knelt opposite him and placed the harp in his hands. "Sing, my lord. In legends, songs have conquered swords. Let your songs fight for you. Sing."

"Legends . . . ?"

"Sing."

There was a fearful compulsion in her voice. While Timeo's mind rejected her command as ludicrous, his fingers floated up to the harp strings under their own volition. He drew a trill from the instrument and sang:

"Under the ocean, under the sea,
Who will come away with me?
Down to the courts of coral and pearl,
Down where the seaweed and porpoises swirl . . ."

The song went on. It was one of his better efforts, a fantasia upon the Triumph of Elaar theme. By and large, he was able to get up to the twenty-second verse before small animals began biting him.

This time, the song had quite a different effect. The mists receded, the island of clear air spreading to include him and Cattail. Timeo looked over the top of his harp to see the men's eyes fixed upon him. Their faces were slack, their eyes glazed. One by one they dropped their nets and gaffs and wandered into the fog. Four splashes sounded from upstream.

Timeo dropped the harp and raced to remove the net from the captive ondine. He blushed somewhat when his hands unavoidably touched her naked breasts, but when she cast her silky arms around his neck and pressed her lithe body firmly against his, his face caught fire.

"My savior!" She nibbled at his ear with tiny teeth. Her

fingers were separated by diaphanous webbing that reached from the base to the first joint, which allowed them to produce the most exotic sensations once introduced to the open neck of Timeo's tunic. "Take me," she whispered hoarsely, "and put me back in the river."

Timeo raised his fish-tailed burden and staggered towards the Salmlis. "Mind my harp, Cattail!" he called over his shoulder. "I won't be long!"

But the barmaid was still waiting when dawn burned off the mists.

Chapter VI

A DROP IN THE BUCKET

"Greetings, Whate. Are they here?" Cattail spoke into the semidarkness of the Marsh and Spring's common room. Even through the gloom, the riverside tavern's less pleasing aspects were quite apparent. There was an all-pervasive dampness, a drizzly atmosphere that coaxed mildew from the thatched roof and furry green mold from the plaster walls. The clientele too looked like they would profit from being taken out and scraped.

Cattail breathed deep of the dank air and loved it.

Whate, the barkeep, was a sodden gentleman with heavy-lidded, protruding eyes and a wide, nearly lipless mouth. He raised his sparse eyebrows at Cattail's question. "Back." He gestured with a thumb the same size as the rest of his fingers. Cattail passed to the rear of the common room, twisted the bung of a wine cask, and pulled open a rack of bottles hiding a small doorway. It glided shut after her. None of the common room crowd seemed to notice.

The back room was darker and damper than the front. Cattail's bare toes splashed through finger-joint-deep water. A lone candle guided her to the table where five figures awaited her.

"Hullo, Cattail. Pull up a glass." Bukor held out an amber wine cup.

Cattail batted it away. "You *idiots!*"

The four fishermen from Timeo's riverbank battle cringed,

but the golden-haired ondine in their midst smiled tranquilly and swished her fishtail through the shallow water.

"What's wrong?" Temble asked. "I thought we did pretty good on that short notice."

"Good? You might've killed him!" Cattail jabbed a finger at the fourth fisherman, the one who had stunned Timeo with his gaff.

"Aw now, missus . . ." He wrung the hem of his tunic. "Missus, it was just t' make it look good. More authentic. We s'posed to just let him spring in there and not hit 'im? Wouldn't look natural. He'd suspicion something."

"*Does* he suspect?" Bukor asked.

"Nothing yet." Cattail was not happy. "It's not the sort of news you startle a person with. If his father were still alive, it would be simpler, but—"

"If his father were still alive we wouldn't need him," the ondine said.

"You . . ." Cattail's eyes glowed green in the shadowy room. If there was any love between her and the fish-tailed girl, it was well hidden. "If there's anyone who overplayed a part, it's you, you sticklebacked slut. Wipe that smug look off your face, or I'll wipe it for you!"

"I was only doing my job." The girl sounded jaded past bearing. "Under *your* orders. Can't get this job done soon enough for me. Why can't we just tell him what he is and be done with it?"

"That's why I do the thinking and you do—whatever it was you did. I don't want to know about it." Cattail hastily raised a silencing hand. "We could tell him what he is in a moment. That's easy. It's making him see that he's ours, that he has a duty to us and to his people—that's the hard part."

"I don't see why." The fishtail curved up to cover a yawn.

"Wake up, Duila," Bukor said. "How would you react if a soul you hardly knew came up to you and said"—here he pressed his hands together, tilted his head prettily to one side, and batted his eyelashes—"'Oh, please, sir, won't you come with me to the Lands Unknown? You're our royal prince, you see, and our only hope for fulfilling the old prophecy of the Vessel of Watersong. Never you mind that no one comes back alive from the Lands Unknown these days. Don't give it a second thought that the whole royal family was massacred—'cepting your father, which is why you're here. Forget that nigh all the folk who might've been your allies over there are helpless. You just come with me.'''

"Oh." Duila was chastened.

Temble sighed deeply. "It'd *be* that easy, not for that cussed spell."

"Cht." Bukor rolled his eyes elaborately in Cattail's direction.

The barmaid lowered her eyelids wearily. "It's all right, Bukor. I don't take it personally, and I quite agree with Temble. Magic would help us no end, if that spell of disbelief would lift from the Lands Unknown. But it hangs on the mind of mortals like a dream, leaving even the wizardly and witchborn unable to believe there was a time when the Lands Unknown were free. Some have even forgotten us entirely. The Waterfolk dwindle to legends in the telling, to nursery tale creatures, even to bloodthirsty monsters, but never to what we really are."

"'S like a fog o' the mind," Bukor said. He chuckled without humor. "There's a rich jest: a fog. And so we need the boy."

"If a lad's to play the hero's part, he can't be plunged into it. Test the waters first, then dive," the aproned fisherman said. He took off the apron in question. Frilly ventral fins did a loincloth's duty below his waist. He peeled the wig from his head and the false eyebrows and whiskers from his face. Skin the color of skimmed milk showed on the patches not stained with walnut juice. He sighed with pleasure. "Much better."

"That looks like a good idea," the fish-tailed girl said, watching her comrade's pleasurable striptease. She proceeded to wriggle out of her scaly tail, revealing celery-colored legs that shone with a thin coating of some oily substance. "Oooooohhh, that feels wonderful!" she gurgled, kicking the fish tail under the table.

"Before you get too comfortable, Duila"—Cattail's voice held a strong warning note—"make your report. I don't like being trapped in this disguise any more than you do. What did you learn from our prince? Did you turn the conversation to his father?"

Duila became very interested in flexing the webbing between her toes.

"Did you talk with him *at all?*"

"I'm bringing him along gently so's not to shock him," Duila said, still not looking at Cattail. "That was the plan, wasn't it?"

Cattail's roar of rage might have been heard in the courts of Elaar herself. "This is what I get for working with nixies!" she complained to the thatch.

Duila took umbrage. "Nothing wrong with nixies. You ondines think you're so perfect! Forcing me into that nasty, tight costume and passing me off as one of you, and why? Think *that* halfbreed's going to know ondine from almondine?"

"Blasphemy!" Temble and the rest were scandalized.

Duila yanked her discarded disguise up by the tail. "Doesn't even look anything like an ondine!" She leaned towards Cattail with a foxy sneer. "Too slim in the tail."

Cattail was unmoved by the gibe. She looked past the unmasked nixie and told the four males, "Gentles, your task is done. You nearly cracked our prince's skull doing it, but we shall forget that. What matters is you have given him a taste of heroism. You have shown him that he can be a fighter, even if his chief weapon must be song."

"Ugh." One of the men winced at the memory. "Did you hear what he did to that poor innocent tune?"

"Comes of breeding on dry land." Bukor took a deep drink. "Beds belong in rivers."

"Mixed blood does not make his claim to the throne any less," Cattail said, very stern. "The royal strain of the Waterfolk will always rise to the top. I myself"—she lowered her eyes modestly—"know whereof I speak. I have some trifling touch of the blood royal in my own veins. It has always been a solace to me in this, our time of trial."

"I'll just bet it has!" the nixie mewed. "Means you're in no danger of being dragged back at old Ragnar's pleasure any time he feels like using Elaar's Daughter to call us in! No, you may have the luxury of calling yourself *exile,* and wander freely through the realms of men!"

"And do I?" Cattail replied sharply. "Elaar's Daughter calls to me in vain, and how do I spend the privilege? In idleness? In luxury? As the spoiled pet of some northern lordling or as queen of a Vairish harem? No! As a slop-wiping barmaid, working for *your* liberation, that's how I use my royal blood!"

She grabbed Bukor's drink from his hand and downed it, then took possession of the whole bottle. "Get out." She was grumpier than a heat-chafed bear. "Back over river, before you turn up missing. Be just like Ragnar to pull one of his nose counts by night. And you, Duila—get back to Timeo."

The nixie scowled, but tugged the false fish tail back on, grousing about uppity ondines and their airs all the while. Bukor and Temble offered to link their hands and give her a lift to the river, but she snubbed them. Nose in air, she hippety-hopped out through a small door at the rear of the room. A loud splash proclaimed just where that door led. The others exited that way as well, leaving Cattail to her thoughts and her wine.

"Make a hero of him," she mumbled, and began to recite a singsong rhyme:

"From a vessel none would fancy,
From a spell both old and strong,
Thence shall come our liberation,
Thence shall rise the Watersong.
Evil powers shall not touch it,
Death shall end the ancient wrong,
From the vessel flows our freedom,
Miracle of Watersong."

She had another cup of wine. "Watersong . . . from Timeo? Gods, there's a fine prophecy for him to fulfill! Maybe he'll sing better once he's on ancestral marshland. Either that, or it's a real miracle we're seeking. Prince or polyp, that one's got a voice like a churn full of cats." She licked her lips. "Not a bad looking churnful, though. Mmmm." Fishy teeth twinkled in the darkness.

Chapter VII

A TIDE IN THE AFFAIRS OF MEN

"He's in love," Ovrin said between sips of beer.

"Good. That'll make him stupid. Ask him for the money now." Fell nodded towards the table where Timeo sat entertaining the mysterious, golden-haired lady. Her beauty was not something seen every day in a tavern like the Chuckling Bear, and she had the full attention of that evening's entire crowd.

"Ask him for the money?" The redhead was taken aback. "Why me?"

"He favors you more, and you know it. Look, you and Keri both hail from his thrice-blasted domain. You ask him for the coin and he'll have the chance to play the grand lord before that lady of his, raining largesse over his humble subject. Nothing better for standing tall with your woman than showing how another man's beholden to you."

"How would you know?" Ovrin flicked a crumb across the tavern table. "Who's ever been in your debt, Fell?"

Fell flashed a short, sharp smile. "You are, Ovrin. Or have you forgotten that your name's on half the wager pledges we've signed in this city?"

"At your instigation!"

"Slack off. Your face turns to raw beef when you get excited. You were willing enough to play when it looked like an easy way to gull the lordling-schoolboys of their candy money. We've better use for it than they, you said."

"It was your prodding made me see it that way. Keri, you kept saying; think of Keri!"

"Well, you thought of him, didn't you? And you signed. If you make a man's bets, accept a man's risk."

"Risk." It was a bitter word for Ovrin. "What have I risked? I haven't coin enough to cover the wagers when the Havror Fenn comes around. All I've risked, and lost, is my honor. My scholarship will be forfeit when this comes to light, and I'll be turned from the university. Then what will become of Keri and me?"

Fell clapped his large companion on the back. *Easy to guide as an ox,* he thought. *Easier.* "At the worst, you'll hire yourself out as a farmer's hand, and all the glories of learning you gathered here will dwindle to dust in your mind. Is that agreeable to you? No? Then I suggest you do as I say, or else you'll be the best educated plow horse ever seen in Lascoe village. Get yourself in front of Timeo's eyes right now and start tapping him for the start of the money we'll need to pay off our wagers."

"Think I should do it now?" Ovrin gazed at Timeo and his lady with envious longing. "He mightn't like being interrupted."

"Get on!" Fell gave him a rough shove. "Mark my words, our Timeo's the sort who can't be happy with a beautiful woman unless he gets to parade possession of her before the world."

Ovrin shoved his mug aside and lumbered to his feet. A session with Fell's plausible words trickling into his ear always left him more bewildered than before, and much wearier. It was less exhausting simply to do as his friend directed.

It wouldn't be so easy, getting to Timeo's table. The Chuckling Bear was packed this night. The academic year drew to its close, the Havror Fenn approached, and already the city of Panomo-Midmists was attracting the usual cut of festival trash, the sweepings of the highroads. Nimble feet and slender hips were called for to cut the zigzag path between the packed drinkers. Ovrin had neither.

As he sidled and bumped his way through the extra chairs, Ovrin saw more than a few unfamiliar faces. He didn't know every university student on sight, but he did know that most students adopted one special tavern as their own early on in their careers and stuck to it more faithfully than some of them would cling to their wives. These weren't the Chuckling Bear's regulars.

The strangers were also too old to be students, or too prosperously dressed. Take that slick-haired jackadandy with the grasshopper legs, for one. Ovrin would either have to step over his silk-sheathed pipe stems, and risk tripping, or ask him to move. Judging from the cut-glass decanter of Sombrunian brandy presently in the stranger's hand, he might prove reluctant to accommodate a tatterdemalion like Ovrin. The rich could be whimsical.

Still, as surely as Ovrin recognized Sterion's famous brandy decanter, he believed it was wrong to prejudge a fellow just because the jeweled chain around his neck might buy the whole tavern or the quartered red and green satin tunic he wore was shot through heavily with pure gold thread. The man might be rich enough to purchase the entire faculty of the Course Sorcerous, but he might also be polite.

Wherefore Ovrin stopped at the fellow's leggy barricade, cleared his throat and said, "Excuse me, may I pass?"

"That's between you and your professors, ain't it?" the young man drawled. Then he slapped his cheek as if awakening from a delusion. "Oh, can you *pass,* did you say? Why yes, you could pass for human almost any day, if you pay closer attention to shaving." The four highly rouged women sharing the table with this wit laughed as if their evening meal depended on it. The legs remained where they were.

"Right." Ovrin's hand closed over the young man's elegantly turned ankles and yanked. The gentleman's rump parted company with his chair and hit the floor as his head thunked a hollow greeting to the wooden seat. Ovrin stepped over his body while he was still blinking at stars.

The redhead found Fell waiting for him hard by Timeo's table. Fell was cross, an emotion not at all flattering to his thin, hard face. "Took you long enough. Why didn't you go 'round the room's perimeter like I did? Always the hard way for you, Ovrin. Now get Timeo's notice before that gilded chamber pot recovers his wits enough to have you booted out of here."

"Steri wouldn't boot me!"

"Steri'd boot his mother to keep one night's custom from someone that gold stinking. Get to it."

Obediently, Ovrin positioned himself beside Timeo's chair and uttered a full choral arrangement of throat noises. The heir of Dureforte Keep was oblivious. All his senses were fixed on the golden-haired lady opposite. Not even a light tap on the shoulder could rouse him as he watched his heart-light down a plate of raw herring.

Ovrin had never seen a lady eat fish heads before. It took him a while to recover self-possession and try getting Timeo's notice again.

"Here's your order!" Cattail slammed down two big wooden tankards between Timeo and his lady. Suds flew, most of them drenching the woman's long skirts.

"Here, stupid! It's a chance!" Fell thrust his pocket kerchief into Ovrin's hand and gave him a shove at the lady. The brawny country lad took the hint and fell to his knees, dabbing at the puddles of beer in her lap.

"Ovrin, really, you don't have to—" At last Timeo was aware that there were other people in the world.

"Oh, let him, darling," the lady purled. Her cool hands framed Ovrin's face for a throbbing instant. "I do so appreciate gallantry." Tiny teeth glittered between curving scarlet lips.

Every thought of asking Timeo for a loan fled from Ovrin's mind. He felt himself being drawn deep into the green pools of the lady's eyes. Something cold and finny tickled its way up his leg and under his tunic as the surface closed over his head. It didn't matter.

The next thing he knew, he was standing with Fell behind Timeo's chair, spilling the whole story of Timeo's abortive entry in the Havror Fenn while the lady made adorable sounds of sympathy and Fell shouted in vain for the barmaid to bring two more beers. Cattail had gone deaf and blind regarding that particular table. In his place, Timeo puffed like a blowfish with pride at having his friends see what a lovely woman had chosen him.

Duila pursed her lips as Ovrin finished his tale. "I think that'sawful. Timeo has a delightful voice, don't you agree?"

"It's not one you'll hear every day," Fell said.

"The old legends simply brim with stories of great heroes whose talents were never appreciated by their own kin."

Duila ticked off examples on her fingers, carefully keeping them pressed together all the while. "Gerhast of Paxnon was a humble turnspit who saved the life of his lord's daughter. He bashed a storm-demon with the family's silver teapot, imprisoning the fiend and all his tempests, too. And Dyved of Sumnerol—where they're all fisherfolk, worse luck to them—he couldn't find the proper bait for catching a cold, they said. Yet he was the one netted the wandering reef beast that was sinking every ship along the coast."

"Heroes all." Ovrin nodded. "We studied their histories in class. There hasn't been their like since the gods departed. The age of heroes is done."

"And what's my uncle, then?" Timeo's small blond moustache quivered with indignation. "King Alban of Sombrunia, Stonesword, who defeated Morgeld himself in battle! What's he, if not a hero?"

"He's royalty. Things are different for princes. They suck in bravery with their mothers' milk."

"My father went nigh every step of the way with King Alban," Timeo declared. "Every step, and he was just a bas—a riverside foundling from this very city."

"A foundling?" Ovrin considered the evidence with just the lofty expression preferred by his professor of Applied Historic Mythology. It made him look ten years more pedantic. "That's even better than being a prince, if you're to be a hero later on. Seven out of ten legendary heroes were foundlings, two were royalty, and only one was of ordinary birth—with legitimate parents and all. Say, Timeo, do you happen to know whether your da was ever nursed by a she-wolf?"

Fell punched Ovrin in the shoulder. "In this city?"

"A bitch would do."

Duila's hand floated over to caress Timeo's cheek. "Well, I don't think every hero has to be a bastard. No more than he needs to prove himself with a sword. Some crowns are meant to be earned by song." She leaned nearer: The long cloak she wore parted. Standing behind Timeo, Ovrin and Fell leaned in to test the truth their eyes were telling them: The lady was stark naked under the pale blue cloth, and her breasts shone like pearls.

Only on the edge of consciousness did they hear her say,

"And the crown Timeo lays at my feet shall be the Minstrel King's."

"Minstrel King?" Ovrin echoed.

"As in . . . the Havror Fenn?" Fell asked. His voice went up so shrilly that it carried all the way across the room to the bar. Cattail heard, and paused in her drying of the wood and glass and metal vessels.

"Of course." The lady shrugged, causing further emotional repercussions in the three gentlemen opposite. "It would be a sin for him to hide his gifts."

"But—he told his mother that—"

Timeo gave Ovrin a hard look over one shoulder. "My mother will have to understand that I am my own man and I make my own decisions. No one tells me what to do." His face went from stern to soppy with alarming rapidity as he turned to Duila. "Isn't that so, my darling?"

"But his mother—she'll—" Ovrin moistened his lips. "She might blame us," he whispered. Mizriel's wrath was not lightly forgotten.

Fell seemed to gain the courage Ovrin lost. A thoughtful look settled over his angular face. He raised Duila's hand to his lips. "Sweet lady, it was a happy day for music when you persuaded our friend that his duty lay in entering the Havror Fenn."

Duila accepted this courtly tribute with a girlish giggle. "Oh, Timeo, I do like your friends!"

Timeo gave Fell a searching look. "What happened to 'Wait for next year' and 'Don't upset your poor mother'?"

Fell's fingers tiptoed into ownership of Timeo's tankard. "I bow to your lady's superior wisdom." He took a long drink. "I see now that I was a fool. A year can change so many things; your voice might be among them. And it will be good for you to adopt a firmer stance with your mother. She'll be glad for it, secretly. Women like to test a fellow's manhood. They're always grateful when you stand up to them and show that you're the stronger." He took another pull at the tankard. "Besides, with such fair inspiration, how can you ever lose?" He saluted Duila with the empty mug.

Duila simpered to receive such homage. "Do sing for us now, Timeo. Sing that delightfully tragic ballad you whipped up last night. You did say I inspired it."

Ovrin had never seen Timeo so quick to answer a request for song, not even when Fell exerted his most doggish flattery. The hand harp was whisked out from under the table, given a cursory tuning, and the Chuckling Bear resounded with "The Braegerd Barbarian's Lament."

It was during the verse where the Malben princess lashes herself to the cabin boy and leaps into the sea sooner than submit to the barbarian's lust that the disturbance occurred. Ovrin saw it coming. The wealthy-looking young man he'd handled earlier was wedging his way between the tables, a doxy on either arm and two trailing behind. He wore an artificial grin, like a shark's leer turned upside down, and his black eyes glittered much too merrily.

"My felicitations, sir," he said. He took the thick gold chain from his neck and dropped it into Timeo's lap.

Dureforte's heir lifted it on two fingers, puzzled. "Your good wishes are welcome, but take your gift back again. I am not one who sings for pay."

"No, no, keep it!" He forced Timeo's hand closed around the gold links and garnets. "The gods know, no one could pay you what your singing deserves! My father, the richest wine dealer in Wickerdale, always told me, 'Zerin, there are some things money won't buy, but who needs 'em?' I don't pay you for your songs, but for something far more precious: Your silence. You sing like a stuck badger."

It was done in an instant. Fell gave Ovrin the old signal, the big student nodded, and Zerin of Wickerdale took an aerial departure from the Chuckling Bear. He landed in the gutter outside, to be joined shortly by his shrieking ladies.

He cast aside their fussing hands. "I'm all right, damn you! Leave off your—" He patted himself all over, to be sure there was no harm done besides a few bruises, then cast a reproving look at the youngest of his trollops. She made a moue and returned his coin pouch.

"That was a mistake." A spectacled boy in student's robes lounged against the tavern doorpost and squinted down at Zerin and his entourage.

"My good fellow, it's to be expected when dealing with these ladies," Zerin replied haughtily. "And I recovered the purse. It's our little game."

"No, not that. I mean insulting Timeo's singing."

"Don't tell me you call that singing!" Zerin leaned on his lady friends as he got out of the gutter. "Are you positive he's not a candidate for the Fool King's crown? Have I come all this way to enter the Havror Fenn—at *great* expense to my father—only to hear that the whole competition's a farce?"

The student pushed his spectacles up the bridge of his nose. "Thought you were new in town. A minstrel?"

"Gods, no! Not one of those waly-waly-woe-is-me birds. I, sir, aim for the higher honor, the greater prize, the belled crown of the Fool King and nothing less. And it shall be mine, as master of the Jest Supreme!" He flourished both arms. A minor shower of gutter filth flew from his sleeves.

"Well, if you want to live long enough to make your jest, keep your mouth shut about Timeo's singing when Ovrin and Fell are about. The two that gave you the free ride, that's they. Anyone who's been in Panomo-Midmists a week's heard about the bet they've made."

"Gossip and students, fleas and rats: the one thick on the other, I've heard. Go on, friend. What bet?"

"That Timeo'd enter the Havror Fenn. Looked fair to go against them, too, until that lady took a liking to his warblings. Of course there's still his mother to consider. It could still go either way. The side bets are springing up already about what she'll do to him when she learns he's back in the competition. A sorceress, she is, and ver-ry touchy about having the family humiliated."

"I wouldn't dare to tell her."

"You would if you had as much riding on this as I do. So if you'll excuse me, I must be on my way to the lady's lodgings. Wish me luck."

"Luck . . ." Zerin's thumb traced the cut of his lantern jaw as his informant waddled off. "And maybe more than luck at work here, for me. Oh, what a jest this may yet be! Come, girls! Let's celebra—"

He was speaking to empty air. He patted himself down again and found his purse had vanished with his playmates. His bony shoulders rose and fell philosophically. A would-be Fool King must sometimes play the fool when he least expects it. Zerin of Wickerdale sauntered back into the Chuckling Bear.

Chapter VIII

BROOKS NO ARGUMENT

For the first time in untold years, the miserable students' lodgings at Gubbo the Sot's were full of the delectable smells of plenty. Keristor sat tailor-style on his pallet, devouring a whole roast chicken under the fond eye of his elder brother. Every so often the boy would look up at the stranger who had brought such bounty to their door, giving him the silent awe due a god.

Ovrin and Fell did not look upon Zerin of Wickerdale as a god. Suspicion and mistrust were in every glance they gave him between mouthfuls of the delicacies he had spread before them. He only smiled when they insisted he eat a bite of every item in the shopping hamper first, and complied. They remained leery.

When he explained his purpose, it struck them harder than any poison's pang.

"That's madness," Fell growled. "Do you know the money you'll lose?"

"And the money you'll win?" Zerin's mouth tugged up at one corner. "I'll cover your bets—all of them—even if my plans don't go as I wish, but if you change your wagers as I've suggested and my scheme does bear fruit . . ." He allowed them to harvest visions of that bright future from their own imaginings.

"Getting him into the Havror Fenn's one thing," Fell

said. ''It's a possibility. I can work with what's possible, understand it, but what you propose—''

''The finals!'' Ovrin looked askance at the grain dealer's son. ''You're not a mage, are you?''

Zerin munched a sliver of blackberry tart and licked his fingers. ''You know the rules. What good would it do even if I were a wizard? Which I am not.''

''You bet *against* Timeo making the finals, yet you say you want him to get that far.'' Even repeating Zerin's proposition didn't help Fell read the tall-stalked youth's underlying motive. He gave up puzzling it out and asked straight off, ''Why?''

''Come, come, if I bet with you in this, folk will keep a sharp eye on all my doings, thinking I'll be using my father's money to affect the contest's outcome. And so I shall, but disguised as one who'd sooner see a pig make the final round than Timeo. I need your cooperation to keep our puppet on the proper strings, your friendly influence with him to make sure he doesn't succumb to a sudden attack of common sense before the contest begins.''

''No fear of that,'' Fell said.

Something in the spindly student's voice made Zerin study him more closely. As an aspirant to the belled crown he had made the world his university, every man a lesson to be learned. *What would you stop at to separate Timeo from his gold, friend Fell?* Zerin mused. *At murder? I doubt it. How much difference is there between you and an alleyway footpad? Or is there any difference at all?*

''So he makes the finals,'' Fell went on, ''and Ovrin and I are rich men when the wagers are paid—yours included. That'll suit us fine, but where does that leave you? Your pardon, Zerin—and I know I should cut my own throat before saying this—but you sound like a fool to me.''

''Not a mere fool''—Zerin held up one finger—''but a Fool King.'' He tossed back his head and laughed. ''To bring a squeal-voiced master of limping doggerel within sight of the Minstrel King's crown—ah! That shall be the crowning jest of all.''

Chapter IX

TRICKLE-DOWN
EFFECT

Duila! Duila!

The nixie sat up suddenly in Timeo's bed, her eyes darting here and there about the darkened room in fear. Timeo had gone out to fetch something to eat. She was alone.

Alone, but for that fearsome voice calling her name.

"Ragnar?" she whispered. "M—Master?"

Not Ragnar, stupid! It's me!

Duila leaned over the edge of the bed. The voice had a distinctively hollow ring to it which at first had lent it that note of dreadful command. Now, however, the nixie realized that it was nothing more than the resonant qualities of the vessel from which it issued.

"Do you know you're talking to me from the chamber pot, Cattail?" she asked, hanging upside down.

It was the nearest water source available. Make Timeo keep his bedside carafe filled, why don't you?

Duila giggled to hear how annoyed her superior sounded. The chamber pot fairly seethed with irritation. "Why should he bother? The water barrel for this whole floor's right outside his door, if he gets thirsty. Well, since you're calling, what can I do for you?"

Report, nitwit. And make it short. I'm standing by the doorway emptying the wayfarer's bucket by dipperfuls.

"Why don't you just nab a bowl of water up to your place in the hayloft and hurl droplets?"

When do I get a moment alone up there? The tavern's packed with hopefuls for the Havror Fenn. Sterion's jamming them in tighter than fingerlings, and the ones he can't fit seven to a bed go out to the stable. When I can find time to sleep at all, I have to do it with one eye open, fighting off the amorous ones. I'd sleep in the river, but last time I tried, they dragged me out; thought I was drowning.

"So you stand by the door and whisper into water. To think I always envied ondines the power of waterspeech! Poor lady, anyone passing by must think you mad."

Crazed with thirst, for all I care. Now report!

"There's little to say." Duila tried shrugging her shoulders from her inverted position. "I've filled Timeo's mind with tales of great heroes who were also great bards and his heart with ambition for the Havror Fenn. Not that he'll last through the first round, with that voice."

That's no concern of ours. The chamber pot was grim. *Let them toss him out in the first trial. We'll win him to our cause all the sooner. Once he's lost, I'll approach him, and while I dish out the condolences I'll make a grand, dramatic revelation: who I really am, what he really is, and that the reason his minstrelry is such an abomination is due to an evil spell laid upon him in the cradle.*

"By Ragnar?"

No, by a milk cow. Of course by Ragnar! Then I shall offer him the opportunity to break the spell, free his people, win the voice his songs deserve, and get a crown while he's at it. And he can have you, too, if he insists.

"No, thanks." Duila made a face.

I trust you've been salting your chats with tales of foul enchantments? We must put him in the proper frame of mind to accept the story about the spell.

"Frame for a blank canvas. He'd buy that whole rigmarole right this minute. He's stupid enough."

Stupid! The porcelain container rattled. *He is no such thing! You will not speak of your rightful king without the proper show of respect, Duila, or—*

"Shhh! I hear someone coming."

The chamber pot would not heed or else the ordinary level

of tavern racket made it impossible for Cattail to hear Duila's whispered warning. The barmaid continued to fulminate upon the theme of Timeo's sterling qualities and Duila's failure to appreciate the same. Duila hissed a second demand for silence, but the knocking at Timeo's door must have obscured it. The hinges squealed as a paltry slip of upcountry manhood crept into the room. Duila dove under the rumpled bedclothes.

"Timeo?" The caller's moist brown eyes squinted badly. He pulled a long lock of oily, colorless hair and chewed nervously on the frizzled end. "Timeo, it's me, Ednyd. Can I borrow your notes from—?"

—just because he's gentle! You want your men covered with fur and muscles, you do!

"Who?" Ednyd masticated his hair frantically. "Me?"

If that's what pleases you, you can get plenty of that kind of attention from the old man's guards!

"I never—! I mean, Grandfather's guards are frightfully nice fellows, and awfully good-looking, but we only talked about—"

You're not worthy to share Timeo's bed!

Ednyd commenced puffing like an asthmatic bullfrog. "Now see here, Timeo, I'm just as much in line to hold my own domain as you, but you don't hear me going around talking about myself in the third person regal; not until Grandfather's dead, at least."

You SLUT!

This last bolt was delivered with such force that the chamber pot exploded with a sharp report. Fragments of procelain shot in all directions. Ednyd yelped as a shard sliced open his trunk hose at the ankle.

His cry was as nothing next to the howl from the bed. Duila leaped straight up, bedclothes and all, her flight inspired by the long, arrowhead-shaped bit of ceramic that had knifed its way through the mattress. Her trajectory landed her on top of Ednyd, who was hopping around on his uninjured foot while trying to stop the bleeding of his ankle. He tumbled onto his back with the naked nixie on top of him.

"You're not Timeo!" Ednyd jerked his hands away from

the nixie's generous curves and waved madly. "Oo! Oo! Oo! Get *off* me, you—you common trollop!"

Duila was glad to oblige. She kicked off from Ednyd's thrashing legs, a kick that had unfortunate consequences for the young man. He writhed doubled up on the floor as she vanished hopping into the corridor. Through his agony, he thought he heard a series of wet slaps, a faint creak, and a splash. It made little sense, for the student residence was well removed from the Salmlis.

He was just getting back on his feet when Timeo strolled in, whistling, with a parcel of lamprey pasties. "Hello, Ednyd. Care to hear the lead-off number I've done for the Havror Fenn? Something humorous, I think. Save the tragedies for the finals. Have a pasty?"

"Feed it to your doxy!" Ednyd was not very imposing when calm, but when enraged he possessed all the fury of a rabid vole. "It's illegal to entertain whores in your rooms. I'm going to tell the proctor!"

Timeo thought fast. "What whore?" He set down his package and casually produced flint and steel to kindle all the candles in the room. He held the last one high, making a broad business of exploring every corner with the light. "I don't see any whore, Ednyd. My bed's unmade, but if you want to complain to the proctor about my habits . . ." His smile was amiable, though his eyes clearly added, *you twit.*

Ednyd went over to the bed and fumbled through the tangled sheets. "I know what I saw—" His voice died away. "I think I did . . . I must've . . . I need a drink."

"Some wine?" Timeo's moustache perked with every sign of affable hospitality. He took a bottle from the chest at the foot of his bed. "From our estates. Not as biting as the stuff your grandfather decants, but I think you'll be amused by its flinty arrogance."

"No . . . no . . ." Ednyd passed a quivering hand over his brow. "No wine." He tottered out of Timeo's room.

"Good riddance," Timeo muttered. He couldn't stand Ednyd in the best of circumstances. The fact that the boy was Lord Thaumas' grandson and heir didn't help matters. Still, it was some comfort to realize that his future rival to the north was such a weed.

Timeo blew a long breath of relief to see him go. It was

relief short-lived. From out in the hall he heard the distinctive, soft creak of the hinges on the floor's communal water barrel, the plunge of the dipper, and an awful cry from Ednyd's skinny throat that was part terror and part triumph.

Ednyd came staggering back to stand in Timeo's doorway, his arms dripping with a half-human half-fish-tailed burden. He was accompanied by every scholar who had been within hearing distance of his scream.

The nixie flopped futilely in Ednyd's desperate grasp. "I *knew* it! I *knew* I saw something! Now I'm not just going to tell the proctor, Timeo." His beaky nose crinkled with evil glee. "I'm going to tell your *mother!*"

Chapter X

ALL WET

Mizriel of the White Hair looked from the sullen barmaid to the rickety ladder and back. "You're sure he's up there?" she asked. "I hate climbing ladders."

"Him and his friends," Cattail replied. "M'lady." It was a grudging addition. "Can I get back to my duties now?"

"Your *duty,* my girl, is to attend me. I've paid your master well enough for your time. There are a number of things I want to have cleared up concerning this whole sordid business. At my son's former lodgings, they told me he had taken up residence in the stable of the Chuckling Bear. They further told me that you were the one to offer him such"— her eyes took in the crowd of travel-stained sleepers snoring in every stall not occupied by a horse—"elegant shelter."

"It's free of vermin, and I've made sure he has space to himself," Cattail riposted. "That's more than I can say for where he put up the last time he left his student rooms."

"The last time, he left voluntarily." The sorceress' jaw tightened. "Tell me the truth: Were you the one Themia's brat found in his bed?"

Cattail's long black braid crackled. "I was not. I don't know who Themia's brat may be, nor Themia either. And I don't share sleep space with him now, if that's on your mind. I've friends elsewhere, including my *master,* as you'd call him. Ask Sterion where I was the night your son got his backside kicked across campus!"

Mizriel's ire subsided a little. She regarded the barmaid

with reluctant admiration. "I beg your pardon. I've been under some strain since I received the news. Shall we go up?" She gave Cattail her hand.

The barmaid accepted the friendly gesture, then gasped as she felt her feet leave the stable floor. Mizriel's magic floated them both up into the hayloft and set them down gently before a startled group of Timeo, Ovrin, and Fell, and an entranced Keristor.

"I told you I don't like ladders," Mizriel said.

"Oh, that's pretty!" the boy exclaimed. "Did you see how she flew? She flew! Ovrin, did you see? That was very pretty. Do it again?"

Mizriel's complacent smile faded to hear a boy apparently in his teens speak so. She lifted her black robe and delicately picked her way over the bundles of hay. Keristor watched her every move with open joy. When she touched his upturned face tenderly, he looked ready to expire from pure happiness.

"I like you," he said. "Your hair is white. It's like the moon. And you fly like the moon. Did you see her fly, Ovrin? Did you, Timeo? Timeo, I remember your song about Sarai and the moon."

"She's not Sarai All-Mother, Keristor," Timeo said softly. "She's only my mother."

"Oh, I know that. Only Sarai is Sarai. But she flies. My mother never flew. She isn't here anymore, but she didn't fly away; she died. I love your mother, Timeo. She must be magic." He took Mizriel's hand and kissed it. A worried look flickered across his face immediately as he did so. "Is it all right? Can I kiss your hand?"

Mizriel raised his face and kissed him on the brow. "It's more than all right, child. It's a princely gift that I will treasure with all my heart."

"Oh!" It was all that Keristor could say. His smile turned his face to a star.

"Ovrin . . . Fell," Timeo said. "I think my mother wants a word with me."

Fell was down the ladder before Timeo finished speaking. Ovrin had to coax his brother away from Mizriel. Cattail came to his aid, promising the boy a treat in the tavern's kitchen. As she backed down the ladder, she looked thoughtfully at the white-haired sorceress.

"So." Mizriel folded her arms. "Not even with a human. I don't know whether to scream at you for getting caught or compliment your originality. From what I hear, the lordling Ednyd had a fit the minute they fetched the proctor, and in the confusion your finny friend got away. *That* would have been worth seeing—her flopping down the stairs and all the way to the river without getting caught."

Timeo said nothing.

"I've heard other things about you as well," Mizriel went on. "Gossip says you're entering the Havror Fenn after all. Is that true?"

"Yes. That's what I was just talking about with Ovrin and Fell, as a matter of fact." He knotted his arms around his updrawn legs and defied her.

"I don't know which is worse: your consorting with a wench who's part codfish or your going back on your word."

Timeo's chin rose by degrees. "I never promised not to enter the Havror Fenn. And Duila is not part codfish. She may look different, but she's human enough to appreciate good music when she hears it! I'm dedicating my first song of the competition to her. If you've come here to try talking me out of it, Mother, it won't work. This time, I'm resolved. It's my life and my choice."

"As you chose to get expelled from the university?"

"It's only a suspension."

"So is a hanging!" Mizriel threw up her hands in disgust. "Oh, what's the use? You'll stick to your crazy notions of music making until you get a smart kick in the teeth. Enter the Havror Fenn; you will anyhow. This is some plot of your scale-tailed sweetheart's making or those two ne'er-do-well friends of yours, though what they hope to gain from it—"

"No one is plotting anything about me!" Timeo maintained. "My ideas and actions are entirely my own."

His mother looked at him dubiously. "If you weren't so young, you wouldn't be so quick to utter the greatest lie any living person ever believed. At your age, I too believed that I was the only one in command of my life. But our lives are all strands of a spiderweb—fragile to the eye, strong enough for their several purposes, and all interwoven in a pattern greater than we may ever guess."

She knelt beside him in the straw and put her arms around him. He tensed against the unfamiliarity of his mother's affectionate overture, then relaxed and returned her embrace. Her hair had the cool smell of spring rain.

"You are my son," she murmured, "and all I have left in this world of your father. No magic I have can shield you from your fate or from the hurts of living. Do as you must, if you can't do as you will."

She pushed away and studied him at arm's length. "Even to entering the Havror Fenn. I suspect you got your stubbornness from my side of the family, but where did you get your stupidity?" Her smile took some of the sting out of the question.

Her unexpected softness heartened him to ask, "Mother, if I *do* give you my word of honor not to try the contest, would you use your magic for me?"

"A bargain?" Mizriel was amused by the prospect. "What would you have in exchange?"

"Heal Keristor."

"Heal—?" There was no amusement on the sorceress' face now. Her eyes filled with pity. "How can you know so little of my art? You grew up with magic all around you, and you never learned the first lesson of the craft: Magic has limits. Some things it can not touch."

"But healing—I've seen you heal other people. Not just those who were injured in body. I remember once when I was small, we were riding down to Cymweh and a madman leaped out of the forest and attacked you, as if our guards weren't even there. He grabbed your horse by the bridle and tried to wrestle the beast down or break its neck—I never knew which. You rose in your stirrups and warned our swordsmen off before they could kill him, then you spoke some odd words and touched his forehead. Oh, Mother, the look on his face when you restored him! The peace that chased off every hidden demon! He was healed, and you never knew who he was. Why won't you heal Keri, too, for my sake?"

Mizriel touched steepled fingers to her lips. "There is a difference between *won't* and *can't*. I can heal a wound, but

I can't cause a man to grow a new arm for one lopped off
in battle. Keristor is not insane; no demons plague the boy.
What he is, is in him and of him as much as stubbornness
is in and of you.''

"*Please,* Mother!'' Timeo pressed her hands in his. ''He's
such a good boy, with a heart so eager to love the world!
It isn't fair that he's shut off from so much! I'll do everything, anything you say, now and forever, if only—''

"Stop badgering me!'' She flung her hands apart to cast
his off. ''Don't you listen? How can you hope to be half the
songmaster your father was if the only thoughts you hear are
your own? My *magic* could not save Lymri! Magic is not
miracle! Some things lie with the gods and some beyond.''

Timeo's whole body slumped. ''I'm sorry, Mother.''

"That's all right.'' Mizriel clipped all trace of passion
from her voice. ''We'll forget the whole thing. I haven't
sought you out to harangue you. I've actually come to take
you to dinner. We have been invited to dine at the Spicebowl Inn tonight, and I want you in new clothes, after a hot
bath. You'll find both in my rooms.''

"The Spicebowl Inn? That's the most expensive place in
town. Who invited us?''

Mizriel's teeth gritted. ''The lady Themia, Lord Thaumas'
daughter—the one who looks like a cow—and her calf,
Ednyd.''

"This tunic will look well in the third round of the
competition,'' Timeo said, catching a glimpse of himself in
the huge looking glass hanging in the entryway of the Spicebowl Inn. ''You get points for appearance, and my third
round song's going to be the wooing of Elaar the Sea-Witch.
This shade of turquoise is very evocative of—''

"One word out of you about the Havror Fenn in front of
Themia and her whelp, and I'll turn you into a turtle,''
Mizriel rasped. ''The bitch is up to something, asking us
here after that incident, and I want to know what. I don't
want you adding to my humiliation by mentioning that
damned twitter fest!''

She tugged her son into the dining room. The Spicebowl
Inn catered to the most exclusive trade in Panomo-Midmists
and boasted separate rooms for eating and drinking, as

opposed to the common room arrangement of other inns. There were even private dining rooms above stairs, curtained alcoves where affluent merchants and visiting nobility could feast in intimate splendor.

"The private rooms cost more," Mizriel muttered as she surveyed the larger dining room. "I'm surprised Themia didn't take one. That'd be as good as shouting how rich she is. If she's receiving us in here, it must be to shame me in front of witnesses. She's going to wake up tomorrow with a pimple somewhere interesting."

"Yoo-hoo! Mizzie!" A fat white arm waved over the heads of the other diners, and a voice by turns shrill and resonant bellowed, "Waiter, there they are! Fetch them!"

"Two pimples," Mizriel said under her breath. " 'Mizzie' indeed."

A servant bearing a silver tray glided up behind mother and son to request, in velvety tones, that they accompany him. He floated across the floor like the most well-bred ghost and seated them opposite the lady Themia and Ednyd.

Themia wore a gown more suited to a midsummer queen—a young one, with firm upper arms, who understood the basic principle that a belt, however wide, was never intended to do the duty of a good corset. The diaphanous yellow tissue did much to make her skin sallower than it was, and her hair was a buttery shade that matched the dress with unfortunate exactness. Timeo stared.

"Wasn't she a brunette?" he whispered to his mother.

"Timeo wants to know if you were ever a brunette, Themia," Mizriel said in a clarion voice. "Don't children say the funniest things?"

Themia patted her limp locks and huffed a bit. "So nice of you to come, Mizzie. Such a pleasant surprise to hear that you were in town, too. You so seldom creep out of that darling weensy castle of yours these days. My sister said you must be dead, but I told her not to presume."

"And how is dear Ykrilta? Still suffering from chronic wind? You know, if you'd lend her a dab of whatever you used on your hair, I'll bet it would make that little beard of hers hardly noticeable, and so much kinder than plucking."

Themia's small mouth got smaller. "Papa sends his best."

"The spontaneous drooling's cleared up, then? I'm

awfully glad. Maybe now he can look into that tedious business of your swineherds wandering into our beech forests. You obviously have more than enough pig feed in your own domain." Mizriel smiled sweetly.

"I can take a hint, Mizzie dear. You're hungry, aren't you? Waiter!" Themia clapped her paws together and rattled off an elaborate order of rare and costly viands. She then returned her attention to her guests.

"I was so thrilled to learn you were visiting, Mizzie. Now that you're finally taking an interest in your boy, maybe he'll amount to something. That's why I asked the two of you here tonight. I wanted to find out whether Ednyd and I should go through with our petition or not."

Mizriel stopped smiling. "What petition?"

"*I'm* petitioning the university governors." Ednyd thrust out his birdlike chest. "I think Timeo shouldn't be suspended for what he did."

"That's awfully nice of—"

"I say he should be *expelled!*" Ednyd choked on his own excitement and had to have Themia pound him on the back. Mizriel looked disappointed as the bluish tinge receded from the young lordlet's curdy cheeks.

"My Ednyd's always been such a moral boy." Themia preened herself. "He doesn't approve of whoremongering."

"Whoremongering's not grounds for expulsion," Timeo said. A small foot kicked him under the table.

"Cross-species whoremongering is. We looked it up." Thaumas' daughter and grandson wore matching smug looks.

"Unless you're enrolled in the Course Sorcerous," Ednyd put in. "We all know about mages and what they do with their familiars." He shuddered with ecstatic revulsion and looked straight at Mizriel.

"Well, Ednyd's bound and determined to turn in the petition, but I said—" Themia paused. The waiter had brought around the soup course. She lifted the bowl by the handles and gulped it down steaming. A limp leaf of watercress clung to her upper lip. "I said that since you were in town, perhaps you'd heard about your son's disgraceful behavior and were going to discipline him at last. If you did, and if you and I might discuss that trifling boundary dispute about the grasslands, perhaps the petition wouldn't be necessary.''

Mizriel spooned soup into her mouth in small sips. "If I were you, Theemy, I wouldn't call Timeo's promised bride a whore where her family might hear you.''

"Bride!'' Themia clapped a thickly beringed hand to her bosom. She looked no less startled than Ednyd and Timeo. "That—inhuman creature?''

"Neither more nor less human than any of the Seafolk, which includes the Mistress of All Waters, Elaar.'' Mizriel tilted her head a little to one side. "How much of your domain's wealth comes from shipping investments, dear?''

"You wouldn't! To stir up storms at sea is monstrous!''

"And a crime. It would bring the wrath of Ayree, Prince of Warlocks, down on me.'' Mizriel finished her soup. "I never would. My future in-laws, though . . . Ayree has no jurisdiction over their sentiments when someone calls one of their daughters a whore.''

The waiter came around with the next course: broiled fish. Mizriel demurred, citing family sentiment.

Themia's portion cooled on her plate as she gasped out apologies. The petition was relegated to oblivion, with many a reproving word directed at Ednyd.

"You really oughtn't be such a prig, my precious,'' she remarked frostily. Ednyd wiggled in his chair, discomfited, while Timeo gazed at his mother with new respect.

"Then, dear Mizriel, might I ask what happy cause brings you to Panomo-Midmists?'' Themia inquired.

"Oh, it's because of me going in for the Havror Fenn,'' Timeo blurted.

"Reeeeeally?'' Themia's plucked brows lifted. "I didn't know you had ambitions to be chosen the Fool King. But he would be a good choice, wouldn't he, Ednyd?''

Ednyd bobbed his head so violently that it looked as if his neck would snap.

"My son is *not* going to be the Fool King.''

"Mizriel, you forget: I have heard him sing.'' The corner of Themia's mouth twitched. "When you visited us for the sheep-shearing festival, remember? Timeo said he had an original pastoral air with which to entertain the shepherds. Father let him. I think that's when the drooling started.''

"It was the first time I ever saw five hundred sheep go bald all at once," Ednyd said. "But it saved time with the shearing."

The white-haired sorceress clenched her hands below the tabletop. The berry-butter sauce over her uneaten fish began to smoke, then to char.

"Surely you're not going to permit Timeo to make a spectacle of himself?" Themia queried.

"Permit him? Ha!" The fish in Mizriel's plate shot across the table, propelled by something more than the force of her laugh. Ednyd squealed as it landed in his lap. "For your information, *some* young men's voices change! Timeo is entering the Havror Fenn with my blessing and *at my request!* And when the Minstrel King's crown is on his head, you'll be the one singing a different tune. Timeo, come!"

Her hair lashed like a blizzard's gust as she swept from the table. Timeo jabbered thanks to his hosts for a dinner hardly tasted and caught up with Mizriel in the street.

"Mother, did you mean that?" he gasped. "Your blessing?"

The little sorceress sagged in her black robes. "Why not?" Her shoulders rose and fell. She gave him a wan smile. "At least now I know where you got your stupidity."

Chapter XI

YOU CAN BANK ON IT

"How much for the harp? Name your price!" Mizriel slapped her hand on the taproom table, her eyes afire with desperation.

The newly fledged warlock chewed his fingertip nervously. Hivrahan of Lyf hadn't been master of his inborn powers all that long, and he was used to having his mentor there to guide him. He was at a total loss to know what to do about this wild-visaged woman who offered him any amount for so simple a thing as a singing harp.

"You're not—one of us?" Hivrahan stalled for time.

"A mage? What else would I be, and staying under the same roof with you here at the Philosopher's Mistress?"

"Then why can't you make a singing harp of your own, my lady? The spells are not complex."

Mizriel stuck her nose into Hivrahan's face. Standing, he would have been nearly twice her height, and well muscled enough, though rangy, to hoist her over one shoulder and carry her away. Not that he would have dared it. Seated across the table from the little sorceress, his slate blue eyes meeting her fox-bright gaze, he felt very small and getting smaller.

"I don't have time for spells of making. I must buy the finished product—charm, song, instrument, anything to do with music! You have the harp, I have gold, so have we a bargain?"

"Sell it to her, Hivrahan." Tiny, cold paws pattered up

the warlock's arm. A purple lizard flicked its tongue in his ear. "It's me—Melki," it whispered. "Ask a fat price and sell it. Come up with a charm to turn ravens to nightingales, while you've got her attention! She's buying up every bit of music-touched magic in this town, the gods alone guess why. Why shouldn't we earn a little extra gold while they're guessing?"

"Gold . . ." Hivrahan brushed the strings of his instrument, and it uttered a coquettish arpeggio. The sound brought his mentor's kindly face and wise words to mind: *Carry your magic as a trust. You do not know whence or why it came to you, and thus you know as little whether it will abide or depart. Treasure it, use it with honor, so that should the day come when you must return it again, you may do so without shame.* Then she had asked him to take his clothes off again.

"Go on, tell her it's one of a kind, worth two hundred in gold, but you'll let her have it for fifty!" Melki, the mage in lizard form, scuttled around the back of Hivrahan's neck to hiss encouragement in his other ear.

"My lady, in truth, this harp is not worth more than twenty-five in silver," Hivrahan said. He heard a very light thud as the purple lizard tumbled from his shoulder in a dead faint. Thoughtfully he pushed Melki under the table with the tip of his shoe so that his friend might not be trodden underfoot before he recovered.

"Here." Mizriel shoved two gold pieces across the table and grabbed the harp. Hivrahan did not let it go. The lady's brows met in a terrifying scowl but still the warlock held fast to his instrument.

"I only cited its worth, my lady; I did not say I'd sell it to you."

"You impertinent pup! Do you think yourself above selling magic? I've heard about you, Hivrahan of Lyf. You're an infant in spells, witchborn son of mortal parents. Without that happy accident of birth, everyone knows you wouldn't have lasted three years past your Naming Day. You'd have been broken to shards on the flanks of the Kestrel Mountains. Well, I can do some breaking too, if you try thwarting me. I've bought charms and enchantments from wizards and witches whose lightest spell would turn you to spit and spangles, so don't hold yourself high with me!"

Hivrahan was cringing by the time she finished her tirade, but he still held onto the harp. "My lady"—he wished he could keep his voice from shaking—"I'd be more willing to accommodate you if you'd tell me why a great sorceress like yourself must purchase small magic from a humble warlock like me."

"Because she's an idiot, and you're another." The purple lizard had recovered and scampered back up Hivrahan's arm. It clung to the warlock's brown curls with all four feet and swung beside his ear. "Sell it and be done!"

"Because Mizriel of the White Hair has more temper than brains," a different voice said. "And if she doesn't live to thank you for not cheating her, like all these other so-called mages, she's a greater fool than I thought."

The air sparkled behind Hivrahan's chair and the falling flakes of brightness darkened to the shape of a bespectacled wizard accompanied by a tall, blond boy in his early teens who stood in the lee of the magician's belling robes, a small lute slung on his back.

"Paragore-Tren!" Mizriel's exclamation was a mix of pleasure, surprise, and irritation. Irritation took over wholly when she demanded, "What do you mean, more temper than brains?"

The old wizard patted his gray-streaked beard and chuckled. "Let's say more haste than prudence, Mizriel. But where are your manners? Don't you see who I've brought with me?"

The boy had a smile to charm and warm, and it only grew wider under Mizriel's distrustful examination. "Have I really grown so much that you don't know me, Aunt?"

"Mother of Mhispan!" Mizriel clapped her hands to her face. "Alveiros, is it you?"

Alveiros' laugh was hearty as a full-grown man's. His voice lilted sweetly when he spoke. "Yes, dear Aunt Mizriel, it's me. All the way from Sombrunia." He came forward to kiss her.

She clutched his arms. "Is something wrong at home?"

"Nothing. My mother and father send their love, though they never thought I'd be delivering it so early. We were going to visit you at Dureforte Keep after the contest. It's a wonderful surprise to find you here!''

Mizriel rumpled Alveiros' sunny hair affectionately. "No less a surprise for me to see you. What contest? You don't mean the Havror Fenn?"

Paragore-Tren nodded, his spectacles sparkling. Surrounded as he was by this impromptu reunion, the warlock Hivrahan tried to creep away, but the elder mage's hand fell on his shoulder, nearly crushing Melki. "Stay, good sir," Paragore-Tren directed. "You asked the lady why she wanted to buy your harp. You're about to have your answer."

Although Mizriel was a grown woman, she felt forever like a wayward schoolgirl when the wizard of the Naîmlo Wood turned his eyes to her doings. Paragore-Tren could not read minds, she knew, but the years had given him a measure of wisdom that was better than any telepathy.

"Timeo has entered the Havror Fenn," she confessed.

"Timeo?" Paragore-Tren exchanged dumbfounded looks with Alveiros, who was speechless. "How very . . . interesting."

"Oh, you needn't say it! I know how he sings—more's the pity, he doesn't. Lymri never would be frank with him, and now it's come to this." Mizriel drooped like old celery. "I'm buying up all the musical charms this town can hold so he won't be shamed too painfully when he comes before the judges."

"My lady, that will never work for the Havror Fenn!" Hivrahan twisted his head violently from side to side, looking at the sorceress, the wizard, and the boy by turns. The purple lizard swinging from his hair turned green with all his gyrations. "The judges make the contestants pass through an arch specially created by the tenured faculty of the Course Sorcerous. It detects the presence of any magical enhancement to a person's singing or playing skills and nullifies them. However many charms you've bought for this Timeo, you've tossed your coin away and been cheated."

"Have I?" Mizriel's voice was perilously quiet. The Philosopher's Mistress had no rule forbidding magic at ground level. Threadworms of blue fire broke from every pore of the sorceress' body and vaulted the length and breadth of the common room. Some snaked out the door, some leaped through the windows.

One zipped just under Hivrahan's earlobe and took Melki for an unpleasant flight ending splat against the far wall. The purple lizard was a singed and sorry stripling mage when he hit the floor.

"I think I'll be getting some refunds," Mizriel remarked, motioning for the barmaid to serve the table. While Zibethica took the orders, the little sorceress said, "I hope you won't laugh at your cousin too loudly when you hear him perform, Alveiros. I know you've always liked good minstrelry, but if we didn't have some contrast, it would—"

"I'm not here to watch, Aunt." The boy's lute was off his back and in his hands. "I'm taking part."

"But you're a child! How old—? Ten? Eleven?"

Again that lilting laugh. "You're thinking of my baby brother Alain. I'm thirteen."

"Fencing with senility." Paragore-Tren's eyes twinkled. "The lute has been his lady since he was five years old. He asked for the chance to try his skill at the Havror Fenn, and his parents gave consent. No one's to know he's King Alban's son. There have been sad cases of influence being brought to bear on the contest in years past."

The boy tuned his lute with the same loving touch Mizriel recalled in Lymri's hands. Without fanfare or overture, he began to sing.

She never did know the words. They were as much a part of the music as each note that thrummed from the lute strings. Sweetness and substance wed, birthing a new being. Melody and words entered her soul by all the portals of the senses and wove themselves into a garland of delight. Mourning folded its dark wings in her heart and died. Hope rose with the sun that brought new life with its light. Kindness sang, and love answered.

The silence of the taproom lay like a lover's hand over everyone when Alveiros ended his song.

A prayer went up from Mizriel's heart as she watched Alveiros set down his lute: *Oh merciful gods, let Timeo fall in the first round of the contest! Don't let him match his songs against this child. Alveiros is everything he longs to be, and never can. Let him learn that he's no minstrel, but not like this! Some dreams can't bear to be broken to blood and bone.*

She became aware that someone nearby was weeping. The tears flowed slowly down Hivrahan's face. "This is true magic," he said. "Beside this, mine is nothing."

He rose from his seat and broke his singing harp against the fireplace stones.

Chapter XII

A WEE DROP OF THE CREATURE

"Well, if that news about your mother doesn't call for a drink, what does?" Duila said, hauling herself out of the River Salmlis. Timeo stooped to give her assistance. She had chosen a tricky bend for her emergence, just below the farmers' market section of town, where cast-off vegetables and miscellaneous leftovers turned the water to soup. As Timeo got his hands under her arms, a heavy wreath of discarded beet greens caught on the nixie's false tail and pulled in the opposite direction.

There was a *schlorp*, and Duila's bare nether limbs wound themselves around Timeo's waist. Man and watermaiden traded startled looks until Duila seized control of her new situation.

"Surprise, lover." Her breath misted his ear, as she turned accident to advantage. "This calls for a drink too."

"Your tail!" Timeo was so horrified by his inamorata's unexpected molting that he nearly dropped her back into the river.

Duila giggled and plucked dead cabbage leaves from her hair and shoulders. "Maybe I should get it back. It wasn't cheap to make." She pushed off from his hips with both feet and arced backwards into the water. She came up right under the drifting fish tail and waved it like a victor's banner before swimming back to shore.

"You're not—you're not an ondine!" Timeo's hand stole forward to touch the dripping fish tail, but jerked away before making contact.

"I am too!" Duila looked offended. She folded the tail over one arm and smoothed down the scales.

"But you have legs!"

"So does a great bronze ape from Vahrd and a Sombrunian stallion and your mother! Why shouldn't I?" Her free arm eeled around Timeo's neck. "I am one of the Waterfolk, my sweet, not one of the Seafolk. Alas for my people, Elaar's firstborn children are the ones most deeply nested in your legends, and they do have fishy tails. We suffer from the confusion in many ways, but none more than this: that every mortal expects all of Elaar's descendants to look like the salt dwellers. Therefore, whenever we venture near your lands, we disguise ourselves so that you may recognize us for what we are."

It was an explanation that only served to confuse Timeo further, particularly as he had always thought disguise and recognition were concepts forever at cross-purposes.

He studied Duila's newly revealed lower form in the faint light coming from a far street lantern. What he saw was something he could understand, and he couldn't say he was displeased. One salient question did elbow itself to the fore. "How could I have missed knowing that you had—I mean, you'd think I would have noticed when we were—" He took the fish tail from her and examined it for gaps from every angle. "How did you do that?"

The nixie linked a leg behind Timeo's knee as if she meant to climb him. "Your mind was elsewhere," she murmured, and set about returning his mind to that pleasantly abstracted state with all the powers in her.

Some time later, a very rumpled Timeo came trailing into the Marsh and Spring tavern behind Duila. At the bar, Whate paid the nixie the supreme compliment of opening his bulging eyes all the way. The outer room customers too were visibly impressed. One gentleman stood up and ceremoniously began to remove his tunic.

Duila shook her head firmly. He made a great deal of pretending that he had only wanted to scratch himself under the rough fisherman's smock before sitting again.

The nixie steered Timeo to a small, unoccupied table and snapped her fingers for service. The sound was not so crisp as it would be if made by unwebbed fingers. However, it was enough for Whate to hear. He hobbled over to serve them while Timeo looked all around the common room with uncommon agitation.

"Why are they all staring at me?" He touched Duila's elbow to draw her attention to the wide-eyed looks focused on their table.

"What an imagination you have, dear one!" She spoke as if to a child who needs to be indulged. "That's the sign of a true minstrel, a maker of powerful songs."

"I don't have that much imagination. Most of my songs come from the old legends. And they *are* staring."

"We shall make new legends, you and I." Duila's small foot ran up the inside of Timeo's leg, leaving the skin damp and tingling even through his hose. "You're the one who's staring now."

"I don't like this place." Timeo forced himself to look away from the many pairs of goggling eyes upon him. Whate came over with their drinks, his wide mouth pulled even wider in an ingratiating grimace.

"Pleasure to serve you, m'lud." His voice was a low, harsh rumble. "Never thought in all my years I'd live t'see this day. Pleasure, pleasure." He rocked back and forth, bowing repeatedly as he retreated to the bar, never taking his eyes from Timeo. Soon thereafter a free round of drinks circulated among all the tables.

"Duila, let's go back to the Bear. This tavern gives me the chills." Timeo knew it wasn't his imagination when all present raised their cups in his direction and drank.

He tried to get up, but Duila reeled him back. "Don't you like my company?"

"Can't I have it at the Chuckling Bear, too?"

"And roll about in the hayloft after? Oh, wouldn't I just adore that!" The nixie's ingratiating softness vanished suddenly as he rose once more. "Sit down, Timeo." He sat, and she was the one to stand. "Now stay. I want to tell them you're here, and that the plans have changed."

"What plans?" His voice squeaked like a crumhorn.

"Never you mind." She crossed to a rack of wine bottles at the rear of the room, twisted the bung of the cask below, and disappeared through the concealed door.

Timeo held onto the table and told himself that there had to be an original song in this somewhere. It was the only thought that sustained him at his post in the midst of a thousand screaming orders from brain to feet commanding *run!* He didn't know who Duila's "they" might be, or the portentous "plans" she'd mentioned, and the longer he sat there, the less he wanted to find out. He hadn't enjoyed suffering poverty, vermin, and short rations for the sake of minstrelsy, not even for a week. He liked suffering suspense even less.

He inched his chair away from the table, but that was as far as he got. A damp, heavy weight fell on his shoulder. He turned his head to see a man's hand, the interdigital webbing shining willow green.

"My lord, I speak out of turn, but the dole of my heart make me bold to approach you, now you've finally come." The face looking down at Timeo was quite human, and although the eyes were a shade more prominent than in most men, the pain in them was real. "I risk everything, coming to this shore to wait upon your need. My wife, my little ones, he has them all in his power. My eldest girl"—his voice broke for a moment—"she's gone; chose the Rock above the shame his men put on her. It's for the others I've decided to come and hasten your return. Accept me, and I am your right hand forever. Through all perils, saving only the call of Elaar's Daughter, I will stand by you against the evil Ragnar."

To Timeo's horror, the man prostrated himself and put the lad's foot atop his head.

"Oh, good," Duila said. "You found something to do while I was gone. Come with me, Timeo. There was a lot of yelling, but I've made them all see my reasons—well, almost all of them. They're ready for you now."

"Uh . . . May I?" Timeo removed his foot gingerly from the prone man's head. His every joint ran liquid as he stumbled after Duila through the wine rack door.

Timeo faced the three ladies seated at the table in the back room. Two were only vaguely familiar. It took him a bit of serious concentration until memory dredged up where he'd seen them before. One was the matronly barmaid from the Philosopher's Mistress, the other a bland-faced housekeeper working for one of the senior professors of the Course Sorcerous.

The one in the middle was Cattail. She didn't look happy to see him. She looked less happy still when Duila wove her arm through his and clung to his side like a whelk to a rock.

"So this is our prince," the housekeeper said, folding pale paws over her swelling belly. All her hair was hidden beneath a starched white cap. Two tiny black eyes in a white, round face made her look like a sugar cookie stuck with currants. "You are sure, Cattail? He doesn't look like much, and if you've made a mistake, we shall have to kill him."

"I'm sure, Nacharis." The ondine was testy.

"If you say so." Plump shoulders shrugged. "Might we trouble you for a little proof of your fortuitous discovery?"

"Tell her who your father was." Cattail's dark eyes flashed at Timeo.

Timeo was still working over in his mind all the implications of "we shall have to kill him." Everything uttered in the back room before or since was effectively eclipsed by that riveting phrase. Cattail had to repeat the question.

"Lymri Riverborn."

"Born where?"

"Here. Found here, that is, on the riverbank."

"There you have it." Cattail's hand swept wide. "Once he produces his father's swaddling blanket, we'll have proof enough to satisfy even you, Nacharis."

"His swaddling blanket?" Timeo asked.

"It is customary to preserve such relics." Cattail frowned. "Isn't it?"

"Um . . . it was, up to a point. My mother burnt it with the rest of the old clothes when we had the great flea infestation of six hundred and sixty-eight." His guileless explanation shattered against a wall of flinty looks.

"His mother burnt it," Cattail repeated.

"But he *was* found on the riverbank." Timeo was emphatic. "Grandma said he was."

"So was my master," Nacharis remarked. "Must we interview every bastard in this town, and all their issue? You've acted rashly, Duila, revealing yourself to this one without consulting me first."

"Why should she consult you?" Zibethica asked mildly. "Cattail has been our leader these past two years and more, not you."

"Two years is only a ripple." The housekeeper's face hardened to a disk of white stone. "Some of us have been with the cause since it began. Some—"

"I was willing to let you hold your leadership, Nacharis," Cattail spat. "You didn't have to resign it to me when I joined you."

"No." The soft hands kneaded invisible dough. "Only to what your father makes you."

Lightning was sluggish beside the slap Cattail dealt Nacharis. "I renounced my father and all he serves!"

The housekeeper's hands remained atop her paunch, though a red stain spread across her cheek. "Blood can never be renounced, or the powers it bestows. Which brings us back to you, young man." Her eyes narrowed near to the vanishing point as she turned to Timeo. "What powers of the Waterfolk are yours?"

"Who, me?" In the circumstances, it seemed a perfectly intelligent question to Timeo. "How should I know?"

Zibethica clapped her hands. "I know! Let's toss him in the river."

"Who, *me?*" There was less bewilderment and more plain terror in the question this time. "But I never learned how to swim!"

"That's perfect, then." Duila gave his arm a loving squeeze. "Don't gape so, sweet fingerling. If you're Waterfolk, it doesn't matter whether you can swim or not: You can't drown."

"And if I'm not Waterfolk?" Timeo spread fingers innocent of any webbing.

"Well, if you're not, we've all made a silly mistake in bringing you here and revealing ourselves to you. You might tell, and a word in the wrong ears on this side the Salmlis could destroy us all. As Nacharis says, we'd have to kill you anyway, and drowning's as good a way as any. So you see, Zibethica's had a simply flawless idea."

Timeo wanted to point out a flaw or two, as he saw them. Any quibbles he might have raised were quashed as the housekeeper stolidly gathered him under one arm like a bundle of wet wash and bore him out the rear door.

Chapter XIII

TAKEN AT THE FLOOD

"Help! Help!" Timeo's cries rebounded from the steeply banked slopes upstream of the city. By daylight, there might have been a passing goatherd to heed his distress, but by night no one frequented this part of the shore.

It was too easy to fall from the bluffs and drown.

The four witnesses to Timeo's struggles sat in a row on the shore and evaluated his progress.

"Duila, save me!"

"He's been in there for half an hour," Duila said, unmoved by Timeo's call. "He hasn't drowned yet."

"That's proof enough for me." Cattail backed up the nixie's words a little too keenly. She leaned far out over the river, her bare toes digging into the bank as if she meant to push off like a racer any instant.

Nacharis' wide, shallow nostrils flared. "Some of these dust-bellies are astoundingly bouyant. Thrashing around like that, who could drown?"

"He's tired out and sunk several times," Zibethica pointed out. "He stayed under for at least— Whoops! There he goes again."

"Two minutes under, by my longest count." Nacharis was not the easiest audience. "I've seen them do that, and not a driblet of our blood in their veins."

"Blood and blood! Why are you so fascinated by blood-lines, Nacharis? Do you breed horses on your day off?"

Cattail demanded. Her fingers jerked up blade after blade of grass from the bank.

"Aye, I can see as how you'd be the last one to have bloodlines mentioned." The housekeeper's small eyes were a watersnake's. "It's your blood that made you our leader—your blood and how it thwarts the call of Elaar's Daughter. There's more of your sire's filthy doings."

"Elaar's Daughter calls to Cattail in vain—we all know that—but not through any of her father's powers." Zibethica tried to charm away the rising storm. "To be immune to the call, you must be of the royal line. The gem's spell can't touch our ruling house."

"What Ragnar's creature left us alive of it." Nacharis' gaze returned to the river, where Timeo had come back to the surface again, spluttering and splashing. "I was only a waiting-maid to the Princess Calla when Ragnar fell upon us. She was no more than four years old, poor love, and sick to death with envy of her newborn brother. I remember having to keep strict watch on her whenever we visited the royal nurseries to be sure she did the infant no harm."

The housekeeper's face hardened as the memories returned. "The day that Ragnar came, his beast in tow, I could not find my little lady anywhere. I ran to the nursery, thinking that perhaps she had stolen away to do some mischief to the baby prince. I found the nurseries empty of all but the infant, wailing in his cradle."

"Where were the servants, the nurses, the rockers?" Duila asked. "Fighting the invaders?"

"Fighting?" Nacharis barked a harsh laugh. "Even as I stood there, looking down into my tiny lord's cradle, I felt the pull. No tide or current ever was half so strong. My spirit rebelled against it, but every thread of resistance was a lance of pain to my bones. I was young, then. I had the strength to struggle against evil, and I sensed evil in the palace that day. Though it cost me much, I strained against the call, and suddenly it was over. I fell unconscious to the floor."

"Nacharis, the tale will keep." Cattail sounded more than a little impatient. "We all know how you saved one prince, but your tongue will cause us to lose another."

"Still afloat?" The housekeeper peered out over the river.

The darkness did not seem to be a hindrance to her sight. "Ah, yes. There he is. Well, it may be you've turned up the right one after all, Cattail."

"Much good we'll get from that! The current has him."

"The current has had him all this while. That is the way with rivers. When I had Zibethica and Duila anchor him to the bottom with a chain of lotus stems, did you think I did it for my amusement?"

"When you called for such an anchor chain, did you think that a healthy young man might not snap it, if he thrashed about in the water long enough?" Cattail retorted.

The ondine was right. Though Timeo had been flailing the water in one spot throughout the course of his ordeal despite the Salmlis' current, he was presently drifting downstream. It was hard to mark his progress, for the fog shrouding the far bank of the river, where lay the Lands Unknown, gave up no landmarks by which to measure it. Still, it was undeniable that he was moving.

"Get him back!" Cattail commanded Duila.

The nixie leaped to her feet, poised to obey, then suddenly drew back from the edge. Her voice contracted with dread. "Cattail, the cross-current has him as well. He's drifting for the other shore."

"So he is." Nacharis shaded her eyes, as if full noon sun were streaming down on them instead of the light of crescent moon and stars. "The mist clings to him already."

"Then what are you waiting for?" Cattail gave Duila a slight shove.

"Don't ask me to do it," the nixie quavered, stepping even further from the water. "Please, not so near the boundary of Ragnar's spell! You can't know how it hurts to feel the pull of the far shore. You never hear the voices calling through your blood, Cattail, and all their pain flowing into your own!"

"Blood again! I am sick of it! We shall lose all, and you lot sit here burbling of blood, blood, blood!" Cattail tore off her clothes and let moonlight drench her opalescent skin. She plunged into the river and lanced across the current after Timeo.

"Well you should hate our talk of blood, my lady,"

Nacharis said dryly to the ondine's wake. "None of us likes to greet the ghosts we have made."

Timeo felt the lotus-stem chain break when he breached the surface for what seemed like the hundredth time. He had grown philosophical about his situation, acquiring that sedative detachment usually vouchsafed someone whose end is imminent. The world removed itself to an aesthetically pleasing distance and allowed Timeo to observe his own fight for life as a fairground puppet show. As the river current came up under him, he relaxed and contemplated the universal questions. Since he would soon be dead, it seemed as good a time as any for such mental twiddlings.

He did think it passing odd that death was being so tardy in taking him up. He'd passed shorter vigils in the registrar's office, awaiting a course change. Dying had turned out to be a disappointingly tedious business. The river closed over his head again, but the old thrill of panic was gone. Where was the poignance and the passion? The unspeakable terror of facing the unknown? The soul-freezing possibility that he would awake among the ranks of Morgeld's captives in Helagarde?

"Death's awful embrace," the incipient poet concluded, "is like kissing your mother. No wonder I can't get worked up about the prince's doom in my epic. Not that I'll ever finish it." A wavelet slopped into his mouth, turning his words to a gargle.

"Duila!" He called his ladylove's name without much hope. He had seen her sitting on the bank with the others, watching him do his serious best to drown. She'd done nothing then, so why should he expect her to come to his rescue now? Shouting for Duila was like praying for rain—you said the words, hoped for the best, and in the meanwhile it gave you something to fill in the waiting.

Now he had the leisure to think of it, he wasn't much surprised by Duila's indifference to his plight. Even in their most fiery couplings, she had remained abstracted and dutiful, like a student serving time at a required introductory lecture. Her caresses left his body sated, but also left a gnawing hunger in his soul. As he rode the river, he felt a twinge of guilt to recall the number of times he'd superimposed Cattail's face on Duila's and summoned her sweet voice to mind in order to perform passably with his paramour.

Fingers of fog began to creep over the river. Moonlight made them into silvery, skeletal hands. Misty strands drifted out to bead Timeo's face with moisture colder than the river. For the first time since the initial shock of his forced dunking, he felt true fear vise his heart.

"Duila! Help me, *please!*"

The fog wound cloudy arms around him. Its touch numbed him to the marrow. The stars shone like tufts of dandelion seed through the blurring canopy over his head, frayed filaments of their light brushing the mist into unfamiliar faces.

A little girl gazed down at him, her dark brows meeting in a petulant scowl. At her back, a moon-faced young woman spoke words in a rippling tongue brighter than any bird song. The fog drifted over the images, pulled a second curtain of vision across Timeo's eyes.

Hush, my lady, the baby sleeps. Hush . . .

No color but the fog's dappled silver, shadowed gray, watered blue. The child's face returned, a ghost among ghosts. The fluted pillars of a palace arose from the river, their capitals ringed with scallop shells, strands of pearl twining up like precious ivy. The child walked proudly through the forest of columns, crystal beneath the pearl, jewel-scaled fish darting up and down within.

The dolomite throne framed by the alleyway of pillars was dark and empty. A slim hand clung to the gray stone base of the throne, a satin banner with a dark, slowly spreading stain covering the rest of the body. The child stopped in her tracks, stared at a ring shaped like a water lily on the hand's third finger. Timeo groaned, every silver petal of the flower cutting into his mind with the child's heart-tearing cry.

She ran forward, carrying him with her, inside and outside her senses all at once. He was with her as she threw herself onto the shrouded body beside the throne. He was elsewhere, with the moon-faced young woman who hid behind a crystal pillar, holding her breath by a spider's thread.

He was with the child again, gradually, horribly becoming aware of the other corpses cast behind the throne, limbs broken, necks snapped. Some were very small. But when the robed man towered out of the darkness and cast his shadow over the weeping child, Timeo's soul was sundered to feel all the agony of the girl's death as a thin Vairish blade pierced her throat, the anguish of the fleeing servant who knew what she must do before she could dare to mourn.

He was warm, then he was cold. He was flying through the air, wind whistling all around him. Beloved warmth comforted him on one side, and he burrowed in towards its source. No milk smell guided him; only the warmth, the cradling darkness, shelter from the unfriendly element of chill air. His small hands pawed at dry breasts.

Then the waters covered him. The impact was sudden, welcome, blissful. His skin seemed to open to the flow, his soul become part of the river's power. All the hunger and the helplessness in his tiny being was obliterated by the water's touch. He was one with its strength, its gift of life. He kicked against the wrappings keeping him from full union with his desire. There was momentary resistance, then grand exultation as he dove free.

But a hand caught him by the neck and dragged him up, up, back into the cold. All his smallness came washing back over him as air filled his lungs. He turned to the warmth of a woman's bosom and sobbed with infant heartbreak.

"There, there," Cattail said, treading water as she patted him on the back. For all her brisk words, her voice trembled badly, as if she too had just passed through sights to try the soul. "You're all right now. We're beyond the fog's reach. Just hang on to me and I'll tow you to shore."

She tried to link her arm around his neck. When he struck it away angrily she couldn't have been more shocked than if he'd bitten her. Sullen and silent, Timeo struck out for the Salmlis' eastern bank with an erratic stroke that nonetheless left Cattail hard put to keep pace.

He hauled himself out of the water, disdaining Duila's dangling hand. By flood-bared root, rocky outcrop, and shallow toehold he climbed to the top of the overhang and wrung water from his clothes.

"Is there a reason why I don't dry off as fast as you lot?" he demanded of the four females. Cattail, fresh out of the river and still naked, was already dry. "My mother's blood, maybe?"

Zibethica and Duila traded a look and fell to their knees in concert. Timeo regarded their bent heads without concern, then turned to Cattail and Nacharis. "Well?"

"Males—males sometimes don't shed water as well as we do," the ondine stammered. "It's a variable trait, like having dark or light eyes."

Timeo shrugged. His gaze came to rest intently on Nacharis. The housekeeper had been watching him with suspicion that receded into reluctant acceptance. Her plump hands spread the wings of her skirt as she lowered herself into a ponderous curtsy. "Your Royal Highness," she said. There was some residual doubt in her voice.

Timeo seized her hands and forced her to stand. To her consternation, it was he who knelt before her. "My thanks, my lady. I swear by the blood of my family, you shall never regret your bravery."

"What do you mean, abasing yourself to Nacharis like that?" Cattail was no less dumbfounded than Nacharis by the young man's words. "She's only Master Gifree's housekeeper."

Timeo lifted one eyebrow in light amusement. "As she was *only* the one who saved my father's life? *Only* the one who dared to risk her own to bring him safely over the river?" He smiled up at the housekeeper, who by now was trembling in every fibre of her body. "Did you keep watch until he was found, my lady?"

"I—I couldn't. I was afraid I would be missed, afraid Ragnar would use Elaar's Daughter to call us all in to him for whatever purpose. He did that several times, in the early days, just to show us how strong his hold was."

She collapsed beside the kneeling Timeo and pressed his hands to her bowed head. "Forgive me for my doubts, my lord. If I had been truly brave, I would have lingered to mark the one who found your father. Then we might have known where he was all the sooner, before . . ."

"My father had his own life and destiny." Timeo made the older woman lift her head. "I have mine." He wrung another shower from his tunic and chuckled. "So I am a prince of the Waterfolk. Won't Mother be surprised."

"*The* prince," Nacharis said in her rumbly voice. "The last of the pure royal stem. There are some remnants of lesser branchlets, but they"—she stared hard at Cattail— "know their own worth to us."

The barmaid's color darkened. She became very business-like. "Your mother must be told at once, of course, sire. She is a powerful sorceress; she must have allies like herself to bring to our help."

"Help—" Timeo's skin chilled. The pictures in the enchanted fog would haunt him forever. He waved at the far bank of the Salmlis. "What I saw . . . over there: Who killed my father's kin? A tall man, dark, heavily robed." A deathly thought struck him. "Was he Morgeld?"

Zibethica and Duila made signs against evil. They had come out of their obeisance to sit at their newfound prince's feet in poses of devout attention. At mention of Morgeld's name, they burst into soft, rustling whispers.

"Silence!" Cattail commanded. She made a face at Nacharis. "Nixies and rush-sprites, all splash and no fish." To Timeo she said, "The one you saw is Ragnar."

"The wizard Ragnar. The murderer of children Ragnar," Nacharis said hotly. "Morgeld's willing servant. There are few such in the Twelve Kingdoms. The wise say that Morgeld can not help being what he is; his blood left him no choice." Her eyes flickered over Cattail. "But those who come into his service of their free will are more evil than the Evil One himself."

Timeo nodded. "Tor was one. My mother told me, and the songs my father wrote. 'Lo! Helagarde Has Fallen!' was the best of them. Sarai All-Mother herself sheds tears for Morgeld's slaves while she lays a great curse on his servants:

> May darkness foul be all their meat
> And death be all their wine,
> May earth and sky their bones deny
> And flame their souls confine.
> May sunlight cast their shadows out,
> May hope deny them rest,
> Their line be curst from last to first,
> And all their slayers bl—"

Cattail's hand cracked across his mouth. Green drops streamed from her eyes. She tried to speak, but her lips opened and closed several times with no sound before she managed to spit out, "*Damn* you!" She leaped back into the Salmlis and swam downstream.

Timeo cradled his smarting lips. "Whuddeye zhay?"

"Only what was just, my lord." Nacharis' sly smile was a cat's. "Let us return to the Marsh and Stream with the happy news: We have a prince."

"Buh—"

Duila was at one elbow, Zibethica at the other. "It was not what you said, lord, but to whom you said it," the rush-sprite told him.

"Cattail is Ragnar's daughter."

A hollow cry of contrition rebounded from the fog and the Salmlis rose in a great fount as Timeo plunged in and swam after the ondine.

Chapter XIV

SOMEBODY LAVES ME

"How dare you? Let me go!" In the false dawn, Cattail churned the river to foam as she squirmed in Timeo's clutches. He had caught up with her under the pilings just north of the fashionable riverside promenade. Here the pleasure boats of Panomo-Midmists' more affluent families tied up, striped silk lateen sails furled. The newfound prince of the Waterfolk would have liked to tie up his obstreperous subject too, but he hadn't the means.

"Release me or I'll scream!" Cattail lodged her threat as a scream, which rather gutted it of menace. "I'll say you tried to assault me and we both fell in the river! You'll be scourged at the gates of the university!"

"If you don't shut up, I'll tell anyone who comes by that you assaulted me first." Timeo was calm.

Cattail laughed him to scorn. "You think they'll believe you?" She drove her nails into his flesh, trying to break his hold on her waist.

"You're naked. Your clothes are the gods know where. And—ow!—look at the scratches you gave me when I tried to protect my virtue. I'm a northern lordling, heir to a rich domain, and for all anyone in this town knows, you're a barmaid out for the main chance like a hundred others. Which one of us would you believe?"

If the look Cattail gave him had been an arrow, it would have carried poison at the tip. She still kicked and jerked mightily, but she didn't scream anymore.

Not that their struggle under the pier was conducted in total silence. Cattail's contortions and Timeo's amateurish attempts to tread water sent waves sloshing against the green-scummed pilings. Two rod and creel carrying gentlemen, dressed as befitted successful merchants, overheard the little maelstrom as they took their places at the end of the dock.

"Biting," said one.

"Mm," the other replied. He cast his line into the river.

Either Cattail was inspired by the fishermen above or the idea was all her own: She snaked her head back and bit Timeo's earlobe. He had gathered her close enough to his own body, his chin resting on her shoulder as he tried whispering reason in her ear, to make such a maneuver all too possible. The resulting yowl did not go unmarked.

"Cats," said the first fisherman.

His comrade took a moment to check the fastening of his empty creel.

Timeo tightened his grip on the ondine. To his horror and humiliation, this necessary close contact brought about a completely natural and inconvenient result. Cattail's eyes widened. His sheepish grin was answered by her outraged stare, though her brows rose and her mouth tightened with too much exaggeration.

"I just wanted to apologize," he whispered.

"For *that?*" It was no use. She could not help smiling as she said it.

He took heart when her sternness melted and he smiled back. "For reciting that bit of my father's epic. I didn't know you were Ragnar's daughter." His hands unlinked, giving her leeway to flee the loosening circle of his arms.

Instead, she pivoted within their compass and faced him. Her own slender limbs twined around his neck. She laid her cheek against his, as if for secrecy's sake, and whispered back, "As you said, my father has his destiny and I have mine. It's I who should ask your forgiveness, my lord. I was a fool. I assumed that the fog's enchantment told you all. So it is, with those whose blood is untainted."

He felt a moisture thicker than river water trickle down his cheek and pulled back to see her shedding those exotic tears. He brushed them away with one hand, the other drawing her ever closer to him. She allowed this, and soon his lips tasted the oily, bitter droplets before mouth met mouth.

The turmoil under the pier changed tenor.

"Slacking off," said the talkative merchant fisherman.

His companion said nothing. His float had dipped beneath the surface. He reeled in the line at a sure and steady rate. Before long he was showing off his catch to his partner.

"Trunk hose?" There was a spell of pensive head scratching.

The successful angler regarded his dripping trophy, then his own massive dimensions. He tossed the garment over the upstream side of the pier. "Too small for keeping." He changed bait and cast his line again.

Cattail and Timeo lay hidden in Zibethica's nest of upriver reeds. "Your poor ear," she murmured, lounging on her stomach as she caressed that abused shell of flesh.

"Bleeding's stopped." He pulled her to him for another kiss. "You never told me you were part shark, lady."

She laughed. "You are ignorant! I am like you, of the Waterfolk, not the Seafolk. We have no dealings with sharks, if we can help it."

"I know all about the difference: No fish tails for us."

"It's more than that, Timeo. Oh, you have so much to learn! I do wish you'd been enrolled in the Course Sorcerous. Nacharis says they make all their students take that survey lecture: On Magical Beings."

"Do some more magic with me." Timeo smiled, looking entirely at peace. His clothing lay neatly folded out of sight on the shore, including the miraculously recovered trunk hose. The river laved his skin with a sweetness he had never really noticed before, and the fragrance of green reeds all around accented the cool, spicy scent of Cattail's luminous skin.

She knelt above him. Her hair had come out of its long plait and hung a curtain of night over them both. "Incorrigible! It's nearly full day. We can't linger here."

"Who's to know? This part of town doesn't favor early risers. They like the dark hours better for their business. Their dusk is our dawn." He reached for her. "Besides, if they do spy us, we're just a doxy and her client—one who's jaded with ordinary bedding.''

Cattail searched the lightening sky for a way to answer such arguments, then shrugged and did as he desired.

Timeo's assessment of the neighborhood was correct. The lone passerby who did glance into the waving reeds was herself a painted daisy—as nice-minded folk called them— and only wanted to get home and sleep.

First, however, there was a report to be made. The doxy trudged through the narrow alleys until she reached an alehouse too poor to be called tavern. Inside, in marked contrast to his surroundings, sat a richly garbed young man. His dark eyes flashed with pleasure when they lit on the girl. He swung long legs off the one table in the place that didn't wobble and greeted her as if she were nobility.

"Stawna, my dear, your poor eyes are ringed with the night's triumph! Did you remember to summon the wizardling after?''

"Where d'you think I been?'' Stawna shoved a frizzy lock of hair out of her eyes. "Little no-talent sodder near ruint the lifter spell, and you told me how it's got to be fresh in my mind for that spell to work! Could feel it goin' stale while he buggered around having second go at it.''

"But it *did* work?''

The girl reached into the deep pocket of her skirt and handed him a curved terra-cotta tablet. Her lip curled as she observed his reaction.

"He wanted you to do *this?* Really?''

"You know piss-all well that a lifting spell pulls out just what happened, and no 'maginings about it. Wasn't it a lifting, used as evidence, sent my poor man Lazedor to the gallows? Look, Zerin, ain't nothing worse than education. Gives men too damn many *ideas.*'' She made a face as if she had bitten a toad. "Make it my normal way not t' take on them universerry types, and 'specially not the perfessers!''

"Enough, my dear!'' Zerin of Wickerdale pressed a gold coin into the harlot's hand. "Salve your conscience with this, and get to bed. There are still a few likely men I'll want you and your guild sisters to visit tomorrow night.''

"Not more perfessers?" Stawna showed irregular fangs.

"Alas, so it must be!" Zerin spread his hands. "So few among the judges come from outside the university community! Cheer up. I shan't make you court any more of the tenured ones. Junior faculty are so much less imaginative. It will be a holiday for you."

Stawna snorted and stumped off, muttering, "Stink-arsed Havror Fenn can't come soon enough for me!"

". . . and it would take about a week under water to drown you—approximately, owing to your mother's mortal blood. But you must've guessed that by now."

Timeo sat on a bale of hay up in Sterion's loft watching Cattail comb out her hair. Everything about her was fascinating, from this mundane grooming ritual to the astonishing way she had summoned Nacharis, Zibethica, and Duila from far upriver just by speaking to water cupped in her hands. The three had arrived as promptly as possible, bearing the ondine's clothes. Duila did not look at all envious when she saw Timeo in Cattail's arms, a fact which still rankled him slightly.

But who could waste time grumbling over the vagaries of a nixie's affections? Not a young man who was in the process of learning more about all the wonders his waiting kingdom held.

"Why haven't I any webs between my toes and fingers?" he asked.

"Oh, likely the same reason that you don't shed water. Though you do have very, very shallow bits of webbing, if you look closely enough."

Timeo did. "No more than ordinary folk. That fellow at the Marsh and Spring, I thought I saw him flaunt better finger webs than a duck's feet."

"There has always been a greater variation of appearance and power among the male Waterfolk than among the female." Cattail studded her braid with flowers Timeo had picked for her. "We females are either ondine, nixie, sprite, or seeress."

"What's the difference?"

"Descending order of powers, though the one power of a seeress could be called the greatest of all. So it would be, if it were subject to her control. All you have to remember, my lord, is that I am an ondine and therefore outrank Duila.''

He handed her another blossom. ''In my heart, if nowhere else.''

Cattail made a moue. ''In your court as well. Bear that in mind, please, for future reference.''

''Are there any with a seeress' power among my male subjects?''

Cattail's gleaming shoulders lifted slightly. ''There have been tales. But male Waterfolk, as I said, are singularly unclassifiable. One may be born with the equivalent of an ondine's waterspeech coupled to a sprite's shape-shifting ability. Another may prophesy better and more frequently than our greatest seeress, only to drown after less than two days' full immersion. We females find it all very untidy of them.''

''Why?''

''Why have I never seen a three-colored tomcat? Save your mind to learn what *is,* and worry afterwards about *why* it is.''

There was one *why* Timeo had that couldn't wait. Very gingerly he asked, ''Cattail . . . if the wizard Ragnar is your father, why have you come to help those who want him defeated?''

Cattail's hands came down, the last flower between them. ''Seek that in the fog.''

Timeo chilled at the memory. ''I don't want to touch that fog again.''

''You will have to, when we pass through it to win back your kingdom. When do we speak to your mother?'' Her face became a mask, impossible to read. The last flower was white pulp and golden dust in her lap.

''Gentlemen, I am most gratified that you were able to find time in your busy schedules to join me.'' Zerin of Wickerdale cut a broadly exaggerated bow, fingertips nearly sweeping the floor. ''Won't you sit?''

Ovrin and Fell tried to act nonchalant as they took their places at the sumptuously laid table. Their host had summoned them to the Spice Bowl Inn by a messenger who bore two new tunics, with all the appurtenances, as well as the invitation. Keristor had sat stroking the heavy slubbed silk for hours until it was time for Fell and his brother to change and go. They had swaggered all the way to their appointment, doing their best to live up to the clothes on their backs, but when they were conducted to one of the most expensive private chambers off the Spice Bowl's main dining room, their confidence faltered.

Zerin allowed them to goggle at the wealth surrounding them, keeping his eyes discreetly averted. He poured himself wine from an amber decanter, its neck curved like the beak of the azanzi bird. The cup passed beneath his wedge of a nose as he pronounced, "A melancholy grape, yet not irreversibly depressed. The bouquet promises future optimism." He served them and added, "I hope you may promise me the same?"

"If the wager drew interest before, now you'd say we were giving away gold by the dipperful." Fell rolled a mouthful of the dejected vintage over his tongue. "I want your guarantee: Will you cover us if this falls through?"

Zerin's mobile mouth quickened. "If I refuse?"

The knife was under Fell's hand on the table before he had finished swallowing. It had darted out of the dark-haired student's sleeve like a snake's tongue, a fine poniard of the sort preferred by the Sisters of Sleep assassins' sorority in barbarian Vahrd.

"Like it?" Fell asked. "I bought it with some of the money you gave us to flash at would-be bettors. I've wanted one of these ever since I took our required Physical Discipline course last year. Very educational. I learned that knives and I understand each other."

"Cold, thin, sharp, and bloodthirsty, both of you: a match of Krisli's making. But my question was as superfluous as yours. You are going to win your wagers, gentlemen, and I am going to win my crown."

"How?" Ovrin asked.

Before Zerin could answer, there was a modified uproar on the other side of the curtain shielding their alcove. The heavy material tossed and belled. Odd shapes thrust against it, and then came a deep tearing as cloth came away from gilt-bronze hanging rings.

Keristor looked up from the mass of curtain under him, cowering like a puppy familiar with the stick. One of the Spice Bowl Inn's incomparable waiters stood over him with a *here*-you-are-sir look at Zerin that transformed Keristor's irruption upon the private party into the fulfillment of the host's own request. So well did he do it that for a moment Ovrin and Fell almost believed that the wine merchant's son had planned for Keristor to show up like this.

Zerin soon disabused them. "Ovrin, my friend, I thought you left your little brother in some keeper's charge when you went among ordinary folk."

The big redhead scowled. "Keri needs no keeper. He can take care of himself when I go out. He just follows us, sometimes, without our knowing it."

"Oh, I didn't mean a beast keeper! Did it come out sounding that way?" Zerin banished the thought with delicate wigwags of his long fingers. "A tutor; I meant a tutor, of course. One able to channel the boy's obviously extraordinary talents. Come here, boy." He helped Keristor from the floor. A cadre of waiters brought a fourth place setting and rehung the tumbled curtains in less time than it took Keri to be seated beside Zerin at table.

The boy's eyes were ready to start from his head in wonder at his surroundings. He touched everything on the table he could reach, then began to pat Zerin's parti-colored cointese. A grimace of distaste touched the would-be Fool King's lips. He forced it into an indulgent smile and draped his arm around Keri.

"If you like what I wear, lad, you shall have a garment just like it, cut to your measure, before the Havror Fenn. Would that please you?"

Keri goggled at this stranger who spoke to him so kindly. "Yes . . ." He hesitated to reply, a little fear behind his gratitude.

"You *do* understand what I'm saying? *This*"—Zerin pulled his dagged sleeve taut to show it off—"for *you*." He tapped Keri's chest. The boy exhaled sharply with surprise, then nodded. "Good boy!" Zerin hugged him. His arm still around Keri, the wine merchant's son poured another measure of drink for all. He pushed a goblet into Keri's hands and raised his own cup high.

"To the Havror Fenn and Timeo's honest victory!"

"Timeo!" Fell echoed wholeheartedly, and drank.

"Timeo." Ovrin showed less enthusiasm. His eyes were on his brother and Zerin.

Keri repeated the toast because everyone else was doing it. "Timeo . . . He's my friend," he confided to Zerin.

"A worthy one. Drink up, boy, drink up." Zerin of Wickerdale tilted the goblet to Keri's lips and held it there while the lad drank, first slowly, then avidly. "A man may be known by his friends, and Timeo shall prove the best of friends to us all. To Timeo, gold, and the Havror Fenn!"

Chapter XV

ONE WHOSE FAME WAS WRIT IN WATER

Mizriel of the White Hair was angry, and growing angrier by the minute. In the past six days she had begged the pardons of every wizard, witch, warlock, wise woman, and miscellaneous sleight-of-hand mountebank in the Twelve Kingdoms, or so it seemed.

She sidled down a row of ominous and exquisite members of her chosen calling, at the same time airing her complaints to Paragore-Tren, who was sidling along behind her. "After nigh a—pardon me—week of this, you'd—excuse me—think they'd try—sorry—to tuck their feet—'scuse me—under the—my fault—benches when someone—pardon me—wants to get—pardon me—by to her own cursed—Oh, I *do* beg your pardon—seat."

They reached what should have been two vacant places in the section reserved for mages and found them occupied. Two very young magic wielders sat discussing the program items scheduled on their handbills while they split a bag of crisp-fried delabru paws. After having inched, edged, and sometimes tripped her way over so many pairs of feet, Mizriel was in no mood to be charitable towards usurpers.

"UP!" Her small hand closed on the collar of the stripling nearest her and yanked him perpendicular.

"Gods protect me, my lady, what have I done to you now?" Hivrahan of Lyf went limp and trembling in Mizriel's clutch as he simultaneously recognized the white-haired sorceress and her red-hot temper.

"Hey! Let Hiv go, or—" Melki jumped to his friend's defense, the illusion of snake fangs already forming in his mouth. He hissed threats, his pupils stretching vertical as a sprinkling of scales spread over his skin.

Mizriel spun a ball of seeing in her free hand, the bright sphere containing an image of a snake with Melki's face having his neck broken by a snow white poison–pounce with Mizriel's. "Or what?" she snapped.

"Or I'll call one of the ushers," Melki mumbled as he sat back down. Scales and fangs withered away.

"Mizriel, my dear, let the boy go," Paragore-Tren told her. "He can't show you his ticket if you've got him half throttled." To Hivrahan he said, "We're looking for places four eighty-nine and four ninety-one, young man. Might we trouble you to check the markings on your own?"

Mizriel released Hivrahan, who gestured nervously at the inscription his forced departure from the bench had revealed.

"Ha! Four eighty-nine!" She savored victory.

"Yes, just like on my ticket, my lady. See? Place four eighty-nine, east tier of—"

"*East?!*" Mizriel dug out her own stub. Her maledictions were hot and inventive when she saw that she and Paragore-Tren had taken the wrong fork in the underground approach to the amphitheater hosting the Havror Fenn.

"I can't believe that after six days I did that!" she exclaimed.

"There, there, Mizriel. You've been under a lot of stress." Paragore-Tren tried to comfort her, but the little sorceress took one look at the barricade of feet she would have to negotiate all the way back to the aisle and burst into dry sobs.

"Oh, my lady, please don't!" Hivrahan gave Melki a sharp nudge. "Give her your place," he hissed.

"Bugger a goat."

"Melki, I'll let you pickle your insides at my expense after the contest. Now give her your seat."

"Oh, all right." There was a mosquitolike buzzing and the purple lizard was back on Hivrahan's shoulder. "Pay all that to come hear the finals of the Minstrelry competitions and I have to be here as an earless reptile,'' he grumbled.

"You only *look* earless,'' Hivrahan whispered as he helped Mizriel into the vacated place. "You can hear as well as I.''

"It's the principle of the thing.''

"Sir,'' Hivrahan said to Paragore-Tren. "Sir, if you would guarantee my safety and Melki's, I'd be willing to transform into a lizard too and give you my seat.''

The old wizard chuckled the offer away. "Guarantee mine,'' he said, "and take your own seat.'' His spectacles glittered in the early sun and he became a large orange tomcat before the last of the dazzle left Hivrahan's sight. The transformed mage curled up in the young warlock's lap. "Best way to get a really good back rub,'' he purred. "Don't forget to scratch between my shoulder blades.''

Hivrahan offered Mizriel the bag of delabru bits. She stopped sobbing and accepted one. "Thank you. I'm sorry about my temper.''

"Your friend said you've been under strain. Might it be something I could help you vanquish, my lady? I am witch-born, not wizardly like you. Sometimes one of my kind has powers that one of yours does not, and vice versa. We must stand together. What ails you?''

"Nothing,'' Mizriel said. "Unless you count the fact that the whole world's going mad all around me and I am the only sane person left.''

Hivrahan mumbled a petition to Ayree under his breath and moved a prudent distance from Mizriel. It was only a finger length, what with the packed stands, but as Melki had said, it was the principle of the thing. Hivrahan made it his policy to put some space between himself and lunatics, no matter how attractive. It had served him well so far.

"Tell me, young man, you've been here for all the days of the Havror Fenn?'' Hivrahan nodded. "You've heard every contestant, from first to last, all the way through?''

"Well, not that. You know how the bouts go on around the clock, spaced so that the contestants may rest between personal matches. I'm not one of these Havror Fenn fanatics who stays up for days with no sleep so he can claim he's listened to every song.''

"Listened to all and heard none," Mizriel agreed.

"But I have heard most of the daylight singers and many of the nighttime contests."

"And in all that time, have you heard the songs of one called Timeo of Dureforte Keep?"

Hivrahan's face turned the color of yeast. "Your son, is he not?" It was Mizriel's turn to nod. The warlock's voice evidenced strain as he said, "You must be very proud of him."

"I don't need to be flattered through my son's achievements, Hivrahan. I need a grappling hook on sanity. Today, before the largest crowd ever gathered during the Havror Fenn, my son will sing for the Minstrel King's crown; my son, whose quality of voice is only equaled by his talent in composition." She nibbled at her fried paw. "What did you think of Timeo's songs, Hivrahan?"

"You must be very proud of him," the warlock repeated.

"I want a straight answer!" Fury formed a silver thundercloud around Mizriel's head. Minor bolts of energy grazed a few of the nearer audience members. An usher was summoned.

"Madam, there is no extrapersonal magic allowed at the Havror Fenn save preapproved stage illusions." The usher carried a thick yellow wand that matched his green-trimmed livery. It was more than a badge of office. "Another outburst and I shall have to reduce and confine you." He tapped the wand. Muffled squeals and scuffling sounded within.

"You and who else?" Mizriel countered.

"Please, madam, I do not think defiance suits a lady of your standing in the community. But if you must know, we have all been given our authority by Fortunata, wardlady of this land. My lord Ayree's sister is a patron of minstrels and a great devotee of the Havror Fenn. Thanks to her efforts, we have set up the barrier keeping witchborn and wizardly spectators from hurling ill-considered spells at the contestants."

Mizriel cast an ill-natured glance down the tiers of seats towards the central arena, where the selfsame barricade tinted the air an almost imperceptible violet by its presence. "I'll behave," she growled. "Keep your tube to yourself."

The usher bowed, and presented Mizriel with a ticket good

for a free gourd of stand-wine. "Your cooperation is noted and appreciated. I don't like sucking up rowdies any better than they like being confined to this"—he tapped the wand again—"for the required twelve hours' punishment. They're bad enough during the minstrelry competition, and the jesting contests are beginning today as well. There are fewer competitors, but you never do know what abomination they'll bring onstage under the aegis of 'wit.' And the gods forbid anyone objecting to the most scurrilous, scatological, cruel, or revolting performance." The usher tilted his head to one side and did a singsong nasal imitation of the jesters' universal battle cry: " 'What's the matter? Can't you take a joke?' Good day, madam. Enjoy the Havror Fenn."

Hivrahan gallantly braved the sea of feet to redeem the complimentary ticket. While he uncorked the stand-wine, Mizriel folded the accompanying sheets of heavy paper into cups. Hivrahan passed his to his shoulder for Melki to share, but Paragore-Tren twitched his whiskers disdainfully when offered some.

"You will never be more than a street-corner mage if you rely on distractions above courage," the orange tom said. "The Lady Mizriel asked you for your true opinion of Timeo's songs. Give it."

"Ugh," Hivrahan said.

"Oh, thank you! The gods bless you forever!" Mizriel embraced the young warlock wildly. For one ecstatic moment he thought he felt the soft touch of lips against his cheek, or was it only a flick of Melki's tongue?

"You don't like your son's singing?" he inquired.

"My son sings as well as I do." Mizriel's mouth twisted. "My late husband always told me I did things to melody that had the night spirits taking notes. He didn't have to tell me what I already knew. My father said that even when my sister Ursula was in her bear form, she sang better than I did. I never tried creating songs. I saved myself from that humiliation, at least."

"But, my lady, the chronicles are full of tales of great poets who couldn't follow a tune with a searching spell."

"They are also full of stories about divine singers without the merest spark of creativity in them." She got the last of the meat off the paw and absently used the claw to clean crumbs from under her nails. "Timeo combines the worse halves of those legends to a frightening degree."

"Yet he is in the final round?"

Mizriel jabbed at the program with the denuded delabru paw. "There's his name, unless I've gone blind as well as mad."

"How could such a thing have happened?" Hivrahan was astounded.

"I am no judge, and the judges are the only ones who decree the winner of each bout below the final level. For this last, for the Minstrel King's crown, public acclaim decides."

"That accounts for the crowds today."

"Taste is more random a thing than any curse, and they claim education alters it." Mizriel raised her paper cup. "I can sit here drinking stand-wine from dawn to dusk with the same appreciation I'd bestow on a bottle of Vair's finest vintage. I do not own an educated palate, and still despise the stronger red wines in favor of the sweeter whites and greens. Maybe that's why I can't value Timeo's singing as highly as these academics seem to do. Then too, my son has come into a great inheritance of late. Perhaps his new expectations have affected his voice and I'm so used to hearing the old one that I can't accept the new."

"Did the old one sound like live pigs being chopped up for sausage?" Hivrahan asked.

"Then you *have* heard Timeo sing!"

"Several times. After the first, always by mistake or a rescheduling not on the program. If his new voice is an improvement on the old, gods spare me from—"

"There is also love, which has come to my boy from the unlikeliest source I ever dreamed. Who can account for the changes love makes in a man?"

"Who indeed?" said Hivrahan, watching the little sorceress with more than polite attention as she crunched up fragile delabru bones.

"I really must go now, my dearest," Cattail said, tying one last love knot in the blue and green silk fringes trailing from Timeo's padded shoulders. "The finals bring even the tavern roaches into the stands, and the charity seats fill up quickly.''

"You don't have to sit among the paupers." Timeo encircled her waist and kissed his beloved. "What did you do with the ticket I bought you for this week's contests?"

"You didn't tell me you'd bought the tickets in a block and given the others to those friends of yours."

"Ovrin, Fell, and Keristor? What's wrong with that?"

Cattail's ivory brow furrowed. "When you've lived among the Waterfolk for a while, you'll be better able to recognize leeches. I mislike them and I mistrust them. They're flaunting more colors than a merchant's whore these days. Where did they get the coin to put silks on their backs? Even Keri's clad in scarlet.''

"Do you begrudge the boy his finery? He loves the sight and feel of fine things so, and the gods witness he's a goodly lad with few enough pleasures in this life.''

"Timeo, you don't understand." Cattail took his hand. "Keri walks forever in a world we can never see, just as I see nothing when I pass through the river mist of my father's making. I don't question his right to enjoy what's come to him; I only question the source. Did you give him the clothes?''

"Me? No. His brother Ovrin keeps him dressed and fed— with a little help from my purse at times, true. But Ovrin and Fell haven't asked me for a single copper lately." A hopeful notion struck him. "Maybe their scholarships were increased.''

"To cover the cost of garb so glorious?" Cattail gave him a fond kiss. "You walk in your own fog, my love. Well, we can sort out your friends' doings later, after the contest. For the time being, just accept the fact that I don't feel comfortable sitting with them.''

"As you like it, sweetheart. After the contest you'll have other things to occupy your mind.''

"Such as?"

"Such as where we're to keep the Minstrel King's crown when we're still stuck living in your hayloft." Timeo rubbed his chin. "Maybe Mother would hold onto it for us until I'm reinstated in the uni— No, wait, she'll have to send it home by spell. She too will have much to do when the Havror Fenn is finished.''

"You jest with me, my precious. We both know the task that awaits us when the Havror Fenn is done.'' Cattail wound Timeo's arms around her and backed into their loving hold. She pressed herself to him and sighed happily. "I can scarcely believe it. Soon the waiting will be over, the chains broken. With your mother's magic fighting for us, my father's misguided spells will have to fall.''

"Certainly, yes. Mother said she would not be the only one to take the Waterfolk's side. She's well respected among her peers. Your father's spell of disbelief won't be strong enough to stand against her testimony. I'd like to see the mage brave enough to tell my mother she was talking fairy tales! She's promised to plead our cause with Paragore-Tren and any other wizards or witchborn of her acquaintance.''

"Paragore-Tren?'' Cattail spun about and faced Timeo. "The wizard of the Naîmlo Wood?''

"You know him?''

"Not by more than name. I think I recall hearing Nacharis say . . .'' She looked troubled. "Never mind. It's almost time for you to enter the green chamber. Fare you well, my love. May the Watersong fill you soon.''

"Watersong?''

But she was gone.

"Prince of the Waterfolk?'' Hivrahan was like one listening to a fairy tale.

"King, rather, although since he has yet to be crowned, their custom is to think of him as a prince only,'' Mizriel said. Her eyes grew sad. "My poor Lymri. When we were young and caught up in great adventure, an evil prince bound him to a stone pillar in the River Koly. He meant for Lymri to drown when the tide came in, or be killed by the montrous Children of Koly. Lymri told me about it later— how the waters covered him but didn't drown him, how small hands undid the bonds holding him to the place of sacrifice, how he thought he saw a sea maiden bid him farewell . . . He put so much of it down to illusion, when it was all real. He never knew. He died, never knowing who he truly was.''

"Many do." The warlock spoke kindly. "Not all are the worse for it." He rested his hand on hers. "My lady, you are not so old to speak of the days when you were young."

Mizriel of the White Hair saw something in his eyes that woke a feeling she had thought impossible to stir up again. Though she had declared her heart dead, embers lay among the ashes. But Lymri was too recently gone for these to kindle into flame.

Wait . . . A small voice spoke to her from the warlock's eyes. Your blood is too young to flow cold. Wait, my lady, for grief to dull and life to sing more than songs of loss. Your spirit is fire, and I have been drawn into that flame. It is my fear and my fascination, and I can not fight what I feel. You feel it too, I sense it. Time is nothing to me, and age only for the magicless to fear. I have time for you to name and accept what you feel. Wait, as I mean to wait for you, even to the last sun, my lady brighter than a star.

She could say nothing, but her other hand came to rest atop his. As if nothing had happened, she proceeded to tell him of her son's need for magical aid if he was to wrest back his kingdom from the wizard Ragnar.

"When the minstrelry contest is over, tell him I am his man," Hivrahan said.

"I'll help," Melki hissed. "It's more glorious work than I'll ever find in these piddling times."

"Paragore-Tren, did you hear—?" Mizriel hushed herself. Smiling, she observed the orange tomcat asnooze in Hivrahan's lap, one paw over his pink nose. Paragore-Tren had heard nothing at all.

The wizard of the Naîmlo Wood slept through most of the introductory minstrelry matches taking place in the arena below. The Havror Fenn was a double-elimination process, and the standings of all those Timeo and his last opponent had vanquished had to be established before the final bout for the Minstrel King's crown.

The minstrelry was interspersed with the first jesting competitions. This was appropriate, since the compleat minstrel was expected to be somewhat of a jester himself, in a minor way. Tradition demanded that each singer warm the audience with a joke or two, or else a humorous fable suitable to introduce the theme of his song. It was not simple, for when one was about to sing a ballad full of foredoomed heroes and woeful happenstance, the number of apt jests leading up to it was limited.

The sun stained the river red before the stage was cleared of runner-ups in the minstrelry bouts. The victor accepted his third-place award—a winged crystal containing the long, somber, stylized face of Insar. Lantern-jawed and pop-eyed, the divine musician's lack of physical attraction was the stuff of legend, yet a swirl of miniature stars within the crystal crowned him with the magic of his song.

The triumphant singer bowed to the several seating sections of the audience, honoring mages and merchants, academics and social parasites by turns. Lastly, he bowed to the judges who had awarded him this token of achievement and to the occupants of the grand box seats above the judges' stand.

"Oh my," sighed the Lady Fortunata to her guests. "Every year it's the same thing: Songs about something wretched happening to a small child always win."

Her sister Senja, witchborn wardlady of barbarian Vahrd, snored in reply. She had nodded off during the fourteenth song in which a sympathetic youngling sacrificed his life for his people. Asapha, the word-sparing lady of Lyf, nudged Senja awake with a leather-clad elbow.

"Is he dead yet?" Senja snorted.

"No, but my rump is," Lucha complained. She had come at Fortunata's invitation from her wardland Vair, where folk knew how to make cushions properly plump and comfortable. "They're lighting the torches. It's the last contest of all, for the crown of minstrelry. Maybe then we can all go home."

"I don't know why I ask you anywhere." Fortunata pursed her lips. "You don't know *art!*"

"No," Lucha replied. "But I know what I like, and I'd like a good laugh 'long about now."

"Hush. The minstrels come."

Chapter XVI

MOIST LIKELY TO SUCCEED

Gorval Bywood of Leyaeli, the would-be Minstrel King who placed fifty-seventh in the competitions, based his prize entry on the legend of how the Havror Fenn came to pass. Either the judges did not appreciate self-referential works as much as songs of havoc wreaked on children or else he lost points for starting his turn with the joke about the frost cat, the wizard, and the armoire.

This was a pity, for the contestant had managed to touch upon all the salient points of the legend, setting his verses in the difficult form of Corintha's couplets. He sang of the battle of Insar, son of Asira, against Neimar, beloved of Elaar the Sea-Witch. These two worthies, later to be allies and friends, met as foes in a wrestling match on the future site of the university city—this in the days when the gods still walked among men.

It was not a gentlemanly battle. Insar had taken his place in the ring only to avenge some slighting remarks that Neimar made about "string pluckers and reed puffers." Though Neimar was brawny, as befitted a man of the open seas, and Insar a pipestem-limbed bider by the fireside, anger transformed the minstrel into a fearsome wrangler in the ring. He was small, wiry, and unprincipled enough to evade Neimar's more direct attacks.

Insar's fight was not all evasion and self-defense. The

legends often painted Elaar's beloved as a giant, hence Insar's ruse of dashing between his opponent's legs, chomping him on the ankle in passing. On his side, Neimar danced about trying to pinch off the poet's head "like a nit's,/Else like the foul disease-bred tick whose bite bears Hagrum's fits." Six of these titanic pinches missed the mark, but did manage to deforest the acreage on which the university city would stand.

When pinching failed, Neimar took to stomping, hoping to "Serve up the versifying pain as men a corncake make,/ Or flatten him in cockroach-wise, and thus his anger slake." This was excellent for converting hills to flat plowland, but not much good when it came to overcoming the ever-nimble Insar.

Neimar's antics were brought to a halt when Insar miraculously stretched the G string of his lute between the two trees the giant had left standing and lured his enemy with a taunting song—played without a G string, of course. Neimar charged, tripped, and plowed out the site of the Havror Fenn arena with his face. After being named victor, Insar showed there were no hard feelings by healing Neimar's hurts with one of his less abrasive melodies.

At this point, one of the more influential godesses watching the whole thing remarked that she was surprised at how stupidly two grown men could behave, given half a chance. To seal their new friendship, and to make sure that future generations of men would not suffer from their reputation, Insar and Neimar then and there founded the university city of Panomo-Midmists. Females were not admitted, having no need to be taught the lesser wisdoms found in textbooks nor the greater sagacity of not behaving like fools.

The Havror Fenn was established coeval with the university. Some claimed this was Insar's wish, so that all further contests on that ground should be of art, not muscle. Some said it was Neimar's desire, because he hated to see such a fine arena go to waste after he had taken such pains to create it. Besides, no one had a better idea of what to do with it.

Time had done much to change the aspect of the Havror Fenn arena since it had been first gouged out of the riverside soil by Neimar's face. The raised platform in the middle of the natural depression was temporary, changed every year, and decorated according to the fashion in stage design. It was torn down after the festival and broken up to be sold as relics to incoming students of minstrelry and jest.

This year the stage was circular, its top rimmed with multicolored scallop shells, the merest suggestion of a railing. All around the skirting was a painted tribute to Neimar, the Chaining of the Beast of the Sea. Two ramps of yellow pine led onto the platform from opposite sides of the arena, a device to guarantee drama when the finalists for the Minstrel King's crown came forth to face each other. Four flexible poles bent over the platform, a cluster of clay oil lamps burning where they joined. Poles and oil lamps were decorated with bright festoons of tissue paper butter-flies, their wings fluttering boldly in every evening river breeze, protected from immolation by a timely fireproofing spell. Ordinary moths and night flyers were not so lucky, but at least the audience remained unmolested. An additional ring of torch-bearing standards stood between the stage and the spectators, casting further illumination over the scene of musical combat.

As Timeo stepped from the green chamber onto the foot of the ramp, he paused to drink deeply of the moment. No dream of all his youth could equal this. If he were to die tomorrow—as he devoutly hoped he would not—he would go a happy man.

Love, music, a minstrel's crown, a king's diadem, and acclaim for his sweet, sweet singing! These, all these his, or as good as his so very soon. He had changed in the course of the many individual bouts that had paved his road here. Towards the last, he no longer stared in startled silence when the judges came forward, grim faced and solemn voiced, to name him the winner of each preliminary match. He had come to expect victory as his due.

"Why not?" he murmured. "I am a prince of the Water-folk. One quality that my people do share with Elaar's subjects of the salt seas is the enchanting power of song. I never even needed my darling Cattail to tell me what every schoolboy knows: All water dwellers are possessed of magically fair voices. Stronger than any sword, more compelling than a wizard's words, headier in the blood than love's first fire— Oh yes, I see now that my talent was simply too overwhelming for those whose ears were unfit to hold such richness. Only you understood me, Father. We shared the blood and powers of our people. You who were the unwitting lord of the Waterfolk could recognize my gifts when no one else could do so. I dedicate my coming crown to you."

He stepped up the ramp onto the torchlit platform and saluted the audience. A roar answered him—unintelligible in content, like most mob noises. He surveyed the many faces of the crowd and imagined how they would sound when they acclaimed him first among Insar's spiritual sons.

"Is this a part of the jesting competition?" Senja asked. She leaned over the edge of the grand box, hawk bells jangling from her tiered satin surcoat. Her keen blue eyes fixed on Timeo. "It must be a trick of the light. I swear I've seen that tone-deaf ganglejohn in more than one bout."

"You did, Senja." Fortunata adopted the eternally patient and condescending manner of a missionary member of the Order of Darg, trying to explain prophecy to a periwinkle. "He won all the other bouts. That is why he is out there now."

The lady of barbarian Vahrd spat with flair and accuracy, right between her sister's kid-shod feet. "Out there to sing again, as he sang every time ere this. When the men of Vahrd hear one of their comrades make sounds like that after a battle, they slit his throat and send him to Twacorbi's keeping. It's kinder to all."

"What waste that would be." Lucha sighed and fanned herself with a frond of ostrich plumes. "I like him."

"You like the way he sings?" Senja searched Lucha's dancing, kohl-rimmed eyes for a moment, then turned to the taciturn Asapha. "I thought Resha was the only one of us who got light-headed on dreamsmoke visions."

"Not the way he *sings*." Lucha's laughter was light as summer rain. "I prefer my men to keep silent and get on with more pleasurable matters than jingles and jaw music."

Senja was in agreement. "I like my men to keep their mouths shut too."

"Oh, I didn't say—"

"You two are impossible!" Fortunata tossed her heavy fall of golden hair. "You have the artistic insight of a clam!"

"One clam between the two of us?" Lucha's penciled eyebrows flew. "La, Senja, this *is* serious."

Unfazed by sarcasm, Fortunata railed on. "The judges of the Havror Fenn have unanimously passed that lad on to the finals. They know more about music than you two will ever learn. They see him as the embodiment of a fresh, new movement in the field."

"A movement away from such silly details as the listener's comfort." Lucha fluffed up her unsatisfactory cushion.

"Not all music is your effete Vairish pipings and twinglings. Asapha, dear"—Fortunata sought her younger sister's support—"the songs of your beloved Kestrel Mountains are also . . . difficult for the uninitiated to appreciate. Surely you see that young man's efforts as a wonderful attempt to hone a new sharpness to the edge of music's sword?"

Her hopeful look was dashed from her face as Asapha wordlessly jerked out her own seat cushion and folded it over her ears.

"Charms! Get your charms here! Guaranteed or your money back curse free!"

"Here, sir. We shall have two of your best." The lady Themia signaled for service with her rolled up program. "Smartly, now. The match is about to begin."

The vendor wove his way through the minor box seats where those most eager to flaunt their wealth held sway. Each installation was an island of superiority unto itself, the banner-hung walls set up to order as soon as the ticket agents knew how many people would require space within the box itself.

Themia's sat two: herself and Ednyd. Her son dithered over the vendor's outstretched tray, turning each charm over and over between his sweating fingers, holding them up to the light, and otherwise pushing the salesman to the edge of homicide.

"They all work the same," he snapped, making the lordling jump in his seat. He spoke to Themia confidentially. "Sifting crystals, as we mages like to call 'em. Spells are outlawed at the Havror Fenn, of course, with two exceptions: If some magician feels like transforming himself to another shape so's to view the competitions better, or more comfy, or just more discreet, that's fine. And if one of the entrants wants to glamour up his presentation—the illusion of a fine costume runs cheaper than the garb itself, sometimes—that's all right so long as the judges know beforehand, so they can take it into account. Nothing but illusion, and the sifting crystals filter it away. Sold a tray and a half of them yesterday, and two trays today already. Everyone wants to tell dream from truth at this Havror Fenn, for some reason.''

''The reason is there.'' Themia pointed at the platform where Timeo still stood awaiting his opponent. Lord Thaumas' bovine daughter chewed the cud of a sticky bun and spoke through a mouthful of honey, nuts, and dough. ''No sane person can believe his eyes or ears when one who sings like *that* shows up in the finals. Will your charms tell me whether the songs I hear *that* one sing are actually coming from his mouth and, if so, whether the way I hear them is the way they are?''

''Guaranteed, ma'am, like I say.'' The vendor held up one of the assorted color teardrop pendants and let torchlight sparkle from its azure facets. ''One peep through this slices right through the prettiest illusion. If you think you're seeing a dream, there's no better way to know for sure.''

''Sight and sound too?''

''Every sense you own, ma'am.''

''I'll take two.'' Themia's pudgy hand closed on a pair at random. Money was passed and the vendor went his way. ''Here, Ednyd, have a look at him through yours. You back me up. I still can't believe that's Mizzie's son down there.''

Ednyd balked. ''I wanted a *green* one to match my tunic,'' he whined. Themia cuffed him, then waved for another seller to bring her more buns.

''Ho! Anis!'' Fell hailed a ragged student making his way to the free seating section. ''Up here!''

The young man stopped, peered up into the finer tiers, and set a chipped sifting crystal to his eye before responding. ''Fell? Is that you?''

"Ovrin with me."

"How do you two come to such prime seats? And—say, is that satin you're wearing?"

"Like it?" Fell chuckled as he showed off his garb. The torches cast swimming shadows over shining cloth and gold-thread embroidery.

"What happened? Someone pay off his bet early?"

"No such luck. Even though Timeo's where we said he'd be, it's traditional that no wager's settled until after the Havror Fenn. When it means holding on to their cash a while longer, you'd be surprised how many folk get sticky about tradition. Speaking of which, we'll be around tomorrow morning to collect on what you put up."

Anis' face went scarlet. "Fell . . . I don't think I can have it by tomorrow morning."

"Tomorrow afternoon, then. We trust you. Just as you can trust us to have a word in the governors' collective ear if you renege. Best hurry to your place, Anis. The charity seats won't take much more crowding." His teeth showed white and wolfish as the poor student shuffled off to squeeze into the free section.

"Fell, Anis is a classmate," Ovrin said. "Couldn't we ease up on his bet?"

"And have the rest find out? Forgive one debt and kiss the rest good-bye!" Fell tapped the top of Ovrin's head. "Is your whole skull wood or just your brain?"

"I don't mean forget the wager entirely. But couldn't we discount the debt or give him more time to pay it? You know how bad a scholarship student's life is."

"All the more reason to keep it behind me. If he couldn't afford to lose, he shouldn't have expected to win. Show a little softness to Anis and our other losers will want the same mollycoddling." Fell shook his head over his partner's goose-brained notions. "What's troubling you, Ovrin? The thought of having coins in your pouch makes you nervous? You haven't sat still the whole time we've been here."

"It's Keri," Ovrin said. "I don't know where he is."

"Is that it?" Fell thumped Ovrin's broad back. "Don't worry about your brother. He always turns up. There's not a soul in this city but knows what Keri is. They won't let him get into any serious trouble. What's more, now he's got our friend Zerin to look out for him too."

Ovrin's face was flint. "You're quick to make a friend of him."

"Who better to count as a friend, you great up-country ox! Zerin of Wickerdale's spilled gold in our laps, all for some rump-sprung jest he means to try at the festival. He's just as daft as Timeo, only we don't have to milk him of his money by dribs and drabs." Fell winked. "If you won't call him friend for that, then do it for your god-touched brother's sake. Keri's fascinated by old locust-legs, and Zerin's taken quite a fancy to the boy, I'd say."

"Fancy! I'll give him fancy if he's so much as—"

"Shut up, Ovrin," Fell hissed. He cast his eyes nervously about to see whether any of the nearby spectators had taken note of the outburst. The better seats were not so closely packed as the mages' reserved section or the charity zone. The folk in the surrounding seats were busy with their own conversations. Still in a whisper, Fell said, "Listen: Whatever turn Zerin's fancy for Keri takes, you think the boy would know what was happening? But if there's no food on the table, he does know it. Hunger he understands. Take the wine seller's brat apart bone by bone for the honor of a plowman's sons, if that's your wish. But you'll only do it after he pays us the wager *he's* got owing us for Timeo's placement in the finals. Is that clear?"

Ovrin did not say a word. The icy fire of his eyes gave Fell pause which the dark-haired student soon covered up with bluster. Just to be safe, he felt for his dagger.

"There, there, you've little to fear anyhow! Timeo always was kind to Keristor, and never the whisper of evil intent about it. Why can't Zerin's affection for the lad be the same? The man can't be all self-interest."

Ovrin remained silent. He no longer fidgeted in his seat. That function had been assumed by Fell. The smaller man almost nibbled his lower lip clean through before the arena entrance opposite Timeo's opened and the other finalist made his long-delayed appearance in the ring.

Chapter XVII

WET AND WILD

Mizriel's squeal of dismay roused the orange tomcat from dreams of mice and magic. "Wha—? What's the matter?" Paragore-Tren blinked slit-pupiled eyes myopically in the dusk. His spectacles, like the rest of his mortal clothing, had vanished with his transformation.

"There, in the arena! See against whom my son must sing!"

The cat padded to the edge of Hivrahan's lap and balanced his paws on the warlock's rather knobby knees. It took a lot of squinting, but at last the wizard said, "Yes? It's Alveiros. Of course it is. For a moment there, I thought something had gone awry."

"But he's in the *finals!*" Mizriel keened.

"So he should be. You've heard him sing. What do you think? If anything's amiss in this year's whole competition it's that—pardon me for saying what we both know to be true—it's that Timeo didn't get asked to leave in the first round."

"I know, I know, but"—Mizriel's pity for her son would have touched the stoniest heart—"but if he must be beaten, why must it be so badly?"

"My lady," Hivrahan said gently. "My dearest lady, before long your son will have greater things to think of than a silly minstrels' joust. Remember, he is a king, and his people await their freedom."

"A king." The word was hollow. "And he was heir to

lands vaster than many a kingdom all his life. It was nothing to him. The longing of his heart was to sing.''

The warlock touched the tear springing from the corner of Mizriel's eye and brought away a flower between his fingertips. Her grief worked its own magic in Hivrahan's heart to give him wisdom beyond his years. To serve her he would cast aside the stripling student that he was and take a grown man's part. What was age to the witchborn?

"He has come this far in the contest. If he falls short of the crown, the memory of all his other triumphs will sustain him. And there is no shame in losing to such an opponent. Insar himself would have to fight to maintain his starry crown against Alveiros.''

"You're right, Hivrahan.'' Mizriel placed the white blossom against her lips. Gratefully she said, "You have the power to comfort me. Is it witchborn magic?''

"It is yours.'' Hivrahan looked away from her while he felt still able to speak. "The chief judge joins them.''

The chief judge of the Havror Fenn was a full professor of the Course Artistic, a graybeard so venerable and cobwebbed that the actual limits of his learning were never questioned. As he was so advanced in years and academic standing, he had long ago ceased to frequent the lecture halls, where there was always the danger of having to deal with students. His place was in one of the huge university libraries, taking notes in a copperplate for multiple volume studies on minute and uninteresting subjects.

He was helped onto the circular stage by several of his underlings, fellow judges and fellow professors of the Course Artistic whose appearances and life works were only an inch or so less dusty than his own. It would not do for the chief judge to ascend by either of the ramps, as this might bespeak a nonverbal inclination to favor one of the candidates.

"Alveiros of Sombrunia, Timeo of Dureforte Keep.'' The judge's yellow eyes sloshed from one to the other as he pronounced their names. Timeo thought he saw a *frisson* shake the old man's frail body when their eyes met, but he ascribed it to the shudders of age. "You have both come this far by the grace of Insar. Now, by the grace of a free and open hearing before this honorable multitude, may the crown of the Minstrel King encircle the worthier brow.'' He raised his hands, took six tottery steps backward, and almost fell off the stage before his assistants could field him.

Two of the junior judges now came onto the stage at the same time, using the ramps. They offered the finalists the customary last glass of wine and last bite of honeycake, if they so desired, then in unison proclaimed the rules.

"You shall agree between yourselves as to the order of your performance. If you can not agree within the space of one sandglass, then you shall strip and wrestle for it, after the manner of Insar and Neimar. You shall not interrupt your opponent's song on pain of disqualification and immediate forfeiture. You shall begin your entry with or without the customary jests of introduction.''

Having had their say, the judges departed, leaving the stage to Alveiros, Timeo, and an upended sandglass.

"Greetings, Cousin,'' the boy said happily. "I'm honored to see our family so highly favored in the Havror Fenn.''

"Cousin?''

"I am your Aunt Ursula's third son.''

"But you're so young! How have you come this high in the competition?''

The boy dropped his eyelids. "The fortunes of song. Do you care which of us sings first? I don't want my guardian taking me home with stories of how I fought my own cousin in the ring like a cattle fair wrestler.''

Timeo felt magnanimous. The boy had a winning way about him, the beguilement of youth, and the snow and gold handsomeness of his father Alban. If Alveiros could sing even a hair better than the common lot and had a bearable way with composition, his charm and good looks were probably the deciding factors in the judges' previous decisions in his favor. It did happen. Judges were human.

But now it was in the hands of the public, and they would recognize true talent when they heard it. They would not be swayed by anything save the song itself. Timeo gave Alveiros a forbearing smile. He had nothing to lose by chivalry.

"After you.''

Alveiros unslung the lute from his back and gave it a swift, though loving, tuning. He was not wearing anything even approaching the grandeur of Timeo's costume. Neither scallops, dagging, slash work, nor embroidery graced the sleeves of his smoke blue tunic. His hose were fine quality, as befit a prince, but unadorned by clocking and both legs the same fawn color. Plain brown leather shoes and a utilitarian belt such as any forester might wear were all the rest of his garb. Compared to Alveiros, Timeo looked like a peacock next to a wren.

The boy bowed with simple grace to the spectators. Without preamble, announcement, or the customary jests, he began.

Timeo was wrapped in his own reveries when his young cousin sounded the starting notes of his song. Having granted Alveiros first go, he retreated into happy daydreams of how wonderful everything was and would be for him and whether he could get a song out of it.

I shall call it 'The Taker of Two Crowns.' I'll have to disguise the hero, of course, so no one thinks I'm singing in praise of myself. Change his hair color, maybe? And make him short and fat—no, just short. Even Mother looked at me with new respect when Cattail told her who I was. Mother promised to help us all she could, after she stopped crying for Father all over again. Just help, no advice, I said, and she accepted my terms! She didn't even try to take over and manage me, the way she always does. If she can protect me from the visions in that awful enchanted fog, though, I'd be willing to listen to a little of her advice. But gods, now I know how a puppet feels when all his strings are snipped! The freedom! The—no, a puppet would just slump over with his strings cut. I need a better metaphor . . . What is—?

The melody did not, could not intrude. Nonetheless, Timeo was suddenly aware that it had been running through his thoughts with the sweet persistence of a lover's lightest caress. Persistent without being insistent, compelling without coercion, Alveiros' music lulled all other thoughts from the listener's mind by gentle degrees. It was the kindest of seductions. Only when Timeo was ready to hear, could he make out the words.

"A heart betrayed where no heart dwells, men say;
Love bribed and banished to the realm of hate;

Sweet mercy sought—a ruse, a jest, a jape—
True joy once found, and lost again, too late.
This thing I am, I did not seek to be.
Birth-bonded to despair, destroy, despite.
What men call truth has set its chains on me,
Unwept, unwanted child of War and Night.
I seek what all must seek if they would live,
Yet find all willing take, none gladly give.''

A knot of shock and exultation burned in Timeo's chest as realization struck. *Morgeld! He sings a lament for the Lord of Despair! Gods, is my cousin mad? Doesn't he want to win this—? Win! He'll be lucky to escape with his life!*

Timeo's eyes swept the stands tensely, waiting for the first cry of outrage, the first improvised missile. Barricades of spells kept the magic wielders from interfering in the Havror Fenn, and those in the better seats were too exalted to lower themselves to more than acerbic comments and dignified withdrawals, but the cheap seats and the charity seats were by far the majority. No spell had been erected to ward off a flung tomato.

And none came.

Timeo's fearful anticipation turned slowly to wonder as Alveiros sang on. No one stirred. The arena held only the clear, pure notes of the young bard's song. Even in the grand box, the witchborn wardladies were silent, pent by an enchantment stronger than any of their summoning. In Senja's hand, a dagger glowed red hot, melted into an iron rose. Dark streaks of kohl smeared Lucha's cheeks. A golden hawk spiraled from the sky to perch on Asapha's left shoulder, its mate following the twisting trail of air down to perch on her right. The birds fastened their copper coin eyes on the singer, their gaze gripping as tightly as their talons.

The first missile flew from the stands: a flower. More fell, a rain of bloom that heaped in drifts of scent and color around Alveiros' feet. The boy sang on.

The knot in Timeo's breast dissolved. The music was a mirror that showed him his own face, his songlets, his hollow aspirations to a crown never rightfully his to wear. *See! This is what song can be, should be, must be!* a voice within him shouted. He saw more than that in the glass of song; too much more. Past matches returned. He saw himself strutting and preening, reaching out to take the scroll of award from the judges' hands, and memory served up a too-clear picture of the old men's eyes as they declared him the victor in bout after bout.

It was never meant to be, he thought, confronting phantoms in Alveiros' melody. They were worse than any horror Ragnar's enchanted fog might hold. *I should never have been named the winner, never come this far in the competition, never disgraced— But why did they pass me on so high? Ah, gods! I can't undo what went before, but I have the power to prevent a greater wrong.*

He threw his hand harp from him in bitter shame. It fell among the blossoms before Alveiros. Above the jangle of its strings he cried, "Cousin, in your song the gods return!"

The spell broke against his words. Silence fell, then shattered. The air rang with the cheers of the crowd, thickened to a haze of petals as more and more flowers flew down from the tiers. The judges swarmed up the ramps, true joy on their faces. The chief judge bore the Minstrel King's crown between his palsied hands, a confection of silver leaves and flowers, their stamens made of gold and pearl.

"By the rule of the Havror Fenn, your opponent has forfeited his right to sing," the old man quavered. There was enormous relief in his voice which Timeo noted for the first time. "Therefore we name you Minstrel King, Alveiros of Sombrunia, with the right to call yourself Alveiros the Bard, Alveiros the Singer, or Alveiros Insar's Son hereafter." In a lower tone he murmured, "The gods bless you, boy, and you may call yourself Alveiros the Savior too, if you like. Your song has been the sword to slay a grievous folly."

"Slay Folly?"

The incredulous voice burst in a deluge of scarlet sparks from the oil lamps above the stage.

"Slay immortal Folly? Are you mad as well as old, sirrah? No sword is sharp enough, no hand sure enough, no man so wise nor death so quick but Folly steps in first to strike him down!"

Every scallop shell ringing the stage spurted pink fire and purple smoke. Strings of squibs materialized just in time to explode with rapid-fire spluttering bangs. In her box, the lady Fortunata summoned her foremost advisor, who showed her the proper preapproval forms for all the illusions now unfolding on the platform below. When she looked back to the stage, the fountains of fire and smoke had dribbled out, revealing a long-limbed man in motley.

He was surrounded by a ring of eleven painted daisies, all wearing gauzy dresses that kept no secrets in the torchlight. They pranced about the stage, tittering and warbling meaningless tra-la-las in more keys and rhythms than seemed possible for only eleven women. If they were there to provide musical accompaniment for their supposed master, they were doing a bone-sorry job of it.

Their real purpose became apparent when one of the judges started with recognition, gasped, and tried to get off the platform. Small hands tightened on the judge's arms and dragged him back to center stage. Their captive struggled, but their grip was harder to escape than an old debt. They were used to holding on. Their dance was a delicate herding maneuver, and they had no qualms about planting a few well-considered kicks and tweaks to keep their dark-robed, gray-bearded charges in line.

"Gentles, greetings all!" the man in motley exclaimed, his voice magic-amplified to fill the arena. One attenuated hand trailed through the flowers onstage as he made his reverence to the audience. "Zerin of Wickerdale joins his joy to yours in this fine lad's triumph." He indicated Alveiros, who was watching the doxies do their turn with a mixture of temptation and terror on his beardless face.

Zerin's smile was lipless tight, carving curves like Vairish swords at the corners of his mouth. "But how can we rejoice with our new Minstrel King when vengeance most royal hovers over this place? My mistress is a proud and jealous lady whose name I must defend. Let Folly not be slighted by the words of ancient men! She has the power to take revenge, you see. Though graybeards scorn and grumble at my antics now and then, a simple song is all I bring with me."

A very amateurishly executed poof of smoke burped up beside Zerin, green and red by turns. From its vacillating roils stepped a tallow-faced wizardling in tatty brown robes. A clatter of baked clay tablets huddled close to his pigeon chest. Every drop of sweat on his brow was visible to the spectators as he began to juggle the ruddy objects—magical juggling, his hands only seeming to touch the clay shards as they whirled through the air in front of him.

There was random applause which so undid the squat little man that he nearly dropped some of the tablets, but he recovered before harm was done. Zerin spared a moment to glower at his assistant before breaking into song:

"A tale of Folly's power I will sing
In honor of your new-crowned Minstrel King!
Yet on a time, my friends, it came to pass
That as the Minstrel King they crowned an ass.
An ear-long ass, a donkey small and gray,
A beast of balk and kick and trot and bray.
How did it happen? Harken to my song:
It's neither undershort nor overlong.
King Mur of Clarem lived so long ago
That few save scholars living ever know
He was a madman, but a madman crowned!
Wherefore, sane men must jump whene'er he frowned
Or lose what made them jump. 'Tis so, alas!
And mad King Mur most dearly loved his ass.
No sweeter sound could reach the royal ear
Then haw-hee-hanh. One day he made it clear
That he would have his ass crowned Minstrel King!
A lunatic's caprice. The song I sing
Would have a different ending were it true
That men will die for honor's sake. —Would you?
No more the judges of the Havror Fenn!
Though they were all the hoariest of men,
Still they loved life, and rather than be dead,
They set the crown upon that long-eared head.
But do you gape, my friends? What would you say
If I told you how close you came this day
To seeing mad King Mur's plot come again:
A jackass crowned, and thanks to these wise men?"

Zerin of Wickerdale snapped his fingers and the doxies laid hands on the judges, hustling them to the perimeter of the stage. It was done with such grace that it looked as if the old men took their places out of free will. The prettiest of the sisterhood linked her arm through Alveiros' and danced him off the platform, whispering secrets that were highly guessable judging from how gladly he went with her. When Timeo tried to follow them off, he was detained.

"Behold, my friends, the ears are shorter, but the tune's the same!" Zerin cast an arm around Timeo's neck, backed up by two of his more muscular ladies. Their flesh glowed with the residual traces of a spell to enhance personal strength, a popular stage illusion of the mind. The recipient believed himself to be more powerful than he was, and somehow faith conspired with reality to make it so. Fight as he would, Timeo could not break away from the women.

"Master Iolo, *if* you please!" Zerin danced away from Timeo and motioned at the juggling wizard. One by one the clay tablets flew from the small man's spell to the tall man's hands where they were juggled in earnest. Zerin winked broadly at the audience.

"Fear is Folly's handmaiden, as we have learned again and again. But at a university, who should teach us better than the honored professors? See them at the lessons which so attuned their ears that Timeo's sweet singing reached the finals of the Havror Fenn! Master Iolo . . . ?"

Zerin jigged around the stage as he juggled, the silver bells on his costume playing a merry tune. Little Master Iolo was built like a wine tun and had to chase after his employer, jags and rags of fiery transformation spells leaping from his plump fingertips to fall short of their marks.

"Too much pyrotechnics," Paragore-Tren opined. He was back in human form, adjusting his spectacles. "Sure sign of a tyro. Less fire, more power, but Iolo will never get that far. He should have stuck to sleight-of-hand, but no, it must be high wizardry or nothing, stupid fellow."

"Who is that horrid man?" Mizriel demanded. "What does he want with my Timeo? I'm going to put a stop to—"

Paragore-Tren restrained her before the angry sorceress could shove her way down the row. "We are warded in here until the contest is over; have you forgotten? Fortunata must signal the ushers to lift the wards before we can get out."

"Why doesn't she?" Mizriel shouted. "Can she mean to let this farce go on, spoiling the Havror Fenn?"

"The Havror Fenn is the festival of music *and* jest." The wizard of Naîmlo Wood glanced toward the grand box. "Besides, have you never witnessed a disaster so overwhelming that all you could do was stand and stare, forgetting your own power to intervene?" He gestured toward the four witchborn wardladies. Fortunata's eyes and mouth were equally round. Her sisters, even cold Asapha, were in little better state.

On the stage, Zerin had finished his patter and come to a full stop. Master Iolo's limping bolts of magic were finally able to hit the tumbling clay tablets. The evening sky bloomed with raucous fireworks as each of the spell-hit shards by turn leaped into the darkness to paint its own preserved scene in crackling fire against the stars.

Even picked out in phosporescence, the features of the judges were eminently recognizable to everyone in the crowd. So were the faces of their female companions, and sometimes more than their faces. Zerin had hired the services of some very popular young ladies. The students in the cheap and charity seats cheered, whistled, and stamped until there was real danger that the tiers would collapse under their enthusiasm.

"The benefits of education!" Zerin shouted as the chief judge's creative effort was splashed across the sky. "The price of a crown! Your pardon, learned sirs, but you'll recall I promised to keep our little secrets only *until* the Minstrel King was crowned. But shall Timeo depart unhonored? After all your judgments in his favor, shall he? If Folly wills it, so it shall be done. Let him not go without his due, sweet ladies!"

Two of Zerin's women produced a chaplet of beet greens and radishes. They jammed it down over Timeo's ears while another retrieved his harp and shoved it into his hands.

"Sing us a song of the new music!" Zerin urged. "If only I had a copper for each soul who claimed there was *something* to your art, Timeo, just because these scholars gave you the nod! No, half a copper for every would-be Minstrel King practicing off-tune, off-step, off-sense songs in preparation for next year's contest. Then I might have coin enough to pay the debt of gratitude I owe to those two fine men who also helped make this day what it is for you and me!''

Zerin nodded, and Master Iolo launched two fistfuls of white fire that winged high to hover over the heads of Ovrin and Fell. The cheers and catcalls from the students twisted abruptly into growls of murderous suspicion. Fell tugged Ovrin's sleeve. They tried sidling out of their seats unobtrusively, but Master Iolo's fireballs dogged them faithfully. A line of young men surged forward to await them at the aisle separating the cheap seats from the better ones. The two retreated, Fell's cries for an usher swallowed up in the mounting grumble of the crowd.

"So merit wins a crown,'' Zerin declared. "Zerin Kingmaker am I, and king I hope to make myself as well. Doubt my powers at your peril! See what I came near to doing this year for my lady Folly's sake.'' He slid down on one knee before Timeo, arms high as if to hail a true sovereign.

"Now see what I shall crown in years to come, if Folly wishes.'' He leaped up nimbly, feet flickering in midair, while his hireling mage threw another indecisively colored smoke bomb. Blinking and bewildered, dressed in a padded tunic that was a ludicrous replica of Timeo's fine garb, Keristor stumbled out of the smoke.

"Play, sweet singer! Play that we might hear the best of him who'll take the crown next year.'' Zerin thrust a pasteboard mandolin into Keri's hands, strung with common twine. The boy stared at it in confusion that was fast turning to panic.

With a great effort, Timeo tore himself out of his captors' hands. His wreath of vegetables sagged over one eye, but he needed both hands to hold his harp like a club, the blow unmistakably aimed at Zerin.

"Get Keri offstage, damn you! Can't you see he's afraid?''

"Afraid? Perish the thought! To fear you must know, and to know requires wit. I doubt our friend here has a grain of it. Speak up, Keristor! Will you go? Timeo doesn't want you here.''

Keri's fear melted to hurt. He pushed himself between the two men. "Why, Timeo? Look.'' He held out the pasteboard mandolin. "Zerin said I can sing. He said I can be like you. I want to be like you, Timeo.''

"And so you shall, crown and all!" Zerin glided sideways, laid a hand on either lad's shoulder, and swung himself into a handstand between them, then vaulted over, landing on his feet. Two more of his ladies planted a matching wreath on Keri's brow, radishes dangling about his ears. "Wise men dance when Folly plays her tune, and Jest is Folly's favorite son. Say, who shall reign as Jest's unchallenged king?" He spread his arms to the arena.

It began as a chant and swiftly grew to a throbbing roar: Ze-rin, Ze-*rin*, Ze-RIN, ZE-*RIN!* Those students not occupied by heading off Ovrin and Fell from all possible exits joined their voices to the swelling tide of sound, their feet pounding out a steady beat, their hands clapping in time.

A procession of elderly gentlemen wearing robes diamond-patched in rainbow colors snake-danced their way out of the performers' entrance and up Alveiros' ramp. Their leader carried a jaggedly pointed crown that looked as if it had been snipped from yellow paper by a child's shears but was really hammered gold. Round silver bells jingled atop each peak and the front was embellished by a leering mask—gold and silver too—whose cold sapphire eyes accentuated how cruel its smile could be.

Zerin inclined his head to receive his due. He got it.

The wave leaped out of the gap between the western seats and the stage. It gushed out of the bare earth to slam down hard on Zerin, Master Iolo, the painted daisies, and the judges. Keri screamed and jumped away, under the lee of a second wave rearing up on the platform's eastern side. Timeo yanked the boy into his arms, closed his eyes tightly, and held his breath as the water crashed over their heads.

He heard the splash; he felt nothing. He opened his eyes and saw that he and Keri were the only dry ones onstage. Doxies gasped and spluttered, spitting water everywhere as their gauze gowns lay in sodden puddles at their feet. Professors of Jest and Minstrelry flobbed and groaned under the weight of water-soaked academic robes, their beards sprouting fish and water weeds.

Master Iolo groaned and screamed alternately, though his predicament at first looked like many a man's dream of bliss. Three lithe young women wound their arms around him, stripping away his saturated garments until he was as naked as they. Their mouths and fingers worked busily over his flesh, and however much he twisted in their grip, he remained prisoner. Sweet prison, until the marks of teeth and nails showed trickles of red. Blue bruises followed where long, strong fingers pinched and poked without mercy. Webbings slapped across his mouth, none too playfully. The wizardling tried to fight off his pretty assailants with magical kindlings. Every spark was drenched to sooty smoke and damp ashes at his fingertips.

"See, my lord, how well we avenge you!" Duila called, waving at Timeo with a small hank of Iolo's rapidly thinning hair. The nixie and her sisters giggled, merry workers.

"Duila, don't! Call yourselves off! Let them go!" Timeo's eyes dashed from one of the Waterfolk's victims to the next. Frogs leaped from the professors' pockets. Fringe-finned men came slap-slap-slapping their web-footed way across the stage to globber unintelligible wide-mouthed endearments at any doxy they could catch. The air reeked of dead perch and dace.

"But we can't call ourselves off, Timeo!" Duila tried to make herself heard above the yowls and pleadings. "We didn't call ourselves *on!*"

A pickerel-headed monster materialized, undershot jaw slashing at anything that moved. It chased the chief judge three times around the platform. Water rose, making a wall-less moat that surrounded the stage. When the chief judge could bear no more of that nightmare pursuit, he had to plunge into the water, robes and all. He snorted and blew miniature geysers from his nostrils as he fought to stay afloat.

"Zerin!" he gasped. "Call off your illusions!"

Zerin too could not call off what he had not called on. The waves had beaten him flat to the floorboards, stunned into stargazing. Only now was he able to push himself up and shake dizziness from his senses. His crown was a crumple, the bells flatter than sand dollars, the evilly laughing mask warped to a grimace of abject misery. Rabbits at bay trembled less than he as he lifted his glance to Timeo. Teeth chattering, he said, "It was only a jo—"

The third wave was for him alone, and it smashed him down again. Foam washed over Timeo's feet, and still they stayed dry. Keri gave a choked mewl and ran away. Timeo could not stop him. From the stands, Ovrin saw his little brother bolt. The brawny student leaped over tier after tier of seats, calling Keristor's name. Deprived of his stronger backing in an argument, Fell panicked and slithered after Ovrin, his knife licking him a clear pathway though angry bettors pelted on his heels.

And as the waves of water and of people ebbed from the arena, a white-skinned woman with water lilies plaited in her endless black hair seeped into sight. She floated over the very center of the stage, higher even than the oil lamps, her braid bridling a gigantic turtle. The creature's head lolled from side to side, like a hound on the scent. Its rolling eye fastened on Zerin, who was trying once more to drag himself upright.

Cattail laughed. "*I'll* put you on your feet, Your Majesty!" The monster drizzled out from under her in a rain of ordinary sized turtles: snappers.

A good sight too late, the lady Fortunata broke the wards holding the magic wielders in their seating section. Those in a hurry to take up their spells again rushed from the stands, none so fast as a little white-haired woman and her companions. Asapha's harsh laughter raked the air.

Cool minds later pointed out the impossibility of it, but in the confusion Cattail and her minions just seemed to trickle away between the fingers of the law. Questioning their victims revealed nothing—those victims available for questioning, that is.

Zerin of Wickerdale was last seen heading north, his progress greatly aided by the number of shelled reptiles attached to his person. If his hireling mage and doxies ever did hunt him down for last reckonings, they never came back to speak of it. Those members of the audience still bound to their seats by courage, curiosity, or simple shock, declared it was the best Havror Fenn in decades. The university faculty racked their brains for months afterwards, wondering what they would be able to do for an encore. Timeo's health was drunk many times over in the student haunts that night for his memorable part in the festivities.

But on the morrow, when they asked where Timeo of Dureforte Keep had gone, no one knew.

Chapter XVIII

TAKING THE PLUNGE

"Why doesn't it work?" Mizriel cried, holding her hands out in front of her and staring at them as if they had betrayed her. "Why can't I find him? Is he dead?"

Hivrahan leaned back on his haunches, resting his spine against a willow. Melki still clung to his shoulder, Paragore-Tren was a scant stone cast away, Alveiros was with him, and the riverside promenade was unnaturally populated for this hour of the night. Yet though torch-bearing crowds surged up and down the eastern bank of the Salmlis, angrily shouting two familiar names, as far as the young warlock was concerned, the shore was deserted except for himself and the Lady Mizriel.

"A searching spell will not always work on a living man," he said, wanting to soothe her the best he could. "Your son isn't dead."

"How do you know?" She wanted to believe him.

"I feel it."

"Feel it!" A sour laugh tangled on a sob. He saw her tears, however quickly she flicked them from her face.

"Searching spells are not all-powerful. Barriers can be erected to keep them off." He stood up and tried to take her hands, but she jerked them away, angry at the world. False dawn stole along the city streets, hastening towards the river. Its light turned her hair the same color as the fog lying close along the western bank.

"See there?" The warlock pointed over the water. "That

is where your searching spells go aground. The mist is a potent barricade. If Timeo has gone through—''

"He did." Paragore-Tren joined them, a firm grip on Alveiros' arm. The boy wore a dreamy smile that made him look agreeably stupid. The wizard had to shake him a few times to wake him from reverie. "Go on, Alveiros! Tell them what you saw."

"It was at her window . . ." His voice trailed away. The moronic smile broadened until sensible folk could hardly stand to look at him and retain dinner. "Atali's window, where her songbirds twitter in their pretty cage—''

Paragore-Tren was not gentle when he shook Alveiros this time. The prince's teeth clacked together; he was completely awake at last. "I was standing there, watching the moon, when I heard the shouting. Atali's room is at the top of a tower in one of the best sections of this city—''

"I know," Paragore-Tren said dryly.

"—with views in all directions. You can even see a little of the arena from there. She keeps a spyglass handy—''

"A lady in her field never does know when to expect callers . . . or their wives."

"Paragore-Tren, *please!*" Mizriel was anxious to hear what Alveiros had to tell. "Go on, dear," she told the boy.

"I picked it up when I heard the ruckus. Something was going on in the arena, but I couldn't see enough of it to tell what. Then the people started to stream out by every portal. I thought I saw Timeo among them, but when I focused the spyglass it was someone nearer my age."

"That poor god-touched child." Paragore-Tren shook his head. "There are times I ask myself the use of magic if it can't change such things."

Alveiros spoke on: "Then I did see Timeo. He seemed to be running after the boy, but when he was almost close enough to touch him, they came to a corner. The boy turned it; Timeo went straight ahead. He was racing for the river." Sympathy showed in the young prince's eyes. "He dove in. His head broke the surface about the middle of the Salmlis, and he kept going. He reached the place where the fog covers the water and went right into the thick of it. I didn't see him anymore. I'm sorry, Aunt."

"Don't be sorry, dear heart." Mizriel kissed her nephew. "You've given me great news."

"But he might have drowned!"

Now no bitterness distorted her smile. "Drowned? Given a week or two. Come, we've time to hire a boat before dawn and cross after him!" She seized Hivrahan and ran upstream alongside the river.

Paragore-Tren sighed and went after them at a more measured pace.

"You see? I spoke the truth. We can not pass."

The wizard of the Naîmlo Wood leaned his elbow on the gunwale towards the stern of the modest fishing boat Mizriel had commandeered and stared morosely into the fog.

The white-haired sorceress gritted her teeth and turned deaf ears to his words. She gathered as much of her power as she could and concentrated it into one mighty bolt of humming force within her. It stabbed from her steepled fingers into the heart of the earthbound clouds. A little of the water vapor sizzled, but the boat bearing warlocks, wizard, and sorceress still remained as if pent in ice. Its owner, manning the tiller, did not look at all surprised by Mizriel's failure to pierce the misty barricade.

"Told y' so on t' dock," the boat keep grumbled as he sucked on a white clay pipe. "But where there's magic, there's no tellin' some folk."

"So it has been from the first," Paragore-Tren said. "From the black day Ragnar conquered the Lands Unknown."

Mizriel sat down in the prow of the boat. "Ragnar. My teacher, old Perquis, once told me a story of Ragnar the master of monsters, a moral lesson against growing too proud of your powers." Her mouth quirked. "Not that my powers were anything to be proud of in those days."

"Master of monsters . . ." Paragore-Tren let the words run over his tongue. "It's no worse than other things he has been called: the renegade, the traitor, the disgrace to all who share the wizard's way." His eyes were small behind his spectacles, but Mizriel could see all the regret in them. "We were students together. He was one of our most learned men. Hivrahan, I hope you know how much more difficult the wizard's way is than that of the witchborn. We are not born with our powers, only with the ability to acquire them after much study. What we do with our aptitude is up to us, and learning how to use it to the fullest is a lifetime's work."

He trailed his hand in the river and watched the ripples spread. "Ragnar was impatient of that lifetime. He had grand ambitions and made no secret of them. He claimed he would read the hidden books of magic that lie in the spaces between the stars. We laughed at him, sometimes—too often—and told him to set more realistic goals. He would not. Eventually word went into the west, and one came to offer him what he desired—one I need not name. He accepted. The next we heard, the Lands Unknown had fallen into his hand, and all access to them was sealed against any magic wielder, witchborn or wizardly."

"And you did nothing, said nothing?" Mizriel could hardly believe it. "You and my lord Ayree, most tireless fighters against Morgeld, could not spare a moment to combat the evildoing of his minions?"

The wizard sighed. "Have you never wondered at the myths surrounding the Lands Unknown, child? A realm of monsters, and yet books abound describing how these regions were well known to humans for ages. Monsters don't just *happen*, like crabgrass. That was the second part of Ragnar's spell, a spell of disbelief as it's called. It is weak but widespread, and most insidious. It affects the mind, so that when the refugees from Ragnar's conquest first presented themselves to the witchborn and the wizardly for aid, we tended to doubt their tales of woe, to dismiss them as malcontents, to fabricate our own explanations for the stories they brought us, even—may the gods pardon us—to convince ourselves that the Ragnar we *knew* existed, did not. Our minds simply refused to grasp the truth, especially the more horrible parts of it. A slaughter of the royal family? Little ones massacred for no other reason than their bloodline? The very attempt to believe in such an abomination churned our guts. It was *physically unpleasant* to believe the fugitives' claims. Oh, consciously we all knew Ragnar might be capable of such excesses, but his spell clove a vast gap between knowledge and belief. Every time someone mentioned Ragnar and the enslavement of the Lands

Unknown, we entered a kind of daydream. We made promises to aid the Waterfolk, sent them on their way, and promptly forgot them, their sorrows, and our promises when we awoke.''

Mizriel protested: "But *I* had no trouble believing."

"You are tied too closely to the Waterfolk for that, by those of their blood whom you have loved. The spell of disbelief touches the mind, not the heart."

"I think I understand," Hivrahan said. "It's only a spell of enhancement, really. What's more human than the desire to believe an unpleasant truth doesn't exist? Ragnar's spell of disbelief merely enhances that."

"Well put." Paragore-Tren leaned forward to pat Hiv's shoulder. "Everything seems to come easily to you witchborn, even words."

Hivrahan was at the oars, though his power alone was what had propelled the boat across the Salmlis' stream. Melki swung from his hair and hissed peevishly at Paragore-Tren. "Don't call the witchborn's lot all honey, master! Born to power, aye, and a lifetime then spent learning to bridle it! No one's favored more than the next in this world: wizard, warlock, or what-have-you."

Mizriel inclined her head. "We do not have even the certainty that the gods still hear our petitions," she said. "Yet pray is all I can do for my son now."

"Y'be wantin' t'go back ag'in, then?" The owner of the boat was untouched by Mizriel's distress and ready to be homeward bound. He leaned on the tiller, hopefully aiming the craft for the eastern shore. "Care t' turn on y' magic oncet, sur? Do beat rowin'."

Hivrahan sighed and nodded. Mizriel picked her way from prow to stern as they crossed the river, wishing to fix her eyes on the fog-shrouded shore that had claimed her son. Her desire put her next to the owner, who was not so inured to a mother's pain once they neared the docks of Panomo-Midmists.

"Now, mum, don' fret so. I know y' boy—whole town knows 'im—*and* the pack he used t' run with, damn 'em f' cheats. Them two gownies—big an' little, rust hair, soot hair, y' know them I mean—they'll look after 'im. Not like he's over in them cust lands alone."

Mizriel was on him in a snake's strike. Her fists twisted the man's thread-poor collar so that his pipe tumbled into the river. "What are you babbling about? What do you know of my son?"

The boat keep pitched backwards like an upended water beetle and came close to falling out of his own craft. "Faith, jus' what I'm tellin' you, mum! And me the sorry victim twice over, if your lot pays me no better for t' use o' me boats than them. 'Twas right at the height of last night's doin's, an' me mindin' me business at the docks. Hear a splash, I do, and fancy I see one who looks like y' boy knifin' through t' waters headin' clean for t'other side! Whilst I marvels free at who'd be mad enough t' brave t' Lands Unknown, *whomp!* T' big redhead plowhorse-sort rams breath from me ribs with an oar, leaps into me best boat, an' it's off wi' him, his witling brother, and t' weasel-faced one. Away *they* go for t' Lands Unknown, and nary more a sight of 'em I see. *Or* me boat. Thieves all!" He spat into the water.

"The Lands Unknown?" Hivrahan repeated. "Granted, they needed to escape this city, but why would they trade the desert for the dragon's maw?" He was young, and an optimistic thought suggested itself. "When they saw Timeo swim across, they must have gone after to help him. They were his friends, after all. Could it be . . . ?" His fingers wandered to the coin purse at his side.

The boat keep's eyes followed them. "Aye . . . Aye, so it might be, m'lud." The warlock's fingers strayed to the drawstring. "Now as I do recall, t' big redhead gasps out somethin' of havin' no time t' linger whilst Timeo's in need of aid. Past kindnesses and all such . . ."

Hivrahan's fingers went where his audience most desired them to go. He fished several coins out of his purse and urged them on a most compliant boat keep. "You should not have to pay the price of their loyalty."

"Hivrahan, do you really think—?" Mizriel grasped whatever hope offered itself.

"Even now they must have found him. They'll stand by him, never fear." Warlock and sorceress smiled.

The boat bumped against the pilings. The boat keep clambered out to tie up his craft, Hivrahan's coins making sweeter music in his purse than any he'd heard at the Havror Fenn. They clinked out harmony with the coins already tucked away—coins that had been given him by the fourth party in his lost boat. The boat keep gave a gusty sigh as he recalled the lady's shimmering charms, so inadequately hidden by her long black hair. And where *had* she managed to carry those coins she gave him as she herded those ne'er-do-wells and the witling boy aboard?

A song rose to the boat keep's lips as he dreamed of the fine new boats he'd buy with his new fortune—two new boats, and everyone happy! If there was one thing a simple man might learn from the Havror Fenn, it was to give the public what the public wanted to hear. Truth only interfered.

Chapter XIX

HE NEVER WOULD BE MIST

The haunting stillness of the Great Rushy Forest was broken by the sounds of unskilled marchers hiking through the brakes. Cattail cast an irritated glance over her left shoulder. "Can't you walk more quietly?"

"Your pardon, my *lady*," Fell replied with anything but deference. "It's not as easy for those of us who aren't naked."

"Strip if you like," the ondine spat. "I promise to keep my terror under control."

Fell felt the cool weight of the dagger still hidden in his sleeve and gazed speculatively at Cattail's unprotected back. He hadn't wanted to cross the river, but his choice had been go where the transformed barmaid ordered or be slaughtered. The fine clothes Zerin of Wickerdale had given him were clammy from recent passage through the enchanted fog, and the ragged tears on sleeve and hose were an ever-present reminder of what the angry crowd of bettors would have done had they been able to hold on to their slippery prey just a little longer.

He would never forget it: Ovrin loping after his brother, he scampering after Ovrin. The up-country lout was Fell's only strength with Zerin out of the picture. The crowd pursuing them from the arena had doubled in number—

trebled perhaps, from the halloo they were raising. It was like being hunted by a pack of grudge-bearing wolves.

The wolves cornered them near the river, just as Ovrin caught up with Keristor. One of the front-runners even managed to latch onto Fell's clothing—a lucky elbow to the midriff knocked him off, not out, hence the rips. There were too many of them to fight, his dagger and Ovrin's strength notwithstanding. They would be lucky to escape with an inch of whole skin.

And then she was there: White as the twinkling lights on high that men called Sarai's Children, she appeared out of a swirl of vapor. The mist she brought whipped itself like an illusionist's cloak between pursued and pursuers, hiding one party from the other. Signaling silence, she whisked them away hotfoot to the dockside and helped them embark. She seemed to guide them, unsensed, through the very midst of their enemies.

Cattail's sudden appearance had been providential. Fell didn't know why she had chosen to save him and Ovrin and Keri—the gods knew, Zerin had made their part in Timeo's public shaming no secret. Until now, he hadn't had the inclination to question good luck.

Or was it so good? He shook when he recalled the moment their boat had first pierced the fog bank. Until shortly before, Cattail had been strolling beside the boat, ambling across the surface of the Salmlis as if it were paving stone. When they approached the fog, she climbed into the craft and wedged herself firmly between Ovrin and Keristor. Stiff as any statue, she waited.

The prow nosed into the mists, the fog drifted over them all, and Cattail's scream dug bloody channels through Fell's already frazzled nerves. He heard Ovrin exclaim that the one-time barmaid had fainted dead away, and his first suggestion was that they pitch her overboard and sail to river's end, into the Opalza Sea.

Ovrin refused. Fell still cursed him for it. The opportunity didn't linger. The fog bank ended abruptly, with an inner boundary as smooth and solid as a wall of smoked glass. Beyond, sky and water alike were clear. The boat no sooner breached the far side of the enchanted mist than Cattail came back to her senses. Ovrin even dared to ask her if she was all right. Fell longed for the strength to make the fellow bleed for his accursed compassion. If the big redhead had only had a little less honor and a shred more self-interest, they might be in full command of the boat right now, coasting southeast for the pleasures and opportunities of Cymweh, instead of tramping through this hideous growth.

Fell called down a variety of supernatural blastings on his luck, his companions, and his surroundings. The boat had beached on a pebbly strand no wider than a tavern wench's apron. The fog was many boat lengths behind them and the sky overhead was a clear dawnlight pink and gold. A palisade of reeds, green and brown and yellow, higher than three tall men, stood sentry beyond the shingle. Cattail recovered at once and took control, ordering them to follow her into the waving curtain.

Fell declined. The ondine said nothing, merely hummed a tune. It would never win its composer the lowest bout of the Havror Fenn, but it sufficed to make the beached boat shoot away from shore fire-fast. It did not go as far as the fog bank—only far enough into deep water for the same invisible powers propelling it to turn it on its stern and sink it in the Salmlis.

"Follow me, stay where you are, or go where you like." Having given them their nonexistent choice, Cattail marched into the reeds. They followed, and had been following her ever since.

"We'll rest here," Cattail announced, sitting down cross-legged in a minuscule clearing among the reeds. "Talk if you wish, but keep it soft."

Ovrin did as she did, unquestioning. He motioned for his brother to sit close beside him, but Keri shook his head. The boy was too entranced by his new world. He ran his hands along the stem of one reed over and over, imprinting the shadings of green, the rough silvery hairs, the piercing green fragrance of the plant deeply into his mind. Tiny insects hovered near, inspecting the inspector. His large, guileless eyes appeared to seek their small, gem-cut orbs and trade secrets.

Fell scowled at the boy. Of the three, Keri's garb alone was just as fresh and fair to see as when it was newly bought. The cold exhalations of the fog bank left no trace

always managed to bring him around. If nothing else works, we've got Keri to play checkmate."

"No. Keri's been used enough. I won't let you do it again."

"Then don't." Fell stepped aside, leaving Ovrin to flounder over a particularly bad piece of ground, every other step a sinkhole. The big man caught his foot in a mud pot and measured his length on the earth.

Fell gave him an arm, with many sympathetic clucks and head shakings. "Better get used to this, Ovrin. You'll be here a long time, if Timeo can't be made to see us home. Keri too. I hope this climate agrees with him. He doesn't swim, either, does he? So many places for him to wander off and pitch into deep water . . . I hope he'll be careful."

"I just hope we reach the village soon," Ovrin panted, wiping mud from his face.

"Reach it? We're in the middle of it." Cattail halted and gave the hummocky bog land a satisfied overview. "Excellent! Everyone's home. Must be a festival, though I don't recall which it could be. I've been out of touch with customs over here since I went east to work for our liberation."

"The feast of the vanishing village," Fell remarked. The land around them was deserted to his eyes. The only salient feature was the large, lichened boulder that lifted its craggy head out of the morass. "I say we climb up there and dry our feet. Mine itch fit to die."

"Touch that and you will die," Cattail stated. "That's the Suicides' Rock. Unless you can prove Waterfolk blood, steer away." With that cheerful caution, she walked lightly past him, her feet skimming the tops of the omnipresent rivulets and puddles. Straight for the Suicides' Rock she went, knelt at the stream bubbling up at its base, and raised a cupped handful of water to her lips.

Keristor wandered closer to see what his pretty lady was doing. He tried to mimic her, but Keri drank the water, where she only whispered into it and dashed it against the boulder's side.

At once there was a thrumming from the earth. Starkweed and willowfly shook. Insects clouded the air, startled from their resting places. The earth itself flowed out from under

Ovrin's feet, pitching him into the mud. Fell flexed his knees, fighting to stay upright.

Webbed hands steadied him, others helped Ovrin rise. Where hummock and watery knoll had been, low domes of shining nacre shed the sludge of marsh and mere from their luminous shells. Their slender bodies draped in flowery gossamers, the exotic variety of the males contrasting sharply with the delicate beauty of the females, the Waterfolk emerged.

One of the more human looking of the males approached Cattail with the dignified mien of a grand oceangoing ship. Thick gray hair in a backswept mane complemented a gaunt face only slightly blue. His bulging violet eyes were the most extraordinary thing about him, though who could tell what lay hidden beneath his thickly embroidered robe?

"Drifting done, Thalac!" Cattail beamed as she scooped more water from the boulder's base and let it pour from her cupped hands into his.

"Drifting done, my lady." He sounded about as sanguine as a gaffed carp. Not even the webbing between his fingers could hold the offered water. It trickled away.

Cattail's smile was gone. "You call me 'my lady,' Thalac? I thought that there were to be no marks of false rank between us."

The elder sighed ponderously. "My lady, you are what you are. You could not choose your birth." He raised his hand. "No more could I choose another way."

Mortal men poured from the huts, helms and spearheads glittering. They laid rough hands on the three young men and hustled them into a deep sinkhole which appeared at a word from their leader, a man with a star-crested helmet. When they emerged from the depths of the hole, it closed after them.

"What is this? Curse it, Thalac, what does it mean?" Cattail lifted her hands, blanketed in a menacing aura of midnight blue. "My father's men here—!"

Two of the warriors came up swiftly to flank her. Rune-carved silver bracelets sheathed their wrists. When their hands closed on hers, all manifestation of her magic powers faded. The signs and symbols on their bracelets absorbed the last drop of Cattail's enchanted rage.

She stared at the bracelets, recognized their meaning. "Elite troops, his own bodyguard." She gave Thalac a hard stare. "I congratulate you. Your betrayal does not lack for style. A lesser man would have settled for having those patrol ruffians crouched in wait here. You rate the palace guard."

"You have been gone a long time," the elder said. Regret bowed his shoulders more than the weight of his brocaded robe. "You left with only half an idea of how things would be for our cause in the lands of men. You never had more than half an idea of how we would fare here when your parents discovered you had gone. You can never know what we suffered, Cattail."

"You think I didn't suffer, over there!" She tried to wave towards the east, but the guards had an unbreakable grip on her hands. "To live as I lived, always with stealth, always fearing my father's agents, always with humiliation—"

Thalac bent his head. He spoke several names very tenderly.

From the largest hut, the children came. They had the faces of half-starved, frightened animals. Some stumbled as they approached Thalac, Cattail, the guards. There were about twenty of them, a considerable crowd, and it took the ondine a while before she noticed the fingers and toes slashed free of webbing, the scars marring the powerful kicking muscles of upper arm and thigh, the cauterized gills of some of the boys, the marks of subtler abuses that showed only in the eyes of the girls.

One no longer had eyes to reveal what she had endured. A little younger than Keri, by her looks, she was guided to Thalac's side by two of her playmates.

The elder embraced the blind girl, then looked back at Cattail. "You remember my Dianta . . ."

Chapter XX

TIME MARSHES ON

Timeo regarded his cell mates with a jaded eye. "The problem with being a condemned man is the class of people you have to associate with."

"Condemned?" Fell glanced desperately around the cell as if seeking a sign that Timeo was only joking. "Detained, maybe, but condemned? We're harmless!"

"I learned how harmless you are at the Havror Fenn." Timeo dug a hole in the marshy floor and absently watched it fill up with water. Keri got down on his belly to observe the phenomenon and dig some holes of his own.

"Timeo, we're sorry." Ovrin sat down beside his former friend and tried to make Timeo look him in the face. "All that money from your domain— You've always been rich. Can you understand our position? No more begging, no more going cap in hand to the governors of finance or to our hometown councils or—or to you."

"So it was more honorable to rent me out as a buffoon than to ask me for coin?"

"Now just a minute! If you hadn't *thought* you could sing worth a dead flea, no force on earth could've forced you into that contest." Fell was glad to have something to take his mind off the word 'condemned.' "We just repeated what you'd been telling yourself for years! And we weren't the only ones, right, Ovrin?"

Reluctantly Ovrin said, "Cattail."

"How much did she get out of it, I wonder?" Timeo

rested his chin on his fists. "That display of hers, the way she turned the Waterfolk on Zerin and his crew, how did it serve her purposes?"

"She was avenging what Zerin did to you!" Ovrin cried.

"I don't believe it. When in my life have I ever run across anyone with a simple motive for his doings? Always grand plots and ploys and plans, with yours truly in the center of them. Pull this string, Mother, and watch me jerk into the perfect obedient son. I'll hold your father's domain against all comers, wed a pleasant girl with an acceptable dowry, and spawn the next generation of land-hungry northern lordlings. Or why not pull this thread and watch me make an ass of myself before the whole university, while my *friends* collect their wagers? 'Bet we can make a corn crake think he sings like a nightingale! Get your coin down now, gentles, and watch the fun!' "

"Timeo, when you lived with us those few days didn't you see how we—?" Ovrin's pleas were for nothing.

"Here's the best string of all!" Timeo's head lolled back as he laughed at the patch of open sky above, an airhole too small and too high up to offer escape. "Pull this one, Cattail, Duila, any of you painted daisies. You'll never guess where it's attached, but the results are unmistakable. One tug, and a man will dance to any tune you play him. Tell him he can sing, tell him he's a prince, tell him he's the savior of his people, and he'll listen. Oh yes, straight to the ear, this string goes."

"Maybe you're condemned, but not us." Fell spoke firmly, as one who seeks to convince himself. "The wizard Ragnar may want you—last of the royal house and all—but he has no earthly use for us. We'll be questioned and set free."

"Who in Helagarde told you I was a prince?" Timeo demanded. "Never mind, I can guess: Cattail. Well, lads, cheer up. We're going to hang together on this one. My loyal subjects up there haven't the foggiest idea—you should excuse the expression—that I'm any different from you. Far as they know, we're all itinerant fools."

"Fools?"

"These many years not one mortal who enters the Lands Unknown comes out again. Who but fools would try?"

Timeo hugged his knees. "My garb's so ragged now it can pass for motley, and I told them the joke about the Malbens and the millstone. They locked me up anyway."

"*We're* no fools!" Fell protested. "We didn't come here of our own free will!"

"No. You came here in company with Cattail. You're liars, villains, cads, opportunists, and kidnappers. That's the least her father'll read it, anyhow. Rumor doesn't reach me too easily down here, but I have gathered that Ragnar never did believe his daughter left court willingly."

"His daughter!"

Timeo gave a half smile. "Didn't she mention that to you, while she was speaking so eloquently of my bloodlines? No, my friends, I'm condemned for trespassing, not royalty, but you'll sail west as abductors. Ragnar will take a personal interest in your embarkation arrangements—very fond of his only child and won't hear anything said against her. My one hope is that his famous rage doesn't blind him to the fact that Keri's innocent in more ways than one." He glanced to where the boy was dabbling in the seepage water, occasionally raising a dripping finger to his lips for a taste.

"Keri, stop that!" Ovrin barked.

"Sorry." The boy tilted his head to one side. "It tastes all right. It tastes clean."

"Oh, do what you like, then." Ovrin's huge shoulders sagged. "What's the difference? It's all up for us."

"So it is," Timeo concurred. "I'm almost sorry to see you sharing the noose with me, Ovrin—if that's how they rid themselves of ill doers in these lands. If it's death by drowning they dish out, they'll do all right with you, but what a surprise they'll have when they get to me! If I'd've been thinking straight, I might've remembered *that* new wrinkle in my life. But no, I took the usual suicide's way: Leap in the Salmlis and bubble on down." He shook his head over his own past folly. "No imagination. No wonder my songs are so poor. I hope the Waterfolk do better by me."

Fell chewed his thumb furiously, brows and mouth knotting tight in thought. *You've a few strings left for me to pull yet, Timeo. I'm getting out of these lands with my skin whole if I have to flay yours off your living back.*

In the dank shadows of the underground cell, his ruminations went unnoted. His face cleared, and his lips lifted imperceptibly.

"So Zerin triumphs after all," he said.

"Triumph for *that?*" Timeo laughed with ill humor. "I saw the drubbing he took. Call that triumph?"

"Timeo, you never took a minor course in Jest, as I did. The Circle of Laughter's no more meaningful to you than the thieves' cant of Ishma."

The way Timeo's eyebrow hooked up in inquiry made Fell think of his boyhood angling days. The bait was being nibbled, and judicious manipulation of the line would make the fish strike hard.

"All jest is basically philosophy," he said, acting as if this was the most easily gotten knowledge in the world. "He who laughs today will weep tomorrow—the way of the world. Likewise he who is the butt of one joke will ride the Circle of Laughter up to jeer at those who mocked him. No jest can be the final one. Even a skull stops smiling after enough years pass."

He linked his hands behind his head and whistled. Timeo and Ovrin waited for him to elaborate. He let them. The big ones only take bait when the angler's interest appears to be elsewhere.

"Well, go on! Go on! Surely there must be more to it than that?" Timeo bit down hard.

"Only the matter of the Jest Eternal. All the professors agree that it is a fallacy, a paradox, an impossibility: the joke where the victim does not rise again to take his laugh in turn. You've changed all that, Timeo. Zerin's pulled it off, thanks to you. He may have some hurts to nurse, but they'll heal. You, on the other hand—you've given up on living to make him sorry, living to show the whole university how wrong they were to laugh at you, just plain living! You've packed your sack with despair, don't care whether you live or die, and off to Helagarde you go! I swear, they'll be laughing at you in the taverns of Panomo-Midmists for centuries to come over this. *After* pouring the libation to Zerin of Wickerdale."

Timeo had a great deal to say by way of rebuttal. Ovrin tried to clap his hands over Keri's ears for most of it, though it was doubtful the boy would understand all the vile words. As Timeo's rage dribbled away, a white-hot coal of determination glowed in his eyes.

"When I go back over the Salmlis, crown and all, we'll see who laughs last!"

"That we will, Your Highness." Fell bowed his head with tasteful reverence. It served to hide a cunning smile. "That we will."

Chapter XXI

NEW WAVE

Things were not going as anyone had planned.

"Look, we all know your new status, Timeo," Fell said, wiping mired hands on the front of his tunic. "But we don't want any of these fishy folk guessing it just yet. Get down here and dig with the rest of us!"

"I did dig. Look." Timeo held out his hands, the nails packed thick with watery earth. He perched on a shelf of giant turkey-tail fungus as thick and hard as a wooden bench. "Escape is *up*. You're burrowing *down*. I may be posing as a fool, but I'm not a damned fool."

Ovrin stood up to his knees in the pit they'd all been digging. "Timeo's right, Fell. Why are we digging downwards anyway?" He climbed out clumsily. "We're already underground."

"I know that! So was this whole cursed village, until the houses came popping up around us like a clutch of toadstools. If we tunnel down a bit, so no one'll see us if they peek into the cell—"

"Peek in through what? There's no door." Ovrin searched the curved walls once more, just to be sure.

"Hear him out, Ovrin." Timeo waved his hand wearily. "The door that *happens* whenever the Waterfolk want to come down here, he means."

"—down and sideways"—Fell glowered at Ovrin's interruption—"we'll break through the wall of one of their submerged huts. I've a great sense of direction, and I know

169

I saw one not too far off that way when the guards shoved us down here. If we're lucky—''

"They could peek in through the airhole," Ovrin said, looking up. "Digging a tunnel downward's pretty visible from up there."

Fell punched him in the arm. "We'll take our chances. Unless you've got another plan?" Ovrin pressed his lips together and said nothing. "I thought not. As I was saying, if we're lucky, no one'll be home, we'll lift a cloak or two, disguise ourselves, and sneak away."

"And if someone is home?"

"How many spawners do you think can squeeze into one of those little huts? They're not barrel herrings. We can handle the few we might meet."

Timeo made a doubtful face. "And if the hut you're aiming at's aboveground for the moment?"

"Better! We'll hit the gap its rising's left beneath it, tunnel up through the floor, and away!"

"What gap?" Timeo asked.

"What do you mean 'what gap'? If something solid's moved it leaves an empty space behind, *that's* 'what gap.' Now will the two of you di—?"

Fell's speech ended in a choked gurgle as the bottom of the pit opened beneath his feet and gulped him into muddy waters. Timeo and Ovrin groped around for him from the surface, but even the tall redhead's long arms found nothing. As the air bubbles atop the brown water grew fewer and less frequent, their groping became more frantic.

"Use Timeo," a high voice said.

"What?" The two men turned and spoke as one.

"Use Timeo," Keristor repeated, his gaze unwavering on the bit of moss he'd scraped from the wall. "He doesn't drown. He said he doesn't. Isn't this pretty, Ovrin? It's green, but it's like fur. Green fur. That would look silly on a cat, unless it was a green cat."

They wasted no time separating green cats from good ideas. Ovrin grasped Timeo by the ankles and used him as a human plumb line to dredge up Fell.

"What gap?" Timeo repeated, pushing streaming hair out of his eyes.

"No more digging?" Ovrin asked as he pumped bilge from Fell's lungs.

"We need another plan," Fell gasped.

Unexpected sunlight cut away a huge wedge of the cell wall. Mossy steps appeared, and flat feet came flapping down to the prisoners' level. Before any of them could take advantage of this sudden exit, a hedge of razor-sharp coral spines sprang out of the muck between them and the visitor, more effective than any iron bars.

He looked to be first cousin to a carp, with a bit of bullfrog thrown in for good measure. Bulbous eyes rotated independently in his head as he scanned the occupants of the cell. "Which one of you's the fool?" he asked.

"I'd say that's up for argument," Timeo replied.

"Right. You're the one. The others I remember. Come with me."

"Am I to be executed so soon?"

"Without the choice being given you first?" The jailor picked at a small fungal growth on his pectoral scales. "Our lord Ragnar'd have our heads for that, manpower growing dearer by the year. You may be a fool, but you look as if you like life and can bear arms."

"Like this?" Timeo rolled up his sleeves.

The jape was even beneath a carp's level of appreciation. "A fool and an idiot too. Nature's a wonder. Try to dredge up something better to entertain the guests, eh? A wedding's supposed to be a joyous time."

"If this is a Waterfolk wedding, I'd hate to see your funerals," Timeo remarked.

"Hush up. Just be grateful for what you can see whilst you can see it. Once we're done with your singing, it's back in the hole with you, my lad. Or d'you fancy you sing fine enough to buy your freedom with it? *There'd* be a wedding gift."

The jailor's less icthyous side showed in his almost human facility of facial expression. Timeo had always considered fish to be the ultimate cardsharps, with no whiff of emotion moving their features. The short time he'd spent among the Waterfolk made him reevaluate his judgment. His jailor looked grimmer than a landlord on rent day.

"Don't talk about what you don't know and you'll do fine. You just go over your jests in your mind, keep them short and snappy, and don't tell any Callis of Clarem jokes. They've been banned."

"So I'd expect." Callis of Clarem was to wizardry what Timeo was to minstrelry. So many merry tales had sprouted of his sorceries gone awry that now no one could say for sure whether there had actually been a real Callis of Clarem or if he was just a catchall for every jest about a magical bungler.

The horrible part of it all was that now Timeo's mind was blank of every joke he'd ever heard except those about Callis of Clarem.

While he beat his brains raw for some other variety of tale, he continued to marvel at the Waterfolk way of preparing for a wedding. The pearly huts were all aboveground, yet not a one was decorated, nor was there any sign of festive adornment in the open space in their midst. A braid of rushes had been draped between the two huts nearest the great rock, and that was all.

The Waterfolk themselves were no more gaudily done up than their village. Even the poorest peasants in Timeo's home domain managed to do proud by bride and groom. If all else failed, they wore wreaths of flowers or berries or evergreen boughs, according to the season. But though Timeo saw a respectable gathering of young and old, not one among them wore any mark to single him out from the rest.

A sweet chord on the hand harp made Timeo turn. A supple youth sat upon the weedy summit of one of the houses, tuning his instrument. His hair was true gold, metallic in the light of day, and his skin the clear color of an aquamarine. He looked like a living bit of goldsmith's artifice that any highborn lady would happily take into her jewel case, and his harp was inlaid with precious stones worthy of such a master.

Timeo sidled closer to the handsome musician. His jailor did not object, likely banking on the fact that even if a prisoner made a dash, he wouldn't get far over the flat swampland.

"Uh, hello, up there. You're the wedding bard?"

Emerald eyes turned their mild, slit-pupiled gaze on

Timeo. "I am to sing them together, if that's what you mean." He spoke Timeo's language with the most charming lilt. "You must be the fool."

"So life proves me. Timeo Landbegot of Norm." He stretched up his hand. It didn't seem respectful to his departed grandsire to link mention of Dureforte Keep with that of his new career.

"I am Wydru."

"That's a queen among harps you have there, Wydru." Timeo could not keep the old longing out of his voice and eyes. "You must have a royal voice."

Wydru shrugged with a fluid grace. "I sing much like the next man. This is the village's harp and it's my cousin's wedding, that's the only reason why the honor's fallen to me. Singing's no grand talent. Now if only I could make people laugh . . ."

"Singing's not bad for that," Timeo mumbled. In a more distinct voice he said, "Which one's your cousin, the bride or the groom?"

A cyan hand went up to shade green eyes. "With all the shape-shifting going on right before the ceremony, your guess might beat mine. My branch of the family never did favor metamorphosis, but Perdica's— Let's just say she was born female and changed her mind a time or two thereafter. I *think* she promised her mother, by the sacred Rock, to stay in feminine form for the ceremony." Wydru frowned. "Of all the stupid times for her to make such a promise . . ."

"There you are!" Timeo's jailor jerked him away from the conversation. "Pick it up and come along. They're going to begin, and they want a few jests to warm the air."

Timeo trod carefully over the unsteady ground. His jailor brought him through the crowd of villagers, past a small table bearing a rose jade bowl, and up to the braided rushes near the big rock. Having positioned his charge so that the performer's back was to the boulder, Carp-face retired, leaving Timeo to confront his first audience since the Havror Fenn.

The silence was cool, deep, and suffocating. Timeo cleared his throat and tried not to think of a fish market. "A funny thing happened to me on my way to the Lands Unknown—" He stopped. "Actually, it didn't."

Goggling stares, flat stares, stares from faces human, fishy, amphibious, breathtaking, revolting, all pressed against him. Several flickered from one form to another, the shape-shifters in the throng either bored or keeping in practice. He gathered his wits to try again.

"How many Braegerd men does it take to sharpen a sword?" He waited for an answer or any sort of response. He got more silence. "Three: One to hold the sword, one to run the grindstone, and one to steal the sword in the first place." The silence became sharper than any sword, honed further by his own voice piping, "Get it? Three? One to steal . . . ? Ahem. One day Callis of Clarem was asked to turn straw into gold, so he went to see the local miller's daughter and—"

"Thank you, young man." Thalac stepped up to the rushy braid and patted Timeo's arms mightily, like a good house-wife fluffing pillows. "We appreciate your jollity at this most happy occasion but time does not allow us to share more of your excellent jests. Wydru, the first chorus: Hurry!"

The song Wydru plucked from the strings of his princely harp was painfully beautiful to Timeo's ear. The Waterfolk began to dance. *Almost—almost as sweet as Alveiros' voice,* he thought. *At least no one can blame me for losing to my cousin. Oh, how I do wish I'd salvaged that harp of mine! Sweet or sour, there's great comfort to be found in a little song. I'd only sing them for myself, now. I was the only one ever did enjoy my own songs. Mother was right. Not even Cattail was honest when she said she liked—*

A realization jarred in Timeo's mind as sharply as any harp string's snap. *Gods above, sweet or sour, when I sang or played, at least I kept the same rhythm throughout. This tune was a pavanne when he began it, slow as a bad winter. Why in Insar's name is he whipping it into jig time?*

Timeo stood awestruck by the turn the Waterfolk wedding took. The majestic cadences of Wydru's song had doubled their meter, tripled it, and presently were a flurry of notes that tinkled like wind chimes in a hurricane. The gliding grace of movement all the guests seemed to share let them keep up with the ever-accelerating tempo, but before long the harper proved too agile fingered. Soon his melody left them all several measures behind. Two or three of the dancers stumbled, and one older female caught her long foot on a hump of marshy earth and took four younger ones down with her.

"Enough." Thalac stood beside the little table and touched the water in the bowl. He spoke the word softly, yet all heard him. He was still in his brocaded robe, the only one there not wearing a simple fore-and-aft of yellow cloth, a belted garment like a knee-length tabard. The bizarre dancing ceased in perfect concert with Wydru's jingle-jangle music. "Our brethren of the Greater River are satisfied."

Timeo poked Wydru's leg discreetly. "River? How can someone see your dance all the way from the Salmlis?"

"No one is in the Salmlis."

"But the Persa's farther yet, and the Carras—"

"*Hst.*" Wydru laid a finger to his lips, then pointed it at the sky. "There lies the Greater River. When night comes, you can see it best."

The elder was speaking again, with much of the dancers' sense of frantic haste in his words. "They bless and bring binding in the sweetness of song. They teach and give tenderness to heart and heart. They open soul to soul, and seal the joining. The shell grows to crumble, the waters rise and fall, the reeds bend and bloom and wither in their time. Only this is eternal. Know it by the change that never comes." He lifted the rose jade bowl.

As he spoke, Timeo noticed two of the identically-dressed crowd edging their way surreptitiously towards the rushy rope connecting the two huts. No one else had touched the green braid until they each laid a hand very lightly on either end of it. A small crowd of Waterfolk moved with them, petals around the heart of a flower. Timeo was perplexed: Not only were they all dressed alike, but several members of each crowd wore their hair in the same color and style as the person presently touching their end of the rope. This was especially striking as one party was all male, with the huge variation of appearances—fishy and human—common to male Waterfolk. The more ichthyous among them wore wigs that fooled no one.

Thalac's eyes rotated rapidly. With a small, swift jerk of his chin he urged Wydru to play.

The azure-skinned minstrel drew a haunting chord from

his harp. He sang, and this time nothing quickened the reverent cadence of his song:

> "From a vessel none would fancy,
> From a spell both old and strong,
> Thence shall come our liberation,
> Thence shall rise the Watersong.
> Evil powers shall not touch it,
> Death shall end the ancient wrong,
> From the vessel flows our freedom,
> Miracle of Watersong."

Timeo closed his eyes, floating on the music. He wished it were as boundless as the Greater River, to bear him on forever. Too soon it was done. He opened his eyes and saw that the two groups of Waterfolk by the rushy rope had moved a little closer to one another. The elder was signaling Wydru to sing again, his strained expression encouraging even more haste.

The first notes of a new tune left Wydru's harp, and crashed aground on a harsh laugh.

"Ain't they cunning though?" A stubbled face, ugly as unboiled blood pudding, leered down at the gathered Waterfolk from the only height for miles around: the great boulder. A grimy leather helmet and armor cast back no glint of sun, but the bright sword in the burly man's hand made up for it.

"Pretty, too," one of his nine companions on the rock said. "Never heard anyone sing half so pretty as these Waterfolk. Knew a tavern wench once who come close, but—"

A third man sat on the edge of the rock, the bent bow in his hands aimed casually at the elder's chest. "Not going to invite us to the wedding, Thalac? That's not friendly of you. And here we bring young Randal with us for his first patrol—as fine a gentleman as you'd find in any duke's court to grace your spawning."

A fourth shoved the young man in question forward. He wore his armor awkwardly, but he held his sword with the ease of long familiarity. "Pity is," Randal's sponsor said, "y' won't find 'im in ary duke's court now. Take a narrer view o' 'is way wi' t' ladies, they did, back in Leyaeli. Quibbles sent 'im here—What's t' use askin' a lass yea or nay when half t' time they changes their minds an' leaves a man all flustered? But Leyaeli's famous fer lawyers—*an'* courts, *an'* executioners—an' so here he be.''

''Where it don't matter much what the ladies say,'' the first man concluded. ''Not once they're caught.''

Randal's throat knot bobbled up and down as he snickered. ''Like fish! Just like fish, right?'' His small eyes lit up with eager glee as he surveyed the crowd below. ''Which one's mine, fellows? Which one's mine?''

''Hand on the rope means bride or groom. Take your pick, honor your first patrol! Go it, Randal! Hurry, you lot, they run!''

The patrol leader launched Randal from the rock with a strong slap on the back. He landed in the thick of the wedding mob and lunged for the group of females. They split up in all directions, screaming as they ran, but Randal had already noted the one who had had her hand on the plaited rushes. The other men with him poured down from the boulder and joined in the chase. Only the archer remained at his post, arrow pointed at Thalac.

The male Waterfolk made no resistance. The most they did was to melt into the scampering crowd of females and block pursuit. The armored men knocked them aside easily, using fist or elbow or the flat of a sword. One of the older members of the patrol soon lost his wind and his patience at the same time. When the seventh Waterfolk male placed himself between the man and his chosen prey, he swore loudly and turned the sword as it came down.

Blood trickled over the earth, tinted the standing water.

Timeo was terrified. He felt helpless, frustrated past bearing, furious with the stolid, passive way of his supposed subjects. *Will I rule a nation of cowards, if I live to rule at all? Why don't they fight? If I had a weapon—*

But he had none, no idea of where to look for one, and the sinking feeling that even if he were armed, he would be no match for ten men. A throng of fleeing females rushed past him and plunged into one of the huts, which immediately sank into the ground. Others followed their example,

but they were mostly those females who had no one specif-
ically hunting them at the moment.

The men worked like good sheepdogs, marking their
victims and concentrating all their efforts on cutting them out
of the herd. The veterans could keep their sights fixed on
their chosen prey despite the interposition of a hundred
Waterfolk males.

Randal was a tyro, but already he showed a master's
knack. The bride was his, a signal honor, and he didn't
mean to lose her. As his comrades one by one made their
catches and dragged them away, he closed in on the female
who was his prize.

Timeo scrambled up to the top of the hut where Wydru
still sat, hugging his harp miserably to his bosom. "She's
your cousin!" he cried, shaking him by one blue shoulder.
"Aren't you going to do a kinsman's part?"

"Thalac is our elder." Wydru was entirely wretched, his
beautiful voice breaking like a boy's. "He still trains his
successor in the old knowledge. If he is slain before the
training is complete, the knowledge dies with him. A village
without the old learning is destroyed. We do not dare to
challenge Ragnar's men when they hold Thalac in peril."

"But couldn't you—?"

"The men don't fight, the women may—Ragnar's men
don't think females can do much, in spite of all the lessons
they've been given. Perdica can take care of herself." He
jerked his head. "See there."

Randal had the bride pressed up against the side of one
of the houses which had not yet sunk. He was much taller
than Perdica, able to use his sword to persuade her into the
crook of his other arm. The blade lay against her ribs. He
laughed to see her try squirming away from it and brought
his lips to hers for a kiss.

The bloody muzzle of a wolf pressed against his mouth.
Heavy paws pushed against his shoulders. Randal staggered
back, too startled to release his encircling hold on the beast.
His sword arm dropped. The wolf staggered with him on its
hind paws.

"Hoy! Randal! Don't let her trickiness cheat you! She
can't shift scent as she shifts shape, y'know!"

The words of encouragement from the archer broke

Randal's astonishment. He scowled and raised his sword once more, crushing the wolf closer to his body.

A moldering corpse leered in his face, lips acrawl with blindworms. She ran green fingers through his hair in horrific parody of a willing lover's embrace, leaving trails of grave mold behind.

Randal swallowed hard, face whiter than the creatures writhing over his victim's flesh. He groaned in horror and disgust, unmanned. Then a cry of a different tenor reached his ear—a high-pitched sobbing scream from beyond the great rock, mingled with the raucous laughter of his fellow soldiers. His looks hardened. He steeled himself and returned the corpse's kiss strongly.

Flames leaped around his face, crept hungrily up his arm. All his clothes seemed to be afire. The blaze engulfed him. Before he could react the flames thrust a mirror in his eyes, a glass that showed him his own face as fire consumed it to running jelly and blackened bone.

He gurgled with fear, and instinctively lashed out with his sword. It pierced the flickering edge of the fire. A mewl of pain answered as the flames vanished. The bride knelt doubled over against the hut wall, clutching her bleeding arm.

Randal's hoarse laugh cried victory. He stopped to sling her over his shoulder with arrogant ease and carried her off the way his fellows had borne their prizes.

"No!" Timeo wrenched the harp from Wydru's hands. He leaped from the top of the hut and ran after Randal, smashing the instrument down on the soldier's head.

It was a light harp, for all its ornamentation, and a good helmet, for all its shabby looks. Randal turned, gave Timeo a look of extreme annoyance, and batted him across the temple with the hilt of his sword.

Darkness sounded close harmony with silence.

Chapter XXII

TIDINGS OF JOY

Timeo thought he was passing through the river fog again. Nothing was solid, and his limbs had that detached, floating feeling, though when he consciously tried to move an arm or a leg, he encountered weak resistance. Sounds had a muzzy quality. The only difference he could see between the enchanted fog and his present situation was that the prowling ghosts in the mist had not been such a bright shade of blue.

"Are you better?" Wydru's emerald eyes were full of deep concern.

"Better . . ." Timeo touched the side of his head and was surprised not to find it tender. "Hey! I thought I was hit—"

"You were. You're lucky he didn't crack your skull."

"Then why doesn't it still hurt?"

"You desire pain?" Wydru screwed up his mouth. "I don't understand dust crawlers."

"I don't *want* to hurt; I just want to know why I feel as if I've done no more than have a bad dream."

"It was no dream." Wydru helped him sit up. Timeo saw that he was inside one of the Waterfolk huts. The doorless entryway showed a day fast coming to its close. Muted glows came from pockets of nacre that were part of the hut walls. Timeo saw other pockets too, larger ones such as might be used to store clothing or tools. Several shelves of russet fungus also protruded from the walls, bearing covered baskets whose contents remained secret. Woven mats made islands of dryness across the floor.

Timeo lay on one, a corpse on another.

"Thalac could not heal him, and he is the best healer among us whose blood is not royal."

Timeo became very interested. "Your kings are healers?"

"Our kings are gone. They were before my time, and it may be all legend. All I know is that elder Thalac said it would take one of the royal blood to heal Elod; he could not." Wydru sighed. "Or maybe Elod didn't want to be healed. The sword thrust wasn't that deep that I could see. Better to die than to watch your child's slow death."

Wydru rose and fetched a familiar object from behind the baskets on the nearest shelf. It was the jeweled hand harp, all its strings broken, some cavities in the frame where gems had fallen out, but otherwise whole.

"No, you didn't dream what happened, Timeo. If you did, then waken, and bring Elod back from the dead, and call my cousin Perdica back from Suicides' Rock."

Twilight cast a tender violet cloak over the nymph who crouched on the great boulder, weeping green tears. Below, the villagers went about their business as if nothing had happened. Timeo stared until he began to suffer the delusion that perhaps he was the only one who heard Perdica's misery.

"Is she— *Why* is she up there?" he asked his guide as they stood on the spot where the rushy rope had been.

"It was her choice," Wydru replied. "She was dishonored before her wedding, and the sacred bowl was smashed." He toed the earth, yielding up small shards of rose jade. "Either one would have been an evil omen, but both together, and the death of Perdica's father too—! No one can fault Mycor for withdrawing his offer of marriage. He's within his rights."

"Just because those animals—? Gods, Wydru, she *fought* that bastard Randal! Spare us all, *how* she fought him! Where I come from, if a woman defends her chastity so strongly and still has the misfortune to fail, she's not looked at as—as something unclean."

"Chastity?" Wydru gave back Timeo's perplexity in blue.

"What's that?" Timeo explained, with the air of a man who suspects his leg is being pulled. When he finished, Wydru commented, "Oh. Interesting idea. Can't be too popular, though. The issue here, Timeo, is as I said: the omens. Some lives are wed to good fortune, some to ill. No one knowingly binds his life to bad luck, and what happened to Perdica's bad enough to serve several lives. A brave man might stand by her, but Mycor's got a yellow liver. Why, there's the final proof of how bad it is—" He indicated the summit of the rock. "It's too much of a bad-luck life even for Perdica herself to bear. That's why she's chosen not to bear it."

Timeo's heart ached worse with every sob that came down from above. "Can't someone comfort her?"

"Speaking to one on Suicides' Rock is forbidden. She went up there by her own choice, and by law there she stays. No one's to dare touch her or splash her or even sprinkle her on pain of death."

"You'll all just let her starve herself?"

"She'll be dead of dehydration long before she feels a hunger pang. The dew may touch her tonight, but by tomorrow's sunset she'll be gone."

Timeo got a determined look in his eye. "Not if I can help it." He made as if to climb the rock.

More hands than Wydru's pulled him back before he could lay a finger on the cold stone. Four Waterfolk males, including Wydru and his old jailor carp-face, linked arms to keep him at a distance.

"Suicides' Rock is sacred to us, groundling," carp-face said. "None but Waterfolk may tread it and live."

"Ragnar's thrice-blasted patrol was tromping pretty free all over it!" Timeo sniped.

"Agreed," carp-face replied. "With this difference: That we could do nothing to stop them, but we can bury you up to the neck in mud if you try."

Timeo sneered. "You're brave enough now. Go on, then, bury me to the neck! Mud's good for the skin, I hear."

"Head first."

Timeo took a voluntary step away from Suicides' Rock. Perdica's weeping still hung on the evening air, every jagged sob tearing at him. The Waterfolk were unmoving, set firm as sun-dried mud in their beliefs and customs. Perdica wept on, a wordless plea for comfort.

A canny look flitted over Timeo's face. "Can she come down on her own?"

"If she chooses," carp-face said. "Which she won't. They don't, as a rule."

"No hurt lasts forever, I've heard. She may sorrow strongly now, but in time—"

"By that time, she'll have dried to dust and blown away. Those that choose Suicides' Rock when their grief's still so fresh on them don't heal from it except with their deaths. I grant you, a word of consolation or reason in their ear might change matters"—fleeting regret touched carp-face's features—"but how's that to pass when speech with them's forbidden? They've chosen, and that's that."

"But if you only try persuading them to make a new choice, a different choice—"

The jailor was well suited to give ignorant statements the fish-eye. "Persuasion makes it the persuader's choice! Look, rock-belly, tomorrow or next day we'll be having lord Ragnar's guards back here to fetch away your cell mates for judgment. That's the same time we'll give you a choice of your own to make, and count yourself lucky you've got it!"

"What's this windfall of good fortune?"

"To join lord Ragnar's service—though I shake to think what sort of soldier they'll make out of a fool—"

"No worse than all the fools some kings have made out of soldiers. And if I won't serve Ragnar?"

"Then you die."

"A pretty choice."

Carp-face turned philosophical. "Not all our choices are pretty, yet they must be made. Streams branch out from their sources, some to seek calm pools, some to find the sea, and some to run shallow and dry, but all by choice. Let no man turn the watercourse of another." On a more practical note he added, "Come along back to prison now, lad. You're healed enough to return, aren't you?"

He tried to steer Timeo away from the rock. His charge refused to budge. "You talk a lot of luck around here, my friend," Timeo said, digging in his heels. "Care for a little wager?"

"With a dust-crawler fool?" Carp-face made a series of short, sharp sounds like a string of bubbles popping, his version of laughter. "Our prisoner besides? What could you have to stake?"

"You say I'll have a choice tomorrow or next day. If you win the wager, I swear that I shall join your lord Ragnar's service."

Carp-face made more bubbling noises. "Now you show how funny you can be! What good does saving your own skin do me?"

"A friend to this village will be among lord Ragnar's troops. A dust-belly who knows the minds of other dust-bellies, and whose words just might persuade his fellow soldiers that some, shall we say, undesirable effects come from too-close association with Waterfolk women?"

"Bah! Who'll believe that?"

"When Randal comes to an untimely end, they might." Timeo folded his hands before him and gazed down at an imaginary corpse. "So young, poor man, and found dead in his bed one fine morning without a mark on him." He winked at carp-face and the rest. "When I was court fool to Count Beveril of Clarem, I had certain . . . other duties apart from entertainment."

Carp-face looked at him narrowly. "You don't look much like an assassin."

"How many have you seen lately?" Timeo replied blandly.

"All right," carp-face said. "Randal's death's a fair stake. And if you win the wager?"

"If I win this wager, I'll let you name my prize."

This time the jailor's mirth sounded like a chain of undersea eruptions. "Done!"

"Without hearing the wager first?" Wydru marveled.

"When I can name his prize if he wins? What do I risk? Go on, lad! Name your wager and prove you're more than a dust-crawler fool!"

"I'll bet I can get Wydru's cousin off Suicides' Rock."

"Are you sure about this?" Wydru asked Timeo.

Timeo touched the battered hand harp tenderly as a new father strokes his infant's cheek. The instrument had been restrung while word of the astonishing wager between jailor and prisoner raced the length and breadth of the village.

"I'm sure." Timeo could not take his eyes off the harp. *How I've missed you!* his heart breathed over the curving wood, the shining strings.

"You won't touch her or talk to her?"

"Not a single spoken word." Timeo set the harp on his knee. "Only song."

"That's been tried before, you know. We Waterfolk— well, you might've heard on the other side about how we're all famed for our voices. Some of us can charm animals and birds with song, and everyone can do a little something to lift and lower our houses."

"Is that how you do it? I thought it was magic."

"Not spell-cast magic." Wydru looked wistful. "If we had that, we wouldn't be Ragnar's thralls. The power we have isn't the same. It just *is* in us. I don't know how to explain it better. That would take one of those university scholars from Panomo-Midmists."

"Don't hold your breath waiting to meet one," Timeo said dryly.

"Hold my—?"

"I shall begin."

He plucked a run over the harp strings and cleared his mind while clearing his throat for song. The Waterfolk formed a semicircle around him. Night came on, and many of them brought shallow bowls of shell and stone filled with a flameless glow. The torches at the Havror Fenn had shone no brighter, but the stakes in this contest were far dearer to Timeo. In this bout he sang against death.

Royal blood is healing blood, Wydru says, he thought. *There are so many legends of songs that heal! Master Insar, if I am lord of the Waterfolk, let this prove it. Let my singing heal Perdica's spirit. Maybe Waterfolk have a different ear for song than ordinary mortals. Maybe Cattail was telling the truth when she praised my voice. Maybe that's why no one appreciated my talents on the far side of the Salmlis. But here—! I am their king, and Wydru claims the least of us has enough power in his voice to move whole houses. Yes, here is where I'll truly find the audience I seek.*

He riffled through a mental catalog of his own compositions and came up with one he thought fail-proof to lure Perdica back among the living: a ballad of heartbreak and its consolations. He had penned it after wandering into the wrong lecture hall at the university.

"Lovely maiden sweet, despair not
Though the bloody battle rages.
Though your lover's gone, pray care not.
Just sit there a-turning pages.
Life goes on through war and battle,
Only hurting now and then.
Yesterday an infant's prattle
Was enough to kill grown men.
He was born a goose girl's bastard,
Though his sire was a prince.
Pretty soon the sword he mastered
And he hasn't dropped it since.
He grew up to be a hero,
Brave and fearless, strong and bold,
Though his brains would count as zero,
He is strong an hundredfold.
Rumors of your beauty led him
Hither on a trail of gore.
Dreams of your fair face have sped him
To promote this little war.
Though your sweetheart now may perish
Don't give him a second look.
Memories are made to cherish.
Just sit back and read your book.
Win or lose, you'll have a master
Who shall be your wedded lord.
Maiden, you are breathing faster.
Maiden, please put down that sword!"

Timeo was very proud of the ballad, in particular of the subtle way the ending implied that the maiden was taking up a sword to fight beside the preferred of her heart. Whether the favored party was her first sweetheart or the challenging hero was intended to remain as piquant a question as Bohemund's immortal "Two Gates and the Headsman."

If he hoped that Perdica would take the hint about

independent action, he wasn't disappointed. The nymph laughed so hard that she rolled off Suicides' Rock entirely under her own power and tumbled right into the waiting arms of her cousin Wydru.

Those of the Waterfolk whose curiosity overruled their smarting ears were witnesses.

"His song saved her life!"

"And what a song to do it. How to explain—?"

"She was whisked from the top of Suicides' Rock by magic."

"Yes, magic, that must be it!"

"I saw a winged lion swoop out of the sky to carry Perdica off the rock! Didn't you?"

"Didn't everyone!"

"A lion with flaming wings, and a sword in his paw, and a skeleton in wizard's robes on his back, and—"

"Magic more powerful than anything Ragnar commands."

"But who could hold such power and still brave the barrier of fog? It rings us on all sides and bars all magic wielders from our lands."

"Only one could pass it. You know who as well as I."

"Only one, the one foretold, the one who brings fulfillment of the prophecy."

"That I should live to see this day!"

"Come out, come all, come see!"

"Miracle! Miracle!" The cry reverberated through the evening air.

Elder Thalac emerged from his hut, nonchalantly removing tufts of fluff from his ears. He knelt in the mire at Timeo's feet.

"The gods pour prophecy into unlikely vessels. Streams twist and turn, are lost in caverns, wander through the roots of trees, to emerge at last in the river of their destiny. The wait was long, but the day foretold has come. Hail, master of Watersong!"

The villagers all knelt with their elder and solemnly echoed his words: "Hail, master of Watersong!"

Timeo smiled a little nervously over the throng of bowed heads and bent backs.

"Does this mean you want an encore?"

Chapter XXIII

AWASH WITH SUCCESS

The feast took place under cover of night, but was no less gladsome for that. Cook fires sprang up in nearly every space between the curve of huts, a glittering mound of glass amphorae was unearthed, and an inner semicircle of patterned spreads took the place of banquet tables within the compass of the dome-shaped houses. All the mature Waterfolk were there, and a few others.

Ovrin changed the position of his legs for about the twentieth time. The big man was finding it hard to adjust to the several embarrassments of sitting on a mat while wearing one of the Waterfolk's abbreviated fore-and-afts.

"I haven't had this much skin to the sky since I was born," he informed Fell.

His dark-haired comrade was built closer to the Waterfolk norm of small and slender. He wore his garment with the arrogant ease of one born to it. "Would you rather we were still in our rotting old clothes?" Yet another twinkling amphora went the rounds of the feasters and he snagged it before answering, "Don't be such a big baby, Ovrin. You shucked down to less than that when we went swimming at school."

"We're not swimming now," Ovrin insisted.

"Swimming in good fortune, and that's enough for me!" Fell filled their goblets to the lip with Waterfolk wine and raised his in a health. "To Timeo! By whatever mad means, he's been our salvation again."

A lovely rushy girl, bearing a fresh round of festive fare, rustled up to where Ovrin, Fell, and Keristor were seated. She knelt with becoming grace and offered her tray of food to all of them.

"Get along, lass." Fell waved a monarch's imperious hand. "We've had enough of your raw fishies." He poured freely from the amphora and drank.

"Raw fish? Do you think we're part otter?" Disgust sharpened the rushy girl's face. She whisked the tray away just as Ovrin saw what it bore.

"Fried fish in honey butter." He licked his lips regretfully. "Every platter at this banquet's better than the last. No one's given us any raw fish to eat. Why are you being such a bastard to these people, Fell?"

"People?" Fell was deeply tickled. "They're more hake than human, more pickerel than person! Being part otter'd count as a step up for them. Put away your indignation, you great country hay bale."

Ovrin grabbed Fell's wrist. His grip tightened with his mouth as he showed just how little he appreciated his comrade's sense of humor. Fell meeped like a spanked kitten.

Keristor touched his brother's huge hand with his small, smooth one. "Let him go, please? You're hurting him."

"I'm teaching him manners." Ovrin was as open to argument as a block of granite.

"All right, all right, I take it back! You're no hay bale!" Fell gave a gasp of relief as Ovrin released him. He chafed his wrist and applied some alcohol to the ache internally. "Take the part of these sprats against an old friend, why don't you?" he muttered. "After all I've done for you and your lackwit brother . . ." *Now it seems I must be in that moss-head's debt as well!* he thought fiercely, glowering at Keristor. "It's me for myself from now on, damn you. Teach me manners . . ."

"What are you saying?" Ovrin demanded.

"I'm saying you've got about as much gratitude in you as a dead crab! What do these Waterfolk mean or matter? I wouldn't share the word 'human' with such creatures. Do you understand half their babble of prophecy and vessels and whatnot? Here's the only vessel of theirs that interests me!"

He jammed the amphora into the marshy ground. "They've set up our Timeo like a godlet—not that I'm complaining about what luck it's been for us—but could you imagine the supposed intelligence of beings who'd worship *him?* Gooseberries have more brains. Here, Keri, pass me that basket of bread."

The boy was seated to Ovrin's right, Fell to Ovrin's left. He was the only one of the four cross-river refugees who still wore the garments in which he'd left Panomo-Midmists. As he passed the bread to Fell, he asked, "Does being smart mean a lot?"

Fell guffawed. "Bless you, lad! There's one question you'll never have to answer."

"Does it mean a lot to be smart?" Keri repeated. "Are you smart, Fell?"

"Smart enough to know when I've earned this feasting," Fell mumbled around a mouthful of the Waterfolk's thick flatbread. "Who was it turned Timeo's head in the cell, eh? Who is it can play more tunes on him than on a harp? Look at him up there!"

Fell indicated the place of honor near the looming shape of Suicides' Rock. In honor of the impromptu midnight feast, the Waterfolk had erected a low wooden platform there. It was no thicker than the *Collected Works of Randu Eluman*, covered with throws of woven grass and beaten bark. There Timeo sat between elder Thalac and his successor-in-training while Perdica and her mother took turns waiting upon his slightest wish.

Aye, look at him, Fell thought. *Were there ever gods, to raise a fool like that so high? He falls into satin from the moment he's born, and out of satin into silk! A taste of my life—the smallest nibble of it!—and he'd have been dead meat in an alleyway before he saw his sixth birthday.* In Fell's veins, envy soured into irrational hate. *The gods give him fortune, but they gave me brains. If I don't use them to make my own fortune, by whatever means, I'm a greater fool than Timeo.*

Timeo didn't look any more comfortable in his strange new garment than Ovrin, and even less so when Perdica's mother took to pressing his hands to her bowed head every time she came near enough to grab them. He murmured something in Thalac's ear. The elder nodded, and Timeo left the platform to join his one-time fellow students.

"Timeo! To what do we owe this privilege?" Fell yanked Timeo down between himself and Ovrin. "Slumming?"

Ovrin passed him a goblet of wine. "What happened, Timeo?" he asked. "How'd you get so high with the Waterfolk, and us out of jail? Did you tell them who—what you are?"

Timeo made frantic shushing motions. "No, Ovrin, no, and I don't want them knowing just yet."

"They *don't know?*" Fell was altogether too loud in his amazement for Timeo's liking, even though the guesting mat was removed some distance from those of the Waterfolk. "What's all this, then, if not a royal welcome? Amnesty for the prisoners too, Your Roya—"

Timeo clamped Fell's hand around the goblet and jammed the rim into his school chum's mouth. Fell inhaled more than he drank and came up choking. Keri crept around and pounded him on the back until he recovered breath.

"I don't want them to know," Timeo repeated in a low, urgent voice. He glanced nervously about to see whether any of his people had overheard Fell's indiscretion.

The Waterfolk were too long starved for celebration to waste this gala night on scrutinizing the ways of dust-bellies. The amphorae danced from hand to hand in the light of glows and flames while songs sweeter than any wine soared to the stars.

"They're ready to follow me, but not because I'm their king."

"Won 'em over with your"—Fell hiccupped loudly— "your personality, did you? You left our cell a fool. Now you're one rung down from godhead. How'd you manage that, my friend? Sing for it?"

"Yes."

Fell collapsed laughing.

"He hasn't eaten a thing." Ovrin felt compelled to apologize for Fell's behavior. "Just been drinking the wine."

"With no water." Keri's eyes were sparrow bright. "The villagers all water their wine. I've been watching." He uncorked the amphora and sniffed it. "Too strong like this, but Fell drinks it so."

Timeo was too put out with Fell to pay much heed to Keristor. "My people will follow me because I am the one promised in the prophecy—a foreseeing more ancient than the evil day when Ragnar and his beast invaded this land and slaughtered my family. I am the Vessel of Watersong. My music is a power greater than any magic."

"*Your* music?" Three voices blended nicely on those rising notes.

"Did you run into a wandering witch with a spare miracle in her pouch while we were underground?" Fell asked, groping for more wine. Keri deftly handed him a cup already half-filled with water from a different amphora.

Timeo scowled. "I will tell you what happened to me from the time I left the cell; you judge the miracle."

The effects of the Waterfolk's wine were not proof against this sudden assault of wonders. Fell grew less inebriated with every word Timeo spoke of the hurried clandestine wedding, the secrecy not secret enough, the attack, the rape, the rescue of Perdica from her own desire to die.

"So that's how godlets are made," he said half aloud.

If Fell meant to say more, it had to wait. On the platform, Thalac stood up with arms raised to the heavens. The feasters quelled their merriment to hear him speak. Perdica fetched Timeo back to his proper place with so much innate finesse and discretion as to leave a corps of royal Malben majordomos sobbing over their comparative servile inadequacies.

"Drifting done, my friends, my children," Thalac said.

"Drifting done," the company returned.

"Done and well done, for we have lived to see the prophecy made truth, the Watersong rising in its chosen Vessel, the freeing of the land at hand." The elder spoke joyfully, but softly, as though he feared the wrong ears might catch wind of a precious secret. "Know that I have been in communication with our brethren. By the Waterspeech, with my child Dianta's aid, I have poured the happy news into a hundred rills of rejoicing. The time is near, and only wants the word. Rise, Timeo Landbegot."

As Timeo stood, Thalac presented him with a drinking

bowl of chased silver. Timeo drank several long gulps from it and returned it to the elder, who circumspectly sipped the spirits within before giving the bowl to Perdica's waiting hands.

"Thus do we make our bond with him," Thalac told the village. "Timeo Landbegot, we are yours to command. Your song will be our salvation. At your bidding, we will unite all the Waterfolk and march against the tyrant's stronghold. Your song shall be our spear and shield, our help and our healing. Pour out, we implore, only the smallest trickle of your promised powers now. Give but a drop of your mending magic to those who thirst. Grant us that much hope, where hope has gone."

The elder knelt, his long robe pooled around him. Timeo watched all, heard all, and comprehended nothing. His head spun with strong drink too rapidly downed. The Waterfolk "wine" left Sombrunian brandy running a poor second— even diluted, it had the treacherous nature of a back-door burglary. The stuff in the silver vessel was outright assassination. He had been drinking erratically watered wine all night, but the last swig from the ceremonial bowl did him in. He was a man pummeled for hours by a small, determined toddler, only to have a marble slab fall on his skull after the child gives up.

Someone on his left was putting something into his hands. He made owl eyes at the battered harp as if expecting it to grow wings and a tail.

"Answer him." Wydru's whisper stabbed his ear. "You can't leave elder Thalac bent down like that till dawning."

"What should I say?" Timeo mumbled out of the corner of his mouth.

"What you say is up to you. He's asking you for a favor."

"Ohhhh." Timeo nodded—dangerous work with a top-heavy head. "Will he get up if I say yes?"

"He'll pass high noon on Suicides' Rock if you tell him to. Timeo, you are the Vessel of Watersong! Anything you say, we will perform. You don't have to grant him the favor; just tell him to get up if that's what bothers you." Abruptly Wydru recalled Timeo's new stature and added, "My lord."

Timeo patted his new friend's blue forearm in clumsy

camaraderie. "Never abuse power, Wydru." His lips had grown thicker since the banquet's beginning—the humidity, he supposed. "I never shall. Lord me no lordings. Be like me. Always remember you're no better than the next fellow. Don't hold yourself high and mighty. Your elder wants a favor, he gets it."

"Will you ask him what it is first, lord?"

Timeo peered at Wydru over the top of a pair of imaginary spectacles. "Never abuse power," he repeated. He tapped Thalac's shoulder. "Get up. Please. I'll do it."

Thalac's face was a study in worshipful gratitude. He left the platform, vanishing into one of the huts. A fluting confusion of excited chatter went up from all the villagers.

"What did I say? Where'd he go? Isn't he going to tell me what he wants?" Timeo turned to Wydru, baffled.

"Lord, all the favors you can give us are your songs." The blue-skinned youth adjusted the harp in Timeo's slackening grasp.

"A song? Nothing easier! I've got hundr—I mean, I think I can find the inspiration." He twiddled the strings for effect and leaped into the music.

As the first notes sounded, Wydru watched Fell raise a wine cup to his lips. His teeth clacked together on the goblet's rim. He dumped his watered wine into the earth and poured a straight measure which he dumped into himself.

Wydru's eyes watered as he heard Timeo strike a chord. Through the blur he saw Ovrin try to bring his little brother near enough to cover Keri's ears for him, but the boy pulled away. "You forget how much I always liked Timeo's music," Keri said with a smile. Ovrin only saw the smile. He was stuffing wads of Waterfolk bread in his ears.

Wydru soon realized that he was not the only one of his kinfolk to react so to their newfound savior's musicale. The Waterfolk heard the harp's pure melody and Timeo's vocal interpretation of the same tune: jaws set, eyes glazed, muscles tensed for fight or flight. One nixie with the swelling middle of early pregnancy went into a hut which sank without further ado.

Thalac emerged from his hut, his blinded daughter leaning on his arm, the other disfigured children crowding behind. Dianta shuddered against her father. Those young ones too beaten and broken to cry only whimpered as the song reached them.

"It should heal." Thalac refused to let go of his faith, though every note he heard ate away the foundations of his belief. "It *must*. He healed Perdica with a song—her spirit, and those wounds run deeper than any hurt of the body. His song *does* heal; it *does!* The prophecy does not promise it in so many words, but the stories, the old tales . . ."

Timeo sang. Dianta could not escape the sound. She felt her father force her away from his side. She sensed the changing textures in the earth underfoot as he pushed her forward, into the middle of the feasting space. Her heels dug in, resisting his efforts to bring her close to that sound. In her darkness, it was the ultimate unknown, more terrifying because she could not recognize or classify its source. She had heard something that came close to this awful noise only once before in her short life. The horror of the sight accompanying it had been one of the last things she had seen.

For that horror, she did have a name.

"*Kya'ar!*" The shriek tore from her throat. She was mortally afraid. "*Kya'ar!*"

Her father's whispered comforts were in vain. She battled to get away, fought him, broke from his arms and ran. She could not see her way, but panic made it no matter. Her heart beat out its desperate command, *Away! Away! Anywhere away from those abominable sounds!* Thalac called her name, she could hear the other Waterfolk rushing to clear her path or to catch her, the wailing of her companions in the hut rose to guide her back to them, and still Dianta ran, screaming, "Kya'ar! Kya'ar!"

Wydru saw her race end with a thump as the armored guardsman emerged from the shadows and laughed as she ran headfirst into his arms. Her fingers found Ragnar's insignia on him and she collapsed with a little moan.

He let her drop. "This one's been done," he called over one shoulder. He stepped over the child's body with as much care as for a fallen log. The troops who followed him did likewise.

By the steady light of glows and the flickering light of flames, twenty of Ragnar's elite troops filled the feasting space. Timeo stopped his song. The harp hung at his side. The Waterfolk were paralyzcd with fear and surprise. Fell was too deeply sunk in wine to do more than swallow air. Ovrin moved Keri behind him with a firm arm and would not tolerate the boy's resistance this time.

The captain of the guard swaggered up to elder Thalac. "Fine loyalty, and constant as the tides. Pledge your faith to our lord Ragnar with one breath and conspire against him with the next." He clicked his tongue theatrically loud. "If not for the *gift* you so recently sent him, our lord Ragnar'd have your whole damned village pounded back into the muck that birthed it. As it stands, you'll get off easy. One coin pays all."

Thalac's violet eyes blinked slowly. He strained to see his child's fallen body, but a sharp blow to the shoulder by the captain brought him back to immediate dealings. "What coin?" he rasped.

"Rumor's a pretty thing. Not all those who pledge faith to our master keep it so poorly as you. Waterspeech, is it called? The way some of your slimers can talk over distance? Spread grand news? A wonderful thing, your Waterspeech, Thalac. Like any speech, subject to eavesdroppers and talebearers." The guardsman grinned.

"We have come for the Vessel of Watersong."

Chapter XXIV

MAKING A SPLASH

They laid hands on Timeo almost immediately, after a cursory glance around the ring of startled faces showed them no one new but he. "Has a harp in his hands, too," one of the men announced, clinching matters. "Come along."

"Let him go," Thalac said. His voice was taut and controlled as a master archer's bowstring.

Ragnar's captain continued to smile. "Old one, count yourself lucky to be alive. We're doing you a favor, removing that one before you all march to your doom in his wake. We're saving you from a very foolish death. Our lord is still master of the magic in Elaar's Daughter. He commands worse things, as you well know. Give up your wild tales of prophecies fulfilled. You'll find your freedom in the grave soon enough. A corpse is a corpse. What difference if he dies slave or free?" To the men flanking Timeo he said, "Take him."

Thalac shouted a battle cry. A chorus of his people answered, voices thrumming on a note that reverberated through the fiber of the Lands Unknown. The land sang answer. Prongs of coral shot fom the ground. Two of Ragnar's men were impaled where they stood, others had their arms and legs ripped open by the whetted edges. Only those positioned nearest the Waterfolk escaped harm. Their swords licked into the light.

Swords of coral and black glass crossed swords of steel. Ragnar's men backed away, surprised to find fight in a

people so long subjugated. The strange blades the Waterfolk
wielded were harder than they looked, glass and coral given
greater density by powers that the wizard's guards did not
know. Elder Thalac's chosen successor threw himself on the
men who held Timeo. His dagger was mortal made, relic of
long-dead trading parties. It was a blade Ragnar's men could
understand, but understanding did not save them from its
sting. Blood ran red over pale green skin.

The wizard's troops counterattacked. Their captain cursed
them out of shock into action. "Hold them back, damn you
all! Make me a path! We'll all die unless—" His men
rallied, four thrusting themselves between their leader and
Thalac. The Waterfolk elder gave a second cry in his own
tongue and a wickedly pitchforked spar of coral burst
through the soil into his hand. He laid open one man's head
from temple to chin, but the captain got away.

Wydru was with Timeo, shielding his left flank while
Thalac's successor fought on his right. "Wydru, give me a
sword!" Timeo cried.

"Dangerous," the blue-skinned youth panted, fending off
one of Ragnar's men. "If you fight—they might kill you."

"They're killing my people!"

"We're *fighting*, blast it! If we die fighting, they're not
killing us like cattle! But if they kill you, we've lost forever
any reason to fight back again."

Timeo protested and tried to wrench up a coral branch for
his own use. His palms came away empty and raw as
chopped meat. He did what he could, swinging his harp over
the heads of his protectors, trying to strike Ragnar's soldiers.
The few blows he landed did about as much harm as the
buffet he'd dealt Randal earlier.

"*Stop* that!" Wydru shouted. "You're only getting in our
way, my lord. Stand still!"

Timeo obeyed, reluctantly. Up on the platform, he had an
excellent view of the battle. He had to admit that Ragnar
trained his elite troops well. They were fearsomely outnumbered, yet they managed to hold the villagers back. Waterfolk females fought beside the males, both sexes showing a
frighteningly wide spectrum of weapon skill. Most of them
were patent amateurs, using their blades like whips or

broomsticks or batons. They left their guard open, and many of them fell to cunning thrusts from seasoned swordsmen.

But there were others to take their places, and others too who knew how to use a sword with concise, deadly art. Some drove Ragnar's men back onto the coral spikes or into the cook fires, some preferred to finish the job with their own blades, and some drew out their private battles, deliberately extending each duel to pay back years of fear, years of torment.

Amid the battle, Timeo saw Ovrin, Fell, and Keristor being hurried out of sword's reach by Perdica. The nixie had no trouble with Fell, who would have outdistanced her had he known the safest way out of the village. Ovrin and Keri kept dropping back. The boy seemed to be seeking something. He dashed away from his big brother, heading the way the troops had first entered the village. Ovrin ran after him, and Perdica followed, changing herself into the semblance of a fire-thrown shadow to avoid detection.

Keri stopped, bent over a small, crumpled shape. Timeo could not see what it was, for dawn was hours off, and many of the standing lights around the feasting space lay toppled by the fighting. Whatever it was, Ovrin scooped it up at Keri's insistence. A shadow touched the big man's arm and turned into Perdica. Fell was right behind her, face like tallow. The four of them sprinted between two of the huts and vanished from Timeo's sight.

Maybe if I sing, he thought. *If I could make myself heard over his racket, though . . . No; better not to try. My people are winning! Let them know their own victory! It will hearten them for our next battle against the wizard. Gods send that more of his men are as cowardly as that captain! If there ever was—*

The earth and the sky and the bones in his body all shook with a roar that covered the Waterfolk village. A shining whiter than the winter moon blazed even the memory of daylight out of Timeo's mind. The battle froze in a lightning bolt's glare that did not fade, but clawed away all possibility of shade or shadow. There was black and there was white, nothing between. There was life and there was death, and not even the whisper of mercy to soften the line dividing them.

"Kya'ar! Kya'ar!" Dianta's panicked cry came thundering back from every side. As a warning, it came too late.

The thing they called Kya'ar was on them.

Timeo saw it in a rush of whiteness, a coruscation of rainbowed energy.

The shaggy mass loomed into the village. Waterfolk fled: Polished black talons scythed them down. Brightness auraed out from a core of burning ice. Ragnar's men cheered hoarsely and flocked to the shelter of the thing's slashing claws. They tore the silver cuffs from their wrists and threw them at it, a weird sacrifice. Pulsing runes stood out, hard black against white shagginess, as the cuffs melted into the creature's body. Its roar skreeked and grated through an impossible scale as the beast came on.

Huts sank to left and right as the Waterfolk plunged into sanctuary. The true-made fighters among them stood where they were, refusing to flee. Timeo caught a flash of his former jailor's face, chinless jaw firm, stance resolute.

It was a flash of sight that ended in a shower of blood. A white paw clubbed down from an unknown height and smashed in the side of its victim's skull. Webbed hands dug into the moist ground in a death spasm.

Brocaded robes flew out behind Thalac in a phoenix tail. He ran to take his place with his successor and Wydru, defending Timeo. A prisming haze of brilliance clung to the Kya'ar. Squint as he would, Timeo's sight could not penetrate it. The beast crossed the feasting space as a cloud of living auroras. Ragnar's men ran beside it, using their weapons to fatal advantage on those Waterfolk temporarily blinded by the creature's brightness or only immobilized with terror. Those too brave or hardy to be felled by mere sight of the Kya'ar fought back. The monster batted them aside, broke their bones like barley straw while the soldiers laughed.

The bravest fled. All the huts were gone, and so they lit out across the marshes, raced for the beckoning shelter of the Great Rushy Forest, headed for the lands lying even farther from the River Salmlis. Eight of Ragnar's troops were all that were left to face Timeo and his guardians, but they were eight in the shadow of the Kya'ar.

Elder Thalac thrust once at the beast with his coral

weapon—and the monster gutted him with one swipe of a paw. The coral pitchfork shattered, shards wounding Wydru. Timeo saw Ragnar's captain in the lee of the beast's right flank, probing the rainbow shell of living light with an iron rod. He wielded it purposefully, directing the Kya'ar's every action. When Thalac died, his jackal smile was nearly as bright as the Kya'ar's aura. He nodded towards the dead elder's chosen successor.

"No!" Timeo placed himself between the beast and the two Waterfolk males still left alive beside him. His eyes burned as he stared into the Kya'ar's brightness. Tears cooled his blazing cheeks. "Call him off," he told the captain. "I will come with you."

"That was never open to debate, my friend," the captain drawled. He twirled his iron wand lazily. "After you."

Timeo left the Waterfolk village conducted by four of Ragnar's surviving soldiers. The captain waited until he thought his prisoner was a satisfactory distance away from the village before giving his remaining three men the nod.

Two more bodies fell.

The royal palace of the Waterfolk was more magnificent than Timeo's fog-borne visions could tell. It soared out of the surrounding landscape like a queen among goose girls, all silver and amber and rose.

The journey had been a short one. Timeo marched with Ragnar's men as night receded into dawn and dawn turned to early morning, but it was not yet noon by the time they reached the palace.

Throughout the march, over bog and water meadow, through blooming stands of outsized chickweed and boneset, Timeo kept glancing here, there, and everywhere around him in a markedly agitated way. At last Ragnar's captain felt constrained to call a short halt and inform his captive, "The beast's not with us."

"Where did it go?" Timeo asked, eyes still rolling, seeing death in every flicker of whiteness glimpsed through the gigantic weeds.

"Back to its master and ours. And yours, if you're smart. All power in the Lands Unknown comes from Ragnar's hands or is destroyed. If a monster like the Kya'ar is under his sway, what can you do against him, prophecy or no prophecy?''

Timeo said nothing. They trudged on, out of the wetlands, over a laughing stream bridged by arches of spun glass that sang eternal harmony with the rushing water, and into the wizard's stronghold.

In the desolation of the Waterfolk village, Wydru groaned and turned over. He felt dawn's sweet dew on his wounds, and smelled the flowery breezes from the east. His blood trickled down over his ribs. He could not resist the urge to touch it, to hold his scarlet fingers up to the newborn day.

"A good hour to die," he murmured.

"A better to live," a familiar voice whispered.

He was dreaming. Dianta's scarred face tilted into his field of vision. She was smiling at him. Her eyes were still gone, yet Wydru could not shake the feeling that she *saw* him. He winced with silent pain—partly to test the dream's illusion, partly because a deep breath set his lungs afire. She startled, registered sympathy, concern. He groped for her and saw her draw away from the blood, then steel herself and clasp his hand decisively. She did not grope for his hand at all.

"Dianta, how . . . ?"

Her lips curved up around a single echoing word: *miracle* . . . The darkness took him before he could question more.

Chapter XXV

OLD MAN RIVER

"So you are the legend," Ragnar said. "I have never met a legend."

Timeo knelt at the foot of the black throne. Two strong guardsmen made sure he continued to kneel. He tried to put on an expression of appropriate sobriety and dedication, a look that would contain respect for a worthy foe without including fear. It was no use. From the moment his escort had allowed him to lift his head and look at the wizard directly, Timeo had only wanted to gasp in sympathy and ask the old man whether he were in much pain.

Ragnar was a coil of twisted bones, a knot of incredibly warped joints and joinings. Whatever should lie straight in a man was crooked, and the rightfully crooked made stiff as any iron wand. Not even the traditional voluminous robes of his calling could disguise it. A gray beard and moustache like hanks of live moss dangled from Ragnar's chin and upper lip, the hair so patchy and thin that the sickness-mottled skin beneath was visible. The hair on his head was a dull yellowish white, streaks of it lying in comet trails over his humped back and canted shoulders.

Only in the wizard's eyes could Timeo see what he had once been. The twinned image of a young man, strong and arrogant and bold, burned crimson in the blue depths where ordinary men's eyes would have pupils.

"You may speak," the wizard said.

"I—" Timeo could find nothing to say. A handful of

ridiculous demands jumped into his thoughts, to be rejected one by one by his common sense: *Release my people! Set the Waterfolk free! Depart from the Lands Unknown! I conjure you by my power as the Vessel of Watersong, begone!* All foolish, all useless.

Where was his power when the guards dragged him over the castle bridge? He had tried singing to them, an impromptu whose refrain was *Go to sleep, go to sleep.* The captain had boxed his ear and told him to shut up or lose some teeth.

I suppose the power might come and go, the way my Aunt Ursula's curse does, he thought. *Or else be linked to contact with water.* He looked down at the river rushing beneath the castle bridge. The arches of the span were ivory, the ribs of some unimaginable monster. He remembered his mother's pet dragon Shkaah, and how the beast had refused to be charmed by the young Timeo's songs. *Of course I was on dry land at the time; not like the marsh where the Waterfolk village stands. There you can't tell earth from water. I shall have to bide my time when I'm in Ragnar's keep. Either I must ask for a glass of water before I sing, or else stall the wizard until my mother can reach me. Her magic must be at least as strong as his.* The idea of being rescued by Mizriel rankled, but it was preferable to the alternatives.

Ragnar leaned forward, still awaiting a reply. Timeo was mute. He was not the man to stand before a tyrant and command him to turn his empire on ear when the power backing his words was undependable. A more sensible statement came to mind—*Please don't hurt me*—and was rejected too as being unworthy, albeit honest.

"Would it help were you to sing your words?" The wizard put a note of false concern into his voice. His hands clawed the arms of the throne like a falcon taking purchase on its perch. "The legends about you are not specific enough for my liking. Still, that is the way with legends. *Can* you do nothing but sing?"

"I wouldn't call it singing," the captain muttered somewhere behind Timeo.

"*Silence!*" Ragnar's voice crackled through the vaulted throne room. The vast hall was deserted except for Timeo, the wizard, the two guards, and the captain. Even the fish that had swum within the crystal pillars in Timeo's fog visions were gone. Slime obscured the crystal. Water weeds choked the inside of the pillars with brown rot.

In a softer voice, Ragnar asked, "Are you what the rumors say? Are you the prophesied Vessel of Watersong? Or are you made from the cloth of dreams—an empty vessel that the Waterfolk have filled with their dearest longings? Are you just another unfortunate who has taken refuge in my kingdom, only to have prophecy wished upon you? You can tell me. I swear on Helagarde that I will not harm you. Surely you have heard enough about me to know that oath is binding."

"You are Morgeld's willing servant." Timeo nodded. "I've heard that much about you."

"True; it is very true." The wizard settled back painfully on his throne. "A servant, alas, long overdue for his proper wages. I took the Lands Unknown at my master's bidding. I hold them at his pleasure, and will do so until he gives me word to move on."

Timeo cleared his throat. "What does Morgeld want of the Waterfolk?"

Ragnar's laugh was the rumble of wave-tossed pebbles. "Of them? Nothing. It is their land."

"The Lands Unknown are rich in gems? Fertile?"

"Is Morgeld a farmer, to covet fertile land? Does the lord of Helagarde, all amethyst above the waves, need a greater jewel? Greed is for lesser beings." The wizard stroked his sparse beard. "The richness of the Lands Unknown lies not in *what* they are, but *where*."

He gestured, and a map of the Twelve Kingdoms burned in the air. "See how the kingdoms of Leyaeli and Glytch lie between the Lands Unknown and the Naîmlo Wood. Glytch in particular is of interest to my master. They say Tor, his most loyal servant, came from there—but sentiment has nothing to do with it. With Leyaeli sealing her northern border and the Opalza Sea her southern, Glytch is by far the most isolated of the Twelve Kingdoms. Oh, she has commerce by sea, but in the season of storms she is cut off. The rulers of Leyaeli recognize their power over her, and do not know the meaning of *enough*. They charge appropriate tolls on all their highways, to say nothing of import duties, taxes on transient goods, export licenses . . ."

The map melted in a shower of stars. "No sane man enters the Naîmlo Wood. No one comes out again who tries. The only free portal out of Glytch is this realm—and thanks to me, it has been shut and locked. My magic guards the door. Much can be done with a man who feels himself alone, forgotten by his fellows. How much more, then, may be done with an entire kingdom? That is what Morgeld desires: a place to begin his final work."

A gentle footfall brushed across the silk rugs spread over the throne dais. Timeo gaped at an apparition so enchanting as to still his heart, so familiar as to crush it. The ondine who floated up to Ragnar's right hand wore a gown less green than her willowy skin, sunbursts of carnelian and chrysoprase worked into the flowing panels of the skirt. Brown topazes like newly turned autumn leaves were held in the web of gold around her throat, the tendriled diadem on her raven hair. A paler, more simply dressed, less overwhelming version of her beauty trailed in her wake. Head bent, eyes downcast, Cattail passed behind her father's throne to stand on Ragnar's left.

The wizard extended his hands to either side. Timeo could hear the joints grate as agony shot across Ragnar's features. "Welcome, my loves. I have the honor to present you with something truly unique for your amusement this day: a captive legend."

The crowned ondine peered at Timeo from beneath heavy eyelids smeared with golden dust. "Is he the Vessel of Watersong?"

"So I have heard." The wizard's mouth twitched.

The ondine shrugged. "Then kill him."

At once Cattail flung herself at Ragnar's feet, head resting in his lap. "Father, no!"

"Be still." The crowned ondine's voice was laden with contempt. "I will not allow further treachery."

"Now, now, Chelona, those are harsh words for our beloved daughter."

"Beloved by you, perhaps," Chelona snapped. Her eyes were harder than stonewood. "Beloved because you are blind to what she's done to you."

"If I am blind, my healing is at hand. And is she the only one?" A dangerously knowing note crept into Ragnar's voice and he stared at the crowned ondine. His glance was a sword to pierce the secrets of the bone. Chelona's haughty look faltered. She leaned a hand on the throne to recover her poise.

"Even if she were, you'd never believe it," she said, forcing her voice to remain firm. "All these years, and always an excuse found for her every failing. For mine, none. Would you be like the gods, my lord, begetting your own consort?"

Ragnar's words were cool and measured. "And should I so choose, wife, who is to stop me? Not even my lord Morgeld questions my doings these days. In these lands, I am more than king. My will is law. Could the gods claim more?"

Cattail raised her head, a delicate shiver running over her skin. "Father, you can't mean—"

He patted her sleek, dark head. "A jest, my love. Merely a jest, such as you know your mother and I delight to barter." His smile for Chelona was rigid.

"Not king for long, if you persist in following bad advice," Chelona maintained stubbornly. "If you would condemn the real traitor—"

"Never mind," Ragnar said. "We are all traitors here. It is only just that we should experience betrayal." He sighed. "Cattail is right, wife. We must not kill him. If he is not the Vessel of Watersong, he does us no harm. He might even make a good addition to our human servants—he could become our court minstrel. I tire of the unreal perfection of every song the Waterfolk sing. He knows how to handle a harp, I'm told."

"And if he is the prophecy come true?" Chelona demanded. "Will you invite your doom to dine with us?"

Ragnar attempted to shrug. His pain shattered the gesture. Stiff-jawed he said, "If he is the Vessel of Watersong, he has healing powers. The tales claim he saved one of the Waterfolk. If this is so, if he can prove the prophecy, then he shall have anything he asks of me, short of the rule of this kingdom. Even you."

"I will never consent to—"

"You will do as I command." He returned his attention to Timeo, but the young man was not looking at the wizard. His eyes were fixed on Cattail, who still clung to her father's knees and kept her face studiously averted from the kneeling prisoner.

"Well, Timeo Landbegot—that is your name?—Good. At least the rumors are dependable so far. You have heard my oath. You are safe from me, and I will see to it that Chelona does not touch you, on pain of her own death. You must excuse my wife. She is of the least branch of the Waterfolk ruling house—the royal blood is but a drop in her veins, not even recognized by her people. She has come to cherish the pretensions of her place as my consort, and will do anything to preserve them . . . and me. Answer me without fear or prevarication: What are you?"

Timeo tried to stand. The guards pushed him back down until Ragnar made a sharp motion calling them off. He rose to his feet. He would not take the coward's path. "I am the Vessel of Watersong."

"Ahhhh." The wizard's breath was the outrushing tide, swallowing the little gasp that rose to Cattail's lips. Joy sparkled in Ragnar's eyes where the image of a healthy, straight-limbed young man still burned. He thrust his ravaged face forward. "Then heal me, and I shall acknowledge two masters. Heal me now, my lord," he rasped.

The throne room grew oppressive with the silence that followed. A guard shifted weight from foot to foot and his armor creaked louder than a thunderclap. Cattail's fingers tangled in a fold of her father's robes.

Chelona broke the silence with a derisive snort. "He stares like a gutted salmon! He can't heal you any more than he can fly. If I die, I die, but I will not choke on what needs saying. You are pathetic, Ragnar! Will you abase yourself to every fool who claims to be this precious Vessel? When you hear the true Watersong, it will be your death."

The wizard jerked a gnarled hand at her. Chelona gurgled and fell in convulsions to the floor. Cattail lunged for her mother's contorting body, but Ragnar seized his daughter's shoulder and held her back with a strength incredible for such twisted bones.

"It will pass," Ragnar said. "She will remember herself

better, next time. Let her be." As he spoke, the convulsions subsided; Chelona lay spent on the rugs. Ragnar's blazing eyes were on Timeo again. "Well?"

"Heal you?" Timeo's mouth worked itself into a half-dozen different shapes as he sought a reply. "But—but you're a wizard! Why can't you heal yourself?"

"Fool! Did you spring full-grown from the Lands Unknown like the Waterfolk's cursed hovels? Do you know nothing of the wizardly and the witchborn? Would I remain in this prison of pain and paralysis if I could heal myself? Magic is change, but those who hold change within their power can never change themselves! That is the boundary at which all magic wielders must stop—a boundary even more solid than the one I myself set around this kingdom, barring all mages from entry while I live!"

"Barring . . . You mean the fog keeps out other wizards?"

"*And* warlocks. *And* witches. *And* any who acquire the hidden arts through birth or study."

Timeo's stomach plummeted. *She won't come,* he thought. *She can't. I'm on my own.* Somehow the realization that he was forcibly free of his mother's interference did not come as the jolt of pure pleasure he'd fantasized.

The wizard was still speaking. "No barrier to those who are magicless or whose magic is their being. Demons and elementals come and go freely where they like, bound by nothing but their whims, and mortals, and those who are more than mortal." A nerve flicked across Ragnar's creek. "Heal me."

"No," Timeo said. Suddenly his way was clear.

"Father, you ask the impossible," Cattail spoke frantically. "He's only a simple mortal musician. He didn't heal anyone. The rumors have exaggerated before. You yourself said that spies often color their reports in hopes of greater rewards."

"Spies who serve me so have their reward in death. I despise a liar; bear that in mind, Timeo Landbegot!"

"I do not lie. I will not heal you."

"Because you can not! Because you mistrust me and think to gain some unnamed privilege by calling yourself the Vessel of Watersong!"

-

"I am no liar. I am what I claim to be." Timeo's calm reply surprised himself. The wizard's tight-leashed look of growing fury did not faze him. He spoke his piece as dispassionately as if ordering lamprey pasties from Mistress Bruling. "My song has already healed one of your subjects, as you have heard. She deserved healing, after being attacked and abused by your men. I will not heal the victim and reward the one who caused her suffering. I will not use a power meant for good in the service of evil. I will not use it to heal you."

"You have no power to use!" Ragnar shouted.

"Believe what you like. I have nothing to prove to you."

"Then prove nothing to me, Timeo Landbegot. Be welcome as guest in my house forever, and only show your power to another of my most welcome guests." He signaled the guards, who grabbed Timeo's arms.

"Take him to the Kya'ar!"

Chapter XXVI

IF IT FEELS GOOD, DEW IT

"Here." The captain of the guard picked up a hunk of cold meat from one of the long worktables in the palace kitchens and tossed it to Timeo. "Don't get killed on an empty stomach." He tore off a second portion of the same unidentified carcass for himself and leaned against the huge fireplace, gnawing.

Timeo turned the fatty morsel over and over between his hands, looking doubtful. The two guards who had accompanied them this far had gone off on an unnamed mission shortly before. He and the captain were the only ones in the kitchens—four separate chambers, each with its own bake oven, hearth, and floor-to-ceiling rack of wine tuns. There were no cobwebs or dust, yet in the lands of the Waterfolk, long disuse left other evidence. Slime molds and fungi in their multicolored profusion spread over every available wooden surface. Lichen and moss slid down the stone walls, and at the bottom, where pooled water lapped two fingers deep, blue-green algae made their home. The only difference between this kitchen and the others through which they had passed was that the tables were clean and the fireplace smelled of recent burning.

"Go on, eat it. It hasn't lain there long enough for the fuzz to touch it. Lord Ragnar's lady felt like giving a royal fête not four days ago to show off her new gown. This was

211

the very kitchen where they prepared the banquet.'' He laughed like a seal. ''A jolly banquet, like the rest of them, with all the guests no more than puppets of the pearl! Oh, they smiled and said how fine she looked, but she could tell the truth of things. Stormed out of her own party early, she did. The garrison's been living on the leftovers since. She never learns.''

Timeo took an exploratory nibble at the meat and found it palatable. ''What do you mean, puppets of the pearl?''

The captain answered with the air of a very bored man with nothing better to fill a waiting time. ''You're an ignorant one. Every fighter needs a shield as well as a sword. A great warrior can have his sword knocked away and still put up a struggle with just his shield. He does it long enough, he might get the chance to take his opponent's sword out too. Our master's got his sword in the Kya'ar, but his shield's Elaar's Daughter. I tell you, you poor doomed bastard, I wish you'd be reasonable with Lord Ragnar and stay alive just long enough so you could see that pearl! I came into the Lands Unknown flying from sixteen counts of thievery, low and high, but I swear I'd risk my skin all over again if I could've been there to watch Ragnar bear off a prize like Elaar's Daughter. They say he stole her from the Sea-Witch's own hand! Ah, she's a princess among gems, blue and cool as the depths of the sea, and filled with sorcery that . . . Well, it'd take more than one wizard's lifetime to study his way into so much magic.''

The heavy step of the other two guards echoed among the elaborately carved stone rafters. They halted smartly before their lounging commander. ''All ready, sir,'' said one.

''And men at the exits?''

''Picked from one of the regular patrol units.''

''Good.'' He threw down his half-eaten meat and beckoned Timeo. ''Come on. Your time's done here.''

Timeo's legs melted. He pressed the gobbet of meat to his chest as if it held salvation. ''Where are you taking me?''

''You heard where, when you made our master lose his temper like that.'' The captain couldn't help chuckling over the memory. ''You're being put into the Kya'ar's den.''

''But he promised! Ragnar swore by Helagarde that he wouldn't hurt me!''

"Morgeld understands the workings of such oaths. Helagarde's more than well populated with men of law, they say. Ragnar won't lay a finger on you. What the Kya'ar does is another story."

All the blood left Timeo's face. A blinding white nightmare covered his sight. He began to shake.

The captain's shove sent him lurching into the worktable. "Bear up, little man! The beast's den is a big place. It might be days before it finds you. You might even manage to pick your way out of that maze of cellars down below us—and the men we've posted to greet you will give you a nice sharp welcome if you do." He snapped his fingers at the two guards. "Take him before he wets himself."

"In this sogged-over place, who'll notice?"

Terror brought a mist more powerful than the cloud Ragnar had wrapped around his usurped kingdom. Timeo felt the guards hustle him over the unevenly paved floors, but only as a peripheral experience: It might have been happening to a stranger. When he finally came back into his own skin, it was to the sound of an iron door slamming shut somewhere above and in back of him. He took a step, trod air, and tumbled to the bottom of a granite stairway. He got up groaning, until he remembered what was lurking down here. Better to ache in silence.

There was light. A yellow alabaster bowl the size of a ladle stood on a shelf a span above Timeo's head. A gentle, steady glow illuminated the translucent stone. It wasn't much, but seen against such total darkness it was sweet as sunlight. He took it down and cupped it in both hands. There was no heat. The bowl was filled with a velvety tousle of plant life that emitted its own radiance.

By the glow's light, Timeo saw the stairs down which he had fallen. Looking the other way his vision stretched through a series of unadorned archways that seemed to go on forever into the shadows. He touched the nearest one and felt cool, smooth marble. Water plashed somewhere ahead. His mouth was dry from fear, and too much salt had been lavished on the bit of meat he'd eaten. If he stayed where he was, he might starve or die of thirst with no guarantee

that the Kya'ar wouldn't find him. He followed the sound
of water.

The captain had spoken of cellars. As Timeo went on, he
saw that Ragnar's man had not lied. Other archways led off
from the main alleyway, some leading into further corridors,
some giving on open storage rooms. Timeo stuck his lamp
into one of these, banishing the dark of years. He saw chests
that had been torn open into slivers of wood, their contents
scattered over the damp floors. Silver threads tarnished,
velvets rotted away.

It was the same story in the next storage chamber he
investigated. Here, there were caskets such as ladies use to
keep their jewels. They had been cracked open like walnuts,
diamonds and other precious stones blinking up dismally out
of the sludge. Timeo thought of the captain and his past
history of thieving. What would prevent one of Ragnar's
men from filling a sack with this bounty and sneaking off to
a new life in one of the larger cities? Enough wealth could
insure that no questions would be asked even by the most
scrupulous neighbors.

He found the answer when he knelt to pick up what he
thought was a ruler's orb. He had never seen one carved
from jade before.

The empty sockets of the greening skull told him the tale
of who stood guard over Ragnar's idle treasures. Deep
parallel clefts rent the mossy bone. He remembered stark
black talons and the Kya'ar's fury.

On he went, avoiding the storage rooms now, fearful of
what he might find. He had tried to keep going in a straight
line, but the alleyway he followed ended at one point,
forcing him to choose between two identical branches. A
little further down the passage of his choice and a three-way
split confronted him. He dared a chamber where ruined cloth
lay strewn about, hoping to unravel a piece and use the
thread to guide him, should he want to backtrack. The fibers
came apart between his fingers. He ventured into another
where unstrung pearls spilled from a broken cask. He tried
dropping a trail of these to mark his route, but they sank
invisible beneath the dirty water.

His feet itched dreadfully. He kicked off his shoes and let
the water cool his toes. Contact with his father's element

made him feel better but did not cause any sudden welling of magical power that he could feel.

How could it? he reasoned with himself. *I am the Vessel of Water*song. *I must combine the two if I am to call upon my powers.* Wistfully he scanned yet another endless corridor of arches. *I wish I could heal my own thirst. This water underfoot's not fit to drink, and my tongue's ready to burst out of my mouth. I wonder if my ancestors kept wine down here? It would be sensible of them.*

The thought of deep-cooled wine spurred him to renewed explorations. The glow he carried was better than any regular torch in that it could never consume all its fuel and go out. At any rate, it showed no sign of failing just yet. Thirst heartened Timeo to look into every storage chamber he passed, and any dead men's bones he found could get their own drinks.

A cat-whisker breeze tickled his skin. He breathed fresh air and hunted it to its source, another of the numberless cellar chambers. No rich cloths, no jewels covered the murky floors here. Timeo counted fourteen fat barrels with their telltale spigots before he dove for the nearest one and slurped gushing wine straight from the tap.

It was Waterfolk wine. It was unwatered.

A little later, Timeo filled the chamber with "Bagonwort's Lament," an original composition of which he was suddenly most inordinately fond.

"And do I sleep or do I dream
Or do I waking wander here,
Out in the moonlight by the stream
Where all the frogs sing very clear?
Oh would my love were in my arms,
And we were far across the sea!
But she is not, and I am not,
And there together not are we."

There was more. There was always more. Timeo must have known on some level of his mind that all good things must come to an end, which was why his songs kept developing further verses and complex codas.

"Bagonwort's Lament" was the worst offender in a series

of ear-affronting compositions. Timeo had been working on it for years, and he still wasn't sure whether he wanted Bagonwort's beloved to drink the potion and have it turn out to be poison or have it turn out to be a sleeping draught, or have Bagonwort *think* she was poisoned and kill himself or only pretend to kill himself, or wander around lamenting until she woke or merely run away with the faithful serving maid who had been saving him from committing suicide every fifth verse or so.

"Star-crossed lovers," Timeo muttered. He sat haunch deep in the water, his arm around one of his wine-barrel audience, and took another handful of the grape to banish that feeling of creeping damp. "Ought to take the lot of 'em out and toss 'em off a balcony."

"It's been done," said a beautiful baritone voice behind him.

Timeo whipped his head around and caught it before it hit the floor. After anchoring it back where it belonged, he peered after the voice but saw nothing more than the oak casks.

"I'm here," the voice returned. "Back of the pile you're leaning on. Just a little to starboard of the port." Rich chuckles bounded from stone to stone of the cellar walls.

"I don't get it," Timeo said.

A sigh gusted over his face. "Ah welladay! I was always better at minstrelry than jest! Come on, seek me, brother. I won't hurt you."

"I've heard *that* one a lot these days," Timeo groused as he hauled himself up by the wine barrels. "Look where it got me." He stumbled around the pile as the voice directed. He found nothing.

"In here, brother." The voice now had a resonant quality and seemed to come from one of the upended barrels. Timeo tapped it experimentally and was rewarded with a deep rattling sound. The lid swiveled up and the voice emerged sounding normal.

"Go ahead, brother, have a look. It's not the first time you've seen a dead man's bones. Be a lot more remarkable if you were to see those of a live 'un!"

If that were meant as another jest, the humor missed its audience. The unwatered wine decided it did not like the housing conditions in Timeo's stomach and pounded on the walls, wanting out. Timeo swallowed very hard, cold sweat trickling down the small of his back.

"Come now! You're not *afraid*, are you?" the voice taunted. "I can no more harm you than fly! Oh, very well. Don't look in the barrel. I'll come out."

"Please—no—you needn't trouble—"

Timeo's protests were passed over. A ghost as soft and smudgy as a gray kitten tumbled out between the staves. He was a small, stout fellow, his thinning hair the same indistinct fog color as the rest of him. Only his eyes shone with mischief's brightness, and the heavily jeweled medallions around his neck shot white sparks from the cut gems' every facet.

"Greetings, brother minstrel," the phantom said. "Tyveen of Sigraton at your service."

Chapter XXVII

DOWN BY THE OLD MAELSTROM

Denial and delight chased each other back and forth across Timeo's tongue. One moment he rejected the possibility that his childhood idol, minstrel of minstrels, could be haunting these subterranean purviews, and the next he was gabbling about how very glad and honored he was to make Tyveen of Sigraton's afterdeath acquaintance.

"I wrote one of my very first songs in your honor, sir! Would you like to hear it?"

"No."

Timeo's face fell with the full weight of Waterfolk wine pooled in his chin. No tracehound ever looked more mournful. In a kindlier voice, the phantom added, "I'd think you'd have better things to do right now than entertain a dead man. I know all about these cellars. I could be more helpful to you as guide than audience."

"It would be good to get out of here," Timeo admitted. "But Ragnar's captain has placed men at every exit. They'd cut me down in an instant even if you did bring me out alive past the Kya'ar."

"*That* thing." The ghost shuddered itself from opacity to transparency and back. "We've crossed paths several times. I was glad of a little company—eternity's longer than anyone ever told me—but the beast has no conversation."

"Few beasts do, sir."

"Aha, but I *sang* to it first." Tyveen laid a finger beside his nose. It passed right through.

Timeo understood. The great Tyveen of Sigraton was famed for charming human speech out of rocks, sticks, even the dour fisherfolk of Sumnerol. If he could not communicate with the Kya'ar, it must be a monster indeed. "Did the Kya'ar . . . kill you?"

"Ten thousand blown bellows, brother, no! I was well and truly a corpse encasked by the time the Kya'ar first fustied up these cellars."

This was a puzzling revelation for Timeo. "The tales and songs all tell of how you sang so well that the sun became enamored of you and swept you into the sky. No one ever saw you alive again."

"Why would they, except as a fall of ashes after the wedding night?" Tyveen floated up and crossed his legs in midair. The ghost of a white clay pipe grew from his lips, and the smoke of good Leyaeli tobacco haunted the air with its distinctive aroma. "Nay, brother, less fiery females than that were the end of me. Like all of our fraternity, I had in my power the minstrel's curse—to condemn a man to love eternally, hope or no hope, the chosen of his heart. I never used it, and I think the curse took offense, for it turned itself on me when I set foot over the threshold of this palace, so long ago."

Tyveen hummed a little tune, conjuring the smoke of his pipe into the semblance of an ondine dressed in regal garments. "She was all the dreams of love and none of its rude awakenings, a princess of her people. I was royalty, in my own way, so I didn't see why she wouldn't want me as much as I did her. I tried to bring myself to her notice in the usual fashion—sad ballads of ladies who don't recognize their humble suitor's worth until too late, and kill themselves for being so stupid. Alas, most of those ladies ended this life by leaping off cliffs into the sea. To a princess of the Waterfolk, that would be a pleasure outing. I persisted, though, blind to the fact that she loved another. I persisted right up until her wedding day. She was made a bride, a wife, and a queen all at once. I went into the cellars during the bridal feast, while they were still drinking her health above stairs."

The phantom minstrel smiled faintly over his past passion. "I drank her health and my death together. The wine flowed too sluggishly from the bung for my liking, so I tilted the lid back and stuck my head in, swilling like a pig. Have you noticed how strong Waterfolk make their wine?"

"Oh yes."

"Well, I didn't until it was too late. I don't know whether I tumbled into this barrel and drowned before I drank it all or simply turned my brains to must and had 'em dribble out my ears. There was drunk for you, brother! I was dead nigh twenty years before I was sober. When I did venture above stairs to see whether my princess was sorry I'd died, I found a human on the throne. Ugly, too."

"The wizard Ragnar. He slaughtered the royal house. I think"—Timeo looked shyly at his idol—"I think it must have been my grandmother you loved."

Tyveen slapped his thighs, to no effect. "All the more reason to help you out of here! Follow me. I know this maze like the Idiots' Galliard." He leaped from his invisible seat and started from the room.

Timeo stayed where he was. "But—what of the guards?"

Tyveen stopped short. "True. Might you threaten them with the minstrel's curse?"

"It's not the worst curse in the world."

"Eternal love and devotion, willy-nilly, not the worst curse in the world? There speaks a man who knows no poetry!"

"Well, the guards know no poetry either, and I'd still have a sword in the guts before they learned how badly I'd cursed them."

"Hmm, I suppose posthumous satisfaction isn't everyone's cup of tea. Very well, then; we'll give you a weapon." The ghost bounded over to another of the wine casks and patted it fondly. It was only half the size of its kin. "Open her up." Timeo hesitated. "*Open* her! My bones are in one barrel alone. I didn't die in episodes."

Now Timeo did as he was told. The lid came off easily, but no pungent bouquet of Waterfolk wine escaped.

"She's dry inside," Tyveen said. "Only thing the Waterfolk make better than wine is watertight casks to keep it pure in. They always have a half measure like this down here.

Sometimes they don't need a whole tun above stairs, or they can't spare all the men it'd take to hoist the big ones. So they decant into these. Reach in, reach in. She's dry, but she's not empty."

Timeo felt around in the small cask and pulled out a leather bag. Something by turns hard and squashy met his fingers as he probed the sack. A sickly look overcame his features.

"No, it's not anything dead," Tyveen said, rolling his eyes heavenward over Timeo's qualms. "Undo the drawstring."

Like some arthritic spider, the object emerged one long, stiff limb at a time, all connected to a saggy middle. When it got up to five, it stopped being a spider and decided to be bagpipes instead.

"The kind you can sing along with while you play!" Tyveen beamed fondly at the splay-droned monstrosity in Timeo's arms. "See the bellows? Pump 'em under your arm to keep the bag going and— But why am I telling you what every good minstrel knows?" His cloudy brows rolled together. "You *can* play the pipes?"

"We studied all the most common instruments of minstrelry at the university, sir," Timeo replied. Two of the drones clacked and clashed against each other in a duel to the death, while the bag and bellows squirmed to escape a stranger's embrace.

"Who calls the bagpipes common? Even with a broken heart and no will to live, I took care to secure my many-throated siren safe from damp and decay before plunging into a sot's demise."

"It's a very nice set of pipes, sir, but . . . against men with swords?"

Tyveen reared back his head and glared at Timeo. "As you are a university man, I will excuse your ignorance. Were I alive and in good form, I could clear a room of fully armed ogres with but a single piped rendition of 'The Hasty Eunuchs' Branle'! When rightly played, there is no weapon deadlier than the primed bagpipe."

Timeo held the glowing bowl high. "Which way now?"

"Through there, then left, then up the flight of steps you'll find in the niche at the back of the storeroom.'' Tyveen's impalpable arm extended itself to three times normal length to describe the way Timeo had to go.

As he reeled in his misty appendage, Timeo asked him, ''Couldn't you come with me? Seeing a ghost would frighten off the guard faster than any bagpipe solo.''

''Perhaps. I can not come, though.''

''Why not?''

The phantom sighed. ''Riddles were never my specialty; I was too fond of knowing all the answers. What happens to a man after death is a riddle with too many responses. I died in drunken despair, yet I did not wake in Helagarde. I died believing in the mercy of Sarai All-Mother, yet none came to guide my spirit on the road beyond the stars. I awoke as a ghost, bound close to the place of my death. I think it happened so because I always did love life so jealously that not even Morgeld had the gumption to wrest me entirely free of the land of the living. And sweet Sarai is too kind to spoil my fun just yet.'' He winked.

''You haven't answered—''

''It is a fact I have observed that often this ugly wizard's guardsmen wear strangely wrought silver cuffs. I wander the palace, betimes, and from a safe distance watch. These cuffs of theirs drink magic. Now who understands the workings of magic fully? Not I. Nor do I understand the workings of this spirit form I inhabit now. Who knows whether those cuffs of theirs have the power to gulp me down as I gulped down my final stirrup cup? Who knows whether the guard at this exit will be wearing the cursed things? Who knows where I will be if my spirit goes down the hatch, as it were, or if I will *be* at all? No, no, brother; that's too many riddles for me. You must emerge through the upper door alone. Here I'll leave you.'' The minstrel stroked the bagpipes Timeo carried beneath his left arm.

''Serve her well,'' he breathed, and drifted away.

Timeo was still not out from under the load of wine he'd taken on before Tyveen's appearence. Midway between full drunk and sober, suffering the worst of both states, he wondered whether the minstrel's ghost really had been there at all. The evidence under his arm was inconclusive. He might have stumbled across the bagpipes on his own.

"Or else they are phantoms too," he said to himself. "I'll stick my head out the door above, squeeze song from bellows not there, and have my moustache trimmed at the neck." He put down the alabaster bowl to pinch himself, but the pain was not proof enough for his sodden mind.

He decided he had to pinch the bagpipes too.

They let out a moan that shook little bits of lichen from the ceiling. Many tiny feet went pattering away in the dark, their owners meeping in shrill terror. Timeo adjusted the drones and fingered the chanter tentatively before giving the bellows a real squeeze. The acoustics in the palace cellars were intriguing, lending the amplified dissonance a nice pear-shaped quality.

Would it hurt to strike up a little tune, by way of trial, before daring to come against the guardsman? Timeo cleared his throat and ripped into rehearsal:

"I sing with heart from night to morn,
For I'm a loyal minstrel born.
I sing for daily meat and bread,
And they'll be sorry when I'm dead."

There was a tricky change in key between the verse and chorus of this composition. Timeo and the bagpipes failed to negotiate it.

"For it's only when a minstrel's dead they're sorry,
And it's only when a minstrel's dead they weep.
Though he's starving on the doorstep,
Far too weak to take one more step,
Oh they bolt the door and blithely go to sleep!"

He returned to the verse, leaving four chords bleeding to death en route.

"I do not ask for fame or wealth,
As long as I enjoy good health.
For music is my ale and cheese,
Though I could stand some money, please."
For it's only when a minstrel's dead they're sorry,
And it's only when a minstrel's dead they—

"Who's there?" Timeo hugged the bagpipes tight in panic. The bellows uttered a squeal to shatter iron.

Only me. Sweet friend, have they come for me at last?

"Come for—?"

Not like that.

The words were not words, yet he understood them. They were pure meaning inside his head, and so delicious that they bathed his brain in a warmth greater than love's most exquisite moment.

After so long, do not torment me with these evil sounds. Mind to mind, as before. Or if you find me soiled by my captivity, then touch me again with your precious gift.

"Me? Touch you? How? What gift?"

Music.

The Kya'ar came into the light of the glow.

Chapter XXVIII

ONE DAMP THING AFTER ANOTHER

Timeo limped through the corridors of the royal palace, his bagpipes under one arm, a heavy leather sack dragging the floor behind him, and something squeezing his ears out of shape. It had to be the worst hangover recorded since the fall of the Older Empire.

Instead of going away or reaching apotheosis in a tidal wave of unconsciousness, the hallucinations just kept getting worse. The ghostly minstrel was bad enough, but to have it replaced by that horrible apparition, the phantom Kya'ar! It had been too real. Timeo could still smell the sharp metallic reek, see the face that was not a face but a swirl of feathery whiteness, feel the brush of shaggy fur that was really millions of flexible scaly shafts. They rasped his skin with absurd gentleness and left it tingling.

Its eyes kept coming back across his thoughts—if they were eyes. He recalled two glowing yellow lights where a proper creature's eyes would be, golden spots of brightness that shifted shade to green and back again. Or had there been a third eye too, a blood-hued glimmer—? No, that had been the deep red shining at the bottom of the frondy white whirl that was the beast's—mouth? Could such a thing be called a mouth, could any being of such alien appearance even be said to have a face? Yet what else could he call the front of that creature's head? Bad enough that it had no distinct neck.

Apelike head and hulking shoulders simply *met*, fused into one another. Timeo's own head ached just thinking about it.

And then, at the top of the steps, there had been Randal.

Oh? Was that his name?

"Go away," Timeo muttered to the presence in his head. "I'm trying to sober up and you're making it plaguey hard. What I'm doing, wandering around these halls in the first place, I just don't—"

What would you have, sweet friend? I will do whatever you ask of me—the thought came plaintively now—*for another song.*

"Don't be ridiculous. It was pure luck I managed to run away from Randal. Of all the guards to meet again! Curse him skin in and skin out, he's too damned handy with that sword."

He hurt you. Timeo's right leg sparkled with sensation reminiscent of the Kya'ar's imagined touch. He looked down and saw the blood flowing sluggishly from the thin deep cut in the fleshy part of his thigh.

"Nearly hamstrung me, the bastard." He gave the bleeding leg another look as he continued to limp along. "I've got to bind it up. I guess that's where I'm going. A mercy it doesn't hurt worse."

It does hurt, sweet friend. I share gladly. A wistful note crept in. *It does not hurt so much as the rod, and the light, and the hunger. The loneliness. This pain is nothing to bear beside the rest.*

"Never again. I am never going to take another drop of wine as long as I live. The day I have to listen to back chat and nonsense from my own blessed hangovers . . . Now where—?" He paused in the middle of a decagonal room. Light from a mullioned glass roof splashed the mosaic of leaping salmon on the floor. Four closed doors waited.

Through there, the voice said. *The one with the silver willow branch handle.*

"And why not?" Timeo said aloud. "I've been sent my way by a ghost and a monster already today. Why not be guided by a hangover?" He opened the door and stumbled into the bedchamber of the lady Chelona's suite.

Cattail's mother was seated by the window, a dainty golden harp on her knees. Cattail occupied a footstool nearby, where she toyed with an embroidery hoop. By the fireplace, Ragnar sat reading a small dun-colored book, his lips moving ever so slightly. It was a heartbeat or two before Timeo's presence broke up that charming familial tableau, then the sight of him struck all three with the same thunderbolt.

Now the time of freedom is at hand. Timeo's head wanted to burst with the fierce gloating that swelled his brain. *Show him! Show him that I am alone no more!*

A strength not his own took over Timeo's arms. Moving like a clockwork toy, he set aside the bagpipes and undid the lacings of the leather sack and without ceremony upended it.

Randal's battered head rolled across the rug to bump against Chelona's slippered foot. The Kya'ar's talons had not made a neat job of decapitation, but a pragmatic one.

Timeo was as surprised as anyone. He laid a hand to his face in shock and encountered the leather earpiece of a helmet. He lifted it off his head; immediately his ears felt much better.

"I guess this must belong to . . ." He looked at the severed head, but Randal was lodging no property claims.

Timeo sat in the dejected attitude of a prisoner who knows he will soon die and has abandoned hope. His shoulders sagged, his head lolled low, and his fingers combed his hair compulsively until golden locks stood out in all directions. From time to time he would raise his eyes to the ceiling and utter a cry that was part sigh, part groan. His whole body shook with it.

He sat in the finest suite the palace had to offer, short of the royal apartments. Every dainty the larders could produce on such short notice now rested on the sideboard. On a smaller table by the window, decanters of five different vintages awaited his pleasure. His robe was thick blue velvet trimmed with snow hare, one of Ragnar's own. The chair he sat in was upholstered in watered silk, its dolphin armrests striped with silver, the beasts' eyes rubies; and the golden bell beside it would summon four of the wizard's finest guardsmen instantly to wait upon him.

He was being treated as befitted a king.

"A mad king," he told the woven faces in one of the room's many hangings. "Mad as a mullet, with a fever of the brain that will not die!"

Oh please, sweet friend! Do not speak so.

Timeo moaned and clamped his hands over his ears. The voice was not to be banished that way.

I am real! I am with you, of you, sharing you as I have longed to share minds with any of your kind. Always the torment. Always the hunger on me, so strong, so shamefully strong! If I did not eat, I would have died. If I had been brave enough to face my own death, instead of dealing out so many—if I had been a warrior, like my mates, my—

There was no word in Timeo's tongue for what the voice said, but the young man sensed his unwelcome tenant meant a bond that was friendship, family, lover, self, all at once.

I am not like the rest. I am a coward. Maybe that is why the wizard snared me, stole me from my own world, brought me here in the chains none of your kind can see. I am punished. Even you reject me.

"What sane man wouldn't reject madness?"

Madness?

For a blissful moment, Timeo's brain felt free. Then suddenly it filled with the mazey dark of the palace cellars, and the coming of the Kya'ar. The luxury surrounding Timeo turned to mossy stone and marble arches. He knew he was in his own memories, sharpened by sober eyes this time. They unscrolled from the creature's appearance to the confrontation at the top of the cellar steps. Randal lunged for Timeo, who had the good luck to stagger tipsily aside. He only got that wound on his thigh. Randal got a good sight more than that, when the Kya'ar filled the cellar doorway. The memory bloomed red.

"Now I remember." Timeo sat up straight as the room came back into focus. "You're no monster!" he told the air. "You dwell with Sarai All-Mother in the places between the stars!"

I do not know this Sarai. I am ignorant.

"You're young." Timeo's voice was tender, full of all the wonder proper to any birth. His words were the midwife's hands to bring forth the truth of the Kya'ar—no more a monster than poor Keristor, except to the truly ignorant, the irredeemably selfish and cruel. "You are from a place so far distant that it hurts my mind to imagine. So very cold, so dark, a sun that shines dull red . . . and yet it is a place of beauty too." He gazed at the chamber's painted ceiling and saw an open curve of sky. "The stars of your night are different than ours, but they are just as fair."

Home . . . Can you send me home, sweet friend? Your powers are great. The cursed wizard himself says so.

"I will. If I can, I will. I must free more of Ragnar's captives than just you."

I will help you.

"Why don't you come out of the cellars right now? With you at my side to face Ragnar, we could—"

There was a piteous cry in the passageways of Timeo's mind, fear and flight projected clearly, without words. *The light! The light! If I come forth into your fierce sun, it will destroy me. By night, or in the great hall of this palace where no windows are, or in those places where shadows linger I may come and go, but otherwise—*

Timeo felt the creature trembling, though the Kya'ar lay so deep beneath the flagstones of this room.

I told you I am a coward, it finished miserably.

"You are not. You're with me the only way you can be, and live. You are—inside me?"

Sharing you. In your thoughts, not your body, though you sense it so. You are the first able to speak to me in the harmonies of my language. Music is thought made sweeter, a free offering of the soul. Yours was the first I could understand. The others—ugh. I could no more share with them than with dust. My thoughts touched yours over the bridge of your music. Once the bridge is built, it lasts forever. We can communicate without song now, you and I, although— the Kya'ar's thought turned coy—*I hope to hear you sing again.*

"Ha! You shall!" Timeo pushed himself out of the dolphin chair and crossed the room to where the bagpipes lay on a satin cushion. The timeworn instrument had received nearly as much pampering as its master from the moment Ragnar got over seeing his guardsman's head turned into a kick ball.

Timeo was warming up, fiddling with the drones, when

the door opened silently and Cattail glided into the room. He looked up and saw his love clad in a white robe as fragile as a gust of dandelion fluff. Her long black hair was unbraided, a sweep of liquid satin on the floor.

"Who are you talking to?" she asked.

"To—" His mouth went dry at the sight of her. He put the bagpipes back on their cushion. "Shall I honestly tell you? Back at Panomo-Midmists you played me for a fool, just like the others did. I know that. But did you ever think I was insane, Cattail?" he asked earnestly.

"Never that. Never any of that. You are no fool, Timeo."

"There's no need to forswear yourself. I'd be your fool gladly, were that your desire." He shrugged. "I'm no minstrel, yet the minstrel's curse seems to have lit upon me. So long as you never thought me mad, maybe I can tell you who I'm speaking to in here, alone."

She came nearer and addressed him reverently. "You are the Vessel of Watersong; no one's fool. You proved it when you emerged from the Kya'ar's lair unharmed, having tamed it with your song so that it killed one of Father's own guards at your bidding."

He laughed. "I did. Oh, that I did!"

"They are both a little afraid of you now, my parents. Father is even more determined to have your powers heal him. The eternal damp of these lands has burrowed into his bones, warped them, set them afire." Her lips curled with distaste. "His petitions to Morgeld for healing go unanswered, as do his requests to leave the Lands Unknown for healthier climes. A fine master to serve so loyally! You are his only hope. Even now he prepares a great feast in your honor, to make a new bid for your healing magic. He will offer you a quarter of his realm, half his treasures, Waterfolk slaves to use as you like." Her voice dropped. "And me."

"A generous man, your father. What's to stop me from singing a tirralay, freezing him magically where he stands, and just taking all his gifts without payment?"

"He has seen that your powers are strong, but no match for his. Would you allow yourself to be put in the Kya'ar's den in the first place if you had the means to prevent it?"

Ragnar's perspicacity took the edge off Timeo's new

confidence. More subdued, he asked. "So you have been sent to plead your father's case with me?"

"No. Mother sent me," the ondine replied. "I am to plead *her* case: that you refuse my father and leave him trapped in a body full of pain. It suits her so, damn her."

"Does it?" Timeo lifted one eyebrow.

"She hates Father. Oh, not for what he did to her kinfolk—for that she has nothing but praise. It cleared her a path to the queen's throne. But she wants more than the trappings of a queen. She sees herself as too grand to be satisfied as Father's consort. She would rule."

"And he sees matters otherwise." Timeo nodded. "How long has she nursed this modest heart's desire of hers?"

"From the moment she felt the consort's crown on her brow." Cattail could not keep the scorn out of her voice. "She will never abandon it. He bars her way, of course, and so she sees his every weakness as a key to unlock that bar. His affliction is one, his mortality another. We Waterfolk hold our youth and our lives longer than humankind. She taunts him with that, when she dares. She can afford to be persistent."

"Not a very fond wife, then."

"Less fond as a mother. If she had loved Father—or only pretended to love him—if she had seen him as more than an instrument of her ambition, it would have been different. But she is a poor actress, and he is no fool."

"I'd call Ragnar something else," Timeo agreed.

"He saw through her early on. Now his pleasure is to play on her weaknesses as she does on his. My birth was just a reminder that she is little more than a breeder, to be used as such at her husband's pleasure."

"Not all men are like that." Timeo yearned to banish the bitterness from Cattail's eyes. She looked at him and her expression softened.

"I know. As I pray you know that all Waterfolk women are not like Chelona. If it lies in my power, I'll set more bars between her and the throne than my father ever dreamed."

"Your mother might have chosen a more sympathetic advocate," Timeo commented. "If you don't favor her cause, why are you here?"

"To plead my own." She slipped the robe from her shoulders and reached for him. "Forgiveness."

He came to her without question, his arms and lips finding their way to where they truly belonged. All that he might have laid to her charge was put from his mind, for the moment. He had walked the brink of death, the wild border of madness. He needed fire strong enough to burn all that away, even the scars.

As they lay together in a whitewood bed hung with emerald damask, Cattail laid her head on her lover's chest and said, "You still haven't told me who you were talking to before. Have you a wench hidden in your rooms? I can be very jealous."

"It's a long story."

"Tell it. I swear not to interrupt."

"I wouldn't mind some of your interruptions."

"Then I'll only interrupt *after* you've told me. If you aren't mad, you're trafficking with ghosts."

Timeo made a forfending gesture with both hands. "I've had enough of that! All right, listen."

He ended his tale and tried to take her back into his embrace but the ondine was distracted by what she had just heard. "You speak with the Kya'ar! You really can do it! Why, this is wonderful."

"I know more wonderful things," he murmured, nuzzling her neck.

Cattail was too caught up with political musings to turn amorous just yet. Timeo nuzzled for nothing. "If you control the monster, there is only Elaar's Daughter left to deal with. Destroy the pearl and my father will be helpless!"

"One minute you're siding with him against your mother's plots, the next you're scheming to overthrow him yourself," Timeo grumbled. "I don't understand you."

"You don't understand my father," Cattail said. Her hands worked as if she were washing them. "He is not an evil man. All my life I have never known him to be unkind."

"Throwing me to the Kya'ar was kind?"

"He is in *pain!* Pain can make the best of men irrational. If he does anything wrong or wicked, it is the pain driving him. That, and my mother's influence."

Timeo frowned, weighing what his beloved said against what he himself knew. "When Ragnar first usurped the Lands Unknown and massacred my kin, he was in full health and he didn't know your mother from a guppy."

"Morgeld's doing!" Cattail snapped. "My father always told me of how dearly he loved the quest for knowledge of the hidden arts. He could not study deeply enough, quickly enough. Morgeld promised him much learning, instantly. He couldn't resist the temptation. Magic is the star that steers his soul, as music is for you. Could you deny its call?"

"I wish I'd been a little less keen eared when the Havror Fenn came calling," Timeo said to himself.

Cattail did not heed. "One mistake! One mistake my poor father made, and he will pay the full price for it if I don't rescue him. Morgeld has abandoned him—that much is clear. He is too sick to hold these lands forever, and when he is overthrown at last, the Waterfolk will kill him. That's why I worked to free this realm. If I could be there, in the forefront of the rebellion, I would know the exact hour of attack and be able to warn him. I would bear him far away, to safety! It's the only way I can see to rescue him from this land, his awful master, even—even from Mother. He's a good man, but stubborn. He's spent so much of his life, his strength, his health here that he wouldn't listen to reason and leave voluntarily. But in the face of a full-scale revolt, he would have to heed me, and escape. I would not let anyone hurt my father."

Timeo's head reeled. Cattail had the hard, determined look he'd often seen on the kneeling tomb effigies of warriors who had gotten their heads smashed in battle for some long-forgotten noble cause.

"Are we talking about the same Ragnar?" he asked.

She gave him an incredulous stare that changed into a knowing smile. "You jest with me, my heart." Her arms were around his neck, and Timeo's confusion was soon set aside in favor of more demanding emotions.

"Where is Cattail?" Ragnar asked his wife.

"Never mind. Hadn't you best get on with the feasting preparations?" The lady Chelona sat at her dressing table, combing out her hair. "I checked with the commander of the barracks, and we haven't a single servant in the palace. The last two ran off.''

"Ran off? That sickly pair of girls?''

"They are gone. Does it matter how they went? We still need more—cooks, carvers, butlers, and servers, besides the more attractive ones to play our courtiers and guests. Have them bring food as they come.''

Ragnar's crabbed hand stroked Chelona's shining hair. "You think of everything, my dear.'' The claw snapped closed; he jerked her head back sharply. A sphere of blue radiance gleamed in his other hand: the great pearl, Elaar's Daughter.

"See that your first thought is always of me.''

Chapter XXIX

CURRENT EVENTS

Ovrin kept parting the curtain of willow branches to peer nervously at the shining spires of the royal palace. Only the little river separated the group of three humans and three Waterfolk from Ragnar's stronghold, and only the low-hanging fronds of the willow grove shielded them from sight. "Are you sure they can't see us from there?" he asked Perdica.

The nixie smiled fondly at him. The big redhead from across the river was as exotic to her as she to him. Both were legends come to life, with the added mystery of legend to make the commonplace more entrancing. He was so tall, so strong, and yet there was a gentleness in him that she had never found in males of her own kind. "I wish I could tell you, Ovrin," she said.

Wydru was the one to answer Ovrin's question. "Ragnar mounts no sentries in the turrets. Even though most of our land is flat, he still gets better intelligence reports by sending out patrols. The rush forests, the bog lands, the water-loving trees are all able to hide a lot more than you might think if your vantage point's that high."

"Aren't you the knowledgeable one," Fell growled. He sat like a grasshopper, legs drawn up, and jabbed at the soft earth with a willow twig. He did not like being conscripted into this rescue party, particularly when he thought that they were all frolicking blithely off to their doom. Timeo's skin wasn't worth the risk of his own. He wished he could

convince at least one of the Waterfolk with them to guide
him back to the River Salmlis. He had tried using his
personal charm to that effect on Perdica and failed. He then
tried persuading Wydru that they could rally an army of
battle-maddened university students to Timeo's aid, once
over the water. He might have saved his breath.

"Wydru knows much about the interior of the royal
palace," Dianta said. The girl still held her head with the
ever-harking attitude of the blind, though in all other ways
she now behaved and reacted like any sighted person. "He
has been called to serve there many times."

"Of course he would, with that face," Fell mewed.

That face turned contemptuously to the dark-haired
student. "When Elaar's Daughter calls, she doesn't sift us
for looks. The pull of the blue pearl ripples out in spreading
nets of magic. They only stop when Ragnar has enough
Waterfolk in the palace to answer his present needs. I had
the bad luck to be caught in the seining four times. I did
what was required of me and left." His beautiful features
closed like an iron gate, discouraging further prying.

Fell disregarded the warning. "And what was required of
you in there, my handsome friend?"

Wydru dashed the complacent grin from Fell's face with
a backhand slap. Fell tumbled to one side. He hand dropped
to the dagger he now hid beneath the wide belt of his
Waterfolk garb. "You slime—" He was ready to spring.

Ovrin stepped between them, his size making the simple
move eloquent. "We have no time for stupid quarrels among
ourselves. We must save our friend." He looked back at the
palace again. "Though how we'll ever do it . . . ."

"*He* will know," Dianta said softly. "I will bring him."
The eyeless girl rose like smoke and gracefully threaded her
way between the trunks of the willows, never once holding
out her hands to guide her.

"Such a miracle . . ." Perdica spoke in a voice of
lingering disbelief as she watched the girl move off. "And
so many more needed."

Fell slumped down in his place. "Why doesn't our little
miracle worker just crack the palace wide open with one
good high note and yank old Timeo out like a peach pit?"
He laid his forehead on his knees and added, "Hard to

believe any miraculous power'd ever choose *that* for its roosting place when it might've had a normal, healthy man to house it."

"Like you?" Perdica looked just like her handsome cousin Wydru when she sneered at Fell.

"Yes, blast it! Like me!" Fell's fists struck the ground. "Why not? Instead of that dish-faced lackwit who still goes about stopping every minute or so to *staaaaaare* at whatever crosses his path crooked. No wonder we've gone on so slowly, with him holding us up."

Ovrin's hands were reaching for Fell. There was a nasty red light in the big man's eye that spoke ill for his comrade's future health.

Fell did not wait for Ovrin's tactile lecture on tolerance. Snake swift, his knife blinked out and slashed Ovrin's hand. The redhead reeled back, clutching the streaming cut. Fell grinned. "Keep them to yourself or lose them, one finger at a time."

Song drifted from the feathery branches of the willow trees. The blood running down Ovrin's hand stopped flowing. Fell's steely smile grew smaller. Wydru slowed as he stooped to pick up a heavy stone, his hate-bright eyes on Fell. Perdica too was caught in the web of sound, her hands stretching out to tend Ovrin's wound, her face showing much more than simple compassion. The song ceased, but not before Ovrin saw how she looked at him.

Keristor and Dianta came out of the grove, hand-in-hand. The boy went directly up to Fell and took the knife away. The bloodstains vanished in the breath of a tune. He gave the weapon back to its owner.

"Don't hurt my brother. You should know how he gets when people speak against me."

Fell regarded Keristor as a man might study a talking dog after short acquaintance. He accepted the phenomenon, but he still could not quite believe it. The boy looked no different than he ever had. Keri had exchanged his clothes for Waterfolk garb, like the rest of them, but he still looked like any marketplace mumbler.

Ah, but when he opened his mouth and spoke—! When he sang—! The change had come slowly. Fell recalled momentary flashes of its development, small incidents that he and Ovrin had overlooked because they were used to ignoring the boy.

Just try ignoring him now . . . Fell thought. A new envy stole into his heart, to join all the old resentments smoldering there.

"I swear, my lord and master, I will never turn this blade against your brother again as long as I live." Fell made an elaborate flourish with the knife before jamming it back behind his belt. His cocksure grin was too much a part of him to stay smothered long.

"Thank you." Keri did not comment on the title Fell had lavished upon him in obvious mockery. He had a new dignity that scorn could not touch, and there was plain affection in the look he gave Dianta—affection she returned with the added glow of worship. They turned their backs on Fell as Keri motioned for the entire party to gather around him. It was his turn to ignore rather than be ignored. He did not choose to notice the envy burning in Fell's eyes.

They sat on whatever dry spots they could find, perching on the knobbly roots of the willows or the patchy rises of ottergrass in the green shade. Perdica sat close beside Ovrin, Dianta with Keri. Wydru and Fell found places as far from each other as the gathering allowed and traded periodic glares across the little circle.

"Before we enter Ragnar's palace to save Timeo, we must prepare," Keri said.

"You will rally our people, lord?" Wydru asked.

"If we attack directly with a large number, Ragnar may kill Timeo before we can take the palace."

"But surely the power of your song . . ."

"I never knew the world could hold so much magic." Keri's eyes took on their old, vacant stare of marvel. "I never imagined that it would touch me. When the power poured itself into me, I thought I would drown in its infinity. But when I was filled, I knew that there was an end to it, and limits past which it could not go. Magic has limits, miracle—*true* miracle—has none and is for the gods alone. I am no god."

"Fooled me, the airs you've been putting on," Fell mumbled to himself. "Bask in your modesty, why don't you? Little snot-sleeve."

"If we can enter the palace, I can try to get close enough to Ragnar to hold him with my song."

"Perfect, lord." Dianta pressed his hand.

"Not so perfect," Ovrin put in. "Keri, you know your songs can heal—there's the proof of it in Dianta, in my hand—but aside from that, do you *know* how far your power goes or what uses it has?"

Dianta regarded Ovrin haughtily. "Nothing is beyond his power!"

"How would you know? By wishing it so? Keri's my brother! Who looked after him all the years when he was—when he wasn't yet your Vessel-thing, eh?" Ovrin threw a protective bearhug around his little brother, a maneuver which amused Keristor mightily. "I'm not having him go against a full wizard just on your say-so unless we know he can win! I didn't watch over him all this time to have him killed by Ragnar's black spells."

"The Vessel of Watersong shall wash the blackest spells away!" Dianta countered.

"Ever hear the nurse tale of the old fool who tried to wash the night clean with a bar of soap? Some things aren't meant to be. Keri himself said he's no god, just full of a special sort of magic, and magic can't do everything. He may be your lover, but damn it all, he's my baby brother!"

"Ovrin, please . . ." Perdica stroked his arm until the little vein leaping in his jaw stopped throbbing so wildly. To the others she said, "Ovrin is right. Do we dare risk our lord's life in any plan until we know his powers?"

"But that's Timeo in there!" Wydru protested, gesturing towards the shining towers. "He saved your life, Perdica. Can you forget that?"

"I didn't say to abandon him, but to wait—"

"For what? How soon before Ragnar learns it wasn't a miracle that saved you, but a good rib-splitting laugh? The wizard's not in the market for a jester."

"And so we should march in and maybe lose Keri's life?" Ovrin demanded.

"I agree with Ovrin," Fell chimed in. "Let's not risk Keri."

"Not risk your own skin, you mean," Dianta sniped.

The argument got louder and fiercer. Keri was the only

one who kept out of it. He sat with legs folded and eyes closed, humming. Bubbles of light the size and color of cats' eyes formed in the air around his head. Each one bobbed off to float above one of the disputants.

Ovrin was the first to call for silence. "Are we fools? If half a dozen of Ragnar's patrols haven't heard this racket by now, I'll be damned."

"Rest easy, Brother." Keri hugged himself over some private joke. "The last one that passed heard nothing." He pointed at the bubbles overhead. They had swollen to three hundred times their original size and looked ready to burst. "I trapped your noises in there."

"With your song, Keri?"

He laughed. "What else have I? So it seems my powers can tap words."

"Spells are words!" Dianta exulted. "Your song can capture Ragnar's magic"—she reached up and plucked her own bubble down—"just like this."

"It's not much . . ." Ovrin looked doubtful.

"It's better than nothing. And Timeo needs us!" Wydru insisted.

"Well . . ."

"Must you wait for his permission to act, lord?" Dianta spoke to Keri as if he were the only one there. "Speak, and we will follow you."

Keri would have replied, but at that moment a blue and red butterfly stole his attention. In spite of the transformation that had come over him since his entry into the Lands Unknown, Keristor was still easily distracted by rare and lovely things. As he watched its wobbling flight in open-mouthed awe, a current of silent, sinister strength flowed over the river and into the willow grove.

Perdica was the first to feel it. She stiffened like a hound on point, then bolted from the cover of the trees. Ovrin called her name; she ran on.

She was too fast for him. The ground of the Lands Unknown was still treacherous for his lumbering steps. When Wydru raced past him, Ovrin thought that he had gone to fetch his cousin back. He stopped, breathing hard, and saw Dianta coming up quickly at his right side.

"It's all right. Wydru will catch her. What do you think made her take off like—?"

The girl ran by as if he were just another willow tree. He shouted after her, then broke back into his clumsy trot over the soft earth. Less than ten strides later, he was stretched out on the ground.

Keri came running to help his brother up. Fell arrived at a more leisurely pace. "What bit them?" the dark-haired student mused.

"Was it the pearl, Keri?" Ovrin asked, scraping dirt from his cheeks. "Elaar's Daughter?"

"Look there," the boy said grimly. They were not far from a well-beaten road, in a runoff gully veiled by wire grass and slipnot growing wild along the verge. Through the waving vegetation they saw many Waterfolk—more than they had ever seen—heading for the wizard's palace. Most of them carried baskets and panniers of food. Some few drew high, light, two-wheeled wagons full of supplies.

"Looks like someone's giving a party," Fell said. "Too bad we're not invited."

Keri scooped a handful of furry green from a gully rock and rubbed it on his thigh. The resulting tint was pleasing. He plopped a second scoop into Fell's hand and drew a streak of Waterfolk-skin over the young man's arm before he could object.

"There's our invitation." He giggled.

Chapter XXX

IT ALL COMES OUT IN THE WASH

"You," the lady Chelona said, leveling a finger at the Waterfolk male who had just dropped the tray of glasses.

"Me?" said Fell. His heart beat fast. He could feel the beads of sweat carving chasms through the mossy green stain on his skin. Though Keristor assured him a dozen times that the tint would not wash away, he still couldn't believe the boy who only yesterday didn't know moss from marigolds.

"Yes, you," the lady repeated. "Come with me." She was too finely dressed to disobey, and the small complement of guards stationed in the kitchen seemed to watch her progress among the slaves with more than passing concern.

Now I'm going to die, he thought as he followed her slender figure out of the kitchen. He was too upset even to enjoy the view, though bits of lascivious surmise licked at his mind momentarily. He was not dead yet.

She led him upstairs, into a snug chamber. The guards had not accompanied them. She was on familiar territory, and Fell got the impression that she did not need armed men to back her. In this room—maybe in this whole palace—she could take care of herself.

He looked around the chamber. If there were any instruments of torture about, they had all been ingeniously concealed. The furnishings were quite ordinary, though luxurious, elegant, rich. The lady seated herself on the velvet cushioned window seat and indicated that he should take a place beside her. She poured him wine, and her hospitality made him more apprehensive than if a masked executioner had stepped out from between the bed curtains.

"Now tell me," she said. "Tell me your crimes."

"Crimes, my lady?" Fell held the wine cup steady. His brain rattled through all the replies open to him, searching for the one that would save him and perhaps pay back a few debts on the side.

"Only criminals enter the Lands Unknown."

He forced himself to laugh. "Then my crime is being born, and my mother was my accomplice."

Chelona sipped from her own goblet. Her winged brows dipped in a scowl. "Do not mistake me for a fool. You are not of the Waterfolk. You are human."

Fell made a great business of indignant denial. "My lady, have me thrown in the River Salmlis if you doubt my birth or my word!"

The lady's smile was lovelier than the frost moon. A trill of liquid syllables danced from her lips. Fell said nothing. Again the musical sounds poured out, and still he sat there, fingers linked around the goblet.

"I will doubt your word," Chelona said at last, "since it's plain you don't understand one word of the Waterfolk speech. I overheard the cooks shouting at you to turn around, and you never responded."

"An affliction of the ear. It comes and goes."

"One of your fellow servants spoke right at you, telling you to take your tray up by the left-hand staircase. You smiled and nodded and headed for the right."

"A poor sense of direction; a childhood weakness."

"You asked to be thrown into the Salmlis. That is not its name, in our language."

"As you were addressing me in the common speech, I thought it would be presumptuous to reply in any other tongue."

"I asked you several questions just now, in our own tongue, and you did not answer any."

"I—I did not think my humble opinions would be of interest to a lady of your standing."

"But they are." Chelona stood and took the wine cup from him. Her gown was tiers and tiers of pink coral sarcenet, foaming with sheer white lace at wrists and breast, clusters of gold ribbons falling from rosettes at the waist. It looked very complicated to put on.

She quickly demonstrated that it was not so difficult to take off.

"They are most interesting to me," she said, "since one such opinion I asked for was whether we should agree together, you and I." Her gesture set a new meaning on the word *agree*.

If this were the path to his death, Fell leaped onto it with winged feet. The irresistible beauty of Waterfolk women was no longer just a vague fireside tale to him. It was more than perfection of shape and feature; it was their fluid grace, their undulating movements, and the fascination of deep water in their eyes. As a human man was drawn to the mysteries of the sea, so he would be drawn to the Waterfolk women. Fell had seen it in even the plainest of their females, and he refused to condemn Ragnar's soldiers for their freehanded way with them. To see such loveliness and resist was hard; to resist after more intimate knowledge of their charms was impossible. In Chelona's arms he satisfied every thirst of his body, and still came away parched for more.

"You—you won't turn me in to the guard?" The question rang hollow. She could do whatever she wanted with him, and he would not have the power to fight her.

"Of course not. We are friends now." She relished the irony. "There are no double dealings between friends. Only favors."

"You want a favor of me?" He did not see how he could possibly refuse her anything.

"No; I wish to do a favor for you." Her fingertip kissed his lips. "But you must tell me the truth. Are there other humans with you or are you the only one?"

"Two more."

"Has there been enough kitchen gossip in the common tongue for you to glean why we are preparing this celebration?"

"Bits and pieces, when the guards chat. They say that there is a great guest Ragnar wishes to entertain. Why that should be, or who he is, I don't know."

"No lies, dear friend."

"Unless . . . it's Timeo."

"Ah." She pulled back a lock of hair from his temple to expose a thin line of white scalp where Ovrin had not been able to rub in the mossy stain. Her nail traced the line all the way to the nape of his neck while he shuddered blissfully. "So you know him. I suspected it. The men who brought my daughter home said that she was accompanied by three humans. They locked you up in the same village where this Timeo was first held. Four humans, and none of them fugitives; I sensed a connection."

"Your daughter? Cattail's your daughter?"

"You sound as if you know her better than Timeo." Chelona was deeply interested. "Tell me more."

The wizard Ragnar sat alone in his study. It was an airy, well-lit room on the topmost floor of the western tower. The windows were narrow, but there were so many of them, floor to ceiling, that the chamber was bathed in sunlight every hour of the day. By night, the great rock crystal chandelier chased shadows from above, while many small jade bowls of glow kept the incidental niches bright. It did not look at all to Fell like the dingy, sinister lair that evil wizards were reputed to prefer. Even Ragnar himself wore a silver-shot cape and sparkling gold ornaments to cheer the dark robes of his profession. He smiled beatifically as he worked, making frequent notes in a large vellum folio.

On the table before him, a very small hand still jerked and clutched in its tray.

Chelona glanced over her husband's shoulder. "I never expected it to last so long. You may be right about the effects of death terror on the vital signs. What a shame you have nowhere to publish your observations."

The wizard pushed himself away from the table. His chair rested on ball casters that rolled smoothly. "Your interest in my research seldom brings you here, Wife," he remarked wryly. He cocked an eye at Fell, who laced his fingers into a dozen nerve-racked patterns as he waited for his introduction. When Ragnar asked, "Who is this wight?" he jumped out of his skin.

Chelona's hand was cool and calming on Fell's shoulder. "A friend of the bridegroom's." Her lips tasted imaginary honey. "If you still bestow our daughter's hand on Timeo after what he shall tell you."

The last trace of benign amusement vanished from the wizard's face. Fell could swear he felt a chill wind blow from Ragnar's hunched body and hear the growl of leashed thunder prowling about the hem of the old man's robes.

"You speak without sense, lady."

"You live the same way," she snapped, "when it's a question of our daughter. Now I have proof to back what you persist in calling rumors! Here is a witness. Question him. Use any method you like." Fell shuddered.

"What manner of witness could you bring but a paid one? I need not ask the coin you used for payment, my lady."

Chelona ignored her husband's reproof. "A witness from her days over the river, a span you have decided to ignore, as though it never happened. You can see as well as I, if you look at him closely enough, that he is not of the Waterfolk. Look at Cattail that closely, and through his eyes! You will see more wonders than all your old books ever held."

The wizard sighed and beckoned Fell to approach. "My lady wife means to try my patience with more nonsense. I shall have no peace until I hear you out. Tell me of my daughter," he said.

Fell closed his eyes and spoke. All that he knew about Cattail—and there was quite a bit Timeo did not know—came pouring out. He told Ragnar of the Chuckling Bear, and of his cousin Sterion, and of the bright and willing barmaid who had come into his service one fine day, from nowhere. He spoke of Timeo, and how he had taken Sterion's place in the barmaid's affections. He mentioned stories that had circulated of other students who had passed into and out of Cattail's good graces before Timeo arrived.

"But all the tales of the Waterfolk do say that the women . . . they're freer than the human—"

"My daughter inhuman?" It was carefully uttered. Fell squeezed his eyes even tighter shut and spoke on, dreading what Ragnar might do to him for that gaffe.

Instead of reprimand or curse, Fell heard: "Why will you not look at me, young man?"

Fell stopped his recitation at that plaintive inquiry. He opened his eyes and saw that tears were running down the wizard's cheeks, dewing his spiderweb beard. The lady Chelona wore a hard, satisfied smile.

"So it is true." Ragnar's words raked over his tears. "I can smell the truth of your telling, young man. It has its own perfume, truth does. It smells of dead things."

Chelona gloated. "Maybe now you will believe me, Ragnar. I only want what's best for us. The fantasy you have woven around Cattail will only harm you and bring you down from your throne. Your daughter doesn't spare you a tenth of the thought I lavish on your welfare, my lord. If you had listened to my counsel all these years, let me share in the rule of the Lands Unknown, you would not now be making a fool of yourself before all our subjects. And over what? Not the Vessel of Watersong! Over your daughter's current bed bright."

"He *is*." Ragnar's nails bit his palms. "He is the Vessel of Watersong!"

"He is Cattail's *lover*! Even now she is with him!" Chelona shouted, drunk on his misery.

Ragnar hardly spoke above a whisper, but the rasp of his voice made Fell wish dearly to be elsewhere. "How sure you are, lady. I will not ask why. Very well. You have won."

The wizard made a small, homely gesture that sleight-of-hand artists used to pluck coins from the ears of village marks. Instead of a copper, a slender scepter of silver, pearl, and nacre materialized at his fingertips. He held it out to his wife.

"When you first came to me, my lady, you feared for your life. You were the last of the royal house, the last with any drop of regal blood. I was young then, and strong, and straightly made. You were very beautiful, as you have remained. When I said you should live, you were grateful. When I said you should be my bride, I thought you would die out of shear thanksgiving. But there is too much water in this land. Water changes everything it touches, fast or slow. You forgot your gratitude. You desired more. You came to demand it, and restless as any river, you ate away at everything solid I tried to put in my life. You would not stop until you had your desire. Well, now you have it. Take the scepter."

The Lady Chelona stretched a trembling hand towards the

silver wand. She clutched it fiercely, swept up by her own triumph. "You will not regret this, Husband. I have greater gifts to give you. Listen to Fell! He has not yet finished his tale. He can give you the truth about the Vessel of Watersong as well as the truth of your precious daughter. Ask him. And then ask her if she ever loved you half so well as she loves Timeo!"

"May you know the answer." Ragnar's words burned dull and hot as boiling lead. "And may it give you comfort."

The magic burst from him, a blast that shattered five of the thin windows, glass panes and stone framings. The scepter flew from Chelona's hands, soaring through the gaping hole in the wall. The lady cried out, as if to bid it back to her, a wayward hawk.

Horribly, it did return, but not as a scepter. It was a spear, silver and nacre and pearl, that shot back into the wizard's study and pierced Chelona's breast. Without losing speed, it bore her with it in its flight back through the jagged opening. She was still alive, still shrieking as she plunged through the air in a tumble of pink and white and gold. Her scream alone was red as blood, but that was soon over.

Ragnar sighed again, and burst into the tears of a tired old man. "She should not have persisted. She thought that because she was lovely, and royal, and sweet in my arms, I would grant her everything. When I would not, she was a child. She would destroy what was dearest to me: my daughter. My daughter as I dream her to be."

"I—wasn't lying," Fell said. His heart had dropped from the tower's height with Chelona. His throat closed as his mind screamed, unreasoning, *Timeo's fault! Always it's been this way, always! Everything for him—gold, good fortune, love—and for me, nothing, as if he drank every drop of luck the gods would have given me. Timeo's to blame for this too, for her death, for the loss of the sweetest love I ever tasted! If I live, I'll pay him out in matching coin, in blood, in death! If I live* . . . He found it hard to breathe. The wizard's tears were appalling.

"Truth is worse than any lie. Lies give birth to dreams; truth murders them. Not the worst of Morgeld's horrors can slay as much as truth." He sobbed anew. "Unnatural mother, to kill her own child that way! Power was everything to her. She could not leave me one dream, and so I sent her where no dreams ever come."

The wizard's reddened eyes lifted. His tears were gone. The pain-savaged face turned to Fell. Ragnar raised his hand. "Truth had an accomplice."

Fell was on his knees. "Lord, mercy!"

"For a murderer?"

"Please, I beg—Lord Ragnar, spare me and I will buy my life with a secret worth a link of gold for every word!"

"What secret? This 'truth' you peddle so freely? Truth about the Vessel of Watersong, my lady said." His eyes slewed to the broken windows. Fell cringed.

It seemed like a thousand years passed before the wizard added, "If you tell me only that Timeo is not the Vessel of Watersong, you die. Pay well for your life, young man, or do not seek to barter with your betters."

The chance of a hope was all Fell needed. His old smile was a hungry ghost, but it was there. He told Ragnar all he knew of Timeo, of Keristor, of the company in which he had come into Ragnar's palace. As he spoke, he drank the wizard's mounting rage like vintage Vairish wine. He said all he had to say and waited in respectful silence, head bowed.

A wrinkle of the wizard's robes wriggled. A dune viper, deadly creature of the great southern deserts, poked its triangular head out from under the draped cloth and slithered over Ragnar's embroidered leather slipper. It crossed the floor in undulations of shining yellow and brown. Fell watched its progress towards him and knew he would not escape. The serpent curled around his ankle, its forked tongue flickering over his naked skin.

Then the snake collapsed in a clang of solid gold links connecting diamonds the color of honey. Fell stared at the priceless necklace ringing his ankle and remained as paralyzed as if it were still a snake.

"Pick it up," said Ragnar. "Take it, I say! I pay my servants well. You are my servant now, aren't you?"

The heavy links were a comfort in Fell's hand. His grin returned. "I am yours, my lord." *Your servant, but master of my own revenge.* Again he said, "Yes, willingly I am yours."

"Or death's, young man; mine or death's."

Chapter XXXI

WATER MUSIC

Cattail wandered through the palace gardens, caught up in the wonders her father's magic had performed. Though she had known these arbors and promenades since childhood, they never failed to amaze her. On ground too deeply steeped in water for such plants to thrive, a hundred varieties of flowers flourished. All the Twelve Kingdoms were well represented in the array of bloom, though by what was right and natural these plants should have lain rotting on the swampy soil. She could not help but be awed by the man capable of such prodigies, and awe overwhelmed the soul in much the same way as love.

"What do you seek, my daughter?" Ragnar came into the garden, leaning on two ivory walking sticks. The cunningly carved, gaping mouths of Vahrdish mount-cats roared silent rage under his gnarled hands. Twin balls of white light glowed at the base of the canes, keeping them from sinking into the sodden earth under the wizard's weight. "What would you have, my dear heart?"

"I thought I would pick a rose, Father; for my hair. But if you would rather I left your garden alone . . ."

"A rose for your hair?" The wizard motioned his daughter closer and stroked her flowing tresses fondly. In spite of all Chelona's whispered venom, all the truths of his new servant's telling, when he was with his child his heart still trembled with a joy that all his magical studies could not name. He recalled her as an infant in the cradle, tended only by servants because Chelona refused to care for her own baby. He had stolen into the nursery by a secret way, not wanting his captive subjects to learn of this one weakness in their lord. Holding her against his heart, already feeling the first twinges of the pain that would double up his bones, he watched in awe as her tiny fingers closed tightly around his. Not even when he had stood in the presence of the dread lord of Helagarde had he felt such reverence, such fear of a power greater than his own. He told himself that he loved his daughter more than any other thing in his life. And the greater miracle was that she loved him.

Yet somewhere in the recesses of his mind a small voice, a voice from other times, whispered futilely, sorrowfully, *And which do you truly love more, when all is told, Ragnar? Which would you choose if choice there came: your daughter or your power?* He ignored it.

"A rose! Where did you learn such high ambitions? Not from your mother, surely."

"Is mother looking for me? I'll be at the festivities."

Ragnar's mouth twitched. "She is not looking for you."

Cattail's fingers went back to the bush where roses the color of sunrise blossomed. Meekly she asked, "Then—may I, Father?"

The wizard dropped his canes and seized her hands in a shockingly strong grip. Cattail exclaimed with surprise and passing pain. "Say first"—Ragnar panted as if he had run the length of the Lands Unknown—"say first if you love me."

Cattail was totally bewildered. "But Father, you know I do! You can't know how much I love you."

"Truth?" His grasp tightened, choking off blood. "Is this the truth you tell me?"

"It is! Truth I can't prove, but still it's true."

He released her hands as suddenly as he had seized them. His twin canes rose back to his clutching fingers by his will's directive. "How many truths . . ." He left the garden, muttering.

Cattail watched her father go, then reached for the half-open rose she coveted. Her fingertips touched it, then retreated. The mad look in her father's eyes had poisoned the flower. She could not take it now.

The great hall had been decked with garlands of lotus and floating lily, the floors strewn with a thin layer of fragrant rushes and mint leaves. All the lights were lit, glow and sconce and chandelier. If there were any windows, it was a well-kept secret. Silk hangings covered nearly every inch of wall, even fell in looping swags from the ceiling. It was like being in a huge tent. Yet air must have circulated through some opening, for the atmosphere was fresh.

The Waterfolk summoned to their master's service were split between those playing servile roles and those chosen to be the wizard's courtiers. Fine garments in the styles favored by land dwellers looked even more exquisite when worn by the most attractive, most human-looking of the Waterfolk. Wydru's blue skin was set off perfectly by the pale rose and white tunic given him. Perdica, in gold and gray, leaned on his arm and played the role of courtier's lady, stirring a breeze with her scarlet plumed fan.

Ovrin, Fell, and Keristor wore the same garb they had arrived in, suitable for menials. None of the other servants was any more fancily dressed. They passed through the crowd of the elect with trays of refreshments.

There was a third division. Over in a corner, to the left of the dais holding Ragnar's throne, a group of ten Waterfolk sat on low porcelain stools shaped like small wine casks. Some held hand harps, some timbrels, one a tambor. They were to be the court musicians, though in a land where the least gifted singer could outshine many a trained bard of the drier realms, it was only the wizard's caprice that selected the players.

Dianta sat among the chosen, a glass-belled timbrel in her lap. Keri managed to pass near her more often than truly necessary. His brother finally took him aside, under pretense of refilling their trays in the kitchen. In the servants' dim passageway, the big man shook Keri vigorously by the shoulders.

"Why don't you just stand up and announce us?" Ovrin hissed.

"I'm not doing anything wrong!" Hot indignation looked

out of place on Keri's face. Ovrin was used to seeing eternal calm there, the absence of emotion. To gaze over a placid pond and see a castle-high tidal wave come bearing down on you was frightening. Ovrin let his brother go.

In a more cajoling voice he said, "I know how you feel about her, Keri. After so long, to have someone to love and to love you, just as if—" He stopped.

"As if I were a normal man?" There was keen mockery in Keri's face as he finished his brother's sentence for him.

Blushing, Ovrin went on: "But you're doing her and us no favors by sailing past her every two seconds. They're no fools here. If they sniff a bond between you two, Ragnar's men'll keep that much keener eyes on your every move."

Keristor snorted. "You exaggerate. And if they smell conspiracy in every corner, let them! I'll put an end to all their suspicions soon enough."

Ovrin bent to look his little brother in the eye. In the damp hallway, he spoke in a voice soft with love and foreboding. "I prayed for this day, Keri. I wore myself out over my books, offering the gods a scholar's greatest prayer: that my studies would find the way to let light into your darkness, that you would one day know the world as other men do. Now my prayers are answered—the gods know how—and I find myself wishing you still wandered the darkness."

Keri's smile mocked his brother's anguish. "Many thanks for your good wishes; I regret that I can not fulfill them. There is a great changing power in the waters that run through these lands—the Waterfolk themselves have magic in them that is neither witchborn nor wizardly. When the gods departed, they left many strange keepsakes behind. It's a spell that I felt from the moment I first touched the Lands Unknown."

"But why you? Why were only you changed?"

The boy shrugged. "To fulfill a prophecy? To satisfy the humor of some hidden god? To offer hope, or to shatter hope if I am the only—witling the waters change? I don't know. When I drank of the waters themselves, I drank knowledge, not omniscience. No, Ovrin; I can no more go back into the darkness than I can part my blood from the water's enchantment. I am god-touched no more."

"Even though you were god-touched, you still knew joy; you still knew beauty. Now you know love, as a man knows it, and pride, and—I fear this most of all—pain."

Keri stared at Ovrin as if it were the big man who had suddenly turned god-touched. "What are you going on about? How can you know what I felt or what I feel? Stand up straight, Ovrin; you look like a fool, stooping like that. What I have become was meant to be, just as I am meant to be the doom of Ragnar. Why all this babble of love and pain and pride? I will be the wizard's death, the saving of this land, and when all is done and I take Dianta for my bride, it will be such a day of feasting as these Twelve Kingdoms build their legends upon. Whisper your warnings then, Brother. Come, hurry up before we're missed." He strode quickly to the kitchens, letting his brother catch up as he could.

In the great hall, the festival continued. Timeo came in under the chaperonage of two guards, an escort of honor rather than a security measure. They carried bows and arrows, not blades. Indoors, where close-quarters fighting was the expected norm, such weapons could only be for show. None of Ragnar's guards in the hall was heavily armed, though the assembled Waterfolk outnumbered them. The wizard's legendary powers were sword and shield enough to keep a beaten people in line.

Timeo was garbed in a cascade of green satin with panels of gold-embroidered cerulean silk, knots of crystal-ringed emerald at his shoulders. He stood to the right of the throne, carrying Tyveen of Sigraton's bagpipes under one arm. Two wooden wings that formed a wide platform had been specially constructed to broaden the throne dais. Samite banners covered its facade, Vairish carpets rippled down the steps from the throne to the hall floor. From this vantage, Timeo scanned the crowd.

Fell saw him. In servant's gear, the black-haired former student rushed to the front of the hall and scuttled up the steps. None of the guards made any move to stop him. He knelt before Timeo, ostensibly offering him the tidbits on his tray.

"Fell! What are you—?"

"Shh! Courage. We're all here to aid you, my friend."

"Aid?" Timeo spoke in the lowest of whispers, yet the guards were near enough to hear it. Astonishingly, when he darted a glance at them, they appeared to be stone deaf. Their eyes wandered conveniently elsewhere—anywhere else but towards Timeo and Fell.

Timeo was never one to question his good fortune too closely. "Who is here? Ovrin? Keri?"

"Hush. You shall see." Fell lowered his tray and tipped a sly wink at Timeo. The gold chain starred with canary diamonds around his neck winked too. *Fool,* he thought. *Soon I'll write you your final song.*

The general hubbub of the hall rose and fell like the waves of the sea. Abruptly, the wash of sound broke into hard silence. A grim-faced guard stood at attention beneath a tapestry. His pikestaff dipped under the weaving's border to draw it aside. An iron-bound door stood revealed.

The crowd ebbed as far from that seemingly innocent door as the hall's space allowed. The guard sneered, and with studied casualness lifted the black latch and swung the door wide.

Friend, are you there? I sense you . . .

The Kya'ar was stronger in Timeo's mind. Even before the beast's snowy presence blazed into the hall, under the jittery guard of six of the wizard's men, Timeo knew his strange new companion was near. The guardsmen all carried the same rods that Timeo had seen them use to control the Kya'ar when they had invaded the Waterfolk village. Not for the first time, he wondered how such slender tools could hold such a powerful creature at bay.

Energy. The inner voice was pathetic. *Power, if that is what you can understand. In living things, in life itself, in the force your folk call magic, there I feed. But these are wizard's work, these bars of my moveable prison. They cannot drink the power from its sources, but they can drain it from me, once I have fed. The wizard has the power to starve me with a touch; to starve me to death, if he chooses. Thus he keeps me docile.*

A second voice sounded in Timeo's ear, distracting him

from the Kya'ar's plaintive mental call. Ragnar's crabbed hand rested on Timeo's shoulder.

"Forgive the insult to your powers, great one," the wizard said. "I know your magic can render the beast harmless, but it would be inconvenient if you had to keep singing throughout this gay gathering. A man ought to enjoy his own wedding."

Ragnar had discarded his two ivory canes in favor of a thick beechwood staff, the wood stained black by years of smoke from untold experiments. He leaned on it like a homeward-bound drunk clinging to a handy tree, and smiled with half-mad abandon to see Timeo's expression.

"Wedding?"

"Yours, lord. To my daughter, my beloved Cattail, my adored child who holds all my heart in one hand, and half my lands for you to take from the other. The other half you shall have when I am gone, if you will have her now."

The wizard signed tersely with his hand and seven nobly dressed and gauded maidens of the Waterfolk emerged from the arch to the far left of the throne. Dressed in heaven's own blue, her veil sewn with pearls and a spray of pearls and silver fanning from her neck, Cattail was led into the hall by her attendants.

She broke from the escort of the seven and came to join her father and Timeo with all haste. Even beneath the veil, Timeo could see how glorious and exultant her smile was, and it was all for him.

Although questioning good fortune was not his way, there were times when luck smiled a bit too broadly, like a skull. Besides, he had been forewarned of Ragnar's impending "gift." He tried to sound very knowing and aloof as he replied, "And the price for all this is that I heal you. You know my answer, Ragnar."

The wizard threw up a forfending hand. "I do not seek to bribe where I may not compel. Come, do you think I am entirely ignorant, young man? I have my ways, my small knowledge. My child loves me as dearly as I do her. Her heart and mind are open to me—is that not so, Cattail?"

Cattail seemed surprised by her father's words. "You— read my mind, Father?" Her fine skin turned notably paler, despite the veil's discretion.

Again the wizard waved away her tremulous words. "A figure of speech. I may not enter into a person's thoughts, no matter how dear to me that person is or what joys I might read there." He patted his daughter's cheek. "But I can read eyes as well as any man. Do you deny you love him?"

Cattail murmured, "I would lie if I denied it."

"And you, great sir!" Ragnar turned to Timeo. "Will you wed my child? No payment asked but an honest answer! Does she please you?"

"Oh, more than life!" Timeo cried without thought or artifice.

Ragnar's beatific smile curled a little at the edges. His eyes narrowed for an instant, then resumed their placid, protective gaze over the two young lovers now joining hands before him.

"Let it be as you desire!" Ragnar proclaimed, sealing their clasp with his own hand. Emeralds and black opals burned on his fingers. "I ask no price of healing for myself, lord. I only hope that once you have wed my child, time will soften your heart towards her father. If it is meant to be, so it will be. Not every prophecy is sung, eh?" He chuckled like the fattest and best natured of innkeepers.

As if prearranged, the guards who had brought Timeo into the great hall raised a shout for the bride and groom. The other guardsmen took up the cheer, and saw to it that the Waterfolk echoed their huzzahs. Only the men warding the Kya'ar did not join in. Their vigilance never slackened for an instant.

"So, a wedding!" Ragnar's hands twisted tightly around his beechwood staff. "No ordinary feast, this."

"Uhhhh . . ." Timeo glanced at the living whiteness of the Kya'ar. "Why don't you have your men take the beast out before the ceremony begins? The joyous occasion and all—well—I'd hardly call it a fit place to bring a monster. Not a blood kin one, I mean."

"Oh, that would be unthinkable!" Ragnar's hands worked up and down the staff nervously, twirling the wood back and forth as if he meant to bore a hole into the carpet. "My lord, you will forgive me, but a king would no more call his court to order without crown on head and scepter in hand than I could stand before the Waterfolk without *that* in their midst''—he gestured towards the Kya'ar—''and *this* in my grasp.''

Ripples of azure light flowed from Ragnar's palm. A blue pearl the size of an infant's skull filled the hall with its aura of calm power.

A sleeve like a great dark wing fell over Elaar's Daughter, cutting off the light. Ragnar's ingratiating leer rose above the black curtain. ''You will excuse an old man his indulgences. And now, as you consent, I shall make the final arrangements.'' He hobbled down from the throne dais with surprising speed.

Timeo laced his fingers through Cattail's and stood with his back to the throne that was his by birthright. ''Why is he doing this?'' The words slipped from the corner of his mouth.

''Don't you want to—?''

''More than anything. I mean that, Cattail. But to give his consent, your hand, half his lands, and ask nothing in return! You told me—''

''You're like the rest, Timeo: You don't understand my father. You hear the stories of the evil wizard Ragnar, and every evil wizard from your nursery tales comes riding out of nightmares to lay his mask over my father's face. He's human, too. More insightful than most common men, but that comes from his years of study. He can *tell* things about a person, and it seems like some black magical power. He could see what I felt for you, what you feel for me. He's changed his mind about bargaining with you, for my sake. He loves me, he knows I love him, and he has brought us together to please me. That's all there is to it! Can't you accept that?''

Timeo was not without insight. He saw in Cattail's eyes, heard in her voice just how desperately she wanted him to accept Ragnar as the man she alone saw him to be. But he could not. He had seen too much on his own. The wizard's soul left its imprint deep on all his doings and marked him for what he was. Timeo still recalled Perdica's ruined wedding, the roving bands of Ragnar's men free to satisfy their desires at whatever cost to a captive people, the true vision of his kin being slaughtered . . .

And from the Kya'ar's mind came more truths, all pouring

over his consciousness with a bright, clean, rapturous light that left him shaking with revulsion over Ragnar's deeds past, the ruthlessness that would make the future more of the same.

He can not feel for anyone but himself. He can imagine no pain of any consequence, no life of any worth, save his own.

Timeo squeezed Cattail's hand. He had no words to tell her all the truth about her father, and no heart to tell her even the smallest part of it. He could not hurt her so.

If she'd believe any of it, he thought. He shifted Tyveen's bagpipes to a more comfortable position on his left hip.

Ragnar stood in the middle of the floor. He lifted his staff and described a circle with it, swaying to keep his balance. The shadow of the wizard's staff cut away the solid rock. Rushes and mint leaves tumbled into the pit that opened. A sharp, commanding gesture from Ragnar, and the guards surrounding the Kya'ar harried it to the pit's edge. Imperiously, Ragnar snatched a rod from the man nearest him and jabbed it deep into the Kya'ar's flank. A horrible roar shook the walls as the beast tumbled into the pit, but only Timeo heard it as a heart-searing plea for mercy where no mercy dwelled. Beside him, Cattail drew in a sharp breath.

"There." Ragnar shoved the rod back into the guardsman's hand and turned a beaming face towards Timeo. "That's done." The Kya'ar was only a head shorter than the walls of the wide pit confining it, but the guards kept their ensorcelled weapons trained on it so that it made no attempt to haul itself out. "Now the ceremony may begin." He returned to the platform.

Sadly Timeo watched as all the ceremonial accoutrements for a Waterfolk wedding were hustled into place. He saw Perdica among the crowd of witnesses, saw her eyes swim more brightly, and wondered if she too were remembering. Ovrin hovered near her, with a look on his face that begged to take away all her pain, past, present, and future.

Yes, that is a face of love, friend, the Kya'ar told him. *Not the gifts love gives, but the hurts it takes away. To spare the one you love pain, even if that pain is your death . . .*

"So!" Ragnar rested the beechwood staff in the crook of

one arm and clapped his hands together sharply. His eyes danced over the waiting couple before the throne, the jade bowl Fell was even now setting down on a small table between them. "What do we lack? Is all ready? Aha! Fool that I am! There must always be song to join bride and groom in a Waterfolk wedding. Is that not so, my loyal people?"

A subdued murmur of assent came from the courtiers and the servants, an inrushing tide of sound that broke on the wizard's hard smile.

"Then let it be so. You! Girl!" The staff spun in Ragnar's hands. A needle-thin beam of green fire shot from its tip and tore a burning track across Dianta's upper arm. She leaped to her feet with a little scream and turned blinded eyes to the wizard with a gaze that was too unwisely steady.

Ragnar did not seem to notice anything peculiar in a blind girl's strangely exact stare. "You shall have the honor of singing for my daughter's wedding. That's how you do it here, singing together bride and groom. All of your kin have sweet voices. Water is but half your life; music is the other. Come, a song, and this shall reward you!" He twirled air into a thread of smoke that hardened into a strand of black pearls.

Another of the designated musicians gasped. "Magnificent! Plundered from our sweet sea mother's own treasury, I swear. Black pearls, child! Sing well." He bent down to retrieve Dianta's fallen timbrel, but someone was there before him. Darting in like a swallow, Keri played the attentive servant. He gave Dianta her instrument, folding her hands around it with his own.

She sang well. As one of full Waterfolk blood, it would have been unthinkable for her to do otherwise. It was a traditional wedding air, lightsome and full of joy, but now and then Dianta sounded a note like a judgment, and her eyes were on Ragnar. Her timbrel rang silver accompaniment to the gold of her voice.

The assembled Waterfolk began to sway back and forth in time to the music in the traditional dance. Their movements were truncated, their habitual grace made into a jerky parody by their fear. They danced from obedience, while Ragnar watched. Short, guttural sounds bubbled out of his withered throat as the dance went on.

Two of Cattail's attendants brought a rope of rushes and gave either end to bride and groom to hold. Timeo recalled the rushy rope that had bound the two huts in Perdica's village, the same rope that Perdica and her intended mate had touched in the final moments of their own wedding ceremony. He sought Cattail's eyes and gave her a tender smile. She returned it shyly, not from any false or expected bridal modesty, but as one who can scarcely believe her fondest dreams are on the point of realization.

Then Ragnar was between them, raising the jade bowl as high overhead as his cramped and knotted body would permit. "So it is—" He stopped. His head snapped around sharply as a striking snake's. The bowl exploded in his hands, water spraying out, blackened blood pattering down over the heads of the assembly. Timeo heard Cattail muffle a scream as her fine wedding gown was spattered with the unholy rain. Even the guards shuddered.

"Blasphemy!" The wizard's bony finger shook as it pointed to the eyeless singer. "Think you that I am ignorant? That your unblessed language is not as familiar to me as my own? I heard your song, girl! I know your meaning! Do you dare to lay a curse upon my daughter on her wedding day and think that *I* shall remain deaf to it? In your speech or mine or the tongue of the Older Empire, the words of a curse still carry their own stink. By the fire that eats my bones, you shall pay for your witchery!"

Dianta was taken completely off-guard. She stood stiff as any spar of rock. The timbrel jangled faintly, nearly as frozen as its mistress by the wizard's abrupt, insane accusation.

On the far side of the platform, Fell crouched like a spider, watching the growing consternation in the hall.

If Dianta's song had hidden any curse, it was so hidden as to be invisible. The Waterfolk had heard nothing but bland good wishes in the words, happiness in the tune.

Cattail looked as bewildered as the rest. She dropped her end of the blood-dewed rush rope and approached the wizard. "Father, the girl sang nothing wrong."

"Keep out of matters that don't concern you!" Ragnar

shoved her roughly away. "You trust too much, child. There is evil where you would never see it. I tell you, she tried to lay a curse on you! Instead she has laid the foundation of her tomb." His teeth gritted together. "To the Kya'ar with her!"

The wizard's command was not instantly obeyed. For one thing, the guards who did not carry the enchanted rods seemed reluctant to come close enough to the edge of the pit to fling anyone in. Those who did hold the rods could not abandon their posts around the pit. Timeo noticed their demur, and wondered whether there was any history of the Kya'ar taking more than its designated due in victims.

An effervescence that was mental chortling tingled through his thoughts, accompanied by the Kya'ar's comment, *You've hit it rightly, dear friend. They have the power to cow me, when the wizard's magical rods are in their hands, but I remember the face of every one that ever drained life from my body. I remember, I wait, and I repay.*

"Ha! Cowards!" Ragnar's scornful look scythed across the great hall. "To the Kya'ar, I said!"

Among the dumbstruck crowd, Timeo observed Keri beginning to edge forward. Courtiers and servants all milled around nervously, cattle scenting the slaughterhouse, but not one of them dared to make a sound. Perdica and Wydru saw him eeling through the terrified Waterfolk, grimly purposeful. Ovrin too saw, and rumbled after his little brother. The two Waterfolk reached Keri first, their purpose no less urgent than his, and seized him in an immobilizing grip. In the incessant roil and shift of bodies in the mob, Ovrin was able to position himself between Ragnar and Keri, deftly blocking his brother's struggles from sight.

Timeo's eyes darted back to Fell momentarily. It was a most disturbing glimpse, perplexing in the extreme. One side of Fell's mouth seemed to draw up in an unpleasant expression as he regarded Timeo. One hand dropped to his belt, though Timeo could not for the life of him assign any significance to the gesture. Before he had time to puzzle it out, Fell slipped from the stage and melted into the crowd. More urgent matters quickly banished lesser questions.

Again Cattail tried to intervene. "Father, she meant

nothing by her song. Fetch Mother to interpret the song's verses if you doubt me.''

"Fetch who?" For some reason, Cattail's words sent her father into torrents of laughter. Timeo observed the wizard's mad humor with a tightly pursed mouth and the unspoken hope that insanity was not hereditary.

Ragnar stopped laughing. He drove his beechwood staff into the stone heart of the throne dais easily as if it were a spear piercing flesh. The wooden platforms to either side groaned, and the stone screamed.

"*I* will give you meanings! *I* will give you new prophecies, and their fulfillments! *I* rule here—not you, not your cursed mother, not even that false lord who abandoned me to *this!*" His clawed hands contained his whole ruined body with a raking gesture. "Morgeld does not rule the Lands Unknown: *I* do! My will is supreme, sole lord above you all, and my will is that she shall die!"

Elaar's Daughter burned brilliant blue in Ragnar's hand. The edges of its power were visible, a halo that stole its color from a spring sky. Then the wizard's will surged into the heart of the pearl, and the radiance of Elaar's Daughter wore a blackening veil.

Dianta gasped and staggered backward, towards the Kya'ar's pit. Step by step, the wizard descended from the throne, holding the pearl before him. The girl whimpered and fell back as he advanced.

"Hunger it!" Ragnar screamed, and his trembling men flung themselves on their bellies to jab their rods into the beast's shoulders. The pit was not wide enough for it to evade the flailing rods. If it sidestepped one, it stumbled into four others. Whiteness flowed up the silvery staves and the Kya'ar's helpless panic rolled through Timeo's mind, blind hunger bound to the natural fear of death. He clutched his bagpipes to his chest, sank to his knees, eyes shut fast with the shared pain, and tried to reach the tormented being.

Resist! Dear—dear friend, resist! The girl is innocent. Wait! Wait, and I will find a way to save—

All that his thoughts could touch was terror, and the instinct to survive. Once the words came weakly: *Friend . . . forgive.*

Hold! Hold fast! If there is any power in me as the Vessel of Watersong, I will give it to you freely! Please, please dear friend, for your soul's sake, do no more of the wizard's evil. There are worse things than death.

Again the terrified moaning whipped through Timeo's mind like an ice storm. The Kya'ar was too young to imagine what could be worse than the end of his own small universe. Dianta trembled on the pit's edge, and hunger stained the beast's thoughts with a rising scarlet tide. It reached up one taloned paw to sweep her in.

And then, the song came. It was a wall of sweetest sound, strong to shield, impossible to deny. The waves of magic pulsing from Elaar's Daughter struck against it and shattered. The blue pearl darkened to bruised purple, then was lightless, as ashy gray in Ragnar's hand. Dianta cried a Waterfolk word of victory and threw herself away from the edge of the pit, away from the groping paw of the Kya'ar.

Around Keri and his song, the Waterfolk gathered with hands timidly outstretched, afraid to touch the miracle. He sang, and the song that poured over them healed all the old wounds, banished the chill, pallid fear that had run through their veins, brought back the hot blood of battle.

"He has come," they murmured. "The Vessel of Watersong has come to us at last." They began to look at Ragnar's guardsmen with more speculation than fear.

On the platform, Timeo found the bitterness of knowledge. *The Vessel of Watersong . . . Keri, not me.* His heart sank under the full weight of sudden truth.

"Truth," Ragnar muttered, staring at the stripling boy with his god-touched face, his miracle-touched voice. "Black haired, black hearted, he told me the truth of the prophecy . . . and of the other." His eyes glanced briefly at Timeo, then slued towards Fell. "He shall have his reward." He raised the enchanted pearl—now rendered useless by Keri's power—and gave a single, curt nod.

Fell pushed two guards aside in his haste to answer his new master's command. They were caught in the net of Keri's song, but not by any magic. The Watersong was no proof against ordinary people, ordinary weapons, but was healing and shelter and strength to bear against darker magics. The guards were merely stunned by seeing a prophecy come true before their eyes. One of them dropped his rod and tumbled too near the Kya'ar's questing claws. Keri's song obscured his final cry.

But Fell had orders that did not touch the doomed guard. His dagger was out, his hands were quick, and Dianta was just as rapt as the rest of her fishy kin. He had her pinned against his body, the dagger at her ribs.

"Shut your mouth, Keri, or she's dead!" Fell shouted.

The song died like a candle flame going out in a cavern. Ovrin saw his little brother's eyes gape with all the worst fears and forbiddings any knowing man would feel. He was too newly, too suddenly come to love. He had no way to prepare himself for the chance of its sudden, violent loss. He had nowhere to hide. The comfortable darkness was gone forever. There was pain to hold power's hand, and the baleful, demonic shadow of a choice to be made, hovering over him.

"Keri . . ." Ovrin breathed. His strength was not enough to save his brother from this.

"Master . . ." The Waterfolk appealed to him with years of suffering in their eyes and voices.

"No," the boy said softly. He stretched his hands toward his love.

"*No!* Keri, not for me!" Dianta squirmed free of Fell's clumsy hands, her bones too limber to be human. A stride took her back to the pit's edge. "Free—" He heard no more of what she meant to say. Her own choice sent her leaping into the depths.

Friend, don't harm her!

The hunger . . . better, a little . . . I'll try . . .

A second pit guard stared at the rod in his hand. It looked different, duller. His shout turned the wizard's attention. A wave of Ragnar's hand and another guard stepped in to take the lost one's place; another, and all the rods regained their shine of sorcery.

The six surges of rekindled light were not a tenth so bright as the realization that now burned to wonderful life in Timeo's mind. "Keri! Keri, sing! Your song destroys his spells!"

The boy did nothing, made no response. It was as if he had clawed the old darkness back around him.

"Keri, you must! You—" Timeo gestured wildly from the

platform. Ragnar laughed, and the sound stirred up rage. "You have to free us! You're the only one!"

"Aye, free *us*, is it?" Ragnar roared. Elaar's Daughter again held its shining spell over the Waterfolk. "*Us*, indeed! See him, my subjects!" The pearl's spell forced every head to turn towards Timeo. "A greater miracle than you know has happened here. Two prophecies come home at once—the cursed Vessel of Watersong, and the last—truly the very last of your royal house returned! Behold your rightful king!" The wizard's merriment was the cachinnation of night spirits.

Cattail tore off her veil and strode to the head of the platform stairs. "It is so!" Desperately she sought to distract her own mind from the mounting evidence of her father's inhumanity. "I was witness! Timeo Landbegot *is* your—is our true king!"

"*Our* king." The wizard spat the words from his mouth like something deathly bitter. "Kneel, then!" Daggers of light stabbed from Elaar's Daughter at Ragnar's jeering command. Knees bent and heads bowed, as the Waterfolk submitted to the pearl's power. Ovrin and Keri, Cattail and Timeo, Ragnar and Fell and the wizard's land-blooded minions remained standing.

"A short reign, Your Majesty," the wizard sneered. He signaled Fell. "Kill him. Seal your service to me with his blood."

Timeo cast around for a weapon as Fell ran to do his new master's will. As he searched fruitlessly, he stammered out the last remnant of his innocence: "Fell, you won't—you wouldn't—! You said you were here to aid me! You said—Fell, you called yourself my friend!"

"And you called yourself minstrel." Fell's dagger was as steady as his grin. "We all make mistakes."

The guards on the platform made free to seize Cattail just as the dark-haired former student vaulted onto the dais, blade ready. Cattail sent a dreadful burning over her skin. The guards hollered, dropping her like a smith's hot irons, but Fell was already on Timeo.

The impact sent them both tumbling. Tyveen's bagpipes came between them, wheezing and groaning as the two men rolled down the throne steps. At the bottom, Fell and Timeo fast beneath him. He raised his dagger and drove it home. There was a hellish death shriek and dying gurgle.

"You lichen-licking bastard!" Timeo panted. "You've cut my bellows!"

His heels came up behind a startled Fell's head and kicked backwards, under the topmost man's chin. Fell toppled, still holding his dagger. Timeo wasted a precious moment staring at the rent in his instrument's body and very nearly got a matched tear in his own. Fell crouched low, stabbing upwards. Timeo smacked him hard in the side of the head with all his drones and the chanter too.

"Idiots! Help that fool!" Ragnar motioned his guards into the duel. Cattail cast a small magic that sprouted coral spikes from the hall floor. "Traitor! False daughter!" The wizard snarled and sent his own powers against her. White cuffs tightened on her wrists, sealing off her spells. Now the guards were free, and they rushed at Timeo again. These were not his bow-and-arrow bearing escorts, but men armed with short, serviceable swords.

Timeo saw them coming just as he gave Fell a final, telling clout with the drones. As his treacherous comrade slumped unconscious, he wondered how many of the oncoming mob he could bash into a similar state before the sword blades bit through the heavy wooden stems of that noblest of instruments.

Someone was at his side, armed with . . . a shield?

It was too flimsy for a shield, but a tray has its uses. When Ovrin brought it down with all his strength on the head of the first guard to reach them, it did manage to stun. A fist to the jaw finished the work and Ovrin helped himself to his victim's sword.

"Join us, damn you, you eel-bellies!" the big man shouted, going into his approximation of a fighter's stance. "He's your rightful king! Fight for him, or it's Ragnar's rule you deserve!" He slashed and stabbed at random with the blade, scoring several lucky hits. The guards fell back to regroup. "Fight for him!"

"Ovrin, they can't fight! They're held by that blue pearl's—"

Ovrin shook off Timeo's excuses for his people. He struck

away a second man's sword and passed it back. "Fight for yourself, then."

They were neither one of them swordsmen. They were scholars who were rapidly learning that books do not teach everything.

The guards took their measure and acted accordingly. They formed a ring around Timeo and Ovrin, who stood back-to-back. Whenever one of the two lunged at their besiegers, the ring melted away on that front and steel jabbed in from another quarter. Before long, both men were bleeding from a host of shallow cuts. Timeo's fine robes were silken rags and frayed golden threads, but they gave up their glory while helping to deflect some of his attackers' lighter, more taunting slashes.

Friend, can't you help us? Climb out of the pit and—

A ghost sobbed behind his eyes. *I can not! I lack the strength. I need to feed, and nourishment is so near, so very near!*

NO! You mustn't harm Dianta!

I have not touched the girl. But—

A renewed assault on Timeo's left flank distracted him from the Kya'ar's sending.

"Father!" Cattail's scream was shrill and harsh. Short wisps of her hair stood out around her pinched face in a wild woman's disarray. "Father, call off your men! They torment them at your orders, I know. Make an end, spare them, banish them from the Lands Unknown, but stop this! It's inhuman."

The wizard acted as if he could not hear his daughter's heart-torn cry. He strolled among the kneeling Waterfolk as if he were their beloved sovereign, conferring blessings and benefits upon his people's bowed heads. At his approach, the guards chivvied Ovrin and Timeo away. Only when he stood over Fell's body did he speak to his daughter.

"You are right, Cattail. It is cruel to prolong a man's death. Or his life, when he has lost the reason to live it." A touch of the blue pearl restored Fell to his senses. A twirl of the wizard's fingers and Ragnar was offering the revived man a short-bladed knife. He nodded to where Keri huddled, still chilled into shock by his loss.

"Father! Not the boy!"

"Keri!" Ovrin heard her, and plunged after Fell, unthinking. A fence of swords pierced him.

Timeo said a prayer and closed both hands on the hilt of his sword. He swung it madly, a berserker. The trained fighter knew that this was not the proper way to use a shortsword. The trained fighter learned that the improper is not always the impossible. The guards who had regarded Timeo's fighting style as a joke got a very sharp punch line. Two of those who had stabbed Ovrin joined him in a heap on the rushes, one of them looking like a man who has literally laughed his head off. Timeo had broken free of the ring and was after Fell.

But not fast enough, not near enough to catch him before he could reach Keri. "Keri, save yourself!" Timeo gasped. "For Ovrin's death, wake! *Keri!*"

Keri thought he heard his brother call his name. He saw Ovrin meet the blades' keen bite, tried to call a warning, and suddenly realized he was too late. He was seeing in his mind's eye a repetition of events he had already seen, but that had not penetrated his sorrow. He cried out for his brother, and all that answered him was Ragnar's laughter. Through mind-slowed time he saw Fell coming for him with a blade, and then he awoke fully. Loss piled on loss turned cold misery to hot rage. He glowered at the laughing wizard, filled his lungs with air, and sang vengeance.

Timeo found his headlong race to intercept Fell itself intercepted. Throughout the hall, the Waterfolk were rising from their knees. A death shout shivered the silk-hung ceiling. They were a wave of a thousand colors, a single purpose. Ragnar stared at the dead gray sphere in his palm, then at the faces rising all around him. He fled while he might, to the protection of his guards.

But the song went on. The Waterfolk advanced, Keri with them, relentless as the hunger of water. A scattering of them loped ahead to block all the exits. Their aim was too singular. They wanted Ragnar and his guards, for the moment disdaining his lesser servants. It was not wise, but Fell had reason to thank the gods for foolishness. He slipped to one side, out of their path, and pressed himself to the wall as they marched against the wizard.

Keri rode the crest of their implacable wave. He was their

prayer and their talisman. Timeo too they bore forward, over his protests and futile gestures at the cowering Fell. He was vital to them too, a man turned symbol, a vessel filled to the brim with promise, hope, a new day to come. A king: a king in tatters, yet still *their* king. Heeding his words could come later.

They had no weapons, but they were many. Many of them died in the first encounter with the wizard's troops, but this time their deaths came in a battle they had a hope of winning. Swords were soon taken from the dying hands of overwhelmed guardsmen. After those first few conquests, it was easy. Even Cattail's maidenly attendants on the throne dais managed to steal up behind the two ceremonial archers and demurely end their lives with nooses of silk and pearl. Cattail's ensorcelled manacles melted away as the Watersong flowed on.

Ragnar stood alone, teetering on his warped bones at the lip of the Kya'ar's pit. Little malicious smiles met his eyes wherever he looked. Cattail saw what they meant to do to her father, and the horror of it stole words from her tongue. She could only utter an unintelligible groan. Timeo's heart hurt for her, but there was no way to deflect this pain.

Soon done with, praise Ambra; there's that, he thought. *When worse comes to worst, at least it's over.*

Keri and the Waterfolk seemed to know this too, and a quick death for the wizard appeared to strike them as scanty payment for his years of cruelties over them. Keri sang to keep Ragnar's power in check, but his hands moved eloquently, directing his attendants. Three of them grabbed Ragnar by the arms and jostled him a little away from the pit. It was an insane ballet, the wizard's ungainly hobble step done to the tune of Keri's supernatural song. Mad or not, it was done: The Kya'ar should not have Ragnar until the Waterfolk had had their due.

Another gesture from Keri, and Perdica flew to Ovrin's side, accompanied by Wydru and two other males who carried the big man's body to one side of the hall, near the throne dais. Rugs were torn from the platform brought by a score of helping hands, so that Ovrin might lie between their silken leaves composed, with honor.

One pair of these hands lingered at the denuded platform,

where two dead archers lay with ropes of pearls cutting into
their necks. No one had thought to take up their fallen
weapons—useless, really, when close-quarters fighting was
going on. The quivers were hardly filled, too. Why bother
to steal a bow and a few arrows from a dead man?

"By the gods, stop hi—!" Timeo shouted in vain.

The first arrow took Keri in the shoulder. Atop the
platform, Fell whooped self-congratulation as the Watersong
faltered and broke off. For a moment, Ragnar's eyes were
on him in just the way the Waterfolk had looked at Keri
when he began his song.

*Yes, Ragnar, remember this moment! Remember me, when
you've got your own again!* Fell crowed and nocked a
second arrow to his string as Keri gasped for breath to regain
his voice. *I may not be good enough to house a miracle, but
I'm good enough to put an end to one!* The boy staggered
a little, but he waved his attendants away. He was young
enough to think that a threatening glare from him would stop
Fell. He would sing again, for Fell's death.

Fell refused to wait for the tune. The second arrow struck
the boy hard enough to send him stumbling backward; too
far backward. He missed footing, and the walls of the
Kya'ar's pit soared up around him.

"Now save us both, Ragnar!" Fell howled, brandishing
his bow. "Hurry! They're almost—"

"They are *mine!*" the wizard howled, and Elaar's
Daughter crackled with a doom of fire.

Friend! The boy—!

*Hunger . . . so much, so much hunger . . . I can not.
Forgive me, but it drives me, and I can not . . .*

Ragnar gazed into the Kya'ar's pit. The Waterfolk stood
like carved ice fantasies around him. He took one of the
silvery rods from a fish-man's unresisting fingers and sent
more of his magic into it to revive the draining spells, then
hurled it like a javelin into the Kya'ar's shaggy side. The
creature's howl turned Timeo's guts watery and wiped his
mind of everything but one wild certainty.

"Hold on!" he called out, and slung himself over the edge
of the pit. "Hold, don't touch the boy, I'm coming!"

He dropped to the stones below and threw a rapid glance
around him. The Kya'ar loomed up in the very center of its

new prison, as monstrously huge as ever. Behind the creature, Dianta lay sprawled, unmoving.

You promised—!

I did not touch her. Her neck snapped in the fall. She was dead from the first.

Keri was a crumpled form to its right, two arrows in him and one leg twisted at an obscene angle. Still Timeo felt his spirit lighten to see the boy's chest rise and fall. He was alive.

He rushed past the Kya'ar as if the monster were only an old, familiar, parkland oak. He placed himself between the beast and the boy. "You mustn't kill him," he said.

Hungry . . . so hungry . . . sick with hunger. Dear friend, I am afraid to die! The hunger is stronger than I.

"Then take"—Timeo swallowed hard—"take what you need from me. The boy must live."

"Must he?" Ragnar looked down upon them, lips more twisted than his body. "Because he is to be the saving of these lands? And here I thought that *you* were the all-powerful Vessel of Watersong, Timeo! With that sweet voice of yours, those deathless lyrics of your own wit's devising, how could you be other? What? No song for me now, Timeo? Not even a note? Sing! Sing for the last time, a farewell performance! Bid my daugher good-bye, and seek to sing your next song in the halls of Helagarde!"

All his life, people had criticized Timeo's singing. From childhood on, he had dealt with more than a bearable share of unsolicited comments on his art. Ragnar's gibe was one note more than his stave could stand. He became angry, and anger shot defiance through his blood.

He would show the wizard how an artist died. He would show him!

"'Hark, my son, the horns of battle
Sound against the birds of dawn.
Why do you put on your armor?
Why declare you will be gone?'
'Father, lord, I can not linger
In our castle like a churl.
I am prince, and bold in combat.
Do not treat me like a girl.'

'Prince you are—the gods defend you!—
And the sole son of my loins.
If you fall, my line is ended.
Heirs can not be got with coins.'
Deaf, unheeding, he rode forward,
Out into the battle's thick.
Soon a sword made for his dooming
Ended his life fairly quick.
Sat his father in his castle,
Black of spirit, brokenhearted,
When the herald came to tell how
His son's head from body parted.''

It was Timeo's masterwork, the epic of the prince's death
that caused an empire to fall. He had never finished it, and
he judged from present circumstances that he never would.
However, that was no reason to spare Ragnar the premier
performance. He only wished he still had Tyveen's bagpipes
with him for a fittingly martial accompaniment.

*Oh, it's wonderful enough without them! Sing on, dear
friend, and waste no regrets over slit bellows. Ah, your song
fills my limbs with strength!*

?

*Power of life, power of magic, power of music as well!
Sing, friend, and I grow strong!* The Kya'ar glowed even
whiter with happiness, imbibing the music.

"Why doesn't the beast destroy them?" Ragnar muttered.
"Perhaps the fool's song grates on its senses as much as on
my own, frighting it off the fool. But it should be starving
by now! Why doesn't it drain the boy instead? If that one
stirs and wakes—"

"Doomed, by the gods!" Timeo exulted, letting his song
go free. He clenched his fists and waved them up at Ragnar,
an elated grin lighting his face. "Keri wakes—he *will* wake
soon!—and when he does, he sings, and when he sings, the
Waterfolk will be on you like hounds on a wounded hare! I
may not be the Vessel of Watersong, Ragnar, but the songs
my spirit holds are enough to free at least one soul from your
thrall!''

"A soul! What soul? That creature?"

"More soul's in him than you'll ever have, Ragnar, and now it's yours no more!"

The wizard's eyes narrowed to chips of amber. "Do you dare try to take what is mine yet again, fool king? My lands! My throne! My child's love!" He thrust Elaar's Daughter back into his belling sleeve and molded a dart of air, tinted with Helagarde's own dismal hue, dripping amethyst fire. He drew his arm back, and Timeo knew there was no way the point of that dark-steeped missile would miss his heart.

The cry from behind made Ragnar freeze, turn, see Fell lurch from the platform, an arrow in his neck. Cattail already had the next shaft in her bow. The second dead archer had given up his weapons while Fell watched the proceedings in the pit, gloating. She swerved her aim and brought the arrow's head to bear on her father.

"Let them go," she said stiffly.

"Betrayer!" the wizard shrieked. "Whore like your mother, I'll give you the same death I gave her! I'll—"

Timeo heard the bowstring twang. A dark shape plunged into the pit, clawing a fiery ball of daylight blue. A vast whiteness, icy as the stars, whirled past him, and life and magic and all the captive power of Elaar's Daughter flowed out of Ragnar's body in one great rush. Timeo felt the Kya'ar's mind-joy rock him to the roots of his soul, but he could not watch the wizard die.

It is over.

Blue as the ocean deeps of Elaar's kingdom, the Kya'ar stood above a crinkled brown shell that was only vaguely manlike. Twig-brittle fingerbones still clung to a cracked, hollow sphere that fell to dust when Timeo knelt to touch it.

From above, he heard a vast cheer, and the sound of one woman weeping.

Epilogue

GO WITH THE FLOW

"Your Majesty! Your Majesty!"

The messenger caught up with the Water King at the very gates of the palace. He bent over, hands on knees, his cheeks puffing like a blowfish until he got his breath back. "They told me you'd be with Lord Keristor, greeting the boatload of new seekers," he said, by way of apology.

Timeo looked markedly uneasy, in haste to be on his way. He patted the messenger chummily and said, "I have more pressing affairs. My presence at the welcome is purely for show. It's Lord Keristor they come to meet. Now, your errand?"

The messenger was not quite ready to speak of that. The openhearted nature of his liege lord, King Timeo, was famed throughout the Lands Unknown, but this was the first direct experience of it he'd had. He intended to bask in the king's friendly favor as long as he might stretch it.

"Lord Keristor himself said you might be by the tombs, it being an Honor Day and all. His lordship might not have one drop of our blood in him, but he's nobler than most, speaking to me so fine and patient, like I was somebody. And him with that whole crowd of god-touched children from the drylands disembarking, even while we spoke! Their kin at the railings with them, 'bout ready to tip that poor old ferry over into the Salmlis! Is it true what they say, Your Majesty?"

"What's that?" A fine note of irritation crept into Timeo's voice.

"That there's aught in our lands that lifts the god-touched into the light?"

"I would rather say that there are many lights, young man; some walk their life's path by one, some by another. Lord Keristor was merely the first to find a passage between. If that passage lies in the very nature of our realm . . ." He shrugged. "The gods have made this world too sweet to be a curse, but too random to be a pure blessing."

The messenger nodded, looking wise as a carp. "I helped guide them off, get 'em in line for the cup of welcome—sometimes that cures some of 'em straight off, and it's a treat to see! Some it takes longer biding over on this side Salmlis, though."

"Your message," King Timeo prompted, "for me?" He sidled closer to the palace gates, but the messenger did not take the hint.

"Well, once I saw Lord Keristor's pretty young helpmeet Filixa come up to take over from me, *then* I was free to seek you by the tombs." He took the king into his confidence by adding, "There's talk nowadays that Lord Keristor's looking on Filixa with more than plain gratitude for the way she makes those dryland children welcome here."

"I rejoice for them both. Now if you *please*—?"

"So, as I said, I went to the tombs. But you weren't there." It was a sad-eyed accusation, made even more poignant by the fact that the messenger had the large, soulful eyes of a snail darter.

"I *know* I wasn't there!"

"But the queen was," the messenger said, too intent on his own tale's unraveling to notice how his sovereign lord squirmed at mention of his wife. "There with all her ladies, laying Honor Day blossoms on Lord Ovrin's tomb. She said she didn't know where you were, but she surely knew where you were *supposed* to be. The whole choir was waiting on your coming for the ceremony at Tyveen of Sigraton's shrine, too, and the boy sopranos already squirming like a netful of minnies."

"Yes, well, I'm going to join her there as soon as I—as soon as I get a little matter settled inside here. Now hurry up and give me your message so I can get on with my business and meet my lady wife!''

So much for the king's reputed affability. The messenger turned sulky. He handed over a small scroll and grumped how it had come by special packet boat from Panomo-Midmists. Duty done, he dove off the palace bridge and swam home in a snit.

Timeo unsealed the scroll. It was from the Board of Governors of the university, soliciting a donation from one of their school's most lambent alumni.

He tossed it into the stream. A tidy-minded nixie tossed it back. Timeo crumpled the parchment and stuffed it into his belt. He had more urgent matters on his mind.

It would not do if Cattail came looking for him, hot on the messenger's traces. She knew nothing of his secret vice, and he intended to keep it that way. Marriages had foundered on lesser shoals. He adored his wife, but a man's passion sometimes had to warm itself at a different fire.

The great hall was nearly deserted, except for a few of the entertainers loitering between meals, in the shadows. Welcome sunlight streamed in from sorcerously opened windows high in the walls, a wedding gift from the king's mother. The crystal pillars again glittered with dancing fish.

A mountebank approached the king as he tried to cross his own hall unnoticed. A trained she-bear tumbled at the jack-a-rag's heels, anticipating the coming night's performance. "Sire, a word!''

Timeo sighed. He could never pass by any player, no matter how disreputable, scruffy, or poverty pinned. He knew some of them were rogues, but all of them shared the same mistress. "Yes, my good man?''

The fellow doffed his patch-and-mend cap and worked it round and round between his hands. "Your Majesty, me and the rest of the players, we was just wondering, like, if you'd be good enough to favor us with a song this night, and if you'd be so kind, to tell us when that'd be so's we can work up the order of our acts?''

Timeo looked from the man to the small she-bear at his feet. She was a winsome creature, with almost human feeling in her eyes. He thought of his Aunt Ursula, which by turns brought his thoughts to his cousin Alveiros. He knew he'd never be the minstrel Alveiros was, but he had come to read men as well as music and hoped his cousin had done the same. He knew the next verse to this tune.

"No, my man. I shall not sing tonight."

"Awwww . . ." The bear keep looked as if his heart would break. His beast felt her master's sorrow and bleated.

"I don't sing in hall anymore. But I shall still give the double pay you've heard of, just the same as if I sang and stayed awake through all the flattery to follow." He rumpled the bear's ears and added, "You and your fellow players change the wording of your compliments a bit, and make them apply to the queen's new gown. You may come by some extra coin that way, and your work not go for naught."

Having disposed of the player, the Water King was able to continue to his assignation without further delay. A tapestry was pulled aside, a door behind opened silently, steps lit by soft glows led downwards into a maze that was Timeo's second home. He only paused to step into one of the many side rooms. From the racks of oilcloth-sheathed instruments, he selected a set of bagpipes.

Friend, do you come? The Kya'ar was a gentle blue radiance just ahead in the tunnel. The rich magic it had drained from Elaar's Daughter was too potent to depart. The creature would nevermore regain its original icy hue.

The Water King found a wine cask and hoisted his regal robes to leap atop it. He sat on his makeshift throne cross-legged, bagpipes under one arm, and made a long business of clearing his throat. The Kya'ar rushed to a second wine cask, previously broached, and filled a gilded goblet with imported Paxnon mead. A sip, and Timeo's throat was miraculously healed.

"I shall sing from my latest composition," he announced. "My own version of the 'Ballad of Rundel's Lady and the Worm of Greyfall.' Ahem:

'Whither wander ye, my lady,
Up and down and up and down?
All the birds have left the woodland,
All the servants gone to town.'

Thus responded Rundel's lady,
Heiress to a vast domain:
'I go forth to seek my lover.
Would you please pick up my train?'
Maid and lady left the castle,
All bedizened and bedight,
Clad in silk and vair and satin,
Diamonds, gold, and some samite.''

Here Timeo stopped. "I know the accent falls wrong on 'samite,' but I couldn't think of another rhyme."

Oh no, don't change a thing! It's wonderful! It's marvelous! Dearest friend, I could listen to you sing forever! The Kya'ar brought its paws together quickly, repeatedly, in just the manner Timeo had taught it. Deep, booming echoes rocked the vaults with reverberations of the star-born creature's acclaim.

Timeo smiled. No thought of extra coin for compliments sullied those words or that sound. No wonder he stole away from his surface life so often, just to hear this! The Water King laughed aloud. He had never been happier, not even when the Waterfolk placed the crown of his forbears on his brow and hailed him as their true king, Cattail his chosen queen at his side. Not even when his mother knelt before him, tears of triumph in her eyes. Some things were worth more than kingdoms: Love . . . friendship . . . fulfillment . . . joy . . .

Applause.

On the Three Orders of Magic Wielders:
A Partial Transcription of Master Baudri of Paxnon's
Introductory Lecture to the Course Sorcerous
As Given at the University at Panomo-Midmists

Gentlemen, I welcome you to the Course Sorcerous in the name of the university governors. No doubt you are all well-versed in the university catalogue by this time and have noted that the Course Sorcerous is strictly divided between the schools of Witchborn Governance Magic and Wizardly Acquisitive Magic.

No doubt you have likewise, by this, become aware of the special insignia assigned you at matriculation which serve as tokens of identification to distinguish witchborn students from wizardly. These you are enjoined to wear for the full term of your first two years at Panomo-Midmists, under penalty of immediate expulsion.

And we'll do it, too.

The reason for the insignia is simple: Many of you come to our fair university with your heads full of ideas. This goes entirely against everything for which a Panomo-Midmists education has come to stand.

I beg your pardon, young man—yes, you in the back row! I was not aware that laughter was an acceptable accompaniment to serious note taking.

As I was saying, both the witchborn and wizardly among you come here with certain—*prejudices,* if you prefer. The witchborn look down upon the wizardly as mere book grubs and scholarly drudges, while the wizardly scorn the witchborn as effete and spoiled wand fops on account of their too-easy acquisition of power. This rivalry is destructive to what ought to be a productive alliance. It also is the underlying cause of more than one disturbance in the refectory, particularly on nights when crookneck squash is served.

Therefore we keep you separated for the first two years—time enough for each school to learn the truth behind the other's management of magic. After that, it is hoped that an attitude of mutual respect and cooperation between your two schools will have been engendered and nurtured, sufficient to allow you all to complete the Course Sorcerous with occassional joint classes.

But that is for the future. Why, you may wonder, are you all now packed into this lecture hall, irrespective of whether your badge be the flowery wand of the witchborn or the open scroll of the wizardly? Gentlemen, what I have to say is for all of you, and whether you come by your powers through birth or study, you will benefit from my topic for today: The Three Orders of Magic Wielders.

There will also be an essay question on it on the final examination.

I would be surprised—nay, shocked—if there is even one among you still unfamiliar with two of the three orders. These two are, of course, yourselves: the witchborn and the wizardly. The witchborn are born with their powers, just as a child may be born with a gift for making great paintings, majestic verses, or a truly palatable lamprey pasty.

Ah-ha-ha-ha. A little joke, there, for those of you who have already encountered the gustatory delights of one of our local cookshops, the Prudent Surfeit.

No, young man, the joke will *not* be on the final.

Having inborn power is not the free gift you gentlemen of the wizardly school might expect. The power is there, but you must learn *how* to make it answer to your will. Discipline! Discipline! The power must be directed, and the witchborn must be taught the best methods for directing it. Without discipline, of what use is all the power in the world? What good to have the spell within you capable of moving mountains if you can not get it to respond to your need when there is a mountain to be moved? What use is the most bountiful well of sweet water if you don't have a bucket?

Just so the born artist has no good of his art if he is never taught the techniques of his craft—the making of pigments, the mixing of colors, the preparation of the canvas, the reassurance of timid models, and so forth. Or think of the would-be poet whose inborn gift dies unsuspected with him merely because no one ever teaches the child to read and write!

The wizardly suffer under a different set of constraints, as you gentlemen of that school will attest. You are born with no magic within, yet you have the aptitude to turn words, gestures, substances, often the very fiber of your bodies, into channels through which the power of magic flows. In you, the path of scholarly discipline comes first. Only through study can you *acquire* knowledge of the proper combination of words, gestures, and so forth, that make a spell to effect a specific change. The longer you study, the more spells you acquire, the more changes you can effect. But the search itself takes time, and you are mortal.

The gift of the witchborn is a raging torrent that must be contained and directed if anyone is to get some good of it. Likewise the gift of the wizardly is a perfectly constructed aqueduct that will do no good unless its builders can find the water with which to fill it. If you waste your lives in envy or scorn of one for the other, you will both parch. Gentlemen, you *need* each other. The witchborn—even the highest—often resort to the wizardly for help when they must find a particular spell through which to focus their powers. The wizardly often draw aid from the witchborn when they have found a necessary spell, but lack the power to effect it.

But enough of that. I spoke of three orders. Some are born to magic, some acquire magic, and some—these last—*are* magic. For the sake of alliteration—always an excellent aid to the memory when final examination time rolls around—I shall hereafter refer to this third group as the wondrous.

You will have heard of some of these: demons, imps, night spirits, Elaar's court, the Waterfolk, peris . . . I could go on indefinitely. Believe it when I say that not all the wondrous of the Twelve Kingdoms have ever been fully catalogued. Just when we think we have them all, another breed pops up and there goes *that* study.

You may be puzzled. Are not those of the third order a subspecies of the witchborn? After all, their powers are inborn, not acquired. True enough, but with these distinctions. They do not need to learn how to govern their powers. Unlike the witchborn, they are born knowing how to use their magic; all of it. Just so, a caterpillar is born "knowing" how to turn itself into a butterfly; or a moth, if it insists. The powers of the wondrous are generally of a limited nature. Unlike the witchborn, who occasionally discover that they have one "pet" spell they can command more easily than the rest of their enchantments, the creatures *of* magic often learn that they have one spell, period. Considering the feeding habits of certain demons, we should be grateful.

Finally, and most important, the witchborn and the wizardly are human, magic-wielding mortals. The wondrous are not. Certainly many of them look human. Many have some human-looking aspects. They are just as subject to destruction as humans, with variations in their susceptibility to mortality according to type. Strangely enough, many are entirely able to *breed* with humans, producing offspring that share the characteristics of both parents. This can be messy.

Yes? Question? . . . Young man, is that a familiar on your desk, taking notes for you? The catalogue clearly stipulates that no familiars are permitted in any mixed-schools lectures. . . . Well, if it is one of our normal, ordinary, common school mice, it is the first time I have ever seen one furred in that putrid shade of green, holding a quill pen in its paws, and putting out its tongue at a tenured lecturer of this university! I will give you one more chance to—

(Here the transcription breaks off. This is a pity, as it was the last lecture Master Baudri gave before his untimely vanishment from Panomo-Midmists. He was last seen entering the Prudent Surfeit. Any information as to his whereabouts should be directed to the board of governors.)

ESTHER M. FRIESNER was born in Brooklyn but left to attend Vassar and later Yale, where she earned a Ph.D. in Spanish. After teaching at Yale for some years, she quit to write fantasy and science fiction full-time. She is the author of *New York by Knight* and *Here Be Demons,* as well as the previous volumes in the *Chronicles of the Twelve Kingdoms: Mustapha and His Wise Dog, Spells of Mortal Weaving,* and *The Witchwood Cradle.*

Ms. Friesner lives in Madison, Connecticut, with her husband, son, daughter, and the obligatory writer's cat. (Pound for pound, it should count as three.) She is a member of the local Society for Creative Anachronism barony of Dragonship Haven and a camp follower of the colonial Fifth Connecticut Regiment. She wishes it made clear that ''camp follower'' is not meant in *that* sense of the word. She is also one of the few writers who has not had a previous life, so she is working very hard on this one.